GLITTER AND GOLD

JILL BEISSEL

Cover Illustration © Nat Mack
Distributed by Simon & Schuster
Line edit by Tina Beier

ISBN: 978-1-998076-43-7
Ebook: 978-1-998672-01-1

FIC002000 FICTION / Action and Adventure
FIC071000 FICTION / Friendship
FIC044000 FICTION / Women

#GlitterandGold

Follow Rising Action on our socials!
Instagram: @risingactionpublishingco
Tiktok: @risingactionpublishingco

For those who have felt the ache of wanting more and dared to follow it.

The wound is the place where the Light enters you.

—Rumi

GLITTER

AND

GOLD

1

Now – August 2018

Mama's grave is barely cold when a face from the past haunts me. Joss Marwood's reappearance is the last thing I expected—or wanted. For a decade, she's been a specter of a lost friendship I tried to exorcise. This Wednesday night, she's very much alive at the Copper Lanes Bowl 'n' Dine, staring back at me, the shell of a long-discarded best friend.

I take a swig from my beer—its bitterness a relief from old memories—and look away, but she's moving closer, taking shape in the corner of my eye. It's too late to escape her crosshairs.

"Delaney Byrne? My God," Joss says, her trademark soft voice punctuated by a vocal fry she never had previously. "Heard about your mom. I'm so sorry. Aurelia was one-of-a-kind."

Her words, meant as comfort, burn like salt in the open wound of our past. She knew nothing about how Mama's cancer had ravaged her body and erased her spirit these last six months, leaving me only with echoes of the vibrant, complicated woman she used to be.

The clacks of bowling balls hitting pins match my racing pulse.

Of course, the years have sharpened Joss's beauty. She became the *Seventeen* models she had once tacked to her bedroom wall. Sloped cheekbones and glassy skin had replaced the youthful, ruddy roundness of teenhood. Her once signature blonde bob has grown to silky lengths that skim her mid-back. I doubt time has been so kind to my Irish skin and auburn hair inherited from Dad.

Ten years of unspoken words could fill the pause before I reply. I've replayed in my head so many times what I'd say if we ever spoke again, polishing scenarios in the shower, on a drive, scrubbing dishes at the diner. Because the pain of our fallout the summer after senior year was so raw, I never thought I'd heal. I thought I'd forever carry the searing hurt of what happened between us.

Sure, I hadn't been a saint. But the last transgressions were hers alone, not mine to fix. Even after everything we'd survived together senior year, she'd stuck a metaphorical knife in my back. Years passed without closure or an icebreaker, strengthening my bitter inner monologue.

I thought I'd have so much to say if I ever saw her again—drill that guilt into her core.

But that's the funny thing about pain. It's at its worst when you're bleeding, or the bruises are freshly purple and blue. When a scar emerges, shiny and raised, it may be tender, but the ache is distant. Not so sensitive to the touch anymore.

Joss is my scar now.

"Yeah, thanks." My decade-long rehearsed monologue fades away in her presence. "Bye."

Her perennial heavy-lidded eyes, which made her look lost in a daydream, flutter with that masterclass of confusion she'd always foisted upon me to skirt blame.

"Whoa, hey," Joss says, "I'm sorry, I'm not like trying to—"

"We're good." I cut her off, pinching the damp label of the bottle. It tears. "It's a few years too late to talk about *that*; it's done. Water under the bridge."

"I know, I'm sorry." Joss looks at her manicured nails, fingers woven together in showy remorse like sinners pray to saints at church. "For everything, honest. Really."

Her need to weasel in an apology—now, of all times—ignites a tiny flame of rage.

"Really?" I say with bitterness, my volume causing a few heads to turn towards us. "I just buried my mom and you're worried about your conscience. Some things never change. Nothing you say now will reverse what you did."

Joss's eyes glimmer. "I thought you'd see the past differently now." She twists her fingers. "I made some shitty mistakes as a scared kid. But I did a lot right by you. Remember?"

I take the last sip of my watery beer, poised to lay a venomous defense on Joss, only to have my twenty-two-year-old sister, Catalina, sidle up beside me, skid-marked bowling shoes in hand.

"Turn these in for me, Laney?" my younger sister says with her pronounced lisp. She curls her tongue at me. "Ready to go home. Need to watch my show. And bed by ten."

If anyone could get me to chill my temper, it's my Cat. She was born with Down Syndrome, and I helped raise her, but she's always the one to keep me grounded—a mirror to show my impetuous behavior. My Mexican mama used to say she's el ángel de tu diablo.

Instead of berating Joss, I take a deep breath. "Good idea. Let's go."

My sister's too focused on her shoes to notice who is speaking to me. Joss moves forward, smiling at her. "Kitty Cat, remember me?"

Cat's face brightens. She'd always adored Joss.

Joss loved including her in everything we did, gifting her peanut butter M&M's, Cat's favorite candy, or finding merchandise from her favorite shows (*The X-Files, Star Trek,* and *Buffy the Vampire Slayer*). Cat squeezes her tight, the top of her wily auburn hair burying Joss's chin.

"Where you been?" my sister asks. "Are you a model now? I missed you."

Joss laughs, closing her eyes. "I've missed you more." She hugs Cat tighter.

"I think Laney misses you, but she won't say."

I roll my eyes, heat creeping up my pale, freckled neck.

"Tell her I miss her, too," she whispers, giving Cat a final squeeze. "Did you ever tell your big sis about that spot you wanted her to look for the El Cobre treasure?"

My heart drops into my gut.

"C'mon, Cat." I glare at my estranged friend, thrusting Cat's dirty rental shoes against the delicate fabric of her pristine ivory blouse, its chiffon refinement out of place in Jericott. "Let's get you home."

Joss steps backward, tucking her hair behind one ear and clutching the shoes in an awkward grasp. I grab my sister's hand and head for the exit, leaving Joss in the walkway that bridges the bowling lanes and the dining room.

"Did you hear Wyatt's back, too?" Her voice echoes between us.

Wyatt. I stop without turning.

"See you in another ten years, Marwood." I shove open the exit doors, holding Cat's hand, charging into the damp night.

If one thing's sure, Joss never lost her audacity. That she has the nerve to face me is annoying. Her arrogance in uttering the words El Cobre is infuriating. And the gall to say Wyatt's name is a gut punch.

I want to forget that mountain and the hoax of its treasure, but I can't. El Cobre peeks through my front yard trees and looms as a constant fixture in my view driving to work. It's a daily, scathing reminder of Wyatt, Joss, Mama, and our last expedition ten years ago and the deadly fallout.

El Cobre Mountain, looming large at every turn, was the impetus for Mama's wish to be ranked among real and fabled treasure hunters: Mel Fisher, E. Lee Spence, Brent Brisben, Dirk Pitt, Indiana Jones, Jim Hawkins, Benjamin Gates. *Aurelia Byrne.* She longed to see her name atop the list of those men who always took the riches of mountains and seas for themselves.

The gilded pipe dream died with Mama after having wasted her time, energy, and the little money she had. A kernel of resentment sprouts in me, as now I'll have to clear our house of its associated clutter, one of the many things her death layers on top of my grief.

Treasure hunting is for fools, and I'm done being one.

"Why are you so mad at Joss?" Cat asks as I unlock her passenger door.

"I'm not mad at her, just over her," I say, hopping into my '86 Chrysler LeBaron.

I have a love-hate relationship with old beater Chrissy-the-Chrysler. Despite her rust-red exterior, white leather bench seats, and loud muffler, the freedom she offers tempers my embarrassment, even if she should have died a scrapyard death before I convinced the owners to sell her for a steal.

"You got four wheels that get you from point A to B, mija," Mama had said.

"She's a relic of a different lifetime," I add.

"Joss is not a treasure box, Laney," Cat says, snapping me from my concentration as I crank the ignition. "And you were mad, doin' that thing with your mouth and chin."

My damn pointy chin.

"See? You're doing it now."

I tuck my chin, trying to untwist my pout at the thought of Joss.

"We just grew apart," I say, painfully aware this isn't the whole truth. I pull onto Grand Basin Avenue, where we pass the half-lit sign of *Jericott, Home of the El Cobre Legend*. It flickers with a pathetic, stunted glory. "And it's not worth going down that road with her again."

"Why?"

Tiny raindrops spit on the windshield, and I press harder on the gas, knowing the desiccated wipers are useless.

"I don't need her or anyone else—only you," I say. "It's all too complicated."

"It doesn't have to be. People are important, Laney. The most."

"*You* are the most important."

"But she's a good person. Deep down somewhere."

Jericott High School's marquee sign recedes into a narrow, glowing rectangle as I glance in the rearview, remembering a time when Joss broke into a hair-pulling brawl when a girl on her cheer squad called me a "ginger-headed twat." I suck my bottom lip in, curbing the memory's irreverent humor.

"Way deep down," I concede.

"Is it worth it?" Cat asks.

"Is what worth it?"

"Being mad at her."

Cat's innocent words are a sucker punch. Fragile righteousness has held me together in these brittle years and preserved me from the disappointment of relationships that came after high school. Cat didn't need to inherit my bitter scars and truisms, though. She's lucky to love Joss still.

I sigh. "Thank you for your TED Talk."

A quick flush breaks across Cat's olive skin; she looks more like Mama as she ages. She fidgets with a loose thread on her polka-dotted skirt, which she wears without fail every Monday, Wednesday, and Friday.

"Sorry, got a lot on my mind," I say.

"I miss Mama. But Real Mama," she says. "Not Sick Mama."

The clicking of the Chrysler's turn signal masks our silence. Real Mama, to me, was still two irreconcilable halves of the same person: one who could be mood-ring-blue, warm and happy; the other, black, cold and restless.

I grab Cat's left hand and squeeze it four times. Its touch is soft, full, and childlike.

"Love you, too, Sis," she whispers back.

I release her hand as I park in our driveway. Dread swells as I spot the millions of imperfections screaming from our small home's façade. Shin-high weeds snake through concrete cracks and rusted junk brims from corners of the carport. Yellow paint curls in shame away from the foundation.

Before Dad died, bottle-green grass carpeted our front yard while beds of bright zinnias and geraniums framed the windows.

I miss him with an ache that makes me wonder if my trajectory would have turned out differently with more years of his love and guidance. Or how life might've been with a different mother.

We climb our stoop, dampened by the gloaming drizzle. The familiar neighborhood musk of rusted metal, stale trash, long-snuffed fire pits, and old homes mask the sweetness of summer blossoms.

As I near the front door, I freeze, my arm stretching out to protect Cat.

"What's a matter?" she asks.

Terror floods every limb as I stare at the mangled casing by the lock and the dark, slivered gap of an open door. Instinctively, I thrust Cat behind me, creeping closer to the entrance.

A strange stillness beckons from inside, like wind holding its breath. Then I catch a glimpse—a tall, elusive silhouette in a balaclava darting through the dimly lit hallway, casting an eerie shadow. A clatter resonates, echoing the swift whoosh-bang of the kitchen door slamming shut, the intruder escaping through the backyard.Adrenaline surges. Without pause, I yell for Cat to call 911 and bolt in pursuit into the wake of the unknown.

2

Then – September 2007

Dad's death defined my senior year of high school, and there I was, stuck with Mama—rudderless without him. Cat and I huddled in the stifling dark of our closet, the only space for breath and solitude in a house overrun with mourners. I refused to come out until the last guest left, when I could clean their Pyrex and freeze their leftovers in peace.

Right now, mourners' cringe-worthy expressions of sympathy, mixed with their morbid curiosities and platitudes expressed through dishes of deviled eggs and tuna casseroles, are the only things that matter.

He'll always be in your hearts.

He's with the angels.

I know how you feel.

At least it happened quickly.

Things happen for a reason.

There was no fucking reason for what happened. He'd dropped dead of a massive heart attack when he'd done yoga—it's all he could do when arthritis sidelined him after working years at the mill—and lived off bland chicken and broccoli. These last few days, I could neither eat nor sleep nor could I mend the gaping hole of pain and depression: my sister needed me.

"Who's gonna take care of us?" Cat asked. The slits in the bi-folded door illuminated the tears on her face.

It wasn't a silly question, given our mother. Her presence paled to Dad's, and he always overcompensated for her. Dad was unlike my friends' fathers in the most delightful ways: just last week, he was applying Band-Aids, kissing Cat's boo-boos, and baking brownies with me. Everything we're indoctrinated to believe that mothers do.

"Mama'll step up. And you know I'm here for you. I'll never ever leave you."

Cat nodded, wiping the tears so hard with her palms she pulled her skin until I could see the insides of her eye sockets. I grabbed both her hands, rubbing my thumbs along her knuckles. "It's you and me always."

The closet door squeaked open in its track, startling both of us. It was Joss, spritzed in her Bath & Body Works glory, armed with a paper plate of hors d'oeuvres.

"Eat up," she said, pushing a daisy sundress on a hanger from her shoulder and sitting beside me.

"Not hungry." I pushed the plate toward Cat, who nibbled at a cheese cube.

Joss closed the door, and the Pearberry air thickened with an extra layer of warmth. "No biggie. But how 'bout just one?" She handed me a cracker with cheese.

The crumbly, creamy combination was both nauseating and nourishing, but it gave me a small ounce of energy—or it could instead be seeing the satisfaction in Joss's face. She leaned her head on my shoulder. "I can sleep over tonight."

A pit of sadness hardened in my stomach at the anticipation of lying in bed tonight, those dark hours when grief kidnapped my loneliest thoughts. "That'd be great."

When Cat finished the appetizer plate, we laid down, squished side-by-side, staring at our cheap array of ill-fitting clothes. There was no room to move, and nowhere I'd rather be.

"One thing I'll miss about your dad? His baking," Joss said. "Those blueberry muffins? So good."

I pushed down the lump in my throat as the sugary whisper of their aroma wafted and faded in my nose, replaced by the distant murmurs of guests throughout the house.

"I'll miss watching *Star Trek* with him. He looked like Chief O'Brien, Commander Data's friend," Cat said. "And now you have to braid my hair, Laney. That's not good."

Joss and I paused at her non sequitur, and everything that bubbled under my stoic surface converged in a strange, manic laugh. "You're right. I suck at braids. I can't do them for shit."

Joss, wide-eyed in bewilderment, caught my laughter, and before I knew it, we were all giggling in the darkness for a few escapist minutes until the sadness seamlessly cycled back around. My smile soured, and I began to sob—ugly, massive tears mixed with snot.

"Hey, bestie," she whispered, clutching me and rubbing my back. "I got you." She twirled the stem of a rose she plucked from one of the stuffy arrangements in the living room. She buried her nose in its soft petals. "Love that smell—""Keep it," I insisted, knowing she loved preserving all things soft and pretty. "For your press book."

Cat gently patted my head while Joss squeezed my hand four times, and I reciprocated—our code between the three of us for "I love you more."

The closet door rattled open again, daylight spilling in like a halo around *him*.

Wyatt Altaha.

My chest hitched as I quickly pulled away from Joss and wiped my face.

I cleared my throat. "Hey, Wy."

Joss sighed loudly through her nose, a dissatisfied purr in her throat. "How nice of you to join us," she said, her tone flat. In fifth grade, she'd staked her claim on Wyatt first, as if saying her crush aloud would make it real. But it was me he paid more attention to, and from that day forward, her resentment—of him, and sometimes me—only seemed to fester. "I got it covered in here, thanks. Why don't you help Aurelia with the guests?"

Wyatt squirmed, a contrast to his usual confidence.

"I—sorry. Your mom asked me to get you." He finger-combed a swath of his shiny black hair away from his face.

Our friendship began in kindergarten, sparked by the innocent joy of chasing each other around the playground. I was first drawn to Wyatt's appearance, so unlike my own: his terra-cotta skin and amber eyes were captivating.

We were two lone puzzle pieces that had finally found their fit. We were both from mixed backgrounds: me, Irish-Mexican American, and him, Irish-Apache Native American.

Everything I wanted to see in myself I found reflected in Wyatt. Mellow kindness, warmth, and patience; it was as if every word that came out of his mouth was fully formed with delicate love and care, gently enveloping me in a safety I had never known before, unlike the stray harsh sentences that often spilled from my own lips.

Too perfect if you ask me, Joss told me recently. *Can't trust anything too good*.

Perfect or not, a crush was inconvenient while mourning the death of my first love: Dad. That sorrow should be all-consuming rather than laced with the guilt of zeroing in on a handsome boy's smile, a foreign heat blooming through my neck and cheeks. I couldn't help how and when the realization hit me—that nameless day a month ago, when my heart and brain saw him through a new lens. It was no longer platonic, but the lovey-dovey filter where my breath caught at his sight and jealousy simmered under the surface when another girl at school laughed with him or brushed against his arm.

"Uh, uh, okay, sure." I scrambled to a seated position.

Wyatt outstretched his hand, pulling me swiftly to my feet, the momentum sending my face inches from his chest. His tall height made me swoon. The top of my head nocked like a fitted puzzle piece beneath his sharp chin. His nearness was thrilling and aching. I turned to Cat and Joss. "I'll be back as soon as I can."

Joss crawled out from the closet and wedged herself between me and Wyatt. "Stay here, D. You shouldn't have to talk to all those people. Let me handle it, and I'll be back quickly. Thanks though, Wyatt."

She stared at him expectantly as he backed away toward the door. My heartache from Dad needled its way back into my thoughts.

"Wait, Wy—" His sunshine, the warmth of his presence was what I needed. I smoothed my sweating palms against the cheap polyester of my black empire-waisted dress. "Stay here with me for a bit. And thank you, Joss."

Joss nibbled the inside of her bottom lip, arching one eyebrow like a cat arches its back. "Sure. Whatever."

She slammed the door shut behind her.

I exhaled, pushing my hair behind one ear. "She can be a little dramatic."

"It's okay. Really." His gaze on me was earnest and genuine, almost unnerving in its vulnerability. "She's very protective of you."

"Hey, Mr. Wyatt, you want to see something cool?" Cat asked. She had moved to sit cross-legged in the corner by her small wooden curio shelf, where she kept her most prized possessions. We're not used to many guests, much less the novelty of a boy in our shared room.

"Sure, show me what you got there." He smiled at me before sitting next to her.

"Do you like *Buffy the Vampire Slayer*?"

"Yeah, that movie was pretty cool."

Cat sighed emphatically and shook her head. "No, no, no. The show."

"Ah!" He flinched. "No, sorry. I'd have to fight too many siblings over TV control. Couldn't watch it if I wanted."

"Get with the program!" she retorted.

I stifled a laugh. "Cat, chill."

She ignored me and held up for him a small plastic figurine as if on a pedestal of her fingertips—a brunette in a yellow and red cheerleader uniform. "This. Is Cordelia."

"Is she a vampire?" he asked.

She giggled, followed by another sigh. "Of course not. Boy, you have so much to learn."

Cat played with the tiny dolls, pantomiming an entire dramatic sequence between Cordelia and a gargoyle figurine, soon becoming so absorbed that Wyatt's presence became irrelevant.

I motioned for him to join me on the bottom bunk, our heads at an awkward angle. He sat close enough to generate a fluttery spark in my chest.

"I'm here for you, Laney," he said after a long pause. "Whatever you need. A distraction. To scream and cry. Sit in silence. Whatever." His pinky inched closer to mine. "I'm not going anywhere."

After a hesitant, sweetly awkward flinch, he took my hand.

My insides warmed with pulsing energy. Did he feel it, too? I glanced at him, but his eyes were fixed on the flower-patterned blanket. If we made eye contact, a first kiss would be inevitable. And they should never happen at a wake.

Adorned in black lace, Mama barged in, smudged mascara under her eyes—ever the quintessential mourner. Joss peeked over her shoulder.

"Mija, the guests are leaving." Her eyes darted warily between Wyatt and me. "Come say goodbyes and help me clean up."

"Asquerosa," Mama muttered, shoveling the Anderson's gloopy chicken tetrazzini into the trash can. "God bless their kindness, but we can't eat that."

I rolled my eyes, scrubbing another casserole dish of its burnt cheese, the sink's soapy hot water wrinkling my fingertips. "It's rude to throw it out, Mama. We can't afford to be picky."

"How can it be rude when they're not here? Want me to scoop it out of the trash for you?"

I scrubbed harder.

"That's what I thought." She set the dish with roux residue next to the sink for me to clean and pulled her smooth, dark brown hair back with a scrunchie. "Besides, we'll never have to eat like that when we find El Cobre's treasure."

The sharp edges of my anger grated at the surface as I slammed the dish into the soapy water and tilted my chin high,

"Jesus, Mama."

"Stop taking the Lord's name in vain."

I gritted my teeth, which was nothing but a tinder spark igniting my fury. "And you should stop talking about the treasure for one fucking day, one fucking day for Dad. His body probably isn't even cold—"

Heat snapped against my cheek—the pain of a hundred rubber bands.

Mama had slapped me.

The shock superseded the shame. I was small, voiceless, and confused. As a Mexican-Catholic mother, she'd spanked me a few select times before, but this, not *this*.

I wouldn't repent for my words. I'd meant them; it was my only retaliation for the sting across my cheek. The one who's hurt never forgets.

"Don't you dare talk like that!" She snapped. "You're one to talk with that boy in your bedroom at your dad's wake. No one loved your father more than me."

I wanted to tell her I doubted that. In her opinion, no one could feel or live as deeply as she did. She failed to see that he had been my and Cat's lifeline, but I lost the courage to be cruel enough to point that out. Instead, I bit down on my tongue until I tasted the pain.

Joss graced the kitchen entrance, a stilted look on her face suggesting she'd encountered a scene she shouldn't have witnessed. Conflict was a way of life with Mama, whereas the Marwoods buried theirs with silent disconnect. In all the years I've known Joss, Mr. Marwood had spoken maybe five sentences to me. Sometimes, I wish that was all I got from Mama.

"Trash can's filled up outside." Joss's voice was light, unintrusive, eyes focused on the linoleum. I prayed she hadn't seen the slap. "I can take any others to the Penny Bucket's dumpster later. Brought in your mail, too."

"Gracias," Mama said. "You are too good to us, especially Laney-Lou." She paused next to me, patting my shoulder before picking up the pile of mail. My muscles tensed at her touch.

"Huh." Mama's tone was curious yet wary as she flopped a glossy brochure on the counter. "Princeton." She whistled. "Interesting. How fancy."

The glossy brochure crinkled between my fingers as I yanked it away, clutching it like a shield against the inevitable barrage of questions. Every page showcased exactly what I'd dreamed of—cutting-edge research labs, passionate professors gesturing mid-lecture, students sprawled on sun-dappled lawns debating philosophy. Then Wyatt had to mention it was on his college list, too.

Despite my excellent grades, Princeton felt like it was slipping away with Dad's sudden death, leaving me uncertain of my place in this new reality or what, if anything, I was supposed to hold together for my family.

Joss still operated under our childhood dreams of inseparable adventure and success together, unaware of my hidden desire for an Ivy League education and escape from our dead-end town.

"It's cool they're interested," Joss said. "Even if Arizona won't give you up that easily."

I cleared my throat, desperate for some water. My cheek still throbbed. "Yeah. Cool."

"Then you should apply," Mama said, perhaps as a subtle apology for the slap. Sorry had never been in her vocabulary. "If it's your dream. Always go for your dream."

"Well, our dream is to get outta here and open our own marketing agency together," Joss said. "Right, D?"

As Joss twirled a chunk of her glossy bob, I realized her escapist fantasies had wormed their way into more conversations lately.

I remembered the cramped trailer she had lived in until fourth grade before coming into family money. Now, the Marwoods lived in a spacious house with sparkling new appliances and multiple cars in the garage—everything that had once been beyond grasp during food stamp living.

Vinyl records, many vintage, lined her shelves: Joy Division, Beach Boys, Lauryn Hill, Prince, Sufjan Stevens, The Clash—their depth and breadth belayed her popular girl persona from school. Behind closed doors, she nerded out over botany, filling journals with pressed flowers. "Vinyl Joss" could be introspective and tender-hearted when no one was looking.

Despite the Marwoods' newer wealth, I couldn't shake the feeling Joss still felt like an "other" who had everything to prove to Jericott.

"Yeah, sure," I said, filling a drinking glass from the tap. "Can we talk about all this later?"

"Don't put it off, mija," Mama said. "Your father would not want your life to come to a standstill grieving him. That's why I'm going treasure hunting in a few weeks. Just me, the mountains, and my dream. The best place to feel and talk to him."

A cold tingle expanded in my chest. I set down my water glass, resisting the urge to squeeze it, imagining that the pain from the shattered glass could rival my shock and anger. Instead, I raised my eyes to the ceiling, marbled with water stains. I shouldn't be shocked she'd say something like that. This was Mama, after all.

"Wow. The nerve."

"I'm gonna go check on Cat," Joss whispered to nobody, and I was grateful she was around to shield my sister from the impending fight.

"Don't start with me, Laney," Mama warned, sitting at our tiny kitchen table, her sanctimonious little pulpit. "Everyone has their process."

"Their process? No, don't turn around and frame your selfishness as some grieving thing. I'm telling you, we need you. Cat needs you. More than ever now."

"And I'm not going anywhere." Mama lightened her tone. "I mean, technically. You need me, yes, of course you do, and this is how I'll provide for you girls. I'm getting so close. This is our birthright."

Jericott rode the coattails of the El Cobre legend hard—trinket-laden gift shops, cheesy signs, guided tours for half-hearted tourists passing through to a bigger destination—but no one held on tighter than Mama. She'd drone on about birthright, eyes lighting up at the mention of it, her voice filled with pride as she retold the stories passed down through generations. To her, the treasure was not just a myth but a tangible piece of family history that she clung to fiercely, determined to bring home one day.

I groaned. "Can you stop with that? Quit living in the past and accept no one's gonna find it, if it's even real. The sooner you realize that, the better off we'll all be. I'm so tired of being the adult."

Mama looked up to the ceiling. "I love you, but you can be so mean sometimes." She wiped the corner of her eye with her finger, darkening it with a mascara smudge. "You act like I don't do anything for you. Like I never labored for days with you and your sister, nursed you, cared for you till I couldn't recognize the woman I saw in the mirror. That I worked shit jobs cleaning toilets and caring for other people's babies when all I wanted was to be with my own. Selling door-to-door so that I could provide for you all when your dad couldn't with his arthritis."

She furiously rubbed remnants of tetrazzini from her hands with the kitchen towel. "It was easier for him to be the favorite, being home with you, and I was okay with that. Because I loved him dearly, and yes, he probably is—was—the better parent. I accept that. And despite everything, I've carried passion through my life, a dream. A dream that's kept me going—and sane. Someday, you'll understand. But don't act like I've done nothing for this family."

I sighed; her guilt trip didn't work on me. "It's not my problem you sacrificed when you didn't want to. And now you feel it's your turn; screw your daughters—"

"Laney—"

"I hate you."

I stormed into the bathroom, slamming the door and locking it to avoid Cat and Joss, too. Splashing cold water on my face did little to help me regain control of my breath.

Dad's love for Mama was the only thing to curb my bitterness. Now, without his strong emotional dam to hold us back, I feared our resentments would drown us all.

3

Now – August 2018

Dim moonlight guides my sprint through the backyard's overgrown grass as I spot the figure for a split frame before it disappears into the shadows. Grateful for the gap in our dilapidated fence, I slip through, my back grating against the rough wood.

Distant sirens whine above the chittering neighborhood silence. I scan shadow after shadow, coming up empty. A sharp left out of the alleyway takes me to an empty stretch of a weed-strewn lot. The streetlight at the far end of the lot flickers, catching the masked silhouette of a figure walking briskly away. An odd thrill burrows into me. And it's almost as if the stranger can sense it, turning their head back to me before running at full speed.

You're not getting away this time.

Heat and humidity weigh against each stride as my lungs burn, my legs pumping toward them through the thick summer air. The person in the shadows held the key. Mama's rivals in the treasure hunt were ruthless and cunning, but none could match her passion, knowledge, or connection to the chase. One duo, in particular, almost ended our lives ten years ago. I can still feel their fetid breath on my skin. They would have snuffed us out were it not for the selfless act of someone who paid the ultimate price for our safety. It's a debt that still weighs heavily on me.

The silhouette must be one of them. I need it to be one of them.

Burning thirst, branches whipping across my face, rocks tearing at my shins anchor the chase. Each pain feels like vindication, a chance to finally banish those phantoms that lurked outside windows and haunted empty backseats. Wanting or needing is insufficient. The stranger gains fifty yards on my strenuous puffing through the labyrinth of foliage and backstreets before climbing the brick wall of the old mill sandwiched between the river and the railway. Police sirens wail louder, making it harder to ignore that I left Cat, confused and alone, in front of our house. Ragged breaths tear through my throat as the shadowy figure vanishes over the wall, leaving only empty darkness behind.

Red and blue lights strobe from Sheriff Shelby's patrol car when I return to my driveway. There's a nauseating sense of déjà vu that hits me, PTSD from when he led the ambulance last week to pick up Mama after I found her unresponsive—another cruel wink from the universe.

Sheriff Shelby stands with his hands on his hips next to Cat, shifting her weight between her feet, twirling her skirt hem into a tight, nervous ball. Each step towards them is heavier than the last, weighted with guilt. The nearly imperceptible outline of our small house at night is only visible from the illuminated windows that display Shelby's officer combing through our belongings.

Cat's face lights up in relief when she sees me. She gets up so we can meet halfway across our unkempt lawn for a hug. "Did you catch the bad guy, Laney?"

"Almost," I say, gathering her wild hair, chilled by the air, and setting it in a neat curtain over one shoulder. "But he won't be coming back, don't you worry about that."

"Is that right, Miss Byrne?" Shelby asks, sucking air through his pointy, crooked teeth. "Got it all handled from here?"

There's more annoyance than usual clinging to his smirk.

"We're poor; we don't got anything burglars want," Cat says.

"They probably had the wrong house," I say. It's hard to keep my tone light and convincing.

Shelby tilts his frizzy mustache toward the walkie-talkie on his shoulder. "Donnell, will you come on out front and take care of Miss Cat while I have a chat with big sis?"

"Yessir." Donnell's voice crackles over the walkie-talkie.

Crossing my arms, I brace for Shelby's inevitable response. He's weathered enough Byrne family storms to recognize the signs. The sheriff's presence loomed at the edge of my vision while Cat's shuffling steps and Officer Donnell's heavy boots scraped across the stoop, fading into silence as the front door closed behind them. The half-moon reflects a metallic stream on the blacktop. Another patrol car putters down the street before turning in the direction of the mill.

"Appreciate you putting your whole squadron of three men on the case," I say.

"Laney, what the *hell* were you doing?" Shelby drops any remaining pretenses. "Running after an intruder's not only dangerous but stupid." He clings onto an extra vowel in *stupid* to underscore his opinion.

"Sorry, I had to." I dig the toe of my shoe into the base of a weed. It loosens easily from the sodden ground. "In case it was one of them. The fugitives."

Even after years, I couldn't speak their names, and the Sheriff knows it. Shelby takes off his hat, where thinning tufts of brown hair cling to the sweat beading on his forehead.

He clears his throat. "Odds of that is one in a million." His tone is gentle but still chiding.

His investment in our family's well-being has always been greater than that of the average officer. In one of Mama's reminiscent moods, she revealed that Sheriff Shelby was her study partner back in high school. The way his eyes sometimes lingered on Mama whenever they spoke around town always hinted at a more profound history, a story neither ever shared.

Though he's fond of us—Mama especially—I could tell babysitting my physical and emotional well-being fatigues him. "Trails leading back to them are ice cold ever since your El Cobre incident. Last sighting was—"

"Alaska, six years ago. Yes, I know."

"But supposing it was them, you really think you should be goin' after that kind of criminal in the dark?"

"With a little more head start, I could've—"

"Could've what?" Shelby's voice grows louder as he hoists his duty belt on his beanpole waist from under his rounded belly. "Captured and arrested him?"

I bite my inner lip. "Could've got a good look at him."

"Well, did you? Anything specific?"

I shake my head. "Tall. Male. Athletic."

"I'm serious, Laney," he pleads, the vague description proving his point. "Quit trying to follow trouble. And I promised your mama—"

His walkie-talkie crackles. "Sheriff, would you and Miss Byrne come inside?"

"Be right there," he calls back, filling me with relief at being spared his lecture. I walk toward the house, Shelby following in resignation.

The intruder exploited Mama's pack-rat tendencies by upending and breaking knickknacks, overturning lamps and chairs, and emptying drawers. Papers and junk are strewn like confetti across our dingy floors, amplifying the existing mess. Our vulnerabilities have been exhumed from cupboards, closets, and corners.

Bile churns the heat of embarrassment as I spot both precious and inconsequential things chucked on the floor. There's a button in an immaculate, tiny zip-lock bag, an insurance policy for a sweater I rarely use and will never repair. Next to it, Donnell's boot touches the edge of a creased, smudged picture of Mama, me, and Cat squeezing our faces into an overexposed frame, a blurry Copper Lanes in the background.

"It appears nothing was taken, Sheriff," Donnell says, shoving his notepad into his jacket pocket. "Money's left untouched, electronics, too." He turns to me, the tips of his buzz cut as sharp as his gaze. "Did you witness the suspect carrying anything?"

The memory of his swift movements through the alleyway flashed fresh—vaulting fences and weaving between shadows like a cat in the night. "Doesn't mean he didn't have something in his pocket."

Cat increases the volume on the thankfully intact TV to mask our voices. She sits in the sagged middle of our sofa amid the living room's mess, the glow of a *Buffy* cable rerun reflecting on her glasses. Her detachment from the burgled chaos is my only comfort.

"Scan through with us and see if anything of note is missing," Shelby suggests.

We move to the bedroom I share with Cat, which experienced the least disruption; a few rifled-through items under our beds, but that's about it. Her shelves of meticulously arranged toys remain untouched. "Looks fine."

Then, we head to the room I haven't opened for a week: Mama's bedroom. They'd touched the dresser only with a tidy reverence as if understanding its atmospheric gravity; the clothes merely thumbed through before moving on to other spaces. Cups, dishes, tissues, and amber pill bottles still burden the nightstand in their haphazard pattern.

The medical supply company has yet to pick up the rental bed. I swallow hard at seeing its wrinkled sheets, almost as if I can still see the outline of her frail body since she took her last breath on them.

"Room's fine," I say before a hasty exit to the hallway.

Mama's den is in the worst shape. Instead of a third bedroom for me or my sister, her dreams of fortune and glory superseded a daughter's need for a space.

Topographical maps of El Cobre, remnants of Mama's years-long treasure hunt obsession, once tacked on corkboards, now litter the ground. Her floor-to-ceiling bookshelves border three of its four walls with old encyclopedias, archaeological and anthropological texts, gemology, numismatics, maritime and early American history, scrapbooks of newspaper clippings, and fictional treasure tales.

The collection overwhelms my senses, evoking the familiar chemical whiff of paper breakdown, cellulose, and lignin every time she cracked open a book. Memories flood back of Mama recounting their stories and how together we devoured her dreams through their musty pages.

Now, these books lay heaped on the floor, their wisdom discarded by the intruder's lack of interest. The old secretary's desk's drawers and cubbies were gutted and abandoned. Like a beached whale, the globe shifts on the wrong axis.

I step gingerly around the papers, reeling.

Why? Were you hiding something, Mama?

"Can you tell if anything is missing?" Shelby asks as if reading my mind.

I tilt my head. "No idea. Mama had a lot of useless shit."

"Seems to me like the burglar was on a mission."

My boot catches on an ancient, yellowed copy of *De Gemmis et Lapidibus* by De Boodt, where pristine white paper edges stick out like modern flags in an antique. The sheet slides free easily as I kneel, revealing elegant navy calligraphy and an intricate logo—an hourglass and compass wound together in delicate lines:

RELICS LTD.

INV. # 1121

TRANSACTION # 0118R3L17AZ84

26/11/2017

AB PAID IN FULL

May this light your true path.

"This," I whisper. "This I've never seen."

The Sheriff nervously finger-combs his sparse hair before putting his hat back on. "Donnell, go sweep the kitchen door area and backyard again." As his eyes follow Donnell out of the room, I can tell he'd rather keep what he's about to say out of his officer's earshot, which hooks my immediate attention.

Shelby gently takes the paper, a flicker of recognition zeroing his attention in on the name and logo in the top left corner. His expression sours, and his upper lip disappears beneath his mustache.

"Now, what I'm about to tell you does not mean it leads back to *them*. Y'hear me?"

I nod, too curious to challenge him.

"There's been an uptick in activity in the dark net treasure-hunting community," he says, handing the paper back. "But especially in the last week. People looking for somethin' as if it were up for grabs now."

The strange receipt trembles in my hand as Shelby's unspoken message hangs between us: since Mama died.

"They talk in code stuff I don't understand much. I know there's an urgency to find something, and this." He points at the hourglass-compass insignia. "And the words Relics Ltd. have been all over. I see 'em just before they find and block me from different chat rooms."

It surprised me that Shelby's involvement in El Cobre was deep enough to be scouring the dark net for activity.

"And you still don't think it's them?" I ask. "Feels like they're written all over it."

He shrugs. "They've stayed away with good reason; the heat's always on them when they come outta hiding." He glances at the receipt. "There are so many others looking for El Cobre answers and artifacts. Other than tall and male, the culprit's still a needle in a greedy haystack."

"I need to know my sister's safe." I fold the receipt into the back pocket of my jeans. "And that haystack can do whatever the hell they want with El Cobre. The well's dried up here as far as I'm concerned."

Shelby scans the graveyard of books on the floor. "Let's hope so. And you know I'll do whatever I can to..." He makes a rolling motion with his hand. Safety is too delicate, too dangerous to promise.

"Better get back to your pencil pushing then." The exhaustion seeps through every word as my petty jab hangs between us, unfair and laden with frustration at another dead end.

Shelby purses his lips as if acknowledging the blunder of his empty promise. "I'll patrol the area myself tonight. Arrange for your stay at the motel—"

"We'll manage. Cat needs her routine."

He turns to me. "Sure?"

Frustration crackles beneath my skin as his concern grates against years of independence. "Always do and won't stop now." The words snap back, worn smooth as river stones from constant use. Donnell scribbles some final notes on his pad before packing up the fingerprinting kit.

Shelby pauses at the door. "I can help stay and clean."

"Let's not draw out our goodbyes. I'm good."

Honestly, I don't know if I am, but having Shelby hover over me won't get me any closer to good.

When Donnell is halfway to his patrol car, Shelby peeks his head in again. "Maybe look at that receipt again. See if it shakes anything loose your mama may have talked about."

"I will."

I shut the front door before leaning against it, surveying the damage through the tenderness of privacy. A gnawing fragility raps at my heart, at what looks like the contents of a pathetic life dry-heaved onto the floors. The bubble of fearful uncertainty grows with each misfortune: Dad, senior year, Mama, this.

Anger burns easier than grief as reality settles in. A dining room chair wedges beneath the broken front door's handle—a futile barricade. Each window lock clicks beneath my fingers, followed by the flimsy back door's deadbolt, all these fragile barriers pretending they could keep the world at bay.

As I collapse on the couch with my sister, our dusty grandfather clock strikes ten. With her own clockwork, Cat gets up, unfazed by the night's disruption. For her, the world turns all the same; a routine is sacred.

"Night, Laney," she says, shuffling to the bedroom.

"G'night, Cat."

Her door clicks shut and the day's deluge floods over. Ten p.m. is the only time to digest my day. Some evenings, it means lying motionless, staring at the popcorn-stucco ceiling, letting thoughts seep out until my neck aches. I call it brain bleaching.

Other nights, too many browser tabs remain open in my head, so I bury my palms into my eye sockets until I see sparkles of color, dimming my thoughts until I can drain them for another day. But tonight, neither coping mechanism works; I'm too exhausted even to fear whoever broke in.

Love bears layers of fear. The first layer is the responsibility for someone's survival, someone who takes up all your heart and fills all the cracks of sadness with joy. The next layer of fear is having limited choices and resources to help them thrive, let alone survive. The choking paralysis of responsibility sears my limbs and chest, wondering whether I'm doing right by my sister.

How am I gonna do this?

My fingers dip into the coin pocket of my jeans, finding the small wooden heart, its edges worn smooth by years of secret touches. Each groove holds a memory of Wyatt, polished by time like beach glass, beautiful and cutting all at once. The memento disappears back into denim darkness where it lives, a constant whisper of everything that slipped away. I'm about to pull the handwritten receipt from my pocket when I hear the familiar creak of our bedroom door.

"I can't sleep," a bleary, rumpled Cat whispers. "Tell me the story of El Cobre again?"

"Sure. Be right in."My legs tremble beneath me as I push to standing, brushing my hands across the grimy denim that's seen better days. Each movement forward might waver, but they come anyway—just like always, just like they have to.

4

Then – September 2007

It was the same tale every night.

When Mama tucked Cat into bed, she told her the story of the El Cobre legend. I could recite it verbatim, predict when Cat asked her questions, and time the same dramatic pauses as Mama to the millisecond. The routine comforted Cat, but the years of repetition wore on me.

I was sick of it—sick of how much it consumed Mama, me, and now my sister. The legend afflicted most of Jericott as well, infecting healthy ambitions to provide for families through hard work with the virulence of a dead-end wish.

Forget the opportunistic gift shop owners, tour guides, or the annual dedicated festival, with their merch emblazoned with El Cobre's distinct peaks and slogans like *Find Your Fortune* or *Where Every Trail Leads to Treasure.*

The epidemic hit the worst for families like the Carvers. Three years ago, Sue Ellen Carver found her husband Lawrence with a self-inflicted gunshot wound through his mouth after a tenth attempt at the treasure. Lawrence had gone from a pharmacist to a desperate hunter running on the financial fumes of a dwindled 401K he used to fund his expeditions.

We saw our local mechanic and Dad's friend, Steven Wilder, on one of Mama's dry runs—smaller treks to test equipment and routes. He was fully geared and smiling, but the next time we saw him was in the hospital after his misstep on the steep escarpment, breathing commands through a straw to a computer.

The legend's contagion was insidious. You didn't know you'd had it until you'd gone too far.

Most nights during Mama's story, I curved my pillow into earmuffs, staring at the sticky-tacked, glow-in-the-dark stars hovering over my top bunk, wishing I was viewing constellations above any other sky. Tonight, a week after Dad's funeral, I listened. After the dwindling casseroles and condolences, a scrap of normalcy felt right.

I get it, Cat. I do.

"Legend goes that Cayetano de Silva, a wealthy, late eighteenth-century Spanish marquis with fervent wanderlust, set out aboard a galleon with a crew of three dozen men," Mama began in her dramatic, storytelling tone, "his sights set on the fabled gold of the American West."

"Galleons look like pirate ships," Cat added on cue. "Jack Sparrow. One-Eyed Willy. Captain Blackbeard."

"Yes, angel," Mama said. "Unlike pirates, the marquis didn't need to steal from others. He was already rich. In Spain, he had three manor houses with libraries and ballrooms. Commissioned portraits and landscapes from classical masters adorned the halls of these residences. He had stables of horses, cellars of fine wine, and taxidermized safari creatures that made ladies faint. Yet, the marquis sought to become wealthier."

"How can you get richer than rich?" Cat asked.

I smiled into the darkness.

"People are hard to satisfy."

I rolled my eyes at her irony. Yet, I had hung on to every word when I was younger.

"Tales of thick veins of gold coursing through the new world captivated the marquis. He wanted to add more wealth and power to his legacy as all the Age of Discovery explorers had done before him. "

"Guys can be so greedy."

"I agree, angel." The bed creaked, and I knew Mama inched closer to Cat for her first revelation. "Treasure was paramount to de Silva, and among his provisions was a chest, which he kept a close eye on."

"Tell me what was in it."

"His priceless family fortune." Her voice echoed in my memory—Mama's brown eyes lighting up, those signature dimples deepening with each word like parentheses of joy around her smile. "Stacks of gold bars, shiny doubloons etched with forgotten dynasties, handfuls of glittering diamonds, fiery opals, huge pearls shucked from giant oysters, and a jewel-encrusted sword. His most prized precious jewel was an egg-sized emerald, passed down from his mother, the Marchioness Isabel de Silva."

"The emerald's my favorite," Cat said. "I like green. More than diamonds—they're the hardest thing in the world. Right Mama?"

"Right. Now the marquis kept his cache secret from his crew—"

"Cross-your-heart, hope-to-die kind of secret?"

"Si."

"Why?"

"He needed them to trek across the wilderness but was afraid they'd kill him and steal what was in the chest. So, he looped a thick gold chain around his neck with the chest's only key, which he hid under his garments."

"Then what?"

There—the part where Mama really indulged in her flare for historical fiction.

"The marquis thought himself of a solid constitution, but the brutal elements could ravage the toughest men. Scurvy took out the weakest men before the sea met the land. As the months wore on, the crew dwindled steadily. Drowned by the swamps of the Deep South. Battered by the storms of the Great Plains. Starved by the hunger of winter. Ravaged by disease from foreign streams. Other men met their fates when their hubris clashed with the native tribes."

Dramatic pause.

"Whoa," Cat said.

Mama's voice got low and urgent. "By the time the marquis reached the peaks of El Cobre in the Southwest, he was down to three crew members who were ready to mutiny for having to carry de Silva's chest over the bare necessities of survival. This angered the marquis, knowing the wonder and beauty of the cache inside."

"Tell me again what happened when he opened the chest."

"He thought it might inspire the crew to keep moving and promised them a share of it to continue. Instead, two men attacked him, saying his riches were worthless to all of them on their journey."

"It was no house—or cheeseburger."

Mama chuckled. "Exactly. Food, water, shelter, and their families were what were most priceless. They all fought hand-to-hand, sword-to-sword, but his men were no match for the military fighting skills the marquis had honed since he was a young, well-trained boy."

"The marquis gutted the first man with his sword, but the second man drove a formidable wound into the flesh of the marquis's abdomen before de Silva sliced his throat. The last man on his crew, an esteemed cartographer named Narciso Rubio, had fought for de Silva and stayed with him for a few days."

"That was nice of him."

I played with a loose thread on the tuft of my chenille bedspread.

"The marquis and Rubio trekked through El Cobre for a few days until a fever weighed down de Silva," Mama says. "His infected sword wound was to blame. Whether in a burst of clarity or disillusion, the marquis told Rubio his treasure was also his ruin. He didn't want the next expedition to meet the same fate as he did."

"He'll learned his lesson."

"Death'll do that, angel."

I clenched my blanket. *If only death taught you, Mama.*

"He asked Rubio to bury the chest before forcing him to leave on horseback. It's rumored Rubio settled in the Tucson territory a few weeks later. As he left El Cobre, Rubio carved directions or blazes in mountain stones and trees, forging from memory an exquisite map so that he could return to the large treasure with an expedition capable of helping him carry it out of the mountains."

"His blazes are what everyone looks for on the mountain."

"You got it. But, it gets tricky. The dying wish of the marquis was to return the precious gems to the earth. At his request, Rubio buried the jewels in the beating heart of El Cobre. He did it piece by precious piece, to render it impossible for some other marauder to retrieve the entire chest in one fell swoop."

"Tricky, tricky."

A phantom image rose of Cat's finger cutting through the air, punctuating each unspoken reproach. "While parting ways with de Silva after the treasure burial, Rubio recalled the marquis's last words: 'I hope thine earth swallows my gold and jewels. Shall the mountain reject it one day and unearth my treasure? It shall belong to a new generation of fortunate fools. Yet may they ask: What is thy true bounty? True in thine hands. Though it cannot save thee. For I shall die with nothing.'"

"You can't take it with you, can you, Mama?"

Mama paused as if it was the only time she'd allow self-reflection. "You can't, but sometimes it's worth it to die trying."

I pulled my covers to my chin.

"Then what?"

"Like I said, Rubio sprinkled blazes, or markers, throughout the El Cobre wilderness so that he could find his way back one day. However, his approach was truly one-of-a-kind. Instead of the universal symbols we all know, my theory is he used his own cryptic symbols with these signposts to throw others off the scent. It's why it's never been found. If you apply the logic of one blaze to another, it could send you down the wrong path."

"And you've seen some of these signs, huh, Mama?"

"Yes."

I'd seen them, too. Complex pictographs and swirls carved into rocks, notched trees, bouldered cairns, or stacks of stones made us marvel at Rubio's strength and ingenuity. They were that tiny flicker of hope for so many pursuing El Cobre, these visible, tangible beacons that a story so outrageous, as if plucked from the brain of Jules Verne, could be real.

"Rubio never had the chance to reclaim the treasure." Mama paused dramatically. "Some people believed a greedy gang seeking answers about the rumored cache murdered him years later in Tucson, while other legends say he made it with a small group to El Cobre, but some unforeseen mutiny or natural disaster fell upon them. Many claim to have seen his map with their own eyes, but it soon disappeared into the ether of hearsay and folklore."

"And?"

"Annnnndddd?" This was where Mama liked to tease her.

"C'mon, Mama."

"And the reason I work so hard for it is because your great-great-great-great-great-grandfather, times like five more greats, was the nephew of the marquis. He followed him to Arizona from Spain, determined to reclaim the legacy of our family, working tirelessly to track it down, track Rubio down. He never came close, but our family hasn't stopped trying."

"It's up to us now that Nana, Papa, and Tío Julio are gone," Cat added.

My teeth dug into the soft flesh of my cheek, holding back the frustrated sound building in my throat. She talked about our family's misfortune like we belonged in history books instead of this backwater town. Sweat pooled in my socks, feeding the irritation that made the whole world feel like sandpaper against raw nerves. "And we'll live happily ever after. Someday," Cat concluded.

"Someday, angel."

Her footsteps and a soft kiss on Cat's forehead drifted from down the hall before her shadow fell across the corner of my vision. "Goodnight, mija."

Rolling away from her brought a bitter satisfaction, the mattress creaking beneath the weight of unsaid words. Her dimples would be fading now, hurt clouding those familiar brown eyes—pain I'd chosen to inflict, pain I could control. This small victory would have to sustain me through her expedition, this tiny piece of power clutched tight in hands that couldn't grasp anything else.

5

Now – August 2018

The break-in forces me out of my procrastination to clear out Mama's stuff, but the Relics Ltd. receipt threatens to reel it back.

Online search results turn up nothing. I've already memorized the invoice number, alphanumeric transaction number, the date of the invoice: *1121; 0118R3L17AZ84; November 26, 2017; AB – PAID IN FULL.*

She's AB, Aurelia Byrne, of course. *But what did you buy, Mama?*

My gut feeling is it's break-in related. The pieces don't add up, though. And we certainly didn't have the funds to buy something last November. I was laid off from the mill's admin office and didn't find a new job until late December. Mama's disability payments didn't kick in until January. She spent irresponsibly when money was available. Unless—

"Hurry, Laney, where's the remote?" Cat couldn't stand to miss the opening credits of *Star Trek*.

"Chill out, I got you."

I set Cat up with her *Star Trek* marathon and plenty of snacks, so she'll leave me to clean. She's like Mama. Everything is a treasure to her; her curiosity undoes any cleaning progress. She'll take an everyday item, examine it, appreciate it, and eventually stow it in a new place. Our house is a lizard's chopped tail—just when I've cleaned the mess, a new one regenerates and takes its place.

At the edge of my sight, I catch the red digital numbers of the clock glowing on our dusty credenza.

Shoot. It's already noon, two hours until my diner shift and so much more to get done. The morning demands a burial of scents and memories, my arms plunging deep into trash bags filled with her abandoned life while last night's chaos waits to be erased. The remains of my tip money trade hands at the hardware store—a sacrifice to make the splintered door whole again.

In the kitchen, I clean out two junk drawers and groan when I meet the last one: the bills drawer. There are crumpled, stained statements dating back seven years, but the fresh ones unnerve me, sending stifling panic into my throat.

OVERDUE. FINAL WARNING.

What I need are extra waitressing shifts to pay for these before the utility company shuts off our lights, but any spare cash is something.

Yard sale it is.

There's still hope I can scrounge enough junk for people to pluck off my lawn to keep the house illuminated, cooled, and plumbed for the next month.

I watch my sister, unaware of how precarious our finances are, too enraptured by the Starfleet's sleek hull orbiting a moon.

Moon. Mama used the lunar calendar in her more pedantic phases; perhaps Relics Ltd. Would, too.

The wrinkled receipt emerges from my pocket, its date aligning with reality—January 2018 on any normal calendar. This was a few months before her health declined, but she received disability money for her back, which was never quite right after her car accident. She was happy at the start of the year, and her secret purchase might've been why.

My cell rings. The medical supply company says they'll be by tomorrow to pick up her hospital rental bed for its next patient. I wonder how many have died on that flimsy mattress.

Steam rises from the asphalt as I heave the last trash bag to join its bloated companions at the curb. The white Toyota rolls up like an unwelcome reminder, gleaming. The scorching concrete beneath my feet offers no escape, no way to dissolve into its unforgiving surface.

"What are you doing here, Joss?"

"Can we talk?" Joss asks, perching tortoise-shell sunglasses on the top of her head.

I grind my teeth, flouncing the trash bags onto the curb, conveniently next to her car.

She scrambles out of her vehicle to meet me on the sidewalk. "I wanted to apologize for last night. Seeing you after so long threw me off. I didn't handle things as carefully as I should have."

I fold my arms across my chest, a useless shield against this moment. Ten years of silence crack open between us, making this confrontation feel like speaking a forgotten language. Words balance with emotions on an unsteady footing, and the dynamic is so different. I'm still closed off from providing her complete grace at this point. I'm okay with making her grovel for it.

"Like I said, water under the bridge." I turn back toward the house, hearing Joss follow with her jangling keys and accessories. "But I can't talk. I must go to work soon and clean up after the break-in."

Joss gasps. "My God!" I turn to see her clasping her delicate hands over her face. "What do you mean?"

Her face crumples in what looks like real surprise, but my steps carry me inside anyway, years of resentment turning even honest concern to vinegar on my tongue.

"What happened?" She's on my heels in the living room. "How can I help? What did the police say? Hey, Kitty Cat." She nods at my sister, who leaps off the sofa to envelop her in a bear hug."Looks like D learned to do pretty killer braids," she says, noting Cat's intricate double-Dutch plaits.

My shoulders sag, knowing it's useless to get her to leave, save for a vaudeville hook.

"Guess you can help clear up that corner with the broken glass," I say, handing her the broom and dustpan.

Joss's jaw is slack as she lobbies more questions about the break-in. It's a twisted satisfaction to dribble the answers to her as she hangs on every word, knowing how she's always craved gossip, priding herself on having the scoop before anyone.

What I won't reveal is how I chased after the intruder or discovered the receipt.

"You think it was—" I know her first suspects were the same as mine. She swallows, glancing out the front window as if saying their names will invoke them like a Bloody Mary apparition.

"Sheriff doesn't think so."

"Oh, what the hell does Shelby know? I wouldn't put it past them to come back. The treasure's their white whale, too."

"Cops picked up prints last night, so hopefully, I'll know soon."

"Oh, really—"

"My turn to ask questions," I say.

Joss brushes a pile of glass fragments gathered in the dustpan into a trash bag and then pauses, awkwardly holding her hands at her sides as if accepting the questions as punishment.

"Why are you really back?" I ask, fluffing open a trash bag. "After all this time?"

Joss chews her lip. "Lots of reasons," she says, looking at her pristine shoes. "Got laid off. Was stupid with my money. No choice but to go home to Mother and Father for now."

Mother and Father. She never lost that formality with her parents, which made them sound ill equipped to comfort her. Still, I want to take the dustpan and smack the self-pity out of her. Joss never lacked a safety net.

"Must be rough." The worn spines of Mama's Louis L'Amour collection thud against each other as they land in the growing yard sale heap, leather covers cracking like old memories.

"Felt like I needed to see you, too." Her voice is now soft. "Like maybe we could fix things."

Monsoon thunder thrums the house's foundation, signaling the afternoon is ripe. The storm coalesces over the mountains, ready to unleash at any moment.

"You keep working on the den," I mutter. "I gotta take care of something else."

I go into Mama's room; the blinds have been drawn since she died. She kept them open so she could look at the mountain, probably dreaming of being on its majestic, pine-encrusted crests instead of withering away in bed with a nose cannula. But now that she was gone, the shadows helped to hide the pain.

I open the curtains once more as they shed glimmering dust particles. The bifold door scrapes along its track, revealing her closet like a time capsule. My fingers find the flannel shirt, its fabric worn to impossible softness by years of climbing mountains and crossing rivers, each thread holding memories that squeeze my heart like a fist. Bringing the fabric to my nose, I inhale her scent, which co-mingles with the outdoors, fresh and earthy. As much as I think I can throw her away, I can't. Instead, I button the flannel over my tee and slam the door shut.

I move to the bedside table, starting with the used tissues, their fragile buds stiffened at the center. Strange how something so pointless continues to give her life even in death as if she were here. Before I pitch them, I squeeze one in my palm until fingernails mark crescents into skin—because the painful grasp keeps tears from falling. Next are the musty bedsheets, half-full pill bottles, drinking glasses, lotions—all salvageable, but I trash them alongside their aching memories.

Next, I check under the bed for any rogue objects that might bottleneck the rental bed's removal, only to be greeted by fluffy clods of dust bunnies stitched with sorrow and static electricity.

But then I spot the smooth continuity of the floor, disrupted. Another memory, once covered in dust and filth, sparkles once more.

A memory ripples through the room: Mama on her knees, chisel biting into the wooden floor as she carves intricate holes and octagons while my small self watches from the doorway. “What are you doing?” I’d asked.

“This’ll be our pequeño secreto.” Mama had shifted from cross-legged into a kneeled position, her voice teeming with enthusiasm. “You know those wooden Burr puzzles I’ve shown you? Where you figure out how to deconstruct it and then put it back together?”

I’d nodded.

“Well, this, mija, is one designed for the floor so that I can keep things safe. Like treasure!”

“How do you open and close it?”

“There’s a harder way. This is the special Laney way,” she’d said, counting three wooden plank spaces to the right of the pattern and three planks above, landing her hand next to the nightstand.

“Then you press down on this.” She’d grunted, pressing a singular square of wood embedded in a wood plank.

The wooden octagon gaped open like a flower bloom. “And listo.”

She pulled at the octagonal edges of her little wooden portal to show a modest cavern. “Maybe there's room for something, like books, in there.”

“What? Why are we gonna put books in it?”

She’d chuckled. “It’s just something you only open in case of an emergency. Until then, it’s a cross-your-heart secret. Comprende?”

“Cross my heart.”

The hidden compartment became just another forgotten relic, its mystery fading like childhood wonder. Over the years, it collected nothing more serious than folded notes from Joss and trinkets, tucked away and abandoned like all outgrown toys. Just one more of her grand plans that went nowhere, a hollow comfort prize for failing to unearth El

Cobre's real treasures. Now, pulse hammering faster, I open it with the curiosity of time capsule exploration, my childlike imagination frozen in time, imagining what I could have left there: Polly Pockets, bouncy balls, or plastic jewels from the market's coin-operated vending machines.

Three across, three up. I push the square behind the nightstand and watch the octagon unfold. My hand fishes between its claws, into the tight dark space, brushing against stiff paper. With a pincher grasp, I pull, unearthing a large, crumpled, taped, manila envelope stamped with the same hourglass and compass insignia as the Relics Ltd. receipt.

Stubborn tape abrades my dust-coated hands as I tear through it. My heart leaps as I unearth a small, weathered leather journal encased in another layer of worn leather, like a water and age-proof bivvy sack. A large, ornate, oxidized gold key slips and clangs to the floor.

My mouth goes dry, my pulse hammering against my skin. Goosebumps surface as I flip through the book's wafer-thin, tanned pages. Mama neither wrote it nor is it lightly vintage: it's centuries-old and etched with a coiled cursive. Some pages show illustrations of El Cobre from a landscape point of view, while others zero in on it from a topographic level. Pictograph symbols mark various areas of the terrain. One page reveals a detailed sketch of the ornate key. It is a replica down to its proportions, as when I set the key atop the delicate page, metal and paper meld into a perfect match. Other ornate inked illustrations include necklaces, rings, brooches, and a sword. The text is Castilian Spanish—which I can read well because of Mama.

This is what she bought.

And I can see why. It's different, *feels* different, from the antique coins, compasses, tools, maps, and texts that she pawned her collateral for to get to El Cobre. If only she'd left me a note, given me the *why* for what makes this artifact worth storing in our secret hiding space. But that would be too easy.

I swallow hard, and a hot flash of realization spreads through my veins, sparked by something she said a few weeks before she died. The thought sears through the hazy web of grief. She talked, and I didn't listen. But I'm listening now.

"The puzzle," her raspy voice had said. "The puzzle place."

I press the Relics Ltd. receipt against the manila envelope, boring the transaction ID into my eyes, wishing their significance would bridge the neural gaps. They're not just numbers and letters. Anyone who used lunar over Gregorian dates is too poetic for that. *0118R3L17AZ84. 0118R3L17AZ84.*

January 2018 is in there: 0118. Receipt date confirmation. AZ stands out. Arizona. 17AZ84. 1784.

The year de Silva and Rubio buried the treasure. I thumb through the journal's first few pages again. This could be that old. But Mama could've never afforded Rubio's authentic journal. The journal was more of a mythical idea than a reality.

And yet.

Maybe Narciso Rubio did make it to Tucson, plotting his recollection of the terrain in this journal. Perhaps he tried to go back.

I take the hairband on my wrist, twisting my waves into a sloppy top-knot. The room is hot, closing in with urgency. My cell phone alarm buzzes, alerting me it's time to leave for work. I press snooze.

I'm still missing details of how and who broke in. Artifacts motivated the break-in, but how did Mama get them, and who knew she had them? If the journal and key are authentic, anyone could be after them. The bigger question is what I'm going to do about it.

“What you got there?” Joss leans in the doorframe, head tilted in curiosity.

My phone alarm sounds again, shrill and demanding.

6

Then – November 2007

"How many applications are you sending out?" Joss asked, her voice edged with something sharp.

We'd been spending lunches in the school library lately, sneaking Doritos and Snapple under the "NO FOOD, NO DRINK, NO LOUD VOICES" sign while combing through scholarship forms. It had been nearly two months since Dad died, and filling out applications felt like one small thing I could control.

"Not many," I said. "Can't afford all the fees. But enough to have backups."

Joss's mouth twisted like she didn't believe me. "ASU will be begging for you."

I smiled thinly; the truth stalled in the back of my throat—that I didn't want the college experience we'd always talked about. I wanted out. Out of Jericott, out of Arizona. Give me ivy-covered libraries, cold winters—a place to disappear into someplace serious and new.

Because Dad's death had cracked something open in me. A quiet hunger for an adventure of my own, a life I could claim for myself. I could no longer unsee the way this town held me down, pressed under its thumb.

"I like to keep my options open," I offered.

Joss didn't answer, her eyes on the envelope she was sealing. Then Wyatt walked up. My heart did that thing again, a warm, racing wallop. He looked at me, not Joss, which made everything more complicated.

"How're your applications coming?" he asked, low and kind.

"She's going to ASU," Joss said before I could respond.

Wyatt raised an eyebrow. "Is that right?"

I fumbled. "Well, I added a few others. Dream schools. Princeton. UChicago. Cornell."

His expression lit up. "Princeton's my number one. But—Delaney, their extended mailing deadline's today."

Panic surged, and the air in my lungs suddenly shallow. "I thought it was next week—"

"Financial aid is next week," he said gingerly.

Joss twisted her body squarely towards me, her face shiny with irritation. "Wait, those are all East Coast."

I couldn't meet her glare. I couldn't explain that I'd already started imagining a life where I wasn't the girl whose dad died, whose mom only got out of bed to chase fool's gold. I didn't want to be the one who stayed behind.

She pointed at my papers with her purple gel pen, her voice too loud. "I thought we were talking about in-state backups."

The library aide shushed us.

Joss sneered at her, rolling her eyes, and curtly gathered her things before storming out. I followed suit, hurriedly jamming papers into my bag while Wyatt distanced himself in the sunny school quad, seemingly safe from an argument that threatened to cause a chasm in our friendship. All the while, my deadline error screamed like a siren in my head.

"Dude." I pulled her by the shoulder to face me. "Don't be like that."

She jerked her shoulder from my grasp. "Like what?" Her voice quivered. "A good, loyal friend? Who's stayed by your side through everything? Now, you're just like, 'Oh, I want to go to a school as far away from you as possible?' Afraid I'll hold you back?"

"That's not fair." I gripped my backpack straps harder, feeling its weight bear down on my shoulder blades, wondering if she was secretly afraid of the same thing. The brisk autumn shade cast by the library amplified my nerves. "You know you're the best friend I've ever had, ever will have. Nothing'll change that."

Joss's eyes filled with emotion, her lips pressed together. "But?"

"But." My heartbeat was in my mouth, throat dry. "I think I want to do my own thing—"

"And what? Follow a fucking boy?" Her eyes flicked in Wyatt's direction.

"This is not about him. I would never—just for a guy? No, you know that."

"Okay, so you study what you want. You could still do it at ASU. In-state tuition's going to be easier for you to afford."

"I could get scholarships."

"You know," she started, her tone equal parts rebellion and resignation, "more than a fancy school can get us out of this godforsaken town."

Her words lingered, and I couldn't tell if they were meant for me or a self-soothing mantra.

My chest squeezed. "Joss. Stop."

"I'm not exactly valedictorian material." Her voice dipped low.

"C'mon, please stop." I was keenly aware my discomfort somehow pleased her.

"No biggie." Her arms folded across her fuzzy pink sweater, a barricade against the world. "Life happens, right?"

There was no winning this fight; we were both going to lose. "Going out of state probably won't work out anyway. But I have to try. Prove I'm good enough, even if I don't go."

Joss's posture softened, and she leaned against one of the library's pillars, tacked with black splotches of old gum. "D, I get that. Honestly, I do. I'm sure everything here in Shitsville reminds you of your dad ... hell I want to get out, too. But do you really want to be so far away from Cat every time Aurelia fails at gallivanting through the mountains? A plane ride versus a car ride?"

Cat and Mama are my weaknesses in all of this. "You don't have to remind me."

Mama left for her expedition two weeks after Dad's death, returning the next day with a fractured ankle. Despite my help and cooking all our meals, she brooded, drowning her sorrows in cheap wine while parked on the sofa.

"Just ... make sure you think everything through. Deal?" She hugged me. "Sorry, I went all crazy. I don't like to think of life-changing without you."

My nose nestled into her flippy bob. "I know. Me too. Senior year's been all kinds of heaviness."

The school bell rang, signaling five minutes until AP History. My mind raced.

"Shit. Shit, shit, shit."

"What?" Joss asked.

I couldn't focus, the bell's knell throbbing in my ears. "I—I have to get my applications sent off today now, but I didn't have time to organize them. Still need stamps, and I've got work right after—"

"You have to do it today?" she asked. "Do they have extensions?"

"Yes, this *was* the extension. Damn, I'm so screwed." My chest was poised to collapse inward as I fumbled my future due to a calendar error.

"I can mail them for you." She outstretched her hands, squared acrylic tips gesturing for the envelopes.

I paused. The offer was generous, but this was my future. "No, I'll take care of it."

Wyatt strolled over, a cautious but warm smile spreading across his face. "Walk to class together?"

Joss stepped back, boxing herself out.

I nodded. "Figuring out how to get these mailed off with work—"

"You know Ms. Valencia will let you use class time to finish up."

The tension in my muscles eased. "You're right, I'll use next period ..."

"You sure?" Joss chimed in. "It's my free period now, and I gotta send off my application, too. It's the least I can do for being bitchy."

"No, Wyatt's right. I'll sort it out, then drop it in my mailbox before work since the post office is out of the way."

Joss smirked, flitting her palms in the air. "Suit yourself. See you tonight to study for the science quiz?"

"You bet."

Joss headed in the opposite direction, toward the school parking lot. She turned her head one last time toward us, her eyes flickering briefly with what seemed like disapproval.

"Ready for your class escort?" Wyatt asked, offering his elbow with a slight smirk and glint in his eyes.

His arm hovered in the air just a beat too long, his fingers twitching as if waiting for my touch. I moved my hand toward his elbow, close enough to feel the warmth radiating from his skin, but I hesitated, letting it fall to my side instead. His stance stiffened a little against the electric charge through my body, betraying the tension lingering from our almost-kiss at the wake. For the briefest second, his smile faltered, but the moment slipped away again before either of us could grasp it.

As he reached for my books, I hesitated at his chivalry, but he gently took them from me.

"Just making sure you have free arms," he teased, smirking. "In case you need to cartwheel or fight off a ninja."

A laugh bubbled up from somewhere deep, spreading warmth through my chest like honey in hot tea.

"Okay, nerd. Or is it so I can do this?" I shoved him, but he rebounded, playfully grazing up against my shoulder, eyes locking onto mine.

"Exactly. See? I've already proved my point."

Heat crept across my cheeks as I turned away, pretending to study the cracked linoleum.

"You and Joss are good?" he asked as we approached the senior wing.

I smiled; he was obviously trying to sound casual and cool with the question. "You know us. We're more like sisters. Things pass quickly."

His chin dipped in silent agreement. "So, do you really think she'll be cool with you possibly going to another school?"

I adjusted my backpack. "I think she'll get there." The daydream unfolded like autumn sunshine, our footsteps synced along Princeton's paths, maple leaves crackling beneath our shoes while October painted the campus in gold and crimson.

He cleared his throat. "And hey, I could carry your books there, too."

My stomach somersaulted. The next four years of possibilities flashed before me—studying together, being his girlfriend. My empty hands disappeared into denim pockets while shame burned away those presumptions.

"Totally," I said. "I don't know if I'll get in. But you, you've got the better grades."

He opened the door for me into the senior hallway, the smell of disinfectant and teenage sweat greeting us.

"Erroneous on all counts," he quipped, falling in step beside me. "You're the smarter one."

We took our usual seats in the back of the classroom next to each other as Ms. Valencia squeaked out a question about Beale's Ciphers across the chalkboard.

Wyatt leaned in and whispered, "Willow Creek this weekend?"

He flipped through his opening his AP History binder as I drew my college applications from the depths of my backpack.

"Wouldn't miss it," I replied, my heart skipping a charged beat. "After my mom gets off her morning shift. I have to watch Cat."

He flashed that lopsided grin reserved for our secret outings, like fly-fishing at the creek or a study session.

I craved the peace of our creek time. What started as a chance encounter of same-time-same-place fly-fishing last summer evolved into a sacred weekend routine, where each other's presence and silence grounded us, the burbling creek and whistling reels carrying the conversation in our own clandestine language. In the creek's shimmering, slender lifeline, I found a piece of my authentic self I'd never met, not even with Joss. We commiserated about the burdens of being the most responsible members of our families and discussed books we'd both read for fun that our classmates might only touch because it was assigned work. Coincidentally, we'd both read Ralph Waldo Emerson's essays around the same time. And Willow Creek was where I'd recently noticed how the muscles in his shoulders rippled as he cast lines.

Joss and I would weather the college thing, though. Like we always did with all our conflicts.

In the row ahead of us, the two Matts, jocks and best friends who played varsity football with Wyatt, huddled close. Their whispers echoed over their nearly matching polos and khakis.

"Dude, no way," Matt B. said. "Did he die—or is he, like a vegetable?"

My ears perked up.

Matt K. shrugged. "They took him to the hospital. Still don't know who did it."

"Took who to the hospital?" I butted in.

"You didn't hear?" Matt B. asked, leaning back in his creaky plastic seat, tanned arm draped over the backrest.

"Someone robbed Kip's early this morning," Matt K. said, fiddling with his yellow Livestrong bracelet. "Beat him to a pulp with the butt of a gun. Bunch of guns missing, and cash and stuff."

My stomach dropped as I slunk further into my chair. Kip's was Jericott's pawn shop on Main Street. Everyone knew the place with its gaudy, giant cowboy boot towering over most nearby buildings, and everyone knew larger-than-life Kip, a fellow El Cobre enthusiast. Him, his wife

Carol, and Mama would sit for hours researching El Cobre antiquities and lore.

"That's awful." His teal pickup had rolled down Grand Basin Avenue yesterday, his wide grin and waving hand catching the afternoon light. "Who'd do something like that?"

"Well, dealing with desperate people is kinda his job," Matt B. said, adjusting his popped collar. "Wouldn't be surprised if it was someone who was really up shit creek."

Heat burnished my neck and cheeks so hot it could've singed the Matts. We've been those up-shit-creek people. Kip had been our financial lifeboat more than once. He never judged the people who showed up at his door; he only honored their immediate needs, seeing every object as a deeply personal story. Something the Matts, with their new cars and Nike sneakers, could never understand.

Matt K. shook his head. "Who knows, man."

Wyatt glanced sideways at me, picking up on my shifting silence. "I'm gonna check with my mom, see if Carol needs anything, dinner or whatever. Laney, you should come, too."

I nodded.

A conspiratorial look filled Matt K.'s eyes. "Possibly connected to El Cobre—"

"Class, you'll have the next twenty minutes to wrap up and turn in yesterday's essays on the California Gold Rush," Ms. Valencia said. "After that, please get out your textbooks. We're on to the Beale Ciphers."

"And they don't know who did it?" I whispered while leaning forward, my throat tightening. "Like nothing on security cameras and stuff?"

"Nope." Matt B. leaned in. "Those were *destroyed*. Someone's not messing around."

Ms. Valencia dropped the chalk in its metal tray below the board; above, the slanted cursive asked: "How do the Beale Ciphers illustrate the human need to seek answers?"

7

Now – August 2018

Joss blocks the doorway of Mama's room as I hunch cross-legged on the floor like a child caught red-handed with my hand in the cookie jar.

Play it cool, play it cool.

"Nothing—some of Mama's items."

My hand reflexively tightens around the journal as every strange convenience of the last twenty-four hours collides with a flash of clarity: Joss showing up on the heels of Mama's death, her El Cobre curiosity, seeing her before and after the break-in. Trusting her has always been a dance with chance. What she did senior year was proof of that.

She juts one hip to the side. "Right." Her mouth twitches. "So, a hole in the middle of the wooden floor and that really-old-looking book in your hand is just some run-of-the-mill stuff?"

"Why are you so concerned, anyway?" I ask, almost shouting. "What it is or isn't...is nothing to you."

Her cheeks flush. "Only curious. You can't blame me, given the way it all looks." She fans her delicate hand at the mess of antiquities on the floor. "And what happened last night."

The key and journal slide back into the envelope, hiding the embossed Relics Ltd. logo beneath crisp paper folds. "Yeah, well, it's real convenient that you'd show up around all this."

"Are you accusing me of something?" Joss asks, her eyes steady on me. "If you are, come out with it. Say it."

"Where were you last night, Joss? Before you saw me?"

Red anger blooms across her face. "Un-fucking-believable." She storms out of the room. "If you must know," she adds, voice echoing from the hallway, "my mom and I had dinner at the diner, then I dropped her off, and then I hung out at the Penny Bucket. Then I came to Copper Lanes. Ask anyone, everyone."

I meet her in the hallway, and her face is downtrodden, her cheeks pale.

"You can't help but look down on me, can you?" she asks.

"I've never looked down on you."

She swallows. "But you do expect the worst of me."

Blood fills my mouth as teeth dig into soft flesh, while thunder rattles the windows like my anger rattles my bones. Each step past her lands heavy on the floorboards, the evidence disappearing into my purse as I storm toward the door. "I gotta get to work. Show yourself out."

Chrissy-the-Chrysler picks the worst times to be temperamental.

The key twists uselessly in the ignition—once, then twice—rewarding my efforts with nothing but a mocking cough. The third try dies with a groan and rattle, my fist landing hard against the grimy dashboard. "Goddamnit!"

Joss angles her face squarely into the driver's side window. The smirk on her face is unbearable as she dangles her keys. I roll my eyes.

"Come on. I'm giving you a ride. Don't wanna be late."

I slam her passenger door and shove the seatbelt into the buckle with dramatic flair, even though the newness of her car makes it impossible with its soft-close doors and smooth mechanics.

"You can't help but need me," she says, tucking her chin as she starts the car.

"Not a word."

I couldn't let Joss being Joss consume me. My focus needed to shift to the discovery under Mama's room, its connection to Relics Ltd., and El Cobre's past. How did it tie to the break-in?

"You think this is all about El Cobre?" Joss asks, keeping her eyes on the road.

My body turns away from her, shoulders angling toward the rain-streaked glass. "We're not talking about this."

"It has to be something, right?" She ignores my request while switching lanes, the rain licking the tires. "Aurelia wouldn't hide something like that for kicks unless it was important."

Raindrops distort the diner's neon glow, but the sight of that familiar tin box sends relief flooding through my chest "Thanks for the ride. I'll find one home."

Instead of pulling away, she parks. As I head inside, I can feel her trailing behind me, a floral vanilla perfume replacing her old Pearberry.

She goes to a booth while I clock in in the backroom. She's going to keep prodding. And poking.

"Had Aurelia gone on any more hunts before she got sick?" she asks when I go to her booth as if our conversation never missed a beat from the car. I plop a sticky laminated menu on the table. "Found any new leads?"

The answer to each question was yes, but she didn't deserve to know that. More locals are filing in for the early bird special, and I'll be slammed with more tables soon.

My cell buzzes in my apron pocket. I glance at the screen to see it's Sheriff Shelby. "Be right back."

I step away into the kitchen.

"Laney, hi," the Sheriff says. I struggle to hear over the din of clattering dishes and shouting.

The phone digs into my ear while Devin glares from behind the counter, his patchy mustache twitching with disapproval. My eyes lock onto his, daring him to say something. "I have good news and bad," Shelby says.

"Order up, D!" the line cook shouts from the kitchen.

I hold up my finger, telling him to wait a moment.

"Good news is, the prints do not belong to our fugitives," the Sheriff continues. My muscles relax slightly. "We were able to rule them out immediately, having their info already in our system. Bad news is, it'll take a couple of weeks to cross-check 'em with the other state counties. These damn systems don't link together like they should."

"Anything else?" I ask. I can feel the line cook's and Devin's eyes still on me.

"Nope, just wanted to keep you up to speed, help you sleep easier."

The call ends as I hurry back to my waiting orders, already wilting beneath harsh fluorescent warmth.

"Shouldn't be on your phone, Byrne," Devin mutters as I pass briskly through the service area.

I hold my tongue and stand over Joss. "You gonna order anything or what?"

"Uh—Diet Coke and burger, medium." She doesn't even glance at the menu. "So, are you going to investigate the El Cobre connection? You can't sit on it."

"D!" Devin interrupts. "Another order's waiting, now!"

I lean over Joss. "It's nothing, okay? I can't do this."

Steam trails behind my path as I hurry the plates to their destination—two tuna melts and a turkey club sliding onto the table beneath impatient stares.

"Order up!" the cook yells.

The kitchen and customers deliver hit after hit.

Four burgers to the following table.

Forgot the side of onion rings.

Table three needs a refill. Order number seven is wrong, the kitchen needs to remake it.

"It's your fault, D," Devin says.

Two new six-tops enter: teenagers. Table one wanted their check ten minutes ago.

Corner! Too late. Devin spills six soft drinks. "Get the mop, D."

"Order up!"

I deliver Joss's burger with my shirt sticky with soda.

She gently grabs my arm, and I quell my anger at the other customers.

"Let's say what you found is connected to El Cobre," she presses. "One last hunt's gotta be worth it, right? I'd do it with you. Few know the mountain better than us."

I spot an old, familiar face in the corner booth, sipping a large mug of coffee: Kip.

The sight of him—rare in the decade since his attack—triggers a tide of memories: his quiet generosity during hard times, his El Cobre knowledge that rivaled Mama's.

"Not going down that memory lane with you, Marwood." The receipt flutters onto their table as my feet pivot toward Kip's corner of the diner.

The other waitress passes me to check on him. I grab her arm. "Hey, I'll switch you tables," I tell her, motioning toward Joss. "And she'll tip you well."

She shrugs and turns back to the service area. Kip looks up, eyes glimmering.

"So good to see you," I say in a delicate whisper, sliding into the seat across from him. I hadn't seen him in months, and he'd skipped Mama's memorial service.

"I'm sorry I couldn't make it for Aurelia the other week," he says with embarrassed acknowledgment, twirling the gold ring on his pinky finger. "You know I cared—"

"It's okay, truly."

He sips his steaming black coffee, eyes fixed on the roiling clouds atop El Cobre. The afternoon light gives a shine to the scar on his cheek, the only visible trace left from his attack. "Hurts that she never found it."

Anticipation rises from my chest. "That's kind of what I'd like to talk to you about."

His bushy left brow rises. “Is that so?” His tone is curious and guarded. Everyone had an opinion about the treasure, but his was worth hearing.

“Does the name Relics Ltd. ring a bell?”

A muted tension stiffens his old bony shoulders, so fleeting I might have missed it if I’d blinked. He looks past my right shoulder as if it was a refuge from the confrontation. “Laney, don’t go down this road, please.”

I fish out the receipt from my apron and plant it on the table. “You know what she bought,” I say, tapping my finger. “Please. Someone broke into my house last night. Does it have to do with this?”

His eyes barely graze the receipt as if its trouble is contagious. Then, Kip leans in. “If I tell you this, promise me you won’t go looking any further.” He twists his pinky ringer faster. “Anything you find, burn it. Not worth the danger that follows.”

“I promise,” I lie.

“It’s no surprise you wouldn’t find ’em online,” Kip whispers. “Relics Ltd. is the vanity company of a much larger antiquities trafficking network.”

“Who runs it?” I ask, trying to ignore Devin delivering food to one of my top-six tops.

Kip shakes his head. “Doesn’t matter as far as you’re concerned.” He combs a roughened hand through his white, slicked-back hair. “Powerful, corrupt people. They care more about the transaction than what one does with the antiquities. They want the money, not the mess.”

“How did Mama get involved with them?”

“D,” Devin interrupts, palms up in exasperation. “Are we socializing or working?”

"She's sitting down 'cause I asked her to," Kip barks. "Don't want to disappoint an old regular, do you, Dev?"

"Consider this a smoke break," I snap. "Like the half-hour ones you take during rush hours."

Devin's mustache puckers. "You have five minutes, D."

Kip shifts in his seat, and I worry he's lost his nerve.

"Please, go on."

He takes another sip of coffee, steeling himself.

"Aurelia was one hell of a researcher. You knew that. They had a sort of ... trade. Her El Cobre and Southwestern knowledge for their muscle and financial backing to find things. And their final transaction, well." He pauses, blowing his nose with an embroidered kerchief. "Even though they'd previously promised it to her, in true business fashion, Relics went looking for higher bidders. She still found a way to get from them what she needed. Honor system, I guess. Stuff I don't even fully understand."

All these months, she never told me, keeping them right under our noses, under our floors.

"You think those high bidders were looking? In my house?"

Kip rotates his thick ceramic mug. "If you were nefarious, desperate, and heard someone had the authentic long-lost Narciso Rubio artifacts, wouldn't you do anything to track them down, too?"

His question sucks the air out of my body.

Just then, Joss slides into the booth next to Kip with her basket of fries.

"Kip." She smiles and rubs his arm. "How's Carol? I didn't realize you were back here 'til I couldn't find D. How are you?"

Kip's smile is stiff as he nods. "We're good, Joss. You in town for a visit?"

She picks up a single fry, biting the tip with her teeth. "You could say that," she says, chewing. She flicks her shiny blond hair behind her shoulder. "What're you two catching up on? Old times?"

"We were," I say. "Thanks for your well-timed interruption, as always." I slide out of the booth. "Thank you," I say to Kip. "If you're around later, maybe we can resume."

He stares blankly at me. "Laney, take care. Please."

I beeline toward the bathroom, shutting myself in one of the two graffitied stalls. The thick cloak of disinfectants makes it hard to catch my breath.

The main bathroom door creaks open.

"You asked Kip about El Cobre, didn't you?" Joss's voice echoes into the stalls.

"I'm pooping," I lie. "Leave me alone." Her doggedness is unbearable.

"Not trying to be nosey—"

"And yet, here you are, tracking me down in a bathroom stall."

"Being back here, I can't escape the wonder. All the what-ifs." In a decade of hindsight, the years that passed without hope or escape from our choices had stripped our lives bare, the richness of dreams gone, leaving only the rugged, lean muscle of survival.

"It was my dream, too, once, you know," she adds.

Trapped in Jericott, I'd starved myself of joy. It sounded like she, too, was trying to fuel herself anew.

The stall door bangs open under my fingers as I push through her space, shoulder first. "I better get back before Devin flips out again."

The weight of powerlessness presses against my chest—no way to fix her life when mine barely holds together at the seams. "If something's stirring with El Cobre, I want in," she says.

A thrill stirs in me, but I push it down. The main bathroom door slams in my wake.

She wants in, but do I?

"Gah-damn, D, order up!" the cook shouts from the service window.

As I hustle to grab the order, my heart drops at Kip's abandoned booth. I push past the service area and rush to his empty seat, a wave of letdown washing over me. So many vital questions still linger. The only thing remaining is a twenty-dollar bill tucked neatly under his still-steaming mug.

I twist around to find Devin's weasel face inches from mine, his hands holding two sodas. "If you don't get your shit together and deliver these sodas," he whispers. "I'll find someone else to do your job."

Devin's patronization, the pressure from Joss, and the revelations from Kip culminate to a boiling point. My jaw clenches, and the rage blinds. Before a deep breath can save me, I take his sodas, throwing them Hail Mary-style straight at the kitchen window—ice chunks and soda spatter the wall and the line cook.

The entire restaurant falls record-scratch silent.

"Guess you'll have to find someone else." I hiss in his face.

My purse swings from the hidden hook behind the bar as I stride toward the exit, chin lifted while Joss's stunned face blurs past in my peripheral vision.

"You're a loser, Byrne!" Devin shouts. "That's all you'll ever be."

"We'll see about that." I wave my middle finger in the air, storming out.

Trudging toward the dumpster, my chest heaves with panic. The monsoon humidity stifles it to the point my breathing aches.

"Keep your nose to the grindstone," Dad would say. "And everything will work out."

Seven jobs later show it's not that simple. And word gets around Jericott fast. My prospects are bleak.

Utility and mortgage bills wait back home. I punch the dumpster siding until it grates off a layer of my knuckle skin, furious and ashamed of the choose-your-own-adventure that's led me here. My legs give out as I slump against the wall, blood beading across my raw knuckles.

Minutes later, gravel crunches from behind me. It's Joss. This is her fault.

"That piece-of-shit Devin deserved that and more," she says. "I'll take you home to Cat."

She had to get my wheels turning about treasure hunting El Cobre. I couldn't fathom returning there.

"No, let it go."

"D, come on." She looks at me with a wry smile. "I have some ideas."

Joss and her ideas. I don't want her to be my last resort. But I don't have another plan, either.

Cat sits with ballerina-straight posture on the sofa's edge, still watching Star Trek.

"You're home early," she says over the sonic, eerie theremin oscillations of the show's theme song. "Hi, Joss."

"Hey, Kitty Cat," she says. "I brought some fries from the diner; want some?"

I frown. I see what she's trying to do—use my sister to buffer my anger.

"Please hear me out," Joss says, stopping short at the kitchen archway, handing my sister the Styrofoam box of fries. Cat happily digs in at the dining table.

My jaw tightens. "I can't go on this merry-go-round with you."

Joss rolls her ankle in a circular motion; I can almost hear her brain working out its next angle.

"What is that?" Cat asks, pointing to the manila envelope sticking out of my purse slumped on the counter. "Is that a present for me?"

"We'll talk about it later, Cat," I say, my throat dry.

My steps falter halfway to the sink as Cat's quick fingers dart into my purse, emerging with the stolen envelope. "Cat, no! Give it back!"

"Laney, you always say no secrets." Cat clutches the envelope to her chest while Joss stands in the corner, silent yet expectant.

"Of course, no secrets with you." I point to Joss. "She's a different story."

"You were best friends once. That shared everything."

"Give me the envelope. This is a family matter."

My sister folds her arms and taps her foot, her hooded hazel eyes narrowing. "It's about the treasure, isn't it?"

My shoulders tense. Cat doesn't know she's forcing my hand, backing me into a corner. She opens the envelope, and recognition spreads across her face.

"It's the treasure chest key!" she marvels. "And Rubio's journal! Mama told me she got the real ones."

"I'll be damned." Joss's eyes widen, twirling a strand of hair around her finger so tightly it turns the tip red.

Blood pulsates through my ears, skepticism converging with excitement. "Wait, what do you mean she told you?"

"Yeah, one night before bed," Cat says nonchalantly. "So, are you gonna go get it?" It's as if it's an errand to run to the grocery store.

She examines every angle of the key, bringing it inches from her face, her eyes crossing. "It's not a fairytale. Joss, look it!"

Joss reaches out her hand, but I intercept the key and clasp it in my palm. "Listen, we don't know the full story of how she got this—"

"She must have known someone was after it," Joss says.

"Please, go get the treasure, Laney," Cat begs.

I shove the artifacts back into the envelope. "It's too dangerous. I should sell it. Key's gold, and I can get some decent cash for it, anyway."

"You can't sell," Cat says between a mouthful of fries. "I won't let you."

"Can you afford to walk away?" Joss's voice is light yet cautious.

"I'll sell the journal and key in a legit way, or get a refund from Relics Ltd., get a nice lump sum—"

"That'll run out in a few months?" Joss counters, her courage back. "Then what? Keep scrounging, scraping by for the rest of your life? Aren't you tired of that? I know I am."

"She hid this stuff from me, maybe as a warning—"

"When have you ever listened to your mom wanting you to do something?" She steps toward me. "It's time to take your chance to go big with a high risk and the highest reward. What's promised on that mountain will set you up for life."

Heat rings through my ears. "Hypothetically... how would I even do this?"

Joss takes a step toward me. "You mean, how are we gonna do this? You don't have to do it alone. We may need the resources of a group. D, you've trained for this moment all your life."

Her inclusion—we—sinks like a brick. We haven't been 'we' for so long.

"The mountain is tough on the body, the heart. You know that better than anyone."

Joss sighs, hands on her hips. It's like she's forgotten what happened. "We have clues, resources, knowledge no one else has," Joss says, using her hands for emphasis. "We can use it. Shoot our shot."

Again, with the we, our, grating my nerves. There is no team, no unity, just Joss's skillful maneuvering and insinuations for her biggest advantage.

"Careful with this 'we' business," I say, my voice grating and loud in the kitchen's echo. I pluck a fry from the takeout box. "This was my mother's key and journal. It's my choice what happens next."

Cat stops nibbling.

Joss clears her throat, stuffing her hands into her designer jeans. "You're absolutely right, D. I'm sorry. I get carried away." She smiles and pauses. "Remember in junior high; we'd talk about everything we'd do after finding the treasure? We wanted to get away from our parents so bad."

My belly flutters. "And how we'd make our own little scavenger hunts with pennies." That old head and heart space are light years behind us.

"That was always my favorite game."

"Stupid, really."

The youthful excitement peters out, a short-lived sparkler.

"Why?" Cat asks, slicing through the silence. "Why are dreams stupid? They're hope that things can be better."

Her big hazel eyes shine with genuine curiosity and unwavering optimism. I can't help but smile as her words soften my thorny heart.

"Go find it," my sister says. "Go find the treasure."

A knot twists beneath my ribs as my throat constricts around unspoken words. "No job, nothing to lose," Joss adds.

"I have everything to lose." I step back, their insistence pressing hard against my fear. "This house, running water, electricity. We used everything we had in the bank to take care of Mama and she'd drained the rest on these artifacts. We're hanging by a thread if not enough income comes in by next month. If I go, it has to work."

"Who says you'll fail?" Joss asks. "The only time to hunt is now. Plus, with the monsoon happening, the mountain has fewer hunters competing for it. They always come in the winter."

"What about them?" I ask. She knows who I mean. "What happened last time we all went up there? I'll bet they know Mama's gone, and they're ready to strike."

"Them who?" Cat asks.

Them—numbers six and seven on the FBI's most wanted list. Their memory ripples across my skin in cold waves, that night from a decade ago still razor-sharp - when death had brushed so close we could taste it. Them—who'd ripped apart my sense of safety for a decade, fearing they'd come for us.

"No one." Joss waves her hand reassuringly. "D, they've had too much heat on them ever since to show their faces in Jericott again. They're older, dead, or looking for low-hanging fruit."

Joss always has an angle, a scheme up her sleeve. Maybe this time would be different. Together, we could help dig each other out of our holes.

“Come on, promise it'll all be okay,” she urges.

This push, in tandem with the mountain's gravitational pull to return, grows stronger, louder. I'm trapped in a cycle of fear: fear of the past, fear of failing, and fear of making things worse for me and Cat. But then, there's Cat, looking up at me wide-eyed, watching my every move. Can I stand by, let it slip away, only to watch someone else succeed at it down the line while we still struggle? Why not me? If anyone should succeed, it should be someone from the bloodline of the marquis.

I'm at rock bottom, and there's nowhere to go except to scratch, claw, and climb my way out.

“Damnit.” Hope percolates and rises in my chest. “Let's do it.”

Joss's eyes flicker with excitement. “We're gonna need a team.”

8

Then – December 2007

"Listen, baaaby!" Mama crooned into her tongs-turned-microphone while sporting a "Nacho Average Mama" apron.

"Ugh, Mama, stop!" I groaned. But secretly, guardedly, I liked it.

Because when Aurelia Byrne was in a good mood, so was everyone, her joy casting a golden aura over the house.

She flipped chunks of tortilla shimmering in the hot oil of the frying pan as she cranked the volume on The Supremes on our shoddy portable radio. Roasted tomatillo and cumin mingled in the fried fragrance of our kitchen, promising a rare feast of chilaquiles.

It was almost delicious enough to forget how dark it got when her emotional pendulum swung. Every bright moment with her cast a long shadow, each laugh holding the echo of what came after. It made her easier to lose when I remembered the poison mixed with honey.

There was only one reason she was in a good mood. Her ankle was better, and she'd set a new expedition date for March, during spring break, and she wanted me to come, be her mule, so she could avoid an injury like last time. She'd act like her best maternal version until then.

Luckily, her maternal instinct kicked in just in time for the winter formal. She could help two clueless, excited teenagers—Joss and me—prep for the dance that evening. After we ate our special brunch, she ordered us to wash and moisturize our faces and put on button-down shirts to avoid ruining our hair or makeup.

As she carefully applied my mascara with surgical precision, I reveled in the attention, her touch, and the whiff of strawberries lingering from her shampoo.

Mama made room in our fridge to store the plastic clamshells containing our date's boutonnieres for the dance.

"Red lipstick or pink gloss?" Joss asked her.

"Oh, definitely red," Mama said before I could chime in to say pink. "You'll look so classic with your hair."

Joss touched a perfect, coiled curl of her bob and beamed. "Thanks."

Despite Mama's flaws, Joss still chose us over Mrs. Marwood in these milestone moments. Their relationship had changed when Joss decided to quit beauty pageants at age fifteen.

I'm not your show pony, Joss'd told her mom.

And you're not the daughter I thought I knew, Mrs. Marwood shot back.

The memory of that night at the Marwoods' haunted the edges of every happy childhood moment in her house, an overheard argument that stained all the years that came before.

"You'll be just like Marilyn Monroe," Mama added.

Joss swiped the red on her lips before twirling her sparkly, white, tea-length dress, as if a trace of her pageantry days clung like Aquanet.

Cat applauded from the couch. Mama was right; the red was perfect. I turned to my own face in the mirror, and a beautiful stranger stared back. Foundation masked my pale, freckly features, and a tousled updo I could never recreate on my own crowned my head.

"Wyatt's gonna love it," Mama whispered at my shoulder.

My palms glided over the silky fabric, its forest green shimmer peeking through black mesh-like moonlight through leaves, each touch trying to quiet the flutter in my stomach.

"Before your dates get here, I have little gifts for you girls," Mama announced, handing us palm-sized boxes wrapped in shiny gold paper. "Senior year is special; I wanted you both to have something to remember it by."

"You didn't have to do that!" Joss gushed.

Inside both boxes sat green cubic zirconia earring studs that complemented my dress.

"For my Glitter Twins," Mama said, her voice thick with emotion. She paused. "Don't feel like you have to wear them tonight. Know that when you do, it symbolizes your bright futures and that big old emerald we'll find one day. The Big Green Egg."

A nameless unease crept through my body as I fidgeted with the mesh overlay on my dress, glancing at the clock. Mama wormed in her treasure agenda whether it was a high or low moment.

She'd coined the term Glitter Twins for us in junior high—she'd caught us lip-syncing to Mariah Carey in my room, doused in cheap, sticky body glitter and adorned in her costume jewelry. She'd radiated joy seeing us like that—carefree, dreaming of fortune and glory, the same way she always had, grateful she'd found a common thread with me. The birth of the Glitter Twins was a rare bright spot for us before I'd racked up resentments.

"Thank you, I love them!" Joss said, undoing the backing of the first stud. "Totally gonna wear them; they're the perfect pop of color."

"You didn't have to buy these," I said. "We don't have the mon—"

She gently took my earlobe and pushed the first stud through the hole. It pinched for a moment. "But I wanted to."

My muscles locked against the gentle sway of standing as she threaded the second earring through tender flesh.

"Got one more thing for you, mija," she said, a trace of giddiness in her voice, retrieving a crumpled gift bag, no doubt repurposed from another gift. "Thought this would be a good time to give it to you."

"Mama—"

Underneath the plumes of wrinkled tissue was a glossy, turquoise-colored bowl the size of a small saucer with thick veins of gold rippling through the surface. It's beautiful and completely impractical.

"Wow, uh—thank you, this is so generous."

"I've had it for a while, got it from Kip before the whole incident."

Uncertainty churned beneath my agreement as the gift's possibilities hung between us. "Thanks, Mama."

"You familiar with kintsugi?"

I shook my head.

She smiled. "It's the Japanese art of fixing what's broken with a gold lacquer. It symbolizes finding beauty in the broken. We don't have to be perfect to be precious."

Mama went quiet as I chewed the inside of my lip. A pretty bowl couldn't mend our relationship, but it was a rare gesture, a step in a positive direction.

"I'll treasure it. Thanks."

At six o'clock sharp, the doorbell rang, and Joss and I squealed with excitement, scurrying into my room to prep for our grand entrance. We pressed our ears to the door, hearing a few murmurs and a chuckle. Cat barged in, stubbing my toe.

"Ouch, Jesus, Cat! Nearly took all my toes off!" I hissed.

"Scared the shit out of us." Joss adjusted her curls into place.

"Ooh, sorry! Not good for dancing," Cat said, her smile so big her eyes are slits. "The boys just look so cute. I wanted to tell you."

"Like super cute?" Joss asked, her frustration melting. "Is Kevin in a white suit to match my dress?"

Cat gives an emphatic nod. "And they smell like flowers and peppermint."

"Girls!" Mama called. "Don't keep your dates waiting."

It was that moment so many romance movies and fairytales promise, the grand heart-pounding entrance of walking toward your date for a school dance, everything dissolving away as his mouth drops and consumes him with yearning, like when Rachel Leigh Cook came down the stairs to an earnest Freddie Prinze Jr. in *She's All That*.

No one warned me of the nauseating excitement that fogged these romantic moments. Wyatt's Binaca and cologne, the pin of the corsage poking my wrist, and the flash of Joss's digital camera were all I could piece together by the time I buckled into Kevin's backseat and took what felt like my first full breath of the day.

Yet by the time we reached the school parking lot, I'd settled back to Earth enough to commit it all to memory. The night hummed with potential, like static before a storm—something different waited in the darkness ahead.

We entered our gymnasium, where the parquet and cinderblock had been converted into a mashup of tulle, twinkle lights, disco balls, and fake flora. The convoluted bipartisan efforts of a divided student council called it Starry Disco Nights Meets Enchanted Forest. Sure, it was cliché, but add Wyatt, the music, and the palpable anticipation thrumming from every group, and it was magical.

The bass pounded between each fast song, anticipation building for that perfect slow rhythm—the moment his hands would find my waist, our bodies swaying close enough for breath to mingle, close enough for that longed-for first kiss to finally bridge the space between us. After a few rounds of just that, the nerves had double-knotted my stomach. I excused myself to the bathroom, a brief respite of sitting while my feet throbbed from heels I never wore. My makeup was still perfectly in place. I squinted at the mirror, then removed a layer of the shimmery eyeshadow with my index finger. For a moment, I felt lighter.

Wyatt waited by the gym entryway as we rejoined the kaleidoscope of sticky bodies on the dance floor. I chided myself for being wound so tight tonight with him. If he was nervous, he didn't show it. We danced in a group, which transitioned in and out of semicircles to about five fast songs before our hairlines and T-zones glowed with sweat.

"Wanna grab a drink?" Wyatt asked.

My neck craned over the crowd, searching for any sign of Joss since she'd vanished with jock Kevin into some dark corner of the night. The too-sweet cup of fruit punch burned my throat. "Spiked already."

Wyatt's eyes flashed wide as he tried his first sip, puckering his face. "Damn, that's disgusting."

It was a far cry from the elementary school juice boxes we shared.

"Lightweight, are we?" I teased, leaning towards his ear so he could hear me.

"If that means never having tried alcohol, then I guess so," he said into my ear.

"Wyatt Altaha, Boy Scout. You are too good for me."

"I wouldn't go that far," he whispered before pulling away with a mischievous smile.

A jolt rose from my belly to my throat.

"Alright, you Jericott Lions." The DJ interrupted from the booth. "We having fun tonight?" A few clapped. "I said, are we having fun tonight?!" A roar erupted. "Now, we'll slow things down before we crank things back up. So, guys, get your ladies on the dance floor for Band of Horses."

The first wistful thrums of "No One's Gonna Love You" dappled to the mirror ball's reflective squares racing across the wall, a fluttery anticipation swelling through me. *I love this song. It's the perfect first dance.*

Wyatt led me by the hand to the center of the floor before linking my arms around his neck. His hands moved to my waist, and I nearly held my breath out of wanting to keep them there.

"I have a confession," he said, his face a constellation of ambient light. "I requested this song. While you were in the bathroom."

"Did you have to bribe the DJ?" My nerves mellowed to a comfortable warmth. Oddly, Wyatt seemed to have tensed up, like he was almost bashful.

"More or less." He brushed a tendril from my face. "I think I'm gonna call you Firefly," he whispered. "Under these lights, goes with your red hair, your spark."

The chorus of the song picked up, speaking for my silence.

The words caught in my throat, prompting a soft cough before I could continue.

"Sorry," he whispers. "I—"

I brought his lips to mine, and like warm tinder catching a spark, his body and his lips relaxed and melted into mine. Wyatt pulled me closer, deeper, his taste laced with mint and rum punch, intoxicating enough that it was just us and our song.

We only pulled away as the final guitar strum faded, and the DJ announced a new song, some oldie like "Unchained Melody" or "Sea of Love." He looked at me with an expression I'd never seen—desire mixed with reverence. I blushed and looked away, but he returned my chin to his smile.

"I've wanted to do that for so long." He pressed his forehead into mine.

I kissed him again. "Maybe as long as me."

His heartbeat kept time beneath my cheek as we swayed together, the music swelling soft and sweet around us. A large group of students congregated near the gym's entrance in a flurry of murmurs.

"D!" Joss exclaimed, startling me from behind. Some students clasped their hands over their faces while others were rubbernecking, attention drawn to the street beyond the parking lot.

"Shit! Where've you two been?" I noted her faded, smudged lipstick and disheveled hair.

Her heavy-lidded eyes were narrower than usual, the whites were red, and an earthy, sweet aroma mingled with her Pearberry body spray. I glanced at Kevin, his mouth open, breathing heavily between stoned, nervous glances around the gymnasium.

"Never mind," I said, my lips pressed in a hard line.

Joss rolled her eyes. "Don't be a hall monitor right now. We're leaving out the back. Some shit is going down—"

"Dude, police and sirens are everywhere," Kevin said. "Ambulances and the coroner sped by like—"

"Shush, let me tell her!" Joss snapped. "I overheard the deputy telling the principal that some hikers were murdered. Curfew's gonna be in full effect."

Worry clamped my throat. Wyatt took my hand, his warm fingers entwining with mine. His touch was reassuring, a silent promise that this was a postponement. "Let's get out of here. We'll make up for this later, okay?" His voice was soft.

The enchantment shattered like glass at midnight, despair rising in my chest as I agreed. Kevin led us to his car, he and Joss radiating stoned anxiety as we moved quickly and silently through the night, each footstep reverberating with uncertainty on the pavement.

The night's interruption was an omen, a personal affront delivered by the universe. I wanted to stay, to relish in our rare moment together. It wasn't meant to be. Even with my own disappointment, the thought of hikers being stalked like prey in the same terrain Mama planned to trek in a few weeks terrified me.

My stomach tightened as we reached Kevin's car, imagining a faceless murderer in the nearby shadows.

It sent a chill up my spine, knowing I had to stop Mama from her next hunt—or go with her.

9

Now – August 2018

Before The Second Expedition

Neon lights illuminate Joss's halo of blonde hair. "I'm excited for you to meet everyone."

The jukebox murmurs in the background as I survey the sprawl of papers littering the expansive table of our leathery booth in Copper Lanes' bar: maps, permits, geological surveys, supply lists, first-aid protocols, archaeological documents. Stale smoke clings around our tactical assembly like invisible velvet. Tonight is the first of three pre-expedition briefings when we'll all finally meet.

Joss has successfully fended off satiating my curiosity by withholding precisely who is joining our team, hoarding the information like a precious jewel.

"They're our ragtag group of superheroes," she'd said. "Everyone I chose brings unique strengths."

The influence of her near decade of experience in marketing and public relations is evident throughout the process. Jargon like "gain alignment on objective and strategy," "foster team synergy," and "roles and responsibilities" are uttered on repeat. I'm the leader, and she labels herself the organizer. Then, she came up with contrived titles like *navigator, motivator, and engineer. Translation: someone who's good with maps, someone who keeps us on track, and someone who knows how to work the equipment.* We know how to do everything, but she insists on the "human power of warm bodies."

"As the leader, shouldn't I know or pick who's going?" I'd demanded.

"As the leader, you should trust in the delegation process."

"Just remember what we promised, you and I." I sip from my third beer, which does little to calm my nerves. Instead, it alchemizes into a bubbly unease.

Joss sips her vodka soda with a sour expression. "Yes," she says emphatically, clearly annoyed. "Even if I don't agree with you."

I'd advocated—no, insisted—we keep the Rubio-de Silva artifacts a secret from our expedition team. The sheriff's and Kip's warnings clarified how small we could draw our trust circle. And to a degree, I only trust myself.

Joss had created notarized contracts for expedition members that stated: *"...in the event of loss of life, splitting the treasure share with the deceased expedition member's next of kin is voluntary and not required."*

An addendum at the end of the contract outlined fields for next of kin beneficiary information or an opt-out.

"It's our insurance policy," she'd insisted, as the hair stood on my neck. "We owe nothing to those who don't get to the finish line."

"But Cat—"

"Then, of course, you can and should opt in to ensure she's taken care of. But I'm not."

A chill had prickled my neck. *Aren't things good with her mom now?*

"Are you expecting anyone not to get there?" I'd asked.

She'd changed the subject.

But I had *my* little insurance policy.

While Joss was gathering the team, I created a decoy map, which Joss thinks models the authentic one in the journal.

If anything went south, Joss or another team member could use the decoys to carry them to a dead-end at Cowboy's Saddle. The true destination was Diego Pass, nestled deep in the higher peak elevations. In the meantime, I'd memorize the real journal before secretly strapping it and the true map to my body for the journey.

"Well, I appreciate your concession," I say, knowing she's used to summoning her wants into existence, bending the stars into willful alignment. "It's too big to trust with just anyone."

The bartender delivers a scuffed plastic pitcher of beer and a stack of glasses. Joss straightens her posture, her dainty fingers shuffling a stack of documents into a tidy pile. "I've always been on your side. Remember that." She glances up at the aged, fogged face of the clock on the wall: seven minutes until the hour. "Any minute now."

I hate to admit Joss's indispensability, but she's always been that hell-or-high-water person who fixates on a goal and achieves it, convincing the universe she's owed it. Class president. Cheer captain. Homecoming queen. Lead actress in the school play. Everyone loves and hates those types.

Her dedication manifested in endless hours of research, countless video calls, and careful vetting until the field narrowed to three solid options. She'd also strong-armed the park services to accept Mama's grandfathered carte blanche wilderness permit for the expedition, something my heated impatience could never have achieved.

The parks stopped renewing and began issuing new permits five years ago to reduce traffic through the terrain. El Cobre's wilderness overlaps with a few jurisdictional dead zones, which became problematic in the deaths of one too many treasure seekers. The double murder of those hikers and our trek in our senior year only strengthened the outcry for stricter legislation.

The bowling pin-setting machine clings with a metallic rattle. Joss diverts her eyes to the door, and she grabs my arm.

"They're rolling in now." Joss scrambles out of the booth; I remain glued to my seat.

A man in his mid-thirties walks in. At first glance, he could blend in with the Copper Lanes crowd with his ragged jeans, solid heathered tee, and mud-flecked boots. However, when he smiles at Joss, he becomes startlingly attractive with his sharp jawline that runs even with his chin-length, mussed brown hair.

"You must be Keaton McLeod," Joss says, her face flushed, their handshake lingering an extra beat. He trails her to our booth.

His gray-blue eyes bounce between us. "Pleasure to meet you." He shakes my hand.

It's firm—a good start. His Adam's apple is pointy, like it'll cut through his skin. He smells of cinnamon and aftershave. A wad of pink chewing gum nestles in the bite of his wide, pearly-white smile. He chews vigorously, enhancing his high, nervous energy. He nods with approval at our war room spread on the table.

"Pleasure's all ours," Joss says, eyes activated into dreamy mode. "Great to meet in person after those video calls. Delaney, Keaton's an equipment expert and will also be in our motivator role."

"Oh yeah? What'd you bring? Pom-poms and a megaphone?"

His charming smile flounders before recovering. "Sorry?"

"That's D's weird sense of humor," Joss says in a low purr, blushing again. "Keaton's from Colorado. He's been on many expeditions and treasure hunts, even in Alaska."

He smirks with pride. "Should've seen me up there. Makes El Cobre look like a kiddie playground. I have a knack for rallying teams and sniffing out artifacts. Few know de Silva and Rubio as well as me. Puts us at an advantage."

Pain shoots through my shin as Joss's boot connects, my derisive sound cut short. "What do you know about the blazes Rubio created?" I quiz this know-it-all.

"They're among the most complex and disputable."

"What do you make of the theory that they put the treasure somewhere in Skyfeather Gorge?" I ask, knowing any true El Cobre expert worth their salt knows this belief is baseless.

"Unfounded." He laughs. "That would deny the existence of the diamond carved in that documented, weird-shaped trail tree at an elevation a thousand feet above the gorge."

I nod in half approval. He's cocky, but perhaps he has the knowledge. "How many successful hunts are under your belt?" I ask. "Where you got the loot or reward?"

He clicks his gum in his cheek again, making me wonder if it's a nervous affectation. "One, actually."

"How much?" I ask.

He runs his hand through his hair, and I can tell he's gearing up with an excuse.

"Well, once we split it between the group of twenty—"

"Hopefully enough to break even," I interrupt.

Joss widens her eyes at me, lips taut. I'm embarrassing her.

"More than enough," Keaton says, not breaking eye contact, as if that will make me back off. "And you? You get the bag ever? Do whatever it takes? Because that's what I do."

The clamor of pins reverberates from the alley, punctuating a triumphant "STTTTTTEEEEERRRRRIIIIKKKKE!" from a patron whose inebriation seems to have improved his game.

My gaze drifts toward the commotion—a cluster of bodies surrounding him, hands landing in congratulatory slaps across his shoulders. "Lucky bastard," I mutter under my breath, unable to suppress a smirk.

Keaton leans in with a conspiratorial grin. "Not as lucky as we're going to be this time next week."

Joss gives a light, airy chuckle. She flips her hair over her shoulder and surveys the scene with amused detachment. I catch myself rolling my eyes at their effortless charm and optimism.

"I'm going to grab something stronger," I announce, feeling the weight of the empty beer bottle in my hand.

Condensation rings on the bar counter glare back at me. Joss joins, propping her wedge sandal on the brass foot rail. "Everything okay?"

My gaze fixes on the scuffed linoleum while irritation bubbles just beneath my skin, each pulse feeding the throb behind my temples. "Just say it!" She snaps.

"Say what?" I grit my teeth as the bartender sets a rye Old-Fashioned on the waxy bar counter.

"Say all your judgments before the rest of them arrive. He can't hear us from over here."

My anger expels like steam from a kettle. "I don't care if he hears me. What kind of oily, braggadocios jerk have you hooked us up with?"

"Rude!" she says, her tone defensive. "That's a big word, even for you. Listen, he's a great guy. Vetted. I promise. It'll be a good group."

"He's here for the wrong reasons."

Joss drums her fingers on the counter. "How do you figure that?"

I lean into her, voice crackling with irritation. "It's a gut feeling. And two women traveling with a strange man or men, is that the safest—"

"Trust me, he's fine." She glares at me as she polishes off her vodka soda and slams it on the bar top.

"Ha, trust you." The tangle of ethanol and sugar drifts between us as I close the distance. "This is *my life.* Everything, everything depends on this."

Joss turns to the heightened clamor of voices in the bar, sighing stiffly while smoothing her blouse. "You're not the only one, D." She fiddles with the gold band on her index finger. "And I know what this means for you. I've changed since we were kids."

The spicy warmth of the Old-Fashioned tickles the tip of my tongue, triggering a memory of Mama, whiskey on her breath, her smiling face, her dimpled olive smile before illness dulled it. Physically, she'd changed, but her heart—unlikely. I don't know to what degree our hearts can expand and evolve before our nature contracts them back into our old habits.

"You know better than anybody the clock we're—you're—up against," Joss continues. "Please. Don't let your attitude or the past ruin this for us." She nudges me with her shoulder. "On that note, come meet our engineer."

We head back to the table. Keaton's flashing a Cheshire grin, chatting with a round, bearded, vaguely familiar man.

"Ladies, I'd like you to meet Tommy Ray Jenkins. Comes recommended by me."

Jenkins. The mention of that name sucks all the air out of the room and replaces it with an irreconcilable mix of guilt and fear—Clyde's younger brother. Tommy Ray extends his meaty, chafed palm, but I can't respond.

Joss recovers on my behalf. "Nice to finally meet you," she says, shaking his hand too enthusiastically.

"Yeah. Sure." His attention is on me; deep, rosy pockmarks border his bushy beard, and his dark, button eyes, like his brother's, bore into mine.

Unease pinpricks up my skin, hoisting hundreds of tiny red flags. *Why is he here?* It never dawned on me until now that Tommy Ray could be responsible for the break-in. He has every reason to hate me, has the know-how to be familiar with an entity like Relics Ltd., the inherent family knowledge of El Cobre thanks to his brother Clyde—and even more reason to avenge him.

I cross my arms. "Were you in Jericott the night of Wednesday, the nineteenth?"

The skin between his eyes crinkles, and his lips curl. "S'cuse me?"

"You heard me," I say. "Real convenient for a person like you to show up after what happened at my house—"

"I don't know what the hell you're talking about," Tommy Ray says, pointing his sausage-like index finger in my face. "But I don't like whatever you're implying. You've got some nerve."

I adjust my posture, pulling my shoulders back as Keaton gently guides Tommy Ray backward.

Joss slices between us. "Will you excuse us again for a sec?"

She ushers me toward the bar. "Okay, so I probably should have warned you about that one."

"You think?" My voice is caustic. "You think he's a good one to have given our last expedition?" My palm slides across damp skin, brushing away beads of perspiration from my neck. "That family's never been the same since Clyde. Neither have I."

Clyde's younger brothers Tommy Ray and Bill lived a few towns over in Verde Valley, where in the last five years, they dodged rumors about starting up alleged racketeering: underground sports betting, loan sharking, and even some counterfeiting. Somehow, they'd always been able to shed criminal charges with town and county authorities—reptiles molting skin and beginning ventures anew.

She sighs and crosses her arms. "He wasn't at the break-in, I swear. I already cross-checked his whereabouts. I wouldn't do us dirty like that. And there're things you have to understand."

I trace a circle from the condensation on my lowball glass. "Enlighten me, oh great one."

Joss bites her cheek before setting her jaw. "Don't do that."

"Do what?"

"Being like, all condescending," she says, dragging that last word.

I scowl. The thick, dingy neon haze of the bar suddenly feels cloying.

"It's not easy finding qualified people," she continues. "Especially with all the—well, history." The same drunk bowler distracts her with another strike. "D, a bunch of wholesome Boy Scouts won't get us to the treasure. The treasure *you* need. We need their money, grit, their special ... talents. The kind looking for redemption. Willing to do anything."

"But after what happened to Clyde? It's like a weird conflict of interest."

She touches my arm. "I get that, D, I do." Her sparkling green eyes soften, imploring. "But you might look at it as a way for us to make reparations, right the past. He deserves to be here." Joss tilts her head, leaning in. "Least that's how I was looking at it."

My fingers lift in a wave, catching the bartender's attention as the order slides off my tongue: "Tequila shot." What's infuriating isn't that Joss is defending Tommy Ray; it's that, in this case, she's right.

The bartender pours the gold liquid to the brim, perching a lime slice on top. I hand the wedge to Joss and shoot it, the burn baptizing my throat and zinging the nerves in my nostrils. She offers me the lime, and I decline.

"Go smooth things over with him. Exercise those PR muscles of yours," I say in resignation. "Better hope we don't regret this."

Victory plays at the corners of Joss's smile before she tucks it away. The tequila burns its last trace of warmth as my hand brushes across my mouth, and then time stops—*his* eyes finding mine from across the crowded doorway. *Wyatt Altaha.*

Feelings I'd assumed forever lost to the misfortunes of youth reignite like the heady rush of a fever dream. I wish it was tequila, but I know better.

"Come to think of it, I should have warned you about our final expedition member," Joss whispers into my ear before biting into the lime.

10

Now – 2018

Before The Second Expedition

First Joss, now Wyatt, to whiplash my heart into the past. He stands here, knowingly, willingly, facing the biggest adventure yet, complete with his Ivy League side-part haircut and those amber eyes. It's the same face I once loved, but there have been so many iterations of him lost, never known, since our final heartbreak. His tears have dried over a decade. Heat floods through me as my pulse trips into a faster rhythm.

"Firefly," he says, now that we're face to face. My stomach flutters at the nickname he coined all those years ago. "I was sorry to hear about your mom."

The bar recedes, wrapping us into our solitary bubble as if we're the only two on our gymnasium dance floor again, blocking out everything but the melody between us.

"Thanks, appreciate that." And I meant it. He'd come to my aid, and by default, Mama's, more times than I could count without any judgment for who she was. "It's been a while." Flutters ripple through my chest.

I want to reach out and hug him, but I hold back, unsure if it's appropriate after so long. He seems nervous, too, the earthy scent of sandalwood lingering around him.

"I—I can't believe you're here," I say, fidgeting with my cocktail napkin.

A flicker of tenderness and memories softens his gaze, tugging at something buried deep in my chest. "Chance to finish what we started," he says, not breaking eye contact.

A warm yearning sparkles from my core, like those first butterflies.

His eyes grow wide with a fiery brilliance, likely in realizing his double entendre. "Finish the expedition, I mean." He rubs the back of his neck.

"Of course, yeah." I sip my drink, but it does little to soothe my cotton dry throat. "How did Joss convince you? Given how you two have always been with each other."

He twitches his mouth askew and looks away, which means I know I'm right about the fact that old grudges die hard.

My eyes trace the familiar landscape of his features—freckles melting into sun-darkened skin, the new shadow of stubble marking all the years between then and now. "I guess we have more in common than we thought," he says, his high cheekbones rising with his smile.

"You and Joss?" I laugh. "I'd like to see you two wax poetic on ancient philosophy."

He leans in. "I think only Hedonism would catch her attention."

I almost choke on my drink. "Ouch. That's a bit harsh."

He backtracks quickly, apologizing for his comment.

"We were oil and water," he admits. "She always had a lot of thunder in her mouth."

I smile, hearing one of his trademark phrases again. *Thunder in the mouth. All talk, little action or integrity.*

"What I will give her is her skill in the art of debate," he adds.

I glance at our booth. Keaton and Tommy Ray bask in her charismatic glow, rapt in reviewing expedition plans. "Can't take that away from her," I agree.

Turning back to Wyatt, I glimpse a large tattoo banding his left arm where his biceps peeked out from under his T-shirt. It's faded, but I remember when he didn't have it. A startling sting of jealousy hits, not just for losing him after vanishing from each other's lives, but for losing him to the ink that tells a story I don't know.

He notices my glance and tugs at his shirt sleeve. "Didn't think I was the tattoo type?" he teases.

I shrug, trying to play it cool. "No, that's not it. I just ... didn't expect it."

He looks away briefly. Those shy expressions of his never failed to send my heart racing.

"It's been so long since I've been here," he says, breaking the momentary silence. "Copper Lanes hasn't changed at all ..."

The disbelief that he's here persists, a thorn pressing into flesh, deep into my heart's muscle memory. The pain sparks a disillusioned hope that I'm a part of his reason for returning to Arizona and joining the expedition. There's never been anyone else who compared to him.

My finger circles the empty glass while chaos churns beneath my ribs, each loop around the rim trying to anchor me against the storm inside.

"So, Mr. Jericott-Success-Story," I say with a playful smile. "Who are you now? What do you do?"

He opens his mouth to answer but hesitates, finally grins at me. "I'm a land surveyor, topographical expert. Still the same old me."

My chest tightens, and I quickly push my hair forward, hoping to hide the warmth spreading across my skin. I want to believe he's still the same Wyatt I knew, but I also know how much can change after so many years. I know what time's done to me.

"That's good," I say, trying to sound nonchalant.

He pauses, looking at me with concern. "Laney, are you sure you're okay with me going on this expedition? I should have asked you separately—"

"Of course," I interrupt him quickly. "Why wouldn't I be?"

But deep down, I know why. And I wish I could take back what I said, like rewinding a VHS tape. What happened between us, how we tore each other apart. I still can't forgive myself for my role in it all, and yet, to this day, I've taken solace in the idea that he'd find the best version of himself without me.

"I ... well, I wasn't sure." He hesitates, shifting on his barstool. "With everything that happened between us. And I have a girlfriend ... well, we're working through some things—"

"Oh, of course, it's all good," I say with forced cheerfulness, hoping he didn't notice my unearned disappointment before I quickly pushed it away. It's not my place to pry into his life now. "Our thing was a lifetime ago. We were babies, you know?"

But even as the words leave my mouth, they taste sour and false. His hopeful look appears to fade slightly, and our bubble of just us shatters against the loud backdrop of the bar.

"We should join the group," he says after a beat. "Only seventy-two hours until fortune and glory."

"Right," I say, my heart aching as he stands so close. "Fortune and glory."

That's the only thing I can hope for from this expedition.

11

Then – March 2008

Before The First Expedition

Murder wasn't enough to deter Mama from her planned El Cobre trek. She seemed to be the only one untouched by the trepidation that clung to everyone in recent weeks. I couldn't, in good conscience, let her venture alone into the wilderness, and she was more than willing to have me along and exploit my labor.

"It doesn't feel right letting you two go out there solo," Wyatt said as we walked along Main Street with Joss, shivering as we sucked down Icee's from the convenience store. We were leaving in three days now that the park was reopened; our trip coincided with spring break. "I'm going with you two."

But there was more than a frozen treat to chill the spring air around town.

El Cobre's double unsolved murders had sown seeds of paranoia through Jericott's residents. The victims were a striking couple of newlyweds from Colorado: avid, skilled hikers and El Cobre legend enthusiasts. Their throats were slit, and the wife had been assaulted before her death.

"Like hell you're going to leave me behind," Joss said, artificial blue raspberry staining her lips. "You need more than a crazy mom and knight-in-shining armor." She slurped loudly, eyes steady on Wyatt. "You need a best friend."

"For the record, 'knight-in-shining armor' isn't my style," Wyatt said before I could jump in. "I'm more of a 'stand-by-your-side' kinda guy. So, no leaving anyone behind—not even if you threaten me with that blue raspberry apocalypse of a tongue."

My palm pressed against my lips as laughter threatened to dribble blue Icee everywhere. Joss scowled, jockeying her way next to me, edging out Wyatt, who walked behind us. I glanced back, and he winked, sipping his drink in satisfaction.

Tension existed between my boyfriend and best friend that I found hard to soften. Joss wasn't used to sidestepping the spotlight, and now she was a third wheel, as Kevin had dumped her last week for Sarah M.

"Sure all your parents won't mind?" I asked, keenly aware that my family's flavor of adventure may seem highly dysfunctional to other families.

"Mom's got the twins keeping her distracted," Wyatt said. His youngest siblings were hellion, three-nager boys. I hadn't seen Orla Altaha flustered by child-rearing until they came along. "And my father can't say anything, being on track for valedictorian."

"I know it's a lot to ask though."

Wyatt's parents had always loved me, but recently, a noticeable coolness overshadowed their warmth and kindness. His dad, in particular, seemed to resent our growing closeness, as if worried it would derail their son, making me uneasy.

"And you know Mr. and Mrs. Marwood," Joss said before slurping on the flattened red scoop at the end of the Icee straw. "If it doesn't interfere with their schedule, it's no biggie. Plus, my uncle got in town today, so they'll all stay busy without me."

"I'd love to have you both," I said as we turned a corner onto a vacant side street.

"Jesus, where is everyone?" Joss asked as we passed a gift shop and two restaurants that were usually open at these hours, their CLOSED signs haphazardly pressed against the window. "Waiting for a freaking tumbleweed to roll by at any moment."

"People are still spooked," I said.

The last of the media left weeks ago, but their presence left the kind of careless mark outsiders can, by illuminating the world's terrors at a small town's doorstep like it was something mundane. Camera operators camped out near the police station, bulky equipment in tow, for days at a time in search of crumbs for updates. Reporters rehearsed and rehashed every gruesome detail for every live update like they were trying to reanimate a corpse, all within earshot of residents walking along Main Street.

But that didn't matter to them; Main Street, with its Southwest charm and El Cobre views, no doubt lured the TV viewers, seduced by the voyeurism of it all. *Glad it's not my town. Can you imagine such horror? If it can happen in a sleepy town like that ...*

And while they'd departed on to the next assignment and without a thought of what lay in their wake, Jericott had become a hollow husk of its golden self.

"What, they really think a killer's going to come out in broad daylight and chase them down?" Joss shook her head.

"My mom's still locking our doors," Wyatt said.

One of Sheriff Shelby's deputies slowly puttered past in his patrol car, his seemingly suspicious gaze masked by wraparound sunglasses. Shelby formed a posse to join federal and state authorities on the hunt for the killer. Everywhere we went, hushed conversations from armchair detectives about the murders fueled the frenzy.

"I was at the diner getting takeout last night, and old Lee Kowalski was spouting off that the killer's a Jenkins," I said. "You know that family from Verde Valley? But Mama thinks it's just his diversion tactic to get more El Cobre competition out of the way."

Lee Kowalski, a bowlegged cowboy in his fifties with a thinning blonde mullet, was an intermittent El Cobre treasure seeker and constant frenemy of Mama's. When he wasn't distracted by his many mistresses or love of whiskey, he trekked the wilderness, seeking out Rubio's hidden blazes or taunting Mama and other treasure enthusiasts on online message boards.

Joss shook her head. "No, there's a code of honor among locals, as stupid and redneck as they are—no one in the last hundred years has murdered for it before. So many strangers come through here looking for the treasure. It has to be someone we don't know." She tossed her empty Icee cup toward a nearby trash can and made it despite leaving sticky blue drops peppering the sidewalk. "Nothing but net."

The conversation came to a natural lull, but the tension remained taut with the weight of our decision to head into the wilderness.

Joss shot me a sidelong glance. "You nervous?" she asked. Her voice was low, a furtive whisper.

"Yeah," I replied, the word a bare murmur, feeling like sandpaper against my throat. "But also ... thrilled. Is that crazy? Don't let Mama know that."

Joss laughed, a sound tinged with her trademark confidence. "No crazier than any of us. If we weren't a little nuts, we wouldn't be doing this, would we?"

"Tell Joss about how your mom let you map out the destination," Wyatt said.

"Is that right?" Joss tucked her hands in her pockets, voice flecked with jealousy.

"It's not that big of a deal," I said.

"No, it is," Wyatt pressed. "It's huge when Aurelia keeps such tight control on expeditions; she loved your idea."

"Come on, spill it," Joss said, looking toward the mountain range. "Would be nice for *all* expedition members to know exactly where we're going."

"Ironwood Crossing," I said, ignoring her dig.

"But wasn't that ruled out by archaeologists like fifty years ago?" Joss asked.

"A lot can change or reveal itself in that time."

Joss looked at me, puzzled, expression dimmed by the lowering sun as we turned down another tree-lined side street.

"Wildfire gutted a huge chunk of Ironwood Crossing a few years ago," I continued. "And if you look at new satellite images, below the dense brush that burned away, you'll see what looks like some unusual, large rock cairns, possibly a cave entrance—"

Joss gasped. "Wait, you're kidding."

Warmth radiates through me as my head rocked from side to side, happiness spilling out despite myself. "Mama thinks it's legit, really worth exploring."

"Hell yeah!" Joss held out her hand for a high five.

"You're built for it, Laney," Wyatt said. "Fortune and glory."

His amber eyes met mine as he took a step to walk alongside me again, our steps as synched as if we set them by a metronome. He squeezed my hand in silent affirmation.

My wrist turns upward, the watch face marking another minute slipping away. "Gotta get home to feed Cat and get her bags packed to stay with the Vances," I said. "Mama's too busy with final prep."

"Three days," Wyatt finally said. "And then we venture into the unknown."

Parting ways that evening felt like the first step into that unknown, into something larger than ourselves, spun from our individual desires and fears, converging toward a terrifyingly and irresistibly uncertain future.

I knew better than to think Joss and Wyatt were coming to support me. Each of us held our reasons for seeking it, each fueled by a hope that seemed both bold and frail in the shadow of recent events.

And there would be no turning back.

12

Then – March 2008

The First Expedition

It was the early morning of our first expedition day. Joss sulked in the front passenger seat while Wyatt and I cozied up in the back, eating breakfast burritos. The trunk was loaded with expedition supplies while Mama reiterated why the mountain was nothing to fear after the double murder.

"It was an isolated incident. We can't live our lives expecting shadows around every corner," she said, her voice wavering momentarily. "Life's too damn short."

As we stepped from the car, the ring of dawn's light haloed El Cobre's mountain range, commanding the landscape with its presence. My heart memorized its outline and familiar patterns, like the lyrics of a favorite song.

The sharp summits rose like castle spires, while a trio of rock formations near its foothills reminded me of the three wise men journeying to Bethlehem. The ridges stretched along the skyline like the spines of slumbering beasts, and the pines that dotted the mountainside formed a pattern that could easily be the wise, serene smile of an older woman. Below, the valleys traced downward, like the stroke of a blue-green crayon, reminiscent of rain trailing across a windowpane. The mountain was both intimate in its familiarity and shrouded in mystery, daring us to tame it.

Joss kept her gaze down as she hoisted on her backpack, puckering her lips as if she was holding back tears.

"Hey," I said, gently touching her arm. "Are you okay—"

The Sheriff's patrol car roared up as we stepped on the trailhead.

"Shit," Mama muttered. Then she turned on her bright smile, dimples winking. "Shelbs, beautiful morning, isn't it?"

"Aurelia." There was a tinge of gentle frustration in his voice. "Come on. What're you doing?"

"Just taking a lovely stroll through this re-opened park. Doing a little light camping. You wouldn't open it if it weren't safe now, would you?"

He removed his hat, nervously palming his frizzy, fine hair before rubbing his eyes. "And taking these kids with you? Damn ... I ... is that the most responsible thing?"

Mama put her palms up, feigning innocence. "We're not breaking the law, and hey, I didn't make any of 'em come. They're here on their own volition."

He scanned our faces. "That true?"

We nodded.

The Sheriff gave a hybrid sigh-groan. "Promise me this isn't no treasure hunt up the peaks?"

“Cross my heart,” Mama said, staring dead-eyed at him, which sent shivers of guilt through me.

He retrieved a two-way radio from his holster. “I know this is a little unorthodox,” he said, his eyes creasing in resignation. “But take this.”

Mama reluctantly grabbed it.

“On a clear day, no obstructions. It's got several miles of range, but it won't work real deep into the peaks. But use it. Please. If you run into any trouble.”

Mama's posture softened. “You've always been too kind to me.”

“We go way back. You know I care about ... what happens to you.” The sheriff cleared his throat. “Good luck out there.”

We spent the morning going along the beginner trails that wound along the same shimmering creek where Wyatt and I fly-fished. Emboldened by an early spring, wildflowers and periwinkle lupines blanketed both sides of the creek. Manzanita trees punctuated the oak groves, their gnarled trunks and branches invoking a surreal Dali-like quality across the lower landscape.

Mama moved with determined steps, hardly looking back, as if her conviction alone would keep away any lurking danger. She didn't notice Joss's sullenness—withdrawn since pickup—or my dread for what lay ahead.

Resolve hardened in my chest before turning to face whatever state I'd find Joss in. “Hey, what's going on? You've been so quiet.”

She stopped abruptly, fidgeting with her sock, before retrieving a pebble from its folds and chucking it toward the wildflower meadow. For the first time in weeks, I noticed she was without her green stud earrings. My own were still in my ears, their cheapness causing warm red swelling.

"Nothing, just tired," she said without conviction. "Hey, Aurelia!" She picked up her pace, catching up to Mama for a conversation, leaving me in dust and confusion.

Wyatt laid his hand on the small of my back, just under my heaving pack. "What'd she say?" His gaze was heavy with worry. "She feeling okay?"

I shrugged, a bubble of guilt growing. "She won't say. Never seen her like this, though."

"Think it's us?" Wyatt kept his eyes on the pebbled path.

I'd been turning down Joss's invites lately, preferring to spend time with Wyatt and make up for our disastrous end to winter formal.

"Who knows," I said. She seemed normal enough when we'd drank Icees on Main Street the other day. "Probably just school and graduation stress. If it's big, she'd tell me."

A silent hour later, we stopped for lunch a few hours from Azure Vista, where we planned to camp for the night. The higher elevation showed its changing face in the large dark stones and leafy oaks that mingled with the sunlight to create a stained-glass pattern on the forest floor. The creek had dwindled to a trickle.

"Kinda romantic here, no?" Mama teased, winking at me and Wyatt.

Joss threw her backpack to the ground with a loud thud, seemingly directed towards me.

"You okay, Joss, honey?" Mama asked.

She nodded, but her face revealed an unmistakable sadness. "Just need to catch my breath."

While Mama and Wyatt ate their PB&J sandwiches on a patch of grass near the stream, I nervously approached Joss, who perched on a large rock, pecking at her white bread while staring into the distance.

"Can we talk?" I asked.

Her steely gaze met mine—the same stare she used to intimidate classmates with whom she didn't get along. "Free country."

It felt like a challenge.

"You don't seem yourself," I pressed. "What's up?"

She gritted her teeth, balling up a piece of the gluey white bread and flicking it into the stream. "A lot."

My chest tightened. "I'm sorry if it's got anything to do with me and Wyatt—"

Joss shoved her half-eaten sandwich back into its Ziplock bag and thrust it into her jacket pocket. "Fucking hell, D. Believe it or not, not everything in my life's about you."

Her dagger-sharp response startled me. "I didn't mean—"

She jumped down from the rock, checking my shoulder like a grazing bullet.

I grabbed her arm. "Joss, please, what is it? How can I help? I dunno what to do if you don't open up to me."

She looked down, her voice thick. "I'll be okay, D. We'll be okay. Let's focus on why we're out here, yeah?"

Shock froze my features before tilting my chin down, dread coiling tight in my gut. A prickle across my skin revealed Wyatt and Mama quickly averting their stares. The gentle sloshing of water downstream pulled my attention away, ripples breaking the dark surface. Beyond the curtain of oak branches came movement and voices. Mama crept ahead of us with her handgun, knees bent and prepped for a silent defense. My body froze.

It's probably just hikers on a nature trek.

An oak twig snapped beneath Mama's boot, and the noises ceased. Except for a subtle click. Someone with a gun; both parties knew they weren't alone anymore.

13

Then – March 2008

First Expedition

"Damnit, Kowalski," Mama said, scowling as she holstered her gun. Lee and his daughter, Kimber, a hulking, toothy blonde who graduated a few years ago, emerged from the grove.

Lee hesitantly followed suit, like being outnumbered by kids wasn't enough to soothe his nerves.

"C'mon Lee," Mama muttered. "It's just me and the kids."

"Should've figured you'd be out here, Byrne," he said. "Feels a little different this time after the reopen." He eyed Kimber, who centered her gaze on Wyatt, mouth agape. Her blonde curls, framing her long oval face, fell like a wily curtain over her shoulders. She didn't speak, much like I remembered from school, and she kept her shoulders curled instead of standing tall.

"God, I don't think I've ever seen her with her mouth closed," Joss whispered. Her sudden proximity sent a jolt through my body, her movement having gone unnoticed until now. "What'd you say, little lady?" Lee asked, his bandy legs stepping closer. "Speak up for the rest of the class."

Joss pointed her head down. "Nothing."

"And nothing to see here, Lee," Mama said, closing the gap so he had no room to approach us. "Let's all be on our separate ways. May the best woman win."

Lee sniffed, a sneer spreading across his leathery face. He withdrew a pack of Camels from his shirt pocket. "Now hold on, Byrne." He slowly, methodically wedged one cigarette between his thin lips as he brought up his lighter with the other hand, his slow draw igniting the smoke's end like an amber pebble. "Not so fast. Let's talk business. Where you headed this time?"

My pulse raced as I felt the map in my back pocket, a leaden anvil. I was sure Lee sensed it. Wyatt drew closer to me, protective as always.

Mama shrugged. "Probably Skyfeather Gorge." She tried to mask any trace of her bluff, moving to gather our leftover trash into our compactor bag and getting us ready to move. "That recent blaze with the bird on it points in that direction."

Lee exhaled a gauzy cloud of smoke. "Bullshit." Kimber snapped her head toward him, wide-eyed, as if she couldn't predict her father more than we could. "There're no 'probablys' with you. And you never do the same destination twice in a row—"

"Never got there last time with my ankle, Lee."

He sucked air through his teeth. "Ain't that a shame."

An idea, fueled by excitement, crystallized by survival instinct, escaped my lips. "Why don't we divide and conquer the Gorge?" I blurted out. Mama tilted her head before a flicker of understanding glinted in her face, pitting one of her cheek dimples. It was my green light. "You see, if you and Kimber take the lower section, we'll take the top." The map crinkled as I eased it from my pocket, my fingers carefully keeping the fold creased over our real path to Ironwood Crossing.

"In fact, this is the perfect location to diverge." I pointed to the creek on the map before tracing two forking squiggles along the topography, the inches a euphemism for the true miles. "We have a better chance to cover more ground in less time, and for that, we could split what we find."

What Lee didn't know was that the same higher-altitude path our group would take would split off again two miles in and take us in the opposite direction to our true destination: Ironwood Crossing.

He dropped his Camel to the earth, squishing it under the tip of his boot. By the squint of his eyes on the map, he was considering it, rolling it over and around in his brain like one of the gems he so desperately sought, scrutinizing every facet for flaws.

"Unless you have a better path," Joss cooed with her languid lashes and full pout on display. She'd caught onto our bluff and dared Lee to deny someone like her.

He looked down, blushing. "Actually." He cleared his throat. "It ain't half bad."

Joss smiled. Bait, snare, trap.

"So, when do we head out?" Lee asked.

"Where we headed to?" a strange voice asked.

We spun around, Mama and Lee with their guns out, looking for the strange voice's origin.

"Over here, neighbors." An eerie, sing-song whistle warbled from just beyond the water's east bank, drawing our attention to another man.

The hefty gear on his back dwarfed him, but the wildness of his appearance sent a single drop of sweat warily tracing down my spinal groove. His brown, matted hair ended where his beard began, grazing his chest. A rope necklace threaded with bird and rodent skulls hung around his neck while his left hand clutched a recurve bow. He wore head-to-toe camouflage, swimming to his knees in a poncho adorned with ghillie, grass-like fibers, and leaves, like someone who was more thing, melded to the feral and the foliage. Not to be trusted.

"Who are you?" I asked, the words spilling out in scared wonder.

Before the man could answer, Lee cocked his gun. "That sum'bitch is Clyde Jenkins."

"Put the gun down," Clyde said as if Lee almost amused him.

And Lee obeyed.

As Clyde edged toward us, crossing the stream's threshold, Mama pulled the three of us closer, fledglings under her wing. The water lapped at empty space as Kimber backed away from the edge, sunlight catching the tears sliding down her freckled face. Everyone was quiet, anticipating Clyde's next move. The trilling birds and babbling water were deafening in wait.

Terror knifed through my chest like a hot blade. At the diner, I remembered Lee's bombshell: Clyde Jenkins was responsible for the hikers' deaths. Mama refused to believe it.Now, we were in the dead center of his crosshairs.

He moved his bow vertically from its horizontal position, and we collectively tensed. "You shouldn't be out here," he finally said, thumbing the bow's string groove as the ghillie on his poncho quivered like tassels. "Dangerous."

Clyde's brown button eyes fixed on Mama, but his expression under the beard and camo was indistinguishable, a mix of emotions I couldn't quite read.

"Why are you out here then?" Mama asked, drawing us closer.

He stretched out another pause as if he had all the time to make us sweat out our fate.

"Hunting," he said.

"So are we," I said, trying to display the same bravery I had with Lee.

His eyes locked into mine, a showdown of silent strength. My heart was pounding, but I wouldn't dare break. Mama and my friends needed me.

The corners of Clyde's eyes finally squinted, blinking before he looked down. "Shouldn't you be in school?" he asked. "This wilderness is only for the aimless."

"We don't need anyone telling us where we should and shouldn't be," I snapped.

Mama elbowed me as Clyde chuckled. "My mistake," he said before turning to Lee.

"Don't you come closer," Lee warned, tightening his grip on the gun as he stepped back.

"And I don't want to, Lee," he said, the ghillie on his cape vibrating in the breeze. "Don't wanna catch the stink of your lies and failure."

Our group exchanged glances, relieved by the diversion but anxious about the unfolding escalation.

"Fuck you, Clyde." Lee sneered while shielding Kimber.

"I know you've been spreading lies about those hikers to get the heat on me." Clyde retrieved and nocked an arrow. "Got ears everywhere. But if I was a killer, you'd have been dead before you reached this group."

Lee gulped.

"Lucky for you, I'm in a generous mood," Clyde continued. "So, you have one chance to pick up and get the hell on your way before I change my mind."

Lee blinked, lowering his gun. Swiftly, he and Kimber retreated in the direction that would take them to the low-lying section of Skyfeather Gorge, but not before nodding at Mama, a silent *I'll meet you there*.

If only I could see his confusion when we never appeared.

But now, we were alone with this wild, burly man, the animal skulls on his chest rising and falling with each breath.

"Interesting," he muttered. "You told him the wrong way."

"There is no right way," Mama said. "We're all out here wandering, hoping to find the same tesoro."

"Are we?" Clyde asked, retrieving a whetstone from his pocket and sharpening the tip of his arrow. "Maybe I'm hunting for something besides folklore."

My breath hitched as I felt Joss tighten her grip on my jacket.

Wyatt cleared his throat. "Are you meaning the mother lion and her cub?"

The rhythmic scraping of Clyde's whetstone stopped. Park services reported multiple sightings of a female mountain lion and her cub over the last few months. Some in Jericott even lived in denial of the murders by blaming the cat.

"Something bigger. A much bigger predator." He blew away the dull metal bits from the arrow tip. "But then again, it's getting crowded out here; maybe I should join your little scavenger hunt."

Now, I felt Joss trembling behind me, trying to stifle her fear.

"What do you want?" Mama asked, her voice irritated. Still, there was a trace of apprehension.

"I want you to know you're not alone out here, and I'm not talking about Lee. Do with that what you will."

"And you?" Mama asked. "You going to leave us alone?"

"Tread carefully," Clyde barked. He looked in the direction where Lee scurried. "Just got rid of that gnat for you, didn't I?" He stowed the whetstone. "I said what I said."

Clyde spoke in strange circles. I looked at Mama, and her hand flinched near her holster.

He spared Lee despite hating him more than us. Hurting us seemed out of the question.

"Appreciate whatever your concern is," Mama said, motioning us to gather our gear. "But all this socializing's put us behind schedule. We'll be on our way—as you should."

Tension rose, crackling like an electric current through the forest air. Maybe he was a predator playing with his prey.

Clyde raised his chin, forehead pinching. "Hope you find what you're looking for." He turned, retreating into the underbrush. "And nothing that you're not."

Clyde was gone as quickly as he came, swallowed back into the wild landscape.

We let out a mass exhale.

"What the hell just happened there?" Joss asked, visibly shaken.

"It's okay. There's going to be bumps along the way," I said, rubbing her arm.

She smiled thinly, our earlier discord now slipping away.

“That’s nothing,” Mama said. “Just men trying to piss all over territory—no offense, Wyatt.”

Wyatt shook his head. “None taken.”

“Mija,” Mama said, cheeks dimpling. “Nice work fooling Lee.”

Gratitude fluttered beneath my ribs. We trekked east for an hour, away from the stream, venturing deeper into dense foliage. “There,” Mama pointed. “This’ll shave off an hour to Ironwood Crossing.”

The path ahead vanished into shadow where Gambel oaks and junipers wove their branches into a dark tunnel, beauty and danger tangled together while goosebumps rose on my arms—from the settling spring chill or from what waited in those depths, I couldn't tell. A sweet, earthy resin tickled my nose as we entered the narrow corridor of cloistered branches. Dappled sunlight filtered through the leaves and flickered over our faces.

“Aquilegia formosa,” Joss breathed, plucking a gorgeous red and yellow bloom. She took her journal out of her pocket, pressing down carefully.

“English for the rest of us?” I asked with a smile, hopeful she was out of her funk.

Wyatt’s eyes widened, amused. She’d never shown her love for botany around him.

She smirked, loving her upper hand of knowledge. “Red columbine. They stand for strength and determination. They thrive in filtered sunlight.”

Mama tutted at us, urging us to keep our lead. The burrow curved upward gradually, but it was hard to see what was beyond.

I flicked on my flashlight as we left the afternoon sun in our wake. The burrow of flora twisted and turned while increasing its elevation. A coati scurried across my beam, and I jumped.

"Nature's heart attack," Wyatt joked.

"Are we sure there's not a better route?" Joss asked.

"No need to be scared," I reassured. "It's just nature."

"Feels like we're in another realm," Wyatt said.

My heart raced with exhilaration and fear as we trudged along the incline. If something happened to us here, Shelby could look for months and never find us. Thoughts of the murdered hikers surfaced, and I lost my footing, but Wyatt was right behind to catch me, his touch reassuring.

"Gotcha, Firefly."

I squeezed his hand in gratitude.

A shuffling, skittering sound resonated from around the bend's dark path. Everyone froze. My pulse hammered against my ribcage as I stepped forward with a flashlight in hand.

"*Mija*!" Mama hissed. "Let me go first!"

I held my other hand, silently signaling for her to stay put and quiet. While fear pulsed through my ears, drowning out any sound, the sweet, earthy scent from the corridor's entrance faded into something more sinister—an eerie rot mixed with the acrid smell of cigarette smoke.

A shiver rippled up my spine as my flashlight beam landed on something not crafted by Mother Nature but imposed upon her territory: a rickety lean-to made from poorly constructed oak branches held together by moss. Littered on the floor were cash, medical supplies, two-way radios, clothes stained with dried, dark fluids—and guns. This kind of cache in the wilderness, possibly with some of Kip's stolen gear, could only belong to someone up to no good—the killer everyone feared. And we'd just encountered two men we couldn't fully trust.

A hand covered my mouth before I could let out a scream.

14

Now – August 2018

Day 1: Second Expedition

My dream last night doesn't help to soothe the unease of my departure. I'd dreamt of a mountain lion encounter. It bared its canines, ears bent in anger, chasing me over the El Cobre terrain. Just when I thought I escaped it by climbing up a tree, the feline appeared on the edge of the branch. It stretched out a large, soft paw before falling.

Sweat cooled against my skin as the darkness pressed in, yellow lamplight pooling from Mama's nightstand while my fingers sought Rubio's journal beneath the floorboards. The leather cover and delicate parchment look even older at this shy hour. I leaf through every page again until I'm nearing the end, where I notice one page feels thicker than the rest. My heart catches as I delicately knife my thumbnail between pages cemented by centuries of secrecy.

A fraction of the way peeled, it resists, and my breath hitches. One shred of impatience or wrong move could ruin its legibility. It takes me countless minutes to splice the pages bit by bit before they finally divide, with only some of the crumbled edges as collateral.

The page depicts a labyrinth of tunnels, sepia shaded and sketched like vicious jaws, crevices and alcoves leading to unknown ends. One twisting, long flourish culminates into an elaborate X. I gasp, hand over my lips.

The treasure is in Diego Pass, but the valley leads to an unknown cave where X marks the spot.

Gingerly, I tuck the journal into my discreet money belt, which I'll strap on in just a few hours, and keep this discovery to myself—for now.

As dawn blushes in strips of peach and periwinkle across the sky, I drop Cat off with our elderly neighbors, the Vances, who are always up before the sun. Our expedition group convenes at six a.m. at Willow Creek Park, which feeds into the mountain's base.

"Mrs. Vance has your TV schedule and enough bologna and cheese to get you through 'til I get back, 'kay?"

I'd already settled her toys, blankets, and toiletries in their spare bedroom.

Cat rubs her eyes. "You think you'll bring back a lot of diamonds and gold? Can I keep the sword?"

"Already claiming the bounty, are we? We'll see."

"I know you'll find it. I got a good feeling."

Doubt gnawed at my edges, making her certainty feel like a different language. The odds lined up, a sequence of dominoes poised to tip. A week to find a treasure my mother couldn't find for decades. Utilities shut off in ten days. Twelve days until the bank comes calling for the house and merging my ex-best friend, the one that got away, and perfect strangers with their secrets and redemptive pursuits.

There is a possibility I won't return or get injured and end up an invalid like Mama. Or something could happen to Cat while I'm there, and I won't know because there's no cell reception.

"Sure you'll be okay without me?" I ask Cat at the last minute, hoping that there'll be a valid reason to excuse me from this whole quest. I brush the long bangs out of her face. "Gotta cut those things when I get back. I can still cancel."

She swats my hand away from her fringe. "Don't you dare cancel," she says, wagging a finger at me. "I believe in you."

My jaw locks tight while grief balls into a hard lump, forced back down before it can escape. "You know ... I'm not like Mama, right?"

She nods. "You won't say it..." she teases. "You love adventure."

I shake my head. "This is different." Mama and I are nothing alike. "And I'll be back for you."

"You're good to me, Laney. Too good. I'll be okay."

On Vance's porch, we stand in silence, the dread of the goodbye bubbling up. We give each other one of those deep farewell hugs intended to embed essence into memory: soft skin, baby shampoo, and her light, lisping voice.

Our group isn't alone as I pull up to the lot at Willow Creek Park. This town can't keep its mouth shut about anything; one whisper in public pollinates its way through Jericott. Word of our expedition ignites the competition and curiosity of other teams.

A smattering of trucks, cars with doors ajar, and people crowd nearly every designated spot. The sun has yet to show its face over the ridge; shadows still bathe the trees and bushes of the park's trails.

Alongside other teams are those who I like to call treasure groupies, sucking up the air and concentration of the serious crews, snapping selfies of the sunrise over El Cobre and chatting up those doing equipment checks, cheering us on as we step onto the trail, like the way I've seen some girls fawn over the local subcultures of bull riders or drag racers.

"Greeting your fans, I see," I mutter to Keaton, who's in the middle of smiling for a picture with a tall brunette in full makeup.

He straightens his jacket as the woman scampers off excitedly. "Just embracing the life," he says. "You should try it sometime."

"Guess some of us are more serious than others," I say. "To survive, you have to be."

Keaton winces, sucking air through his bright teeth. "Yes, Captain." He turns and heads over to Tommy Ray.

The mountain has always been a fierce protector of its secrets. Too steep and craggy to navigate by all-terrain vehicles, El Cobre chews up and spits out their mangled metal cages and toylike tires like a predator who guts its prey and leaves the bones.

"How the marquis navigated El Cobre with a sword wound, I'll never know," Mama used to say.

But having stood on its peaks, breathing in solitude and touching the earth, I can imagine how he and his men did it. Their oneness with wilderness, both by choice and in the absence of it, was unencumbered by modern distractions—just them and the mountain, working in rhythmic connection.

We burden ourselves with securities now. Keaton and Tommy Ray do equipment and supply checks—fastening metal detectors to backpacks, strapping shovels and trowels, furling ropes and stowing rappel devices. Joss smiles and weaves between everyone, marking items off a checklist. As she sips between the slender curls of steam from her insulated tumbler, she stuffs extra rolls of gauze and medication packets into her sizeable first aid kit. Fancy GPS watches adorn every wrist except my own, a tether to modern comforts in a landscape out of cell range.

You can never be too careful or prepared.

Mel Fisher wannabes especially flock to El Cobre during the mild fall and spring months, as the mountain lies in a unique dead zone—it sits in neither a state nor federal park so that no government can stake a significant claim in any findings. At least half a dozen times every year, I hear the signature *thwap-thwap-thwap* of a rescue helicopter chuffing through the air, headed to the park to retrieve naïve, dehydrated souls, some of which I see here: townies in jewelry and impractical footwear with small plastic water bottles. They won't make it more than a day.

Shelby's patrol car slowly pulls into the lot, heading directly toward our staging area, and I get a sinking feeling. Joss, Keaton, and Tommy Ray eye me with varying degrees of wariness, begging, *why's the cop here?*

I meet him in the middle of the lot to reduce any contact or questions with the others. I approach his driver's side, and he rolls down his window.

"You think this is a good idea? So soon after your mom and the break-in?" he asks, forehead wrinkled with concern.

"Have you found out who broke into my house?" I ask. "With all due respect, sir."

He taps his fingers on the steering wheel, scrutinizing the group in his side mirror. "The mountain's vicious this time of year, the weather so unpredictable."

"Got it covered, Sheriff. You should worry more about these other people than us."

"I know they won't get much farther than the creek, where they'll try to pan for gold." He pinches the bridge of his nose. "I don't wanna have to get county helicopters to pluck you off the peaks in a few days."

"Then don't send them because there'll be no need."

"Only trying to look out for you, Ms. Byrne. Take my radio."

His genuine kindness and interest in my well-being should be comforting, but they're unnerving. A microscope zeroed in on the cracks in my pursuit. A flood of memories, saturated with death and failure, resurface at his offer.

"I have my own this time, thanks," I say. "Though it didn't save everyone the last time." I flash the one holstered onto my waistband. "Let me know what you find out about the break-in, Sheriff?"

I back away, heading toward the group. Sheriff Shelby frowns and rolls up his window.

As the patrol car leaves, an old, white Ford truck rumbles up, and Wyatt hops out of the passenger side before removing his backpack and survey equipment from the bed. My heart somersaults against my will. He gives the exterior a few heavy pats and the driver takes off without a word.

"One of your brothers?" I ask.

"Yep." He scratches his head. "Can't remember which," he says, grinning.

"Glad I'm not the only one—"

"D, sorry to interrupt," Joss says in her go-getter mode. "But I think we'll be ready to push off soon, so you'll want to get everyone rounded up."

"Gather round everyone." My strange new congregation shuffles towards me. "Today's objective is to follow the riverbed to Parson Ridge. There, we'll camp out, and it'll be our shortcut for tomorrow to the Naranja Valley—"

"Wait a tic," Tommy Ray says, tilting his head. "Thought we were takin' Harp's Ridge? Like we discussed?"

I cleared my throat. "True, but I went back over the topography, and we've got the miner bridge near Parson as the shortcut—"

"Harp's is even shorter   "

"Steeper, too," I insist. "Could get slow and problematic with the amount of gear we have."

"Agree to disagree."

"I disagree," I say. "We're doing Parson Ridge."

Tommy Ray inserts a toothpick in his mouth, the stick furiously twirling. "Already a dictatorship, I see," he mutters.

A larger part of me wants to press the argument further, tell him what I know, and show him he's wrong. I think better of it, refusing to play into his goading to see a woman hysterical or upset. Our shared history regarding Clyde is a buffer padded with guilt, and I know he's apt to hide his anger behind it.

"Like I was saying." I glare at Tommy Ray, who is thrusting out his chest. "We'll cross over Shadow Canyon bridge from Parson Ridge, which will lead us to Naranja Valley before the limestone cliffs of the escarpment, which are identified on both the map I gave you and the contour maps Wyatt provided."

"Weather's supposed to be nice for summer today, high 80s," Keaton chimes in while smacking his gum, this one an indistinguishable mint. "But keep an eye out with those monsoon clouds."

I bite my tongue, vexation building at his interruptions.

"Anyway, keeping your eyes out for everything goes without saying," I say. "This is prime season for wildlife—snakes, insects, mountain cats."

Tommy Ray snickers. "I'll eat 'em for breakfast."

"I'll be in the lead, with Wyatt bringing up the rear for this first leg." I ignore him. "We'll I.D. a rest stop in about an hour and inventory how everyone's doing with the pace. In the meantime, communication. It's critical. Speak up if you have a problem. Remember, there's no cell reception once we reach Parson Ridge."

Their faces are inscrutable, and I wonder if I'm biting off more than I can chew. I'd be faster without most of them. I need them just as much as they need me, though. Their expensive gear, their money, their brawn—a commodity in trade, to my knowledge. Encouragement radiates from Joss's face, her gentle nod and soft smile supporting my every word.

"And uh—let's go find some fuckin' treasure."

Keaton whoops, and everyone moves like worker ants bounding off each other and gathering their items.

"Nice speech," Wyatt whispers into my ear. "Right up there with *Braveheart*."

He winks.

"Shut up." I nudge him with a playful elbow. A warm energy runs through me.

Stepping onto the shale-colored, pebbly Willow Creek trail feels like arriving at an old friend's welcome mat. It's been years since I greeted the mountain face-to-face. Life got in the way. And as much as I love the outdoors, this patch of earth's chokehold on my family made it hard to return.

Yet as the sun's first piercing ray reaches my face from behind the peak, a heady mixture of wonder and heartache swells from my core. I blink back a film of tears, quickly wiping any rogue drops.

Mama *is* here with me, but she should be here. Her journey is now mine. In this moment, my anger and frustration at her imperfections part like a biblical sea, and I understand her dreams, desires, and need for redemption, to have achievements and adventures separate from her family.

Over her family.

With that, my stunted grief floods back, a nagging high tide of resentment.

A gloved hand grasps mine, and I flinch. It's Joss, now by my side. She gives me a knowing squeeze, her eyes glistening, too.

15

Then – March 2008

First Expedition

Fear choked me until I recognized the rough, familiar hand pressing against my lips.

"Laney," Mama said, her voice low and urgent. "It's me. Stay quiet. And keep moving."

I nodded, trembling, as she slowly removed her hand. Joss and Wyatt stood still, eyes wide with terror.

Mama retrieved her gun from its holster, silently motioning for us to follow her through the tree-lined corridor. She brought up the rear, her head continuing to snap back at the stockpile. She paused.

"Mama!" I hissed loudly. "Come on!"

She hesitated, then sprinted towards the stash, shouldering a rifle.

My eyes widened. "What the hell—"

She shushed me before forcibly shepherding me along the remaining hundred feet of the corridor. Sweat gathered at the nape of my hair, knowing the tenant of that shelter could be nearby—that they must be the murderers of those hikers. No one else would keep that cache in this wilderness. And worse, we'd stolen from him.

The ground swelled in ascent, leading us into a sun-drenched clearing surrounded by russet boulders that seemed to watch our every move. Mama searched every corner and cliff edge for any sign of danger, her gun pointed forward. Wyatt surveyed the ground for tracks—a skill his grandfather taught him. Finally, Mama nodded and holstered her gun.

We exhaled in unison, but I couldn't shake my unease.

"I can't believe you did that," I said. "We're gonna really have a target on our backs now."

"We have to protect ourselves," Mama said. "If we meet whoever it was."

"And they're going to be pissed!" I exclaim.

"I can take the rifle," Wyatt volunteered. "But maybe we should keep moving."

Mama's eyes smiled, but it didn't reach her lips. She handed Wyatt the rifle.

"We need to go home," Joss pleaded. "I ... I ... need to get out of fucking Jericott. I shouldn't even be here. This isn't worth it."

"She's right," I said, averting my eyes from her scared face. I was the reason she was out here. I should be the reason she gets out alive. "We need to go back."

Mama pressed her palms together.

"Or at least give the Sheriff a head's up?" Wyatt asked, motioning to the two-way radio secured on the side of Mama's backpack.

"No, not yet."

"But I'm spotting two sets of tracks," he said. "I think you should call us in."

"So, like, not that weird Clyde guy?" Joss asked, burrowing her hands in her pockets. "Unless, oh God, there's another one of him."

"The only pair we know out here are the Kowalskis," Wyatt said. "I'm not sure Kimber's shoe size, but the second set seems a little smaller than hers—"

"Oh my God," Joss said, tears welling in her eyes. "It's someone else. A *pair* of murderers? We're gonna die. We're gonna fucking—"

"Cállate!" Mama's stern gaze silenced her. "Let me think, just a sec."

Moving closer, my hand found Joss's shoulder, her fingers instantly wrapping around mine. Our old signal passed between us—four squeezes given, four returned, speaking all the words we couldn't say. "Mama!" I refused to put my friends in any more danger. "This is crazy. We have to go back. It's not safe. It's not fair to them."

I grabbed the two-way radio. She tried to block me, but I was too quick. My thumb pressed hard on the push-to-talk button as I frantically spoke into its crackly void. All that came back was a mocking tone. Out of range.

"I will protect all of you," she said, not backing down. She plucked the radio from my grasp. "I promise."

"Bullshit, this is serious. These hunts have never been like this—"

"You don't know what these hunts have been like," Mama said. "This land is our biggest threat, not people. I'm so close, that cave at Ironwood's it." She paused like something was on the tip of her tongue. "I took another look at those satellite images. Had a buddy run it through some enhanced imaging software. There's something humanmade near, possibly within those caves, but I can't find any indication in my map archives that anyone's trekked back there in over a hundred years. The treasure's there."

"Maybe it is," I said, with the jolting realization that our tunnel visions were disparate. "But let's explore it when it's safer after we report what we saw."

"No!" she said with such force Joss, Wyatt, and I jumped. "Qué, I shouldn't have let you come—"

"I couldn't let you go by yourself!" I shouted. Even in the turmoil, Mama still placed a finger over her lips, reminding us to be quiet and cautious. "We've already lost one parent," I whispered. "I can't let Cat lose you, too."

"And you?" she asked, eyes dropping to the ground.

A dull ache whirred from within. Honestly, I didn't know. Part of me felt that I'd been without her entire presence for so long it shouldn't matter. But Cat mattered. I shook my head, glaring at her, before turning away.

"Whatever we choose, we should probably keep moving." Wyatt's insistence sliced through our exchange. "Based on their sharpness and lack of debris and disruption, those tracks are very recent. They could come back any time."

"Are they turning toward or away from Azure Vista?" Mama asked.

"Away," Wyatt said.

"Does that matter?" asked Joss.

"It's too late in the day to turn back to town now," Mama reasoned.

"How convenient," I snapped. "But tomorrow at dawn, my friends and I are leaving. With or without you."

By the time we set up camp on Azure Vista, night had imposed itself on the golden horizon. We huddled in a subdued semicircle on chilled boulders, pecking at our cans of cold beef stew, trying to gulp down its unappetizing glop. Everyone knew that starting a campfire could attract unwanted attention.

I couldn't shed the feeling of being watched. The shuffling and skittering before coming upon the makeshift shelter wasn't from coati or other animals. It was bigger, more pronounced. An involuntary shiver ran through me. Had our presence spooked them? Were they crouching nearby, watching our every move, aware that we had seen too much?

"You okay?" Wyatt asked as Mama left our grouping to sweep the area once more.

I sighed, pushing some soft chunks of potatoes through my thick stew. "Counting down the hours to get out of here. Nothing like a brush with danger to put things into perspective."

Even if the stockpile owners had left everything, there were three more people they knew who could pick up the weapons and use them.

I glanced over at Joss as she emerged from her tent and zipped her jacket to her neck. If Princeton didn't work out, maybe going to Arizona State with her wouldn't be so bad—anything to be miles from here.

Mama approached, hand over her holster, the rifle's strap slung on her shoulder. "I'm going to monitor our perimeter," she said. "That way, you all can get some sleep."

"What about you?" I asked without meeting her eyes. Bitterness over her choice lingered—treasure winning out over our lives—but there wasn't room to hold both the hurt and the rage. Something had to give. "I can take a shift. If you don't recharge, you'll be no good to us tomorrow."

"I'll be fine," she insisted.

My determination wavered for a moment as I looked into her eyes. But I pressed on. "Then you'll be able to get a good night's sleep once you leave the mountain with us," I urged.

"I know what you're trying to do." Her lips formed a taut, straight line. "Believe me when I say everything I'm doing, I do for you and Cat."

I scoffed, resentment forging a hard knot inside me. She dug in so deep, ignoring how much her daughters needed her—I didn't know how many other ways I could express how I felt, only for her to ignore it. She tried to kiss my forehead, but I pulled away. I could see in my peripheral how she hung her head, shoulders slumped, moving toward her lookout spot near the bluff.

Joss, Wyatt, and I sat close in the cramped tent, a thin nylon barrier between us and twilight's chill, watching Mama's warped silhouette shift off and on the canvassed walls.

Wyatt fidgeted beside me, his knee brushing against mine as he settled in.

"Truth or Dare," Joss said, breaking the silence. "I'll ask first."

Wyatt cocked his head. "Now?"

Joss rolled her eyes. "Oh, let me guess, you all would rather be sad, weird, and existential." She scooped her bob into a purple scrunchie, shiny flaxen sections spilling out. "We need a good distraction."

Wyatt laughed, shaking his head.

"What?" she asked crossly.

"Funny coming from you is all. You've been the most scared. Now you're okay with worry taking a backseat."

Joss's mouth gaped, cheeks flushed as if he'd slapped her with his words. Then, she straightened up, eyes narrowing into a mask of bravado.

"Maybe I am scared," she admitted with a defiant tilt of her chin. "Who isn't? But I'd rather do a stupid game than moping in the dark. So, are you in, or are you going to be a buzzkill?"

Wyatt shrugged. "Fine."

Dread thudded through my heart as I wiped my sweaty palms against my jeans. She was going to pry about my and Wyatt's relationship.

"Take it easy, though," I said, trying to keep my voice level. "No dares. It's been a weird day."

Joss knocked her shoulder against mine playfully. "Geez, chill, it's not like you're on trial."

I loved her, but I knew better than to let my guard down.

"Fine," I said, careful and measured. "Let's do truth."

Joss enjoyed being in control, but I wouldn't let her take over completely.

"Wyatt, you go first," Joss said, the challenge in her voice clear.

He inhaled sharply. "Okay then." He turned to Joss. "Do you hate me?"

"Yes," she said.

A stone dropped through my chest as Wyatt's chin dipped in silence, his face a blank wall. Then Joss's voice cut through the moment before I could find my own. "I'll go second," she said. She turned to Wyatt point blank. "Do you hate *me*?"

The tension was agonizing. His brows pulled toward one another, and he didn't speak.

"You heard me. Do you hate me? Your girlfriend's best friend."

He swallowed, scratching the back of his neck. "I don't hate ... I don't hate anyone. I think we have to get to know one another better."

She laughed, the pitch hollow. "Such a diplomatic response ... alright then. You hate me. Cool. Feeling's mutual."

"You have a lot of thunder in the mouth," he said.

She glared at him. "I'm not afraid of a little storm." She turned towards me. "D, your turn."

My pulse beat fast and warm in my ears, gathering the strength for an answer I already knew. But this game, I couldn't help she knew what was coming. "Are you going to be mad if I don't go to Arizona State with you?"

"Yes," she said. "But you will go, so I'm not worried."

My frustration began to simmer. "Seriously? Like ... friendship-ending mad?"

"Maybe," she whispered, her voice thin, like ice over deep waters. "Because you promised me," Joss said, her voice wavering. "We made the promise in eighth grade to always stick together. To escape from here, start a new, better life, and now you're just abandoning me—"

"It was a promise made as young kids!" I exclaimed, struggling to keep my composure. "People change, life changes. I have a right to change my mind and try to be friends. You should wanna support—"

"You ungrateful bitch." Her venomous words lashed with rage. "After everything I've done for you, been the one constant in your life, let you cry on my shoulder when your dad—"

"Enough, Joss, stop," Wyatt interrupted, his voice loud and steady. "No one's trying to break your bond with Laney, but it shouldn't be a chain."

Joss sniffled, glaring at Wyatt. "Ironic, coming from you."

"I have one more follow-up truth question," I said. "Is the college thing why you've been so upset?"

Joss shifted in her cross-legged position, pulling at a hair strand at the nape, which she only did when upset or feeling vulnerable. "No," she mumbled. "Moving on. My turn again."

"Isn't it Wyatt's?"

"My game, my rules."

I scoffed. "What's new."

She ignored me. "D, are you a virgin?"

It was a cruel taunt born of pain and jealousy between us both. She knew the answer; I wasn't. Lost it to my freshman-year boyfriend; a painful, awkward, thirty-second interlude in our three-month relationship, a concession made more for his satisfaction than mine.

Wyatt must have assumed it, but we never talked about it. I hoped and prayed that his love for me would not change.

"Stop it, Joss."

"My turn again," Wyatt intervened. His voice was clear and strong but tinged with ... something else. "Joss, did you somehow sabotage Delaney's chances at Princeton and the other East Coast schools?"

"Whoa, Wyatt, come on," I said.

She couldn't—wouldn't do that.

"You've made it very clear how you feel," he pressed further. "And everyone's heard back from their schools but Laney."

"What's that got to do with her?" My pulse hammered against my ribs as the question tumbled out.

"Besides me, who were you in class with? Who knew where and when you were dropping off your applications?"

His question was bewildering and illuminating at once. I snapped my head in her direction.

"Excuse me?" she asked in a higher pitch, a microcurrent of shock and fear over her face.

Fuck. She was avoiding. Lying.

He's right. She knew I was putting them in my mailbox following a lunch break in the library and after AP History that day. She probably stashed them in her backpack while we studied for our science quiz.

"Answer his question," I said, embers of rage tingling behind my eyes. "You were so quick to answer the others."

"What are you talking about?" she asked, pressing trembling hands to her chest. "I would never."

"Did you remove the applications from my mailbox?" I asked, taking over the questions. "Funny how I only received my ASU response."

Her mouth gaped, but no words came out.

"Joss, it's a simple question," I said. My heart pounded in my throat.

She picked at a loose thread on her jeans. "So, I *may* have taken them out of the mailbox—I panicked, okay? I saw those East Coast schools and thought, this is it. She's leaving me. Not just Jericott. *Me.*"

I clenched my fists, anger building. "What the fuck?" My mind was reeling.

"I regretted it and tried to mail—"

I crossed my arms. "How much later did you mail them? Huh?"

She opened her mouth again, reaching for an answer. "D, I regret it and didn't know how to tell you."

"Oh my God," I groaned, about to be sick. "You are so selfish, I can't even—"

"Let me ex—"

"How did you think you would get out of this one?" My fists were balled with rage as I recoiled back to the corner of the tent, wanting to be as far away from her as possible. "Explain that. Were you gonna type up rejection letters from forged school letterhead? Like what the—are you out of your fucking mind? You've ruined everything! God, I can't believe I was so stupid to trust you."

Joss's eyes were glistening as she pulled her jacket tighter. "It's wrong, I know. I was scared, like a reflex." She wipes her cheeks with the back of her hand. "You know my parents. You're like the one person who's been there for me since forever and to not have you around? When I saw you acting all giddy with him the way you've been with *us* ... I don't know. I freaked out."

"You couldn't handle being happy for me, could you?" I glared. "I'm not gonna let you drag me down with you. Get the hell out. Now."

Joss tearfully grabbed her sleeping bag and rushed out of the tent, ducking into Mama's.

Wyatt and I sat in silence as he rubbed my back.

"Hey," he finally said after several minutes. "I should've mentioned my suspicions earlier; I'm sorry about the timing."

My knees drew up tight against my chest while hot tears carved silent paths down my face. "It's not your fault." I bend my head to wipe the tears against my forearm. "I'm the stupid one to have trusted her. It's like you knew something wasn't right."

"You couldn't have known she'd do something like this," he said gently. "I was hoping I was wrong, but I had a gut feeling."

"She's always been jealous," I said, my anger regaining steam. "Even if she has it all. She can't stand that I had something she didn't."

"She cares for you a lot, even if it's in the worst way."

The anger, still steaming, made me want to bathe in complete hatred for her. But underneath it all, I understood, even as I resisted that grace. She hadn't done it to hurt me. It was terror that I'd outgrow her, find a new future without her in it. Maybe that was for the best.

He laced his fingers in mine, a comfort within the darkness. "What are you going to do next?"

"Call the schools when I get back. Hope for the best." I curled closer into Wyatt and his warmth. "And tomorrow, when we get off this mountain, I never want to see her again."

We sat in silence, darkness shrouding our tent. Time lost its shape and structure as I lay awake grappling with the betrayal. My best friend did a horrendous thing. But Wyatt was there—my sanctuary. With him, I found safety, understanding, and empathy to ease the pain, if only for a moment.

"I love you, Wyatt," I whispered into the void, heat flushing through my body. It didn't matter if he said it back. I needed him to know how much he meant to me.

A cold draft swept along one side of my body. He'd sat up. Suddenly, his face was next to mine, his lips hovering so close to mine that I could taste his breath. "I've always loved you, Firefly," he whispered back. "Ever since that first day of kindergarten, when you were flying high on that swing, your red hair in the wind."

And then we kissed—a kiss so passionate that I pulled him onto me while struggling awkwardly with the barrier of the sleeping bag separating us before finally giving in and throwing it off altogether. The desire for him to be pressed against, melted into me, was stronger than ever. His tenderness was intoxicating. Layer by layer, we shed our dusty, sweaty clothes, flesh touching flesh with agonizing warmth, the risk of being caught by the others yards away only adding to the strange, newfound excitement.

"Are you sure about this?" he whispered.

Mama stood watch on the perimeter, and Joss was asleep in the other tent by now.

I nodded. "Do you have ...?"

He nodded, reached into his pocket, and drew out a foil square. When he was ready, I continued kissing him fervently, my legs wrapped tightly around his hips. I'd never been so sure about anything—every cell yearned for nothing but him.

In our clumsy innocence, we were magical as one, moving in perfect rhythm, a harmony of passion and deep connection that transcended pleasure. Adoration glimmered in his eyes through the twilight, a reflection of my own. It was the kind of pure vulnerability of two lost souls finding their way home to each other. Nothing else mattered for those brief moments out of reality's scope.

"This is all I've ever wanted," he said after, tracing a figure-eight infinity loop on my bare shoulder with his finger. "To love you."

My soul shuddered at the permanence of being with my oldest and truest heart—like I was star-written just for him. I kissed him, relishing its fleeting beauty before slowly edging toward sleep, dreaming of the future.

16

Now – August 2018

Day 1: Second Expedition

The contrast between the calm, gorgeous scenery and our group's rigid, awkward tension is stark. Five near-strangers thrust together as a team that *should* work in perfect unison.

The din of cicadas and ripples of the parallel creek help carry our small talk. Wyatt comments about lilting clusters of orange wildflowers while Keaton boasts his last Colorado hunt—the mountain "twice as high and covered in snow." The water shimmers with diamond refractions made by the morning sun.

Joss people-pleases with chirpy responses — "yes" and "oh, is that right" as her running-on-repeat commentary, seemingly enraptured by Keaton's stories. Tommy Ray grunts about needing to "stop and take a piss" soon. I remain silent. I have a good excuse, leading with the map and all. Only the skittering of dead, windward leaves and rubber soles shuffling over rocks punctuates the lulls in conversation.

Two buzzards soar overhead as Joss quietly sings a Sufjan Stevens song about a tower above the earth, the hum vaguely familiar from one of her vinyls she'd always have playing. Two hours into the trail, we hit a rhythm with a sizable lead ahead of the group.

"I still can't get over how we're making this happen," she says. "Literal childhood dreams coming true."

"Slow down there. We haven't found the X yet."

"We're manifesting that shit. The Glitter Twins are finding gold."

I blow a raspberry.

Joss rolls her eyes as I stare at the gold studs now occupying her earlobes, Mama's green stones long gone. "Come on, I loved being a Glitter Twin."

My hand flicks across my skin, batting away the persistent insect. "Does adding Wyatt to the group make up for me not telling you about Tommy Ray?" Joss asks.

The swirling heat and rocky trail make it hard to connect the dots. "What do you mean? You pulled the rug out from under me and invited him, too."

"I didn't tell you for fear you'd back out. But I knew all bets were off when you saw Wyatt."

"I'm surprised you'd even be able to stand each other," I say, kicking a large pebble with my boot.

"I'll put up with a lot for treasure," she says, hip-checking me playfully. "That bitterness fades a little after all these years, ya know?"

"Sort of," I say. "Doesn't matter. He's got a girlfriend now."

"Minor detail, D, you're the star, you know that," she says, vocal fry surfacing back into her vowels. "Did you guys ever—*talk* about that summer?"

I pick up my pace as if that'll fight off her questions. "Nope, not going there."

"Even after all these years?"

My face twists into a glare as her hands lift skyward in mock surrender. "What's there left to say?" I ask. "Can't take it back, much as I want to. And I've come to terms with knowing I'll never have something like that with anyone again."

Joss uses her wrist sweatband to wipe her brow. A mischievous smirk emerges. "Nothing like some mountain time to rekindle something, huh?"

"Not happening."

"I wouldn't be so sure," she teases in a sing-song voice.

"How about you?" I ask, emboldened by her inquiry. "What's your love life like?"

A slow smile blooms across her lips, the kind that tells me she's keeping a secret.

"Oooh, that juicy?" I ask. "Is he hot? Is he packing?"

Joss laughs with that genuine full-belly sound that drew me to her as a kid, where she's not worried about her looks or how she sounds.

"He's ... unlike anyone else I've ever been with," she says in a low whisper I can barely hear. "We met at a bar—"

"Of course, you did," I rib.

She chuckles, straightening her posture. "Anyway, we met in this Scottsdale bar in the VIP section. He's an entrepreneur and loves the outdoors. *Great* in bed. He's super charismatic and spontaneous, which is incredibly sexy. We have a good time out, and his friends always have the hook-up. It's exciting."

All the things she ever wanted, and I never did. And yet, here she is, though, sweaty and covered in dirt, and I know the only thing keeping her here isn't me. I'm a means to an end. It's the treasure.

The bitter truth settles in my chest—her wounds run just as deep as mine. "Wow, that's ..." I struggle for the words she wants to hear. "That's amazing. Sounds like you found something special." My pulse picks up as I find an ounce of courage to be vulnerable. "How long have you two been together?"

She sighs, looking toward the eastern peaks before hanging her gaze on her boots."A while. We've been through some things."

"Yeah?"

"I spiraled when he disappeared into some late nights and noise," she says, eyes fixed on the horizon. "Picked fights just to see if he still cared. Stayed out too late with people I barely knew. Sketchy parties, pushing limits I didn't know I had. Anything to feel something—control, maybe. We hurt each other more than we'll admit. But somehow, we clawed our way back. Came out stronger. I think."

I stay quiet for a moment because it wasn't what she said that caught me. It's how she said it. So rehearsed it could be a mantra practiced in a mirror. Like her version of the story is the one she needs to believe to keep moving forward.

The pack slides against damp skin as I adjust its weight across my shoulders. "So, he's all for treasure hunting?"

An unfamiliar flicker glimmers in her eyes. I know Joss's tells, but not this one. It's a part of her she's never revealed, or it might've developed when I was out of the picture.

"He's super psyched for me," she finally responds. "You know, he's probably more into the lore of it than I am."

"Surprised you never asked him to tag along. Share the adventure with you."

She shrugs. "It's my time. To 'do me.'" She bends down to triple-knot her bootlaces. "Guess we should wait for the slowpokes to catch up."

Three hours later, sticky heat rises, replacing the morning chill. Sweat glues my cotton tee to my spine, and my backpack suddenly weighs more. The climbing temperature moves into our group like an invasive species: chit-chat whittles to a halt, replaced by panting and plodding, gnats whining in our ears.

We descend a long, sloping hill, the last before a stretch of flat terrain that leads us to Parson Ridge. A mosaic of tree needles, leaves, and juniper berries canvas the steep path. As I scan the horizon and take a careful step, it happens: a whisper of a wire catches my boot, the sudden biting of invisible teeth around my ankle.

I yelp, falling backward as the momentum whips me around. My head hits the ground, leg suspended above me, with nothing but blue sky in my purview. The pain constricts sharply around my ankle, reality finally absorbing the shock: I fell into a snare trap.

Wyatt rushes to my side, Joss trailing him, pale.

"D, oh my God," she says, blinking rapidly. "Is your head okay?"

She pulls me to a seated position as Wyatt slashes his pocket knife furiously against the trap wire. The sharp, vice-like pressure around my ankle begins to dull.

"Let's see what I can find in the kit to patch you up," Keaton says.

He looks at me as if new judgments snap into focus with every click of his incessant gum—*leader's the first one down*.

"I'll be fine." My tongue is thick in my mouth, the heat slicking a sheen onto my forehead. "Just a little water would be great."

"Who would do this?" Joss asks as Wyatt finally frees my ankle.

"Prolly some novice," Tommy Ray mutters. "But Miss Delaney falls for any trap, don't she?"

Wyatt and Joss flinch, freezing in their tracks. Tommy Ray stands motionless, arms defiantly crossed as if daring me to confront him.

The retort rises hot in my throat—something cutting about sabotage and his childish whining—but pride dissolves on my tongue. Better to swallow the words than crack the fragile trust holding our group together.

"It was well-concealed," Wyatt says, motioning to the now-limp wire secured around the base of an old juniper. "Could've happened to any of us."

"But who set it?" Joss asks, scanning the landscape for any sign of danger. "Should we go back and let the Sheriff know?"

We shoot down her suggestion with a resounding "no." It's too early and minor an issue to concede a defeat—we've dealt with much worse.

As I stand up, Keaton offers me an ibuprofen, but I brush off his gesture. I can't show any weakness, especially in his alpha male presence.

"Let's not jump to the worst conclusions," he says, stepping a bit too close into Joss's personal space. "It's probably from some game hunter or jealous, competitive little asshole crew tryin' to scare us." He steps even closer. "They don't know who they're dealing with."

Joss blushes and takes a step back, smiling at Keaton's bravado. "You're right." She rubs the bared skin on her neckline, glowing from the rush of it all. "I got carried away."

"Maybe we should stick around to see who might have set it," Wyatt suggests. "They might come back and prove themselves harmless before we continue."

"I'm fine, really," I say firmly. "It's not worth the daylight we're burning."

Like Keaton said, it's a minor setback, a mix-up by another hunter or petty retaliation of a small rival. Embarrassing and annoying, but that's all.

And yet.

The snare's bite still throbs, echoing our grip on a dream we foolishly think belongs only to us. We're trespassers, too. This immense, ancient wilderness has seen countless entitled seekers like us, all hunting for riches that hold no real value except to ourselves. And with the realization of our shared greed comes a whisper of fear: out here, someone else might be desperate enough to do anything to claim it for themselves.

Tommy Ray doesn't argue with me this time. "Let's move," he says, eager to take the lead.

I grab his arm firmly. "I'll lead."

His brown button eyes transfix on mine, even as he spits a wad of chaw at my feet. Saliva, the color of motor oil, dribbles from his lips and into his beard. "Okay," he says. "We'll see about that."

17

Then – March 2008

First Expedition

As the sun rose, a bittersweet ache thudded in my ribcage. The night with Wyatt was magic, but Joss's deceit pierced me like a thorn in the light of day. Her meddling in my college plans was unforgivable. Determined not to let my emotions cloud our situation further, I quickly packed our gear.

Wyatt winced as he wrapped his thumb in a bandage.

"What happened?" I asked, gently taking his hand in mine.

He pulled away shyly, retrieving his knife and a small piece of wood.

"I was making this for you and got careless," he confessed, showing me the heart-shaped wood carving in his uncurled palm. "It's not much, but it's a promise. Our night together meant everything."

I smiled, placing my hand over his. "I love it."

"You ready to move soon?" Mama interrupted as I leaned in to kiss Wyatt's cheek. Her tired eyes betrayed her sleepless night.

"Been ready," I said.

Wyatt stepped back awkwardly. My gaze lingered on him as he stowed his knife in his backpack's mesh pocket while I tucked the wooden heart safely into my jeans.

"Did something happen last night?" Mama asked.

Her question hung in the air as discomfort squirmed through me. *Everything* happened last night. I'm sure she heard one commotion or the other and was trying to play it cool to nose her way to answers. The argument with Joss would have been a heart-to-heart shared with Dad, where I could cry and commiserate without fear of going on the defense.

It's never been like that with Mama. She couldn't just say, *I hear you, I feel for you*. She was the devil's advocate, and today wouldn't change that.

And as for Wyatt, our night together was for our hearts only.

"Nope, everything's fine," I lied with a tight smile. "Just want to get going."

I refused to look at Joss, ignoring a few of her feeble apology attempts, ones she had undoubtedly rehearsed since last night. It was childish, I knew, with communication being a survival tool, but the anger was too intense and blinding. As I trekked behind Mama's lead, Wyatt was a comforting diplomatic barrier between us.

Rather than double-backing around the dangerous stockpiled camp, we scaled the other side of Azure Vista toward Willow Creek again. It was a steep hill packed in rust-colored soil. Normally, such a challenge was a thrill: scaling hills, racing the wind. But last night changed everything.

Mama started with effortless, controlled footwork and a strong forward lean, but I stayed put, my feet rooted into the ground. She looked up from the bottom, her eyes questioning. I could usually match her pace, step for step, but not today.

When she reached the bottom, Joss volunteered to go next, and I was too angry to give her an argument. She took longer, using a zigzag pattern to maintain control, a technique I knew well but somehow seemed to have forgotten. She was showing off, flaunting her more naturally athletic abilities than mine. It stung more than I wanted to admit.

"Go together?" Wyatt asked, pulling me from my spiraling thoughts.

I nodded gratefully, my swirling brain affecting my limbs as if they were detached from my control. "I think the zigzag pattern is best."

"A forward lean will get us there faster," he pressed, his eyes filled with concern and challenge. "And you'll have my hand there to ground you."

The thought of relying on someone else, of admitting that today I wasn't my usual self, made my stomach twist uncomfortably. "Please, no." I flick my wrists, shaking away the nerves, attempting to dislodge the unease clinging to me like a second skin. "Let's just take it slow."

He exhaled, a sound heavy with unspoken words. "Okay. If that's what you're comfortable with." His agreement was a small comfort, but the tightness in my chest remained.

Side by side, we made our way down the ridge together. Wyatt's larger hand clasped mine as we avoided the loose rocks and knotted roots scattered before us. At a quarter of the way left to go, my boot dislodged a rock from its caked earth, sending my foot forward into a smattering of pebbles, triggering panic as my grip slipped from Wyatt's, and I stumbled forward, struggling for balance.

Wyatt cried out as I braced for a painful fall in slow motion, but then Joss was there.

Her arms wrapped around me in an unexpected safety net, her grip firm, saving me from a would-be faceplant.

My lungs burned for only a moment's pause while my heart thrashed against my ribs like a caged bird fighting for freedom. Recoiling from her embrace, I stood upright. Coppery dirt dusted my jeans, which I brushed off. My face burned with a heat that had nothing to do with pain and everything to do with embarrassment.

Mama approached, placing a hand on my drooping shoulders. "Okay, mija?"

My feet carried me away as a trembling breath escaped, sweat cooling into icy trails down my neck while I fought to gather the pieces of myself back together. Frustration gouged deeper into my chest with each throb of pain, this stumble marking another crack in my armor.

Wyatt joined me. "Laney, I'm so sorry, I messed up back there," he said, his voice heavy with guilt.

The lukewarm water slid down my throat as my head moved side to side, trying to scatter the dark thoughts rather than acknowledge his worried gaze. "Not your fault. It was a stupid rock," I muttered.

"Maybe we should take a break?" Joss suggested, her voice reaching from a cautious distance.

I paused, the water bottle halfway to my next sip. Instead, I closed it with a definitive snap. "No," I insisted, fueled by a stubborn refusal to show more weakness. The last thing I'd let her do was control the situation. "We keep moving and might make it to the creek right after noon." The words were more a declaration to myself than anyone. I needed to move, push forward, and leave the faltering—and the mountain—behind.

The next two hours dragged, the landscape reluctantly sluicing us through its obstacles, its beauty lost through the tension. There was contempt for the wildflowers, their bristly stems worming their way into my boots and the sloping watercolored terrain, only filling me with anger at their obstinance of being in my way. I stonewalled every attempt at Mama or Joss trying to engage me, at which point they turned to Wyatt, who gently redirected their conversations with the patience of a saint.

A stack of fallen logs and a cluster of thorny brush disrupted our intended path, appearing too conveniently placed, as if by someone's deliberate design rather than the random chaos of nature.

"God!" I groaned. "It's like I can't get out of this fucking place fast enough!"

"Language!" Mama shouts. "The Lord's name *and* that dirty word. If I had soap, I swear to Santa Monica ..."

She surveyed the obstacle, her furrowed expression carrying a hidden question as if considering their origin. "Huh. Strange. Think someone placed these here? Deliberately? *Maliciosamente*?"

Her words in the warm, muggy air set my skin tingling with a strange unease. It can't be true; we're seeing things at this point. We just needed to keep moving toward Jericott.

"I'm sure it's fine, right?" I insisted. "Wy, do you see any tracks around it?"

He crouched down, sharp amber eyes scanning for broken twigs, displaced stones, or embossed earth that might tell a disturbing narrative. Finally, he rose.

"Looks clear to me, no human prints." He cleared his throat. "Excuse me, Mrs. Byrne—Aurelia, I think we could use this detour." Worn-down vegetation from an animal path, flanked by rocks, curved down to our left and around a small hillside. "And we'll be back on track in twenty minutes, tops."

Mama gave him a slight nod as if re-appraising him. "You're a good boy, Altaha."

Following the animal trail, we found a narrow clearing encircled by ponderosas with sharp, dried needles carpeting the earth. I cursed under my breath as the pine duff snagged my socks.

"Okay, that's it, I'm sick of your attitude!" Mama shouted as we came upon the shaded trees atop a small hill. "I'm not going any further until you tell me what the hell is going on."

I stayed silent, headed toward the low clearing. She wouldn't understand.

"Is this about me wanting to keep going?" she asked. "I'm going to get you to safety and head back—"

"But why now? It's the worst timing ever being out here with who-the hell-knows—"

"That's exactly why!" Mama exclaimed. "I didn't come this far to have some pendejos like Lee or Clyde take it away from me!"

"God, it's not all about you," I groaned. "And I can't believe you'd just drop us off. It's like you don't care."

"Of course I care!" Mama snapped. "That's all I do is care. Finding financial security through our birthright. I want so bad for you not to have to struggle the way I did."

"But did you ever think if we had more of you, the less we would need any of that?"

Mama's nose flared in a way that I knew helped her mask tears. She wasn't going to admit any flaws in her logic. She might walk out of the wilderness with us in a few hours like I'd never begged her to. For now, she deflected. "So, what's going on with you two?" She wagged an index finger between me and Joss.

Joss burst into tears. "It's all my fault, Aurelia."

Mama snapped her head between us, torn between comforting Joss's tears or pacifying her daughter's irritation. "We're working this out right now," she announced. "There can't be anything in this world big enough to come between the two of you."

"Guess again," I said.

Mama gritted her jaw, cheeks dimpling. She turned and moved forward. "Keep talking, we'll keep moving—"

"I'd rather not—"

A metallic skitter followed by the taut pull of a cinch snapped through the stillness, rustling the dead pine needles. Joss screamed.

Next, my feet touched air, not earth. I was falling, the ground meeting my belly and forehead with a brutal punch. I couldn't consume enough air like the earth had swallowed my lungs when it gave way. More screams and shouts echoed from above. Mama wheezed a groan beside me, attempting to uncurl from her fetal position.

"Mama, you okay?" My breath had returned, but it hurt to inhale too deeply. "What happened?"

My fingers curled around her elbow, steadying her weight as she rose to sitting. "A trap." Her breath was ragged, eyes glazed, like this deceit, this trick, was an old frenemy. "Set for us."

As the shock began to recede, the reality of our surroundings seeped in. We were at the bottom of a hole, five or six feet deep by about eight feet wide.

The world tilted violently as I pushed against gravity, each heartbeat sending fresh waves of dizziness through my skull. "Wyatt! Joss!"

Their vocal distress just moments before was now silence. Except for footsteps. Slow, deliberate, confident.

Two dark figures, palming their holsters, ringed in daylight, peered down at us in the hole.

18

Now – August 2018

Day 1: Second Expedition

We reach Parson Ridge in the late afternoon, the sun baking our backs and burning off clouds on the western horizon. The ridge has always been one of my favorite vistas: tiny twinkles from Jericott can be seen through the verdant brush below the distant tree line as El Cobre's wrinkled capes rise from the earth—hibernating monsters marbled by the shifting colors of the sunset. It makes the world both gigantic and intimate.

A chirruping vibration breaks through camp, and Joss fumbles to muzzle something in her pocket.

"Sorry, phone alarm still on," she mutters.

"Might wanna keep that down," Tommy Ray says. "Don't want to bring any unwanted attention from animals or ..."

His eyes flicker at me before he turns to pound stakes and weave tent poles together. A smiling Keaton returns from a bathroom break to help

Joss unpack and meal prep, and by the way she preens and flips her hair, I can tell she's loving his attention. Wyatt and I venture beyond the campsite to gather kindling for the campfire in anticipation of dinner and plummeting night temperatures.

"I don't know how he's going to be able to cooperate with me," I say, eyes darting in Tommy Ray's direction. "I understand the misplaced hate, but it's gonna screw us over if I need to depend on him."

"Think it'd be worth talking to him tonight?" Wyatt asks. "No one ever gave him or his family a full picture of what happened that day. There was too much chaos—"

"We were reeling," I whisper. "And it was an ongoing federal case."

Wyatt breaks a large oak bough. "Maybe it would give him some closure."

Closure. It's a luxury that eludes me, one I can only hope to tie off with the treasure. Everything that has frayed my heart converges in this place: Wyatt, Joss, Tommy Ray. And the ghost of Mama.

The juniper branches crack between my fingers, releasing their sharp scent into the air. "Maybe."

"Speaking of which," he starts, amber eyes fixed on me. "It's a good time for us to catch up."

My pulse courses thick and heavy, with the words left unsaid between his dialogue.

"Sure." I clear my throat, busying myself with unnecessarily stripping the bark from an innocent bough.

"I was miserable at Princeton."

"Is that supposed to make me feel better?"

"Sorry, no, of course not. For better or worse, I just, well." He pauses, looking at the western horizon, his muscled bronze forearms rippling from his nervous hands. "Thought you should know I carried you with me for a long time. Before I found some kind of happiness."

My cheeks burn, and I divert my eyes to our growing heap of kindling. My past regrets are a hot coal in my core. "So, you're happy?"

He's silent. The decades-old butterflies flutter to life. But I tamper them with the cautious wisdom gained over the years.

"I mean, with being on the expedition," I supply.

He smiles. "Yeah. I'm happy to finish what we started."

Stars poke through the inky sky as our bellies swell, full of dinner. The scents of sweet, smoky pine and charred meat mingle in the air above the crackling campfire, which we stare at in satisfied silence. A shared meal has a strange power in balancing the differences among a disparate group. Mealtime conversation is pleasant, mellow. The earlier tension unknots itself like a rigid muscle loosens under pressure.

"You can cook, girly," Tommy Ray says, pointing his toothpick toward Joss. "I'll give you that."

Joss smiles, thanking him.

A terrifying wail carves through the soft darkness, and everyone sits straighter, eyes wider. The anonymous cry ricochets everywhere like a disembodied woman meeting her demise.

"Someone's getting killed out there!" Tommy Ray exclaims.

My muscles coil tight as the sound transforms—a woman's shriek twisting into something feral and wild—while Wyatt's head shakes in silent denial. "No one's dying," he says. "It's the mountain lion's mating call."

An uneasy energy shifts over our group. Tommy Ray and Keaton rise, chests puffed, scanning the dark landscape. Joss shifts closer to me as chatter erupts: Mountain lions—do they attack people? Should we move our camp? How can we scare them off?

"Nothing to be scared about. The only thing she wants to hunt for tonight is a boyfriend," Wyatt says. "We're taking lookout shifts tonight, anyway."

I clench my fingernails into my palm, trying to curb the nerves and the smoky meat rising from my stomach. In all my years, I'd never heard a mountain lion cry out here.

The mountain lion dream.

While I'm not worried about a frame-by-frame reenactment of my dream, the boundaries of the unearthly and the wilderness are warping, threatening to swallow me whole, as if the great expanse has inverted.

Besides carrying the revered platitude that there's something bigger than us in the universe, I was never particularly religious. But right now, I pray for the omens to cease. I'll absorb my parents' Catholic truisms and refurbish them into my version of God and destiny. A deity who I'm putting my faith in to protect me across this terrain.

I flinch when Wyatt touches a hand on my tense shoulder.

"Hey," he whispers. "That lion won't hurt us, I promise."

My chin bobs too quickly, overcompensating, while nervous energy still skitters beneath my skin. Joss huddles close, squeezing my hand in a quick succession of four, our old love-you code with Cat. Nowadays, those words are too hard, too unearned to speak aloud. But it soothes my nerves instantly.

"Let's hope that lion gets some tonight," Joss says, a light pitch entering her voice.

Everyone chuckles as Tommy Ray and Keaton sit back down.

As we settle into a cautious lull around the fire, I watch Tommy Ray propped on one elbow. He squints hard at the flames as if he's begging for them to deliver him something. My guilt rises, sour like bile.

"I'm so sorry about Clyde," I blurt. "I wish I could rewind that day. But he's a hero. And I'll answer for whatever I can. I want us to be able to depend on each other out here—"

"Unlike the past," he snaps, sucking air through his teeth. "Ain't that convenient."

I swallow hard. "I deserve that. But if we can't talk through it now or put a pin in it, we're never going to succeed—"

"You don't get to tell me what to do," he says with a growl. "If you hadn't been so careless—"

"No," Wyatt interrupts. "Don't put that on her; we were all there, and it wasn't that simple—"

"No doubt following orders from that greedy mother of yours."

Wyatt and I launch toward Tommy Ray, ready to jump the flames to get at him. Keaton and Joss hold us back when a loud snap pierces the quiet. We freeze as more loud snaps follow the crunching of pebbles. Everyone's eyes widen. Destiny just stepped closer.

19

Then – March 2008

First Expedition

It's not Lee, Clyde, or Kimber staring down at us.

It's two new faces.

The man's eyes were narrowed, and he had a thick neck and an oversized brow ridge. The woman's face was twisted into a cruel grin, and something in her expression suggested she held all the power.

The infamous El Cobre killers, armed and dangerous. My heart raced as I realized this was not the encounter I had anticipated. Not by a long shot.

"Sorry, friends, for the inconvenience here." She was tall, her voice deep and strident. "We just had to know who was traipsing on our turf, stealing our stuff." She flashed a yellowing smile, brown grime nestled between every groove of her gumline.

I trembled, thoughts festering of Wyatt and Joss dead beyond our trap. "My friends—"

"Who are you?" Mama asked with a glare.

The woman tapped her dirty fingertips to her forehead facetiously, her vivid blue jay eyes widening. "Gosh, where are my manners?"

Long, scraggly chestnut hair peeked out from under her black cowboy hat as her thin frame, wrapped in head-to-toe black, prowled forward, the hem of her duster nearly grazing the dirt. A deep, freckling tan and layer of dust betrayed her true age—she looked fifty, but she could be in her late twenties.

"Harriet," she said before pointing at the man who now had the rifle Wyatt had carried. He was about a half-foot shorter than her. "And this is my husband, Norm. We're the Callahans."

"The Callahan pirates," Mama said, her voice fringed with alarm. "It's been you terrifying our whole town. You're the murderers."

I snapped my head in Mama's direction. She looked braced to lunge at them. "Mama?"

How does she know who they are?

Harriet's eyes flickered with amusement. "I'm so flattered our infamy's reached your shit town." She placed her hands on her hips, examining Mama head to toe. "And I'll be damned, I think I know you, too."

Mama swiftly drew her gun, aiming it squarely on Harriet as Norm matched her threat by pulling his gun. Harriet didn't flinch, only casually raising her palms in the air.

"You know nothing," Mama said. "I don't do what you do, leaving a trail of blood between here and Central America, that temple shootout—"

"Easy, lady," Norm growled.

"It's fine, babe," Harriet said as Norm stood down. "We're just getting to know each other. Aren't we, *Aurelia Byrne*?"

Harriet drew her holstered gun lightning quick. Mama clicked her hammer.

"Yeah, I know of you," Harriet crowed. "The legit hunting circles are small. God, I can't believe my luck right now."

Mama slowly shifted her way in front of me. "I think your luck's run out—"

"You know I've got no use for these kids." She smirked.

My pulse quickened. This was it. I was going to die in a hole and be buried in it.

Harriet motioned Norm with her head. "So, I'd sit tight and listen up if I were you." She squatted down, as close to eye-to-eye as she could with Mama. "Because you're gonna lead us to the de Silva treasure."

Norm now held Wyatt and Joss by their collars. Silver tape had been slapped across their mouths, and rope bound their wrists. Fear and guilt pinched me from the inside, my anger at Joss taken off the burner; they wouldn't be in this danger if it weren't for me. We were only two hours from the park entrance, but now, this dark tide was pushing us back into the belly of the wilderness.

"If you so much as look at one of them wrong," Mama said, the weapon never wavering. "You might as well hand me your gun, and I'll pull the trigger on myself. And you'll never get what you want."

Her ferocity both startled and softened me. Growing up in the shadows of her dreams, I drifted under her radar, the spotlight only shining when she needed something. Now, she was ready to lay her life on the line, and I dared my heart to like that feeling. That, she, too, could be engineered with the unbreakably loving thread between a mother and child.

Harriet sucked air between her teeth, eyes narrowing. "I can't have anyone dispensable."

"He can track blazes, animals, and read a map like no one else," Mama said, motioning to Wyatt. She was doing what she could to buy us time. "She's insanely agile—" pointing to Joss. "Can get into the tightest spaces. And my girl—" her voice broke, meeting my eyes, pursed lips reining her emotions. "Is smart and strong as hell. Knows just as much, probably more about de Silva, Rubio, and El Cobre, than any of us combined."

I'd be happy for the praise if I weren't so scared. She'd never said anything like that before.

"Too many mouths to feed," Norm grunted while his gaze lasciviously stretched the length of Joss.

"Let me worry about the details," Harriet chided. "You just do your job, huh?"

My eyes widened. Before the four, in the foliage, a small figure rippled in the blink of a frame, a jump cut playing tricks on my eyes. It was a whisper of movement, a ghost in the forest. Slowly, meticulously, a human peeled itself from the habitat like a sticker from its backing.

It was Clyde in his ghillie suit, an arrow aimed at the duo. His eyes signaled Mama and me, an unspoken alliance of survival. I quivered, poised to spring into action.

Clyde's arrow whistled through the air, striking Harriet's hand. She dropped to the ground, screeching in pain and dropping her weapon. Norm whirled around as Wyatt head-butted him before kicking him in the groin.

Mama was scrambling up the dirt wall, taking hold of an exposed root. I helped push her the rest of the way out before she hauled me up.

"Cover Wyatt," I said to Mama as I headed to Joss.

Clyde was nocking another arrow as Mama kicked Harriet's gun out of her reach. It skittered precariously along the ledge of the hole.

"Run!" Clyde ordered.

Joss sprinted towards the outcrop of trees, but I turned back to see Wyatt wrestle the gun from Norm's grasp as Harriet sent Mama to the ground with a punch. She scrambled for her weapon.

"Mama!" I ran toward them, heart hammering.

Harriet clasped the gun and whipped around in the direction of my voice, firing. Mama screamed over the shot's thunderclap. The milliseconds stretched in languid terror. I felt nothing, only saw my line of vision to Harriet blocked.

The bullet found its mark before reaching me.

Clyde's body jerked, falling gracelessly to the ground, crimson pooling over the browns and greens of his camouflage as he became one with the forest floor.

"No, no." My throat tightened like a noose, the pain and horror at his sacrifice sinking in deep. I placed my trembling hand over the wound, his warm blood coating my hand. "We're going to get you help."

Mama rushed to our side, removing her flannel and replacing my hand with it over Clyde's wound. My gaze lifted to find Wyatt cradling Joss against his side as he moved toward us, Norm's gun gripped tight in his free hand. The Callahans had slipped away under the cover of chaos.

"Hang in there," Mama whispered. "You're going to be okay."

Clyde's face had paled. He shook his head. "Leave. Get out of here," he rasped.

The sight of his blood seeping into dirt paralyzed me, each pulse of my heart screaming that I'd chosen wrong—that I should have fled toward the clearing with Joss instead of charging toward them, should have done anything but what instinct drove me to do. "The radio!" I exclaimed. "Keep holding the wound, Mama."

Static crackled from the radio as my fingers fumbled through the backpack, searching for salvation. "This is Delaney Byrne. We need immediate rescue about four miles northeast of Willow Creek Park. We have a man down. Over."

"Wyatt, the GPS," Mama ordered.

"Help is on the way," Joss said, placing her jacket under Clyde's head. She was holding back tears.

Clyde's blood seeped through Mama's shirt, his eyes rolling back in his head.

"Copy, Laney," the Sheriff's static-filled voice replied. "Hold your position. Extraction en route. Over."

"Incoming coordinates headed to you, Sheriff," I said as Wyatt handed me the GPS device. "Over. Quick, get the flares ready, Joss."

She removed the safety pins from the flares before striking the igniter against the cap. Their eerie red glowed to life as the encircling pines shuddered in the breeze.

"Hold them away," Mama ordered. "Set 'em away from all the pine needles."

The flares sputtered and hissed amidst our silence for several minutes. We dared not move from our spots; Joss and I took turns applying pressure to his wound, scrambling to find anything that might help from our first aid kit. Wyatt and Mama scanned the perimeter with their guns in case the Callahans decided to return.

"This is all my fault," I whispered to Clyde. "I'm so sorry."

Clyde's skin now had a mannequin's sheen. He no longer held the same intimidating presence as before. His body seemed smaller, his lashes curled and his once fierce eyes now a warm shade of brown.

This fate wasn't meant for him—it was meant for me.

"The choice was mine," he said, barely above a whisper.

The hum of a distant copter murmured in the air.

"Hang on just a little longer," I said.

"Go," he said.

His breath stuttered before hitching, suspended between life and death. Then he stilled, and so did the world.

"Mija," Mama said, her voice low. "He's gone."

20

Now – August 2018

Second Expedition

Tommy Ray draws a pistol, and Keaton unfurls a large glinting pocketknife. My hands clutch the earth as I hold my breath, fearing any noise will draw whatever is out there closer. Flinty footsteps grow louder.

They are less cougar and more human.

We smell them first: acrid and earthy. Then the curtain of darkness parts to reveal two familiar, weathered ghosts lit by the campfire flames.

Harriet and Norm Callahan.

I gasp as old nightmares come to fruition and dread multiplies in my cells. We clamber to our feet, forming a defensive line. Tommy Ray's face reddens as he clicks his gun's magazine into place.

"Well, well, well." Harriet grins, new age lines carved into her face. She spans her gun across the group so we make no mistake about who's in charge. "We have ourselves a little reunion up here, don't we?"

"Been waitin' ten years to kill you for my brother," Tommy Rays says with a growl, ready to pounce. Keaton holds him back.

"Who?" Harriet says, her voice flecked with mockery.

"Clyde," he says through gritted teeth, his breath unsteady. "He wasn't supposed to be there."

Harriet's vivid eyes brighten with recognition. "Oh, the hairy guy in the camo." She chuckles.

Tommy Ray erupts with a guttural roar, the vein bulging in his head. A jab of guilt twists my side.

Norm points his gun at Tommy Ray, a warning.

"Easy, little brother," she says to Tommy Ray. "Wasn't personal. Wrong place, wrong time. But I'm sure you knew that."

She winks at me like she's confident to poke bears and come out unscathed. Rage pounds through my ears, deafening. I'm ready to give it all up for a shot at wringing her neck.

Norm snickers, slinking toward Joss with his gun. "Ain't you grown up," he says with a predatory sniff. Joss jumps backward.

"Get away from her!" Keaton protests, waving his knife.

The Callahans grin smugly.

"We've got unfinished business; we're not going anywhere," Harriet says boldly as she stops short when her bluejay eyes meet Wyatt's. "And say it isn't so! Our Apache pal, too ... still hanging out with these bitch-es?"

Rage explodes through my veins as my fists ball tight, fear burning away beneath white-hot anger. My gaze snaps to Wyatt—I could barely make out his face in the darkness, but I felt his rage burning a hole through Harriet's skull.

Harriet clicks her tongue, savoring our reactions to her goading, her feral grin stained a darker shade of brown since we last met. "Was real sorry to hear about your mommy, dearest," she says, her glinting boots halting before me. "I've gotta confess ... the news of her death through the dark web grapevine was what brought me back here. The idea of returning to find the treasure she never could—"

"Spent years on the run 'cause of you," Norm interrupts.

"You ruined lives!" Tommy Ray shouts, his face pinched.

My heart knows that expression—the one you wear when a big piece of you is ripped away.

"You would've been on the run anyway," I mutter. "Criminals. Murderers. Knew it was you that broke into my house."

They scoff. "We're not small timers," Norm says.

"But we are at an impasse," Harriet adds. "Let's cut to the chase. You give us Rubio's journal with the map. And the key."

Uneasy whispers ripple through the group, Keaton and Tommy Ray exchanging glances: *journal, what journal? And a key?*

Harriet rocks back on her heels, surveying the suspicious atmosphere. "Sounds like all of you have a communication breakdown. Didn't share the Relics Limited assets, I see." She clicks her tongue. "Trust issues. Sure you wanna be in business with Miss Red?" Her eyes dart between Keaton and Tommy Ray.

My neck stiffens. "What journal and key?" No one could know, not yet. Keaton and Tommy Ray could mutiny if they think I lied to them.

Harriet turns on her heels, gazing up at the dark sky. "Don't trifle with me. I know things."

I step forward, jaw set in anger. "You don't know a damn thing."

"Spicy, like your mom," Harriet's eyes flicker. "I can respect that. In another lifetime, I think we might be friends."

"You're not going to get away with this," I say. "You're outnumbered."

"Are we. though?" She fans out her palm, examining her dirt-laden fingers like a manicure. "We could have an ally in the darkness watching right now." The mask of night chitters in its stillness. "Your little trio doesn't have the guts to do what it takes to remove obstacles like us." She motions to Keaton and Tommy Ray. "That leaves Pretty Boy and Potbelly here. Our two guns to their one. I think we'll take our chances—"

"And we'll take ours," I say.

A campfire spark flares to life with an airy crackle, distracting everyone just long enough for Keaton to sprint forward with lightning precision at Norm, slashing his cheek with his knife.

Norm yowls, losing his grip on the gun. It flings into the darkness. Hand now free, Norm punches back, fist meeting flesh. Keaton's knife drops into the dirt.

Joss scrambles into the darkness, screaming.

I need to find a weapon, a rock, anything. Harriet aims her firearm and winks an eye at me. I leap to the side just as she pulls the trigger.

Tommy Ray gets a clear bullseye shot of Harriet but flinches, forehead doused in sweat. Harriet doesn't hesitate, firing at Tommy Ray and nicking him. He howls, clutching his shoulder. Fear spreads through me as Wyatt leaps in to help him. *God, if he gets hurt ...*

Keaton and Norm writhe like embattled snakes before Keaton gains gun control. Norm twists Keaton's wrist, and he cries out, sending the weapon into the dark. Keaton desperately palms the whiskery brush while shoving and punching Norm with the other arm.

Harriet charges Wyatt and Tommy Ray until Joss slams her back with a melon-sized rock. Harriet falls, her face nearly grazing the campfire flames, gun limp in her hand. I jump at the opportunity and seize her gun just as she tries to curl her fingers around it. Keaton gains the upper hand on Norm, his body planted on his chest. He sends rapid-fire punches to Norm's giant jaw.

I fire the gun—*crack, crack, crack*—into the night sky.

Nervous silence fills the air. I shift my aim to Harriet, her arms now pinned by Wyatt. Tommy Ray scrambles to his feet, his upper arm stained crimson, his forehead bleeding freely down to his eye. The dancing light and shadows of the fire amplify Joss's trembling.

"We're calling Shelby," I say.

Wyatt finds the two-way radio from our gear, only to be met with static dead air.

"That ain't gonna do, anyway," Tommy Ray says, clutching his bloody arm. "Gimme the gun, Byrne. They need to be put out to pasture. We all know it."

The Callahans blanch.

"It's what we should have done years ago," Joss says.

A gust of wind slants the roaring flames, distorting our hulking shadows against the rocky backdrop.

"No," Wyatt says. "That's not our call."

"Exactly," I say. "You can't be serious." Their punishment should be an easy choice. Bile creeps up my throat as the Callahans stand with arms raised in surrender, a faint echo of the monsters in my dreams. "Hold on—"

"Leaders got to make the tough choices, Miss Delaney," Keaton says, keeping Norm's gun aimed at the men while handing Tommy Ray rope to tie the Callahans by their hands. "Follow through."

"I've waited too long for justice," Tommy Rays says.

His desperation is palpable. He is hesitant to wield the weapon in his hand yet unwilling to leave the Callahans' fate to chance.

"We're not killers," Wyatt says, his eyes tinged with mercy. "We can't do this."

"What else are we gonna do?" Joss says. "I don't want to do it, but look what happened last time, what happened to Clyde. Not to mention the chaos they've caused since."

"Let the FBI handle it. We'll get the reward," I say, trying to appeal to their greed. The bounty pales in comparison to the net value of the treasure, but it would be a guarantee that we don't have with the expedition. "We could turn around now, split the money."

Joss exhales. "Yes, that could work."

Keaton scoffs. "And you really trust the government to take care of us?"

Tommy Ray grunts, shaking his head as he forces the Callahans to the ground. "Nope, too many variables, too hard to transport, many things could go wrong."

Wyatt and I argue for several minutes with Keaton and Tommy Ray over the fate of our prisoners, flanked between us and kneeling stone-faced in the dirt.

Wyatt and I cling to our moral high ground, pleading for compassion and mercy instead of succumbing to violence like the Callahans. The campfire thins, a chill filling the air. Joss remains silent, her arms crossed tightly over her chest like shouldered angels and devils battling for her soul.

"No, absolutely not!" I say. "End of story. Legally, morally, this is wrong. We're not judge and executioner here."

"Different laws apply out here in the wild, D," Keaton says. "But we'll add a touch of civilization. Make our little jury. We vote."

My stomach churns as the night seems to catch fire in my veins, my leadership stolen.

Keaton raises his palm. "All in favor of getting rid of the Callahans, say 'aye.'"

Tension builds like a storm—his "aye" strikes first, then Tommy Ray's follows like thunder. My eyes lock onto Joss's shuffling feet, the sound of her clearing throat sharp as breaking glass. Her arm rises through the thick air, slow as a noose. "Aye," she whispers.

The word is a knife in my back as fury rips from my throat: "Joss!"

Harriet's head droops in defeat.

"You and Wyatt are officially outvoted." His chin lifts with smug victory, finger rolling his gun. He moves closer, whispering into my ear. "If we don't do this, the expedition's over, especially for you."

His words are a threat, blushing my ear with the heat of fear. If we don't do what he wants, he could be all too willing to turn the gun on us next. It's a forced blood pact.

"Without question, we take this to the grave," Tommy Ray says, pulling the angry, dejected Callahans up by their collars. "I'm coming with you," he says to Keaton. "Look 'em in the eyes one last time."

"Tommy, no," Wyatt says. "Think of Clyde. It's a line you can't uncross."

"He wouldn't have wanted that," I say. The last thing he needed was for the Callahans to infect the memory of his brother any further.

Tommy Ray's face darkens with rage. "You didn't know shit about my brother, you don't know what he'd want—"

"I know he had a clear shot of both of them and chose to disarm them instead," I retort. "Please don't. I saw you hesitate on Harriet."

"I didn't—"

"You're injured, though." Keaton sniffs, eyeing Tommy Ray. "I'll handle them, and we need you guarding the perimeter. Looking out for that third they mentioned."

Tommy Ray narrows his eyes. "They were bluffing."

"You wanna take that chance?" Keaton asks. "You guard camp, survey the perimeter. Keep your head in the game."

Tommy Ray grimaces, clutching his bloody arm in resignation. "Fine, I'll do my part, but I ain't your personal army either." He turns to me, wincing. "Don't think for a second I don't see the mess you've got us in. You're keeping secrets, playing us for fools. I ain't forgotten, and we ain't square."

My mouth goes dry, my palms slick with sweat, fingertips still cold. Between his bitter words, the raw truth gnaws at me. Sharing the treasure is sharing the blood and guilt. We watch the dark, dusty backs of the Callahans recede into the maw of wilderness with Keaton.

"D," Joss begins, cautiously treading toward me. "My vote was—"

"No." A lump of betrayal hardens inside. Joss reels me back, only to disappoint me every time.

"Yes," she presses, trying to meet my averted eyes. "I spent years in therapy trying to get them out of my head, scared they'd come back—"

"We've all been scared; doesn't make it right to kill them—"

"D." Her tone is desperate, begging. We move out of Tommy Ray's earshot. "We open up a whole new set of problems if we go against these guys."

"And whose fault is that?" I snap. "I didn't pick them."

Joss's face pinches.

A tear threatens to fall as their silhouettes fade into darkness, powerless to stop their march toward death. "It scares me when we lose ourselves out here," I whisper.

"More secrets?" Tommy Ray approaches, a fresh red drizzle of blood running the length of his arm.

"You should go patch yourself up." I shove past him and Joss, the harsh clarity of our situation illuminated—either kill or be killed.

21

Then – April 2008

After First Expedition

For three weeks now, I've woken up screaming, haunted by dreams of undead Harriet and Norm, their skeletal fingers poised to choke me, their all-white eyes staring greedily from rotting sockets while maggots wriggled out from their slack jaws.

This morning was different.

The smoke alarm's eardrum-splitting whine shrieked before a sharp, charred odor of burnt plastic and fabric hit my nose.

Cat's bed was empty, which fueled my panic as I scrambled out of the room. A charcoal-colored plume of smoke mushroomed from the kitchen. Cat was bounding in frenzied circles, helpless and coughing, hands over her ears. I removed her from the kitchen before retrieving the fire extinguisher below the sink Dad placed there years ago. Pull, aim, squeeze: the hose released a soapy foam, reducing the smoke to a few dying gray curls.

"It's safe now," I said, coughing.

Cat huddled in a corner of the living room, tears glimmering. "I'm sorry," she said with a tiny whimper.

"Come here, you're okay." She ran over, the brute force of her embrace nearly knocking me down. The house was quiet. "Where's Mama?"

Mama's absence after the expedition wasn't a surprise to us. Failure weighed on her more heavily than Clyde's death or our run-in with the Callahans.

Instead, she was restless with the idea that the Callahans were still in "her" mountains. Back in full force were the crazed late nights of drawing up new topographic maps, pouring over the pitfalls of the trails we took. Alcohol spurred these studious benders, so half-empty liquor and beer bottles littered side tables and shelves. I even plucked a humid amber bottle from her shower caddy yesterday.

Survival demanded motion—cooking meals, scrubbing floors, mothering Cat between classes. But even as routines fell into place, El Cobre's shadow stretched long across every carefully reconstructed piece of normal.

Local and federal authorities had zeroed in on their suspects for Kip's break-in and a triple murder, only to have them vanish. The media buzzed with theories about the mountain incident—sleepy Jericott thrust back into the spotlight. We stayed silent, and Sheriff Shelby kept us out of the headlines.

A key scraped aimlessly against the front door lock. Peering through the gauzy curtains, I saw Mama armed with a large paper bag. My chest tightened. She'd been to the corner store for liquor, no doubt.

Mama flung open the front door, entering with a brown bag in one arm. She set it down with an exhausted sigh. The green necks of glass bottles bobbed from the paper rim. Her hair's black waves were shiny with grease, dulled at the ends in a haphazard bun, under-eyes and cheeks sallow. The new gauntness in her face turned her dimples into marks of hunger and darkness.

"What's that smell?" she asked, nose crinkling.

"You left Cat alone in the kitchen," I said, hugging my sister tightly. Her soft body was still trembling.

"Me?" Mama said, blinking languidly. "That'd be you; I wasn't even here. Why weren't you up with her? I told you I had to run to the store."

"You didn't," I said. "You didn't wake me up. It's not even seven. Have you already been drinking?"

Mama began opening windows. "Stinks in here."

"Geez, Mama," I said, my jaw and head throbbing. If I gritted my teeth any tighter, they'd chip. "And we're okay, by the way; thanks for asking."

She rolled her eyes. "Don't be so dramatic. I'm gonna hop in the shower before work. Fix me something to eat? Or grab me a granola bar."

Before I could respond, she picked up the bag, took it to the bathroom and slammed the door shut.

"That's what I was trying to do," Cat whispered.

"Do what?" I asked.

"Make oatmeal."

Mama had left for one of her cleaning shifts, and I fought the urge to scold her so I wouldn't add any more stress to Cat.Instead, I sent my sister out into the fresh April air, thick with warm cedar and penstemon, watching as she meandered over to the Vances' pristine porch to play with their golden retriever.

The front door creaked open as I peeled a burnt potholder from the stovetop grate.

"Laney?" Wyatt's voice echoed with concern.

"In here."

He's been my one bright spot post-El Cobre, a refuge from the noise in my head. His presence was comforting—it was healing to be loved and worshipped and simultaneously liberating to forget everything haunting me.

We constantly sought each other out for stolen moments of passion: in a deserted locker room or dark school theater closet, in the dusty bed of his family's pickup truck, or thrusting on top of my twin mattress when Mama and Cat were elsewhere. The thrill of exploring each other intensified with every encounter.

"God, what happened? Are you okay?" He grabbed the nearby trash can for me to place a handful of scorched remains.

"Cat, this morning ... Mama wasn't here."

The words caught like thorns behind my lips, but Wyatt's presence carried understanding deeper than explanation. "You have another pair of gloves?" he asked.

Wordlessly, we cleaned the ashy foam from the floors and countertops. Every scrub pushed the mess into wet, sooty swirls that looked more like abstract art than progress. My eyes stung from the cleaning products and chemical retardant.

"Probably not doing this right," I muttered, furiously scouring a stubborn spot.

Wyatt placed his hand over mine, stilling its motion. "I'll run home in a bit to grab some supplies to take care of this. But let's take a quick break."

The mattress dipped beneath his weight as exhaustion dragged me down, my empty stomach protesting while pain pulsed behind my temples.

"Can I get you something to eat?" He started up from the bed, but I pulled him back.

"Not hungry," I said. "I just need this right now."

He nuzzled into my neck. I closed my eyes, resting in silence for several minutes.

"Have you contacted Princeton yet?" he asked, brushing a curl away from my face. "I'm sure you could plead your case."

I opened my eyes and groaned, turning away from his gaze. The thought of the school refusing my application filled me with dread; I couldn't bring myself to take that risk. "Not yet."

Wyatt bit his lip, deep in thought and strategy. "It can't hurt to try. If they can't see how amazing you are, then make them see it, give them a little nudge." He paused, propping himself up on one arm and tracing a figure-eight around my navel with the other hand before continuing in a softer tone. "We're going to get you to Princeton one way or another." He kissed my eyelids, but it didn't ease the fear coiling inside.

"Can we not talk about this, Wy?" My fingers press into the phantom warmth his lips left behind.

"Shit, my house almost just burned down."

As loving as Wyatt was, his tunnel vision for Princeton was a luxury I couldn't afford. He didn't have a fragile family or the haunting guilt of someone taking a bullet for him, consuming every thought.

"Sorry." He pulled away, fiddling with the hem of my covers. "I wish I could take it all away."

"I'm sure it's all real inconvenient for you." I turned away, my back facing him.

It was a low blow, but it was easier to be frustrated at him than face the tug-of-war between desire and duty.

He didn't take the bait. Instead, his firm grip pulled me back in toward him. I tried to resist, curling into a ball. He enveloped me in his arms, rocking me.

"You know I blame myself for that day too?"

I pulled away. "What? No. Why?"

"If I hadn't taken us down that path—I led us right into their trap." He pulls at his jet-black hair. "I've never been so wrong. Can barely sleep; it just plays over and over."

I wrapped my arms around him. "Don't do this to yourself," I whispered.

"I could say the same to you."

Somehow, granting him the grace I couldn't give myself was easier.

He created a canopy over us with the thin sheets, his handsome features sharpening in the diffused light as he kissed my neck, edging ever closer to my lips. I wrapped my legs around him as he hardened against my inner thigh.

"You can't push me away, Laney," he said between kisses as I moaned with longing. "I'll just pull you in harder. You are my future. We belong together."

His words echoed in my head as I melted into his embrace. It all seemed too simple, too perfect. Joss's betrayal had freed me from any desire to stay in Arizona. In my clouded mind, she remained undeserving of forgiveness after the expedition.

Yet I couldn't shake the needling sensation that I needed to stay in Jericott, that invisible familial thread tugging hard.

"Cat, though..."

After our expedition, I retreated into my shell. The thought of leaving Cat behind in the dysfunctional tornado of Mama's spiraling was suffocating. I had to be the rock because Mama couldn't. This morning was proof of that.

Wyatt inhaled sharply. "I know." He kissed my cheek before breaking our cotton canopy. "We'll figure something out. Maybe the deferral would help in taking her with us."

Hope jolted through me.

"You mean it?" I asked.

"Loving you means loving your sister, too," he said without hesitation.

Could I convince Mama to pull Cat from this chaos? Frame it as enabling her to pursue El Cobre and her freedom. Everything she's ever wanted. If I could find a way to make Mama sign her rights over to me—being eighteen and all—and if I got a second job for the summer and applied for a loan from Jericott Bank, then I could certainly take Cat away. If push came to shove, the kitchen fire was the perfect leverage to show authorities that she was unfit as a mother. Cruel, yes, but I wasn't above it.

My lips traced eager paths across his skin as my arms pulled him closer. "Thank you, thank you, thank you."

Feet clomped up the front stoop. Cat. We sprang off the bunk bed, knowing she could ruin things by telling Mama that Wyatt was here.

Mama was strict about alone time with Wyatt despite her neglectful parenting. I had to get him out before Cat caught us.

Wyatt followed me to the window, where he clumsily tried to escape without making a noise, but Cat came in just as he was about to flee.

She grinned from ear to ear. “Naughty, naughty,” she teased.

I put my index finger to my lips as she pantomimed, zipping her lips and throwing out the imaginary key.

Wyatt gave us a half-smile as he clambered out the window. He cupped my jawline with both hands. “Be back with the cleaning stuff. Everything’s gonna work, trust me, okay?”

22

Now – August 2018

Second Expedition

We hunch in the rigid silence of forced camaraderie around the dwindling fire. Questions roll in my mind: *where is Keaton? Where did he take them? How is he handling them? When will he be back?*

Tommy Ray retrieves a flask from his coat pocket, breaking the silence. "Care for a little refreshment?" he asks, the flask glinting in the flame, begging for takers. He takes a swig, wiping a dribble from his beard.

I reach out my hand, giving in deeper to abandon, but not before cleaning the lip of the flask with my shirt.

"Think I got cooties or some'n?" Tommy Ray asks, half-amused, half-offended.

"Of course you do," I rib, and everyone smiles, momentarily breaking the tension. "I don't know what you've had in that beard."

The bourbon burns, sweet and sharp, sliding down my throat, liquid fire spreading through my body with each greedy swallow. Joss asks for the flask and takes a large gulp, cringing after. Wyatt returns the flask to Tommy Ray before suggesting we take shifts for watch duty.

I nod. "I'll go first."

Two gunshots ring out. I picture one bullet going through Harriet's gaunt jaw and another piercing Norm's giant brow ridge. Every muscle tightens in my body, fighting against how wrong it all feels as the wilderness resumes its usual hum.

No one moves or speaks until we hear the swish of Keaton through the dark brush thirty minutes later. At the foot of the flames, he drops a blood-soaked cowboy hat and gray button-down covered in dark red—Harriet's and Norm's, respectively.

"It's done," he says. Specks of blood freckle his cheeks, and streaks stain his hands; a layer of dust coats his clothing.

Fluid heat crawls from my stomach to my esophagus, and I rush to the fringe of the campsite, vomiting Tommy Ray's bourbon and our barbecued dinner.

Wyatt's soft touch meets my back, and he gathers my curls away from my face. "It'll be okay," he whispers.

The bitter aftertaste puckers my mouth as I wonder to what ends Mama would have gone. *Would she have allowed the unthinkable, too?*

"I don't know about that."

My shift on watch is quiet, save for the nervous shuffling of sleeping bags inside tents. Yet without everyone's unease exposed to the open air, the darkness is gentle, subdued. It's a waning moon, and with the campfire now smothered, millions of little stars stand watch, too.

Cold stone anchors me in place as Harriet's pistol presses reassurance into my palm. From this vantage point, no one can sneak up from behind, and I have a 180-degree view of potential threats to our campsite twenty-five yards down the ridge.

No one's getting into our camp while I'm awake.

Being on first watch also distances me from our earlier actions and from everyone, including my tent mate, Joss. Maybe the distance from camp would birth a fresh perspective, validating what we'd done or, at the very least, helping me process the emotional weight of it.

And claustrophobic quarters with Joss are a sore reminder of sleepovers where the late to early morning hours were ripe for spilling our deepest dreams and secrets. Dreams of leaving our little town, loaded with El Cobre's riches. Secrets of hushed fights between parents, Mama's unpredictability, and Joss's father having an affair with a younger woman. Those nights, we hugged each other tight until we fell asleep.

We couldn't piece things back together. At least not in the same way. Tonight had all but ensured that.

I adjust my body, shaking the sleepy pins and needles stabbing my limbs. The temperature drops further, the cold boring deeper into my skin. Heat packs crackle to life in my gloved hands, and their warmth seeping deep while winter gear wraps close. Tension melts from my stiff muscles as comfort spreads through aching joints.

A scream wails through the pitch black, but I can't move or see. More rapid-fire screams, first louder, then muffled. My brain is slow, syrupy. Consciousness mingles with dreamland, both dark and exhausted. I can hear it, but what's—

Shit. I'd fallen asleep.

Loose stones scatter beneath my feet as I sprint toward camp, hands ripping against gravel as I catch my fall. The screams pull me forward through the dark until my tent comes into view, its fabric sagging beneath the weight of moving shadows.

"Joss? Wy?" I cry out. My lungs are raw from the cold and terror as I aim the gun into the darkness. *What happened? Is everyone okay?*

Wyatt has a flashlight on her. She's curled in a fetal position, but I can only see a disheveled blond mass as everyone else crowds around.

"Joss!" I scream.

She turns her head, right cheek rouged, tears staining a clean path down her dirty face.

Joss flinches at my touch, trembling in shock. "God ... what ... I ..."

"You're going to be okay." I hope I've said it with enough conviction.

Tommy Ray paces the perimeter with his flashlight and gun.

Keaton turns on a battery lamp so we can better assess the damage, squeezing in between Joss and me. "Tell me what happened."

The ready-heat blanket from the emergency kit crackles as I spread it open, pushing past Keaton to reach Joss's trembling form. Next, Wyatt checks for any signs of injury.

"Joss, you're gonna be okay," he says. "Checking you over right now. You're going to be fine. Deep breaths."

Joss ignores him, continuing to tremble and rock back and forth. Wyatt turns to me. "Maybe you can keep her steady while I inspect her, see if she'll respond to you."

"Look at me, Joss," I say as her fearful, distracted eyes turn to mine. "Breathe. Come on. Breathe."

She takes a labored inhale and shaky exhale.

"Again, honey."

She mimics my deep breathing for a few more rounds, wincing as Wyatt gently wipes away the tear streaks.

"Alright, let's see if she'll talk," Keaton says, his nervy impatience splintering our attempts to handle her with fragile care.

An owl hoots in the distance like an eerie midnight soundtrack. Tommy Ray returns from beyond the perimeter.

"Didn't find nothing out there," he says. "No tracks, animal or human."

"Some—someone was in my tent," she trembles. The words linger in the chill night air, their implications crystallizing.

It could be one of the rival groups we saw in Willow Creek's lot or the possible third group member the Callahans referenced. My attention flickers between Keaton and Tommy Ray, the two strangers in the group.

"Yo, whoa, whoa, whoa," Tommy Ray says, indignation steaming from him. "I'm a lotta things, but I ain't no fuckin' creep."

"And I would never," Keaton says, palms up. "A safe, unified group is everything."

My suspicion softens its grip as Joss's features relax, her small nod easing the tension in my shoulders.

"Did you see or remember any specifics?" Wyatt asks. "What did this person look and sound like?"

She squints, hugging her knees to her chest, as if that muscle tension will help her memory find a face, like grasping at fragments of half-forgotten nightmares.

"I dunno. They were looking ... going through my stuff, and D's—"

"Stealing something?" I ask.

The possibility of theft jabbing like an icy finger into my spine. *The journal. The key.*

Between the tree lines and jagged rock cliffs, every shadow morphs into a potential threat beyond the reach of flashlights. If it wasn't the dead Callahans, and it wasn't Keaton or Tommy Ray, how many enemies lurked out there?

"Supposing it was someone," Tommy Ray says. His belly, all crinkled hair and sun-scorched skin, dances beneath the hem of his shirt. "Think they were after the same thing as the Callahans? This journal or whatever?" He turns to me. "You need to spill what you know."

His small, mole-like eyes flicker, pressuring me with unspoken curiosity, defiance, and begging. *What aren't you telling us, how dangerous is this trek, really?*

Keaton slides into the tension like a diplomat, his lean frame melting into a crouch at Joss's side. His hand skims her knee, a gesture of reassurance. "What I'm supposing happened," he says with an undercurrent of precise control, "is that we're all super tired and shaken from the day. I think you probably had a nightmare that felt very real."

"I know what I saw!" Joss's words tremble on her lips. "It was real!"

Keaton nods, his expression earnest for once. "I know what it feels like, believe me," he whispers. "Sometimes our minds just need time to process everything that's happened."

Her eyes glass over, shaking her head. "It was real, Keaton."

"We're still going to watch the perimeter all night," Wyatt adds. "Someone will always be watching, so you don't need to worry."

Joss presses her lips together, her face tightening. "Weren't you supposed to be on watch, D?" She leans away from me toward Keaton. "This happened on your watch."

Keaton presses his hand to Joss's shoulder—a silent plea to remain calm.

"I—I don't know what happened. I didn't mean to. I'm so sorry. Please—" I lean toward her, my hands slick with sweat. No matter what she's done to me, this feels a million times worse.

But Joss isn't done, her focus sharpened by ire. "Whoever it was," she says, "they were after you—not me!"

"No!" I exclaim, eager for absolution and to keep my secret safe. Wyatt's touch pulls me back, and he asks Joss to stand down. She's hurt and betrayed by what happened, but revealing too much about the journal and key could doom the entire expedition. "That's not true, the Callahans are gone. Who the hell else? The group *you* handpicked?"

Her mouth gapes like the wind has been knocked out of her; our low blows at each other swirl like toxic fog.

"That's what I thought," I mutter. "Like Keaton says, it was probably your twisted dreams."

"It's good to know what a great lookout you are." She turns her head to Keaton. "Can I stay in your tent while you're out on watch?"

Keaton flicks his eyes toward me as if asking for permission. I groan, her immaturity grating.

"Sure," he says. "Why don't you grab your sleeping bag? I'll start my watch now."

I rise, adjusting the skewed tent poles before seeking their refuge. Once inside, I lock my knees on my chest with my arms, a shield against vulnerability. The guilt simmers, but there's something more insidious stewing above it, like oil rising to the top of water. It's not just the shock of Joss's accusation. It's the gnawing uncertainty that the attack, dream or not, wasn't making sense.

I always knew Joss as a light sleeper. She never talked or walked in her sleep when we were kids—in fact, she'd joke about all my nocturnal mumblings. She would know a dream versus reality. So that begs the question, who was it: an insider, one of us? Another marauder hidden in the wilderness?

"Delaney?" Wyatt whispers from outside the tent.

The tent door whispers open as he folds into a cross-legged position beside me, his breath warm against the night air—something electric dances down my spine at his closeness. "You doing okay?" His voice is soft.

I exhale. "Yeah, I'll be alright."

"I don't want to speak out of turn, but ..." He inhales. "What's this journal and key they were talking about?"

I pause too long to decide whether to let Wyatt in on the truth. "Nothing, rumors."

He smiles. "I know you. And I hope you know you can trust me."

I look down, fidgeting with one of my bootlaces.

"Laney."

He's feeling like the only one I can trust, who has my back. And aside from Cat and Joss—sparingly—he's the only *someone* who's ever cared.

"In Mama's stuff, I found the real Rubio journal," I concede, lowering my voice. "It has the real map. The chest key was with it." I fish it from under my shirt, dangling from the thick chain. Then, I show him the journal taped to my abdomen. "By my knowledge, all but confirmed by Kip, they're legitimate. The map in the journal diverges from the group map we made at Cowboy's Saddle. Joss knows about the artifacts, but she doesn't know I altered the group map. I couldn't reveal the entire truth for the expedition ... because—"

His jaw tightens. "You didn't trust everyone."

"It's not like that, not with you." I grab his forearm before checking myself and pulling back. "I had a feeling about the others, and I wanted to be sure." I pause, wrapping my fingers around the key. "Mama once said nothing brings out someone's true nature like surviving the wilderness together. For her, I had to protect it until I knew. I didn't want to bring you into danger if I didn't have to. And with the Callahans—it's a good thing I didn't."

"Except someone attacked Joss, most likely looking for them."

I hang my head. "I feel horrible."

"I didn't mean that in any way—"

"No, you're right."

"You don't trust her?"

Joss had kept her word about the journal and key with the larger group, even under duress. But many other red flags over the years, and now with the Callahans, are hard to ignore. "It's not that simple with her."

He nods. "Never has been, has it?"

"There was also a break-in at my house after Mama died," I continue. "It has to be connected. The treasure-hunting community is small, with an even smaller underground network."

Wyatt listens.

"I feel awful about the Callahans, the attack, then with everyone piling on... don't know how I'll regain trust. Or the lead, for that matter."

"If anyone can get us through this, it's you. I'll help in any way I can. And your secret's safe with me."

My shoulders sag with relief. "Thank you."

"You need sleep. I'm gonna set myself up outside your tent so you can rest," he says. "And so you're not alone."

"You don't have to do that."

"I want to."

He slips back into the night as I lay there, restlessly staring up at the fabric dome, all of today's failures replaying in my head like a sizzle reel—hoping sleep will win out this time.

23

Then – May 2008

After First Expedition

Graduation week crept up like an unwanted surprise.

It was the itchy, heavy gown weighing on my shoulders. The cap bobby-pinned onto my scalp, the stiffness of my mother's hug, and the bestowal of my diploma on stage, guillotining my last connection to high school.

It should have been a thrill, being salutatorian behind Wyatt's valedictorian status after spring break's upheaval. I could carry on with A-plusses and surface-level smiles with classmates, but no one knew better.

My brain, my sense of place, was still stuck in a distinct pattern, blocking out what was happening around me to craft an existence from my design.

The summer's second job promised escape money—enough to fund the East Coast dream with Wyatt while proving to the courts I could support Cat if needed. Legal knowledge gathered between shifts, preparing for that moment I'd face Mama with *the question*. In the best-case scenario, Mama would voluntarily relinquish her rights. Worst case, I'd have to testify about her inability to meet my sister's needs, which'd hurt both of us to dig into.

The final loose thread to tie off was the Princeton deferral. It all hinged on their acceptance of my late admission and approval of the deferral request.

While Mama and Cat trudged inside after the graduation ceremony, I'd bee-lined to the mailbox to find a thick envelope from Princeton. My heart expanded, and anxious fingers opened it to find two letters within.

The first letter from the admissions office congratulated me for my late acceptance to Princeton, promising further details will be mailed in the coming weeks.

The second letter, however, denied my deferral request due to the number allotted each semester while asserting that my admissions offer still stood.

Disappointment and joy collided in a heady swirl. Here was my ticket out of Jericott, but its terms and conditions paved the way for the next obstacle: affording tuition loans, housing, and caring for Cat. It couldn't be any more complex than what I'd juggle if I remained home. I couldn't hold off the discussion any longer.

"Can I talk to you for a moment?" I asked, my voice barely audible over the blaring television as Mama sank into the worn-out couch next to Cat, a Corona dangling lazily from her fingers.

She sighed and took a sip. "Yeah, sure. Aren't you supposed to be getting ready for the big party?"

"In a bit." I swallowed, my throat tight. "Cat, why don't you go to your room or play outside? Just some boring grownup stuff we're gonna talk about."

My sister's brow furrowed in a miniature protest, but she complied, the old screen door rattling behind her.

"Damn, must be serious, mija," Mama said, her mouth stiffening. She kicked off the scuffed heels she'd worn to graduation. "Please don't tell me this is one of your 'interventions.'"

Her use of flippant air quotes caused my nerves to slip away, but I steeled myself. I was now an adult who could deal with mature problems and conversations.

"More like a proposition."

She settled deeper into the cushions, re-homing her beer on the stained coffee table. "Okay, I'm waiting."

I broke the news about my Princeton admission and deferral rejection. Then, the case for Cat came out in a nervous rush of words, each trying to outpace the other, desperate to articulate all my points before she could shoot them down. I talked to Mama about her chance to live out her treasure-hunting dreams while Cat could return after a successful El Cobre hunt. I rattled on about Cat's wish to move, my readiness to bear the financial burden, and the wider resources a larger city would offer Cat. It was a grand plan for both of her daughters to achieve success and make it big.

When I rested my defense, Mama stewed in silence, her knuckles marbling white as she clenched the neck of the beer bottle. Her wild emotions filled the air between us, heavy as gathering storm clouds.

"What are you saying, Delaney?" Her voice had taken on a shrill tone, the color draining from her olive skin. "Voluntarily relinquish? Are you suggesting I'm a bad mother? That I can't take care of my children?"

I exhaled slowly, steadying my resolve. "Mama, it's not about you. It's about what's best for Cat. *I'm* the one that takes care of her day-to-day. *Me.*"

Mama's hearty laugh was now sharp and bitter. "You? An eighteen-year-old girl? You think you can replace a mother's love with your foolish notions of responsibility?"

"You want to talk responsibility? Where were you when our house almost went up in flames?"

"Hey—you were here too—"

"But she's your daughter, and you were too busy buying booze!"

Mama narrowed her eyes in defiance. "You're so ungrateful. Punishing me because we see the world differently. And you think you're some big shot now with your Ivy League school."

"It's not about me!" I shouted, losing my cool. "And it's not about you! Cat deserves more care and attention, not some half-drunk mother more interested in a legend than the flesh and blood who needs her. I already applied for a loan from the bank so I won't need anything from you."

Mama shoved the coffee table with her foot, upending the beer which dribbled on the carpet. She stood up, chin tilted in defiance.

"Oh, and you think she'll be better off cooped up in some Jersey apartment while you live it up in college? And at your classes all day?" She waved a dismissive hand through the air, a smirk etched on her face. "Please."

"I'd never—"

Mama had already turned away, effectively ending the conversation. "I won't hear any more of this bullshit. *I'm* still her mother, and *you're* still an ignorant kid who thinks she knows better." She looked back at me, her brown eyes heavy with unprecedented callousness. "As for you, *you* can leave and never come back for all I care."

"Don't you worry. You're the worst mother in the world! I hate you and this town! I'll be so much better off."

Her bedroom door slammed shut, and I flinched. My fist connects with wood as desperation surges through me, but only silence answers from behind the locked door, my words dying in empty air.

Cat came bounding in from outside, the sweet scent of mock-orange flowers blooming off her clothes; its petals were tiny stars in her hair. "You done with your grown-up talk? Where's Mama?"

"We are. For now," I said, plucking a few tenacious petals from her strands through a film of tears. "She's lying down for a bit with a headache."

"Another one. Big surprise."

I swallowed hard, rubbing her arm instead. "I'm sure she'd like to watch something with you tonight when she's feeling better."

"Will you make me dinner before your party?"

"Of course."

False cheer clawed its way onto my face as celebration swirled around me, every second away from Cat feeling like ammunition in Mama's arsenal against our future. My hateful declarations to Mama had carved a hollow, queasy ache in my stomach. Hatred tangled with understanding in my chest—not for her, but for the cruel twists of fate that had carved her into this shape.

String lights ribboned the sycamores and ponderosas dotting the Altaha acreage, the buttery vanilla scent of their bark is still strong from the heat. Students filled the clusters of Adirondack chairs and picnic tables while family members served frybread tacos, roasted corn, and fresh melon.

When Wyatt spotted me, he rushed over. "There you are!" He kissed me. "Glad you finally made it."

He sensed something was wrong before I opened my mouth and quickly ushered me to a more secluded spot beneath a tree. I spilled everything that had happened at home.

"Damn," he said, draping his arms tightly around me and kissing my forehead. "We'll come up with something. Think it over tonight, talk to Aurelia in the morning ... maybe in the light of a new day, she'll listen?"

Agreement moved through me like muscle memory while dread pooled heavier in my gut at his words. Even Wyatt's steady presence might not have been enough to untangle this mess.

"Water," I managed, as nausea twisted sharp and urgent.

When Wyatt disappeared into the throng of partying graduates, my heart tightened as I looked at Joss across the sprawling landscape. Her smile quickly faded as she realized I saw her, too. Our gaze locked for a few agonizing seconds before she extracted herself from a cluster of cheerleaders, threading her way toward me.

A torrent of memories surged—the silly inside jokes, the urge to reach out whenever something reminded me of her—while I also imagined a better future without her. We stood on opposite sides of an invisible divide, our soldered hearts now splintered and solo.

"Didn't mean to distract you from your new crew." I cleared my throat, but a sour taste still lingered.

Joss shrugged. "They're kinda boring, anyway." She plucked a purple lupine at her feet, another specimen for her press book. She stroked the petals with once-glossy fingernails now chipped and bitten. She looked thinner, fatigue blanching her face. "Miss you. Like, a lot. How are you?"

"Got into Princeton," I said. "Late admission."

She hung her head, her chic sandals tracing arches in the dirt. "Great. Good for you. You deserve it. Really. I still regret all that."

"And you?" I tried to sound casual. "How's everything?"

Her glassy eyes caught the shimmering lights winking in the trees above. "Umm. Okay. Hard not having my best friend to talk to."

"Yeah, it's been tough to put behind everything that happened in El Cobre—"

Her eyes snapped back to mine with a rare fire. "God, it's not that—" she spat. She clenched her fists. "It's so much worse."

A chill wormed over my skin as she turned her head away, dabbing the corner of her eye with her knuckle. Nothing could be worse than our disintegrating friendship and encounter with the Callahans. Or had she made another horrible mistake?

I crossed my arms. "I've been having a rough time too—"

"God, D, I get it." Joss's face looked pinched. "But sadness and hardship don't belong only to you."

Shock froze me in place as her mood whiplashed between tenderness and steel, her approach catching me off guard when she was the one who'd sought me out.

"What is it then?" I cleared my throat to stave the queasiness and annoyance. "What did you do? What's going on?"

Joss laughed hollowly, crossing her arms, her face fringed with hurt. "Wow. What did *I do*? Okay. You know what, Delaney? Fuck you."

She turned on her heels, her silhouette dissolving into the dim outskirts of the party. Minutes later, her headlights pierced through the darkness as she drove away, leaving me bewildered.

My nausea surfaced higher in my chest, causing me to spit saliva. I hunched down in the grass, taking careful, measured breaths, but I was still reeling. If it wasn't about our expedition or fractured friendship—what was it? What sent her to seek me out tonight, only to turn on me?

A touch on my shoulder yanked me from my thoughts. It was Wyatt, holding a clear plastic cup. "Hey. Sorry. Took longer than I wanted, got stopped by too many chatty cousins." He offered the cup, which I took, swirling a mouthful of water before spitting it out. "And I saw you and Joss talking, didn't want to interrupt," he added.

"I wish you would've," I said.

"That tense?"

Before I could reply, Wyatt's mom came rushing toward us, cordless phone in hand, panic canvassed across her face. Visceral dread ripped through my insides.

"Laney, it's the Sheriff." She panted. "Your mom and sister were in a car accident."

24

Now – August 2018

Day 2: Second Expedition

Wyatt's silhouette stands against the pre-dawn haze as I stir from an uneasy sleep. He'd relieved Keaton a few hours earlier. Last night's memories went in a torturous loop. The camp's hushed quiet belies the turmoil gnawing beneath the surface, fraying at my conscience.

The mountain is different in my bones this time, too. A headache throbs nail-sharp behind my eyes, and my hamstrings and lower back are stiff. Beneath the scratches left by the snare trap, my ankle's evolved into a deep shade of purple. I wonder if Mama felt this battered.

I make a batch of instant coffee and bring Wyatt a small tumbler, our fingers brushing against one another in the exchange.

He flinches as if struck by static electricity. "Thank you," he whispers. "Need a boost right about now."

We gaze across the ridge, the peaks and foliage painted in soft strokes against the early morning light. Morning seeps into my bones, pine and dew dancing in the air before others stir from sleep.

"The calm before the storm," I say, absorbing the stillness. "A new day."

"Here's to a better one," he says before turning to me. "Thanks for opening up last night. I hope we can have more of that. For our friendship."

"Me too." My sip of coffee is extra bitter. *Friendship.* He was so much easier to read ten years ago. Since Copper Lanes, it's been a daisy-petal oscillation of feelings. He loves me, he loves me not. But friendship? It leaves no more petals to pick. He loves me not.

Even if it falls short of my hopes, friendship feels strange with how we left things all those years ago.

Joss emerges from Keaton's tent, hair smoothed into a high bun. My breath catches, and I wonder how she'll act towards me and what her boyfriend would think of last night's sleeping arrangements.

My steps pull away from Wyatt as Joss catches my gaze, her soft greeting belied by restless hands. "How are you feeling?" I ask.

"Tired." Her voice is barely audible. I spot two parallel tracks of scratches stretching from her brow to her cheekbone.

We continue our dance around what happened last night, guilt and frustration tiptoeing around apologies until she wraps her arms around me in a brittle hug. "I know, I'm sorry." Her voice cracks. "I don't blame you. I was scared and angry."

I squeeze her back, her perfume now replaced by antiseptic and sweat. "We need each other's backs out here, Marwood," I whisper.

"I see we've kissed and made up?" Tommy Ray says, emerging from his tent, hair and beard askew. "Sorry, I missed the kiss part."

"Shut up, Jenkins," I say.

He "oohs" and snickers.

"Easy on 'em," Keaton adds, emerging from nearby bushes, zipping his fly.

No sleep-deprived haze roughs Keaton's face. His eyes are clear, their slate-gray depths offering no hint of the guilt that should yoke him after last night. His greasy hair is scraped into a haphazard ponytail, lending him a rugged rockstar charm.

Joss stares at him for an extra beat before looking away.

"I'm just messing around," Tommy Ray says, pouring his coffee. "Ladies can't take a joke."

I pat Joss's arm before walking away to pack up the tent.

Keaton takes me aside, his brow stitched together. "You want to see where I buried them?"

The instant coffee curdles in my stomach. "No. I wanna move forward."

He nods. "No one's gonna miss them."

We leave Parson Ridge shortly after six a.m.; only a smattering of footprints and a sand-soaked fire pit suggest we were ever there. A conglomerate of gray-blue clouds grows over the far side of the mountain range near the escarpment.

"I don't like those," Wyatt says from mid-line. "They've been over there all week, dropping rain."

"It's why hunters rarely come here this time of year," Joss says. "Can't help feeling a little nervous."

Keaton casually dismisses her apprehension. "Doesn't mean we'll get much rain. I'm sure we'll be fine."

"We could be next to the storm and be okay," I add. "Or it could be dozens of miles away, and a flood comes tearing through."

"Any strategies we're taking to avoid one?" Joss's voice is thick with skepticism.

"Staying as high as we can, when we can," I say. "Some washes we can't avoid. But it's good to stick to any banks we see."

"Whatever gets us there fastest," Tommy Ray says.

Wyatt forges ahead, his knife slicing through overgrown branches as we push towards the thicket. "This route will get us through faster to Naranja Valley from the bridge," he declares.

"I hate crossing those old miner's bridges," Joss grumbles.

"It beats climbing," I reply, scanning the group map. "And there's a Rubio blaze nearby that could lead us on the right track."

Mama had always believed that Rubio's symbols were meant to be deciphered, not taken at face value. Years ago, she'd shared an old Polaroid of the blaze, a triple-carat formation carved into a rock side. Three kilometers in the opposite direction, she'd theorized.

Now, with the real journal in my possession, I could confirm she was on to something, just not quite the *right* something.

"High risk, high reward," Keaton chimes in, popping a bubble in his gum.

But my mind is focused on the triple-carat formation sketched in the journal, which aligns with a sepia sketch of the Copper Peak escarpment.

We stop for lunch near a clearing I know well. It's littered with tall, jade-green grass and ochre-colored boulders, as if giants carefully piled up Jenga rock blocks.

"Remember when we came through here once?" Joss asks me between bites of a peanut butter sandwich. "I think we were about ten or eleven. We were with your mom ..."

What's left unsaid of the memory feels too fragile, too innocent to carry. A bittersweet lump sticks to my words. "I do."

I picture a still frame of that day. It was fall. We played "scavenger" among the grass in a season when it was dead, wheat-colored. We engineered this game where we'd hid plastic jewels under the boulders, practicing for when we found de Silva's loot. Mama's laugh while watching us play ricochets in my brain.

Joss's eyes skip around the group, landing on each face briefly. "Let's shift gears," she suggests with a tempered smile. "What's everyone doing with their piece of the treasure?"

Wyatt chuckles. "Always the optimist and manifester, huh?"

Joss's smile flickers, her excited gaze more green than blue in the shade. "Belief can be powerful."

"You start then." Tension coils beneath my words as I study her face, bracing for whatever truth waits in her words.

She twirls a stray lock of hair that escaped from her topknot, her voice dropping its affected vocal fry. "It's a chance to rewrite some chapters ... a fresh start." Her eyes catch mine briefly.

"Seeking closure," Wyatt murmurs, understanding more than he lets on.

Again, *closure*. I feel a twinge, recognizing the buried pain of 'what-ifs' we all carry. Our shared past feels like a closed book; none of us know how to reopen.

I clear my throat, but Joss leans into the growing intensity. "That's why you came too?"

He toys with a twig, his focus inward. "I've been behind a desk too long. Guess I'm chasing a feeling ... of home, of purpose."

Tommy Ray's scoff cut the moment short. "C'mon, no one's sharing the real deal?"

Wyatt's sigh is his only concession.

"Fine, Tommy Ray," I say, secretly appreciating his levity. "Tell us what to do with a treasure."

"Think," he says, leaning in, his beard filled with crumbs from lunch. "What's a gap in the north-central Arizona market?"

No one answers, waiting for him to tell us his plan.

"Strip clubs," he says, his grin meeting his eyes. "A kingdom of 'em. The gift that keeps on giving."

Joss wrinkles her nose. "Gross."

The rest of us laugh—politely—letting him have his crass dream.

Keaton eagerly shifts the attention to himself. "It's the rush for me, always has been." He folds a new piece of gum into his bright white teeth. "And I've had a hell of a time these past several months. But this'll turn everything around."

His eyes catch mine, offering up a piece of gum. I wave it away. "What about you, Miss Delaney?"

My throat tightens, thoughts drifting to the fragility of my needs, much less dreams. Sharing any was exposing a vein, leaving me open to bleed misinterpretation or manipulation.

"Continuing a legacy," I manage. "There's honor in that."

"Not trying to interrupt, but look at that horizon," Tommy Ray says, a welcome respite from the introspection.

Sooty clouds hover over the mountain rim ahead, its microburst cascading below like a gossamer blanket.

"Let's get going," I say.

We pack up without a word, thunder grumbling in the distance.

An hour later, we reach a familiar bend—the old miner's bridge is just beyond. Clouds blot out the sun, but the sky above us remains blue. Terror slams through me as I clear the bend, the sight hitting like a physical blow.

"No, no, no," I say, picking up the pace, my backpack weightless as a jolt of alarm shoots through me.

Ahead of me is no bridge, only a gaping divide. Crumbling, mildewed wood and rusted metal dangle from each side. Keaton reaches the chasm next, cursing.

"Goddamnit, what happened? Where is it?" Tommy Ray asks.

"I ... I dunno," I say. "It's always been here ..."

Wyatt peers over the edge. "Wonder if a big microburst took it down."

"Looks like it's been this way for a while now," I say.

"Doesn't matter who or what broke it, it's not an option now," Joss says.

Keaton turns to me and Wyatt. "So, what's plan B? How far does this put us back?"

Wyatt removes his map from his back pant pocket. I lean over his shoulder, sensing a magnetism in his body language as he leans into our proximity. "Well, we have two choices."

"More like one-and-a-half." I point toward another bridge four miles north. "That bridge is in the worst shape of all around here. Shit, it could even be down too, and then we'd have to double back to our only other option."

"Which is?" Tommy Ray asks.

"The creek bed through the canyon," I say. "But—"

"It's more dangerous," Wyatt supplies, finishing my thought.

"More dangerous, how?" Joss asks.

Wyatt looks up at the sky. "Fewer places to seek high ground if the storm gets worse."

"But the creek bed has lots of trees for good shelter if we need," I say. "And high ground isn't so great for lightning. Though neither are trees."

"We're screwed." Joss fidgets with her manicure. "I don't like being in a riverbed that could run at any minute."

I couldn't blame her for hesitating. "Just let me think for a second."

The boulder with Rubio's triple-notched carats stands a few yards away. I crouch eye level at the symbol, hoping it'll affirm the tough choice I'll have to make. I wink one eye, then the other, before staring with both. Each time, one-carat points perfectly to the same spot in the Copper Peak escarpment. I look down at the map. The place it points to is near Diego Pass.

My heart hammers in my chest. I'm onto something. "There's no way to get to where we need to be except through that bed."

"Should we check that other bridge in case?" Wyatt asks.

"And lose all that time?" Tommy Ray counters. "Hell no. Saving time is everything. Obviously, hunters have already gotten wind of what we're doing, and now they can get to the treasure before us!"

"There's gotta be a third way," Joss says.

"Maybe rock-climbing steep canyons, but then again, we'll have to go through it, anyway." I thrust the map into her hands. "If you think you can lead us by a better route, by all means."

I loosen and refasten my hair into a bun, my tunnel vision peaking. Wyatt's pause for concern and Joss's undermining shouldn't nip at my own judgment. I hadn't prepared my heart for them to agree on something.

I am the leader.

Keaton folds his arms, nudging dirt down the precipice where the bridge once stood. "I hate to say it, but I agree with Delaney and TR here. Most of us are seasoned enough to deal with the storm if it passes through." He looks at Joss. "And we can help the rest."

Joss's cheeks turn pink as she folds the map, conceding to the hard truth. "I just don't know; something doesn't feel right."

"Let's vote," I say. "Canyon, all in favor say 'aye.'"

Tommy Ray and Keaton raise their hands. Wyatt's concession is half-hearted—putting up a palm before walking away.

"I'm going through the canyon bed, hell or high-fuckin'-water," Tommy Ray mutters.

He turns around toward the canyon path, equipment jostling on his back.

Keaton follows him, stepping one foot in their direction. "Faster to the treasure, faster to financial freedom."

Images of Cat's crinkled smile flash through my mind as tension balls in my chest, hope wrestling with fear that this gamble might destroy everything. "Sorry, Marwood. Let's go."

The dry creek bed's lower elevation is a new world. Boulders and rough grass give way to the canopy cover of willowy trees and sandstone cliff sides while smooth gray pebbles jut from the tacky mud. Downed tree trunks flank our path. Joss grumbles and sighs loud enough to ensure we all hear her irritation.

"Watch your ankles, everyone," I say. "It's easy to slip between these rocks. The best thing we can do right now is keep paying attention." I turn. "And that means keeping the chat to a minimum."

Joss trips, hands splintering on a dead trunk that braces a fall. "Damnit!" Her lips pucker. "Knew this was a bad idea."

I sigh. "Funny how you were more than okay about stuff last night, and now you put up a fight."

She brushes off her hands, shaking her head indignantly.

"You want to go there about last night?" The question is a challenge. "Let's go."

"Quit being childish!" I snap.

Keaton tries to calm Joss, patting her shoulder and helping her over rocks.

We now trek over the smooth stones, fissured clay beds, and protruding trunks in silence. Within twenty minutes, the silence becomes a rhythm, a symphony of heavy breathing and trudging footsteps. The occasional thunder peel stops us in our tracks.

Banks dotted with trees and stubby brush dwindle to a choke point of sparse and claustrophobic canyon walls, the dry creek now spanning only thirty feet in width. We take a collective deep breath. There's nowhere to go but forward.

"How much longer is this stretch?" Keaton asks.

"About twenty minutes if we move fast," Wyatt says.

"Okay," I say. "Let's pick it up. Eyes and ears open."

We walk for ten minutes, the canyon narrowing with every step. Wind whips and trills off the acoustics of the surrounding stone facade. Sweat clings to my neck and forehead, and my heart beats heavily. I'm a stranger to this canyon path. Mama never enjoyed cutting through them.

"Can't trust who or what's around la esquina," she'd say.

A low, bass-like rumble reverberates beneath my feet and off the canyon walls. I freeze in fear. Everyone stops. The sound and vibration halt before returning with a boom.

"Run to the sides!" I scream. "Flash flood!"

They're my last words before a wall of water hits Joss's body.

25

Then – May 2008

After First Expedition

Wyatt drove me that cruel and hot night to the scene of Mama's accident, my last hateful words toward her burning a hole in my heart. Dark possibilities spun through my mind like poison, each scenario more crushing than the last.

What if my words were the last running through her head? What if those words drove her to drink more before getting behind the wheel?

Scorched rubber assailed my nostrils when we arrived. Our old Buick's hood was accordioned against a neighbor's tree trunk. Sheriff Shelby's officers and a handful of tow truck attendants were busy treading over the shards of broken glass, a crystallized carpet over the blacktop.

Tears of relief fell when I saw Mama and Cat sitting huddled next to one another in the back of an ambulance, bandaged and silent.

Sheriff Shelby pulled me aside before I could reach them. He told me Cat's shaken confession—Mama drank too many "spicy drinks" and suggested they go for ice cream, but she was too afraid to go. Mama insisted, promising her as much ice cream as she wanted. My guilt twisted deeper, having told Cat the white lie of Mama's alcohol being "spicy" so she wasn't tempted to try it.

They made it only a half mile down the street before Mama lost control, stepping on the gas instead of the brake.

"I hate to do this," Shelby said. "But I'm gonna have to charge her with a DUI."

My fingers tightened around Wyatt's while grief pressed sharp against my ribs. "I wanna go talk to them."

Wyatt stayed behind with the sheriff, only for Mama to avert her gaze when our eyes met. I could tell the shock of the accident had sobered her up significantly.

Cat nearly leapt out of the ambulance when she saw me. She squeezed my neck so tight, her little body shuddering, that I couldn't hold my emotions back any longer. When we released our embrace, I scanned her for injuries.

"Don't cry, it's just scrapes," she said. "It was scary, but I'm really strong in accidents."

My lips pressed against her warm cheek as she playfully wiped away the kiss, pulling a smile from deep inside. "Yeah, you'll be just fine."

My gaze found Mama's ravaged face—skin mottled pink and red, scattered with glass cuts, her dominant arm hanging useless in its sling. "Thank God you're okay."

She dropped her chin to her chest, masking her guilt-ridden face. "You must be so angry," she whispered. "I would be."

"No," I assured her. "I'm too relieved."

She looked up. "But our fight earlier—"

"Don't worry about it."

"You'd have all the ammo you need to take her—" Her voice broke, face crumpled with remorse. At that moment, she looked so small, so fragile, like Cat. Her vulnerability tugged at my heart as she melted into my hug.

"I feel so helpless sometimes, and I don't know how to fix it."

"I know," I whispered into her hair, my words taut with forced maturity. "I know the feeling."

The next few weeks were a stifling blur—the pressure of doing and being everything for my family squeezed into all my thoughts and actions. I had barely enough time to eat, and given the added stress since graduation, I could not really stomach much.

Mama not only had a broken left arm but also badly tweaked her back, which made easy tasks like going to the bathroom or showering a challenge. And with the fire incident, we were lucky to only have a sash of soot along the kitchen wall. Still, I needed to scrub the remaining dark spot from sight; if only I could also wipe it from my memory.

I had other things to clean instead. I had picked up some of Mama's nighttime cleaning shifts at the different county buildings so we could pay the bills, a reluctant agreement from her employer after the DUI.

While the hustle seemed to diminish my fears over the Callahans lurking around the corner, it only exacerbated my indecision over the next semester. Even the ever-waiting Wyatt could only be so patient—he needed to know my plans and Cat's so he could put down a security deposit on an apartment in Princeton; reserving a one or two-bedroom place made a significant difference on stretched budgets.

For Wyatt, it was a matter of choosing between bedroom quantities. Tonight, as I squeegeed and mopped the bureaucratic grime from the courthouse's speckled terrazzo floors, I wondered if I was kidding myself about Princeton, deluded by what could happen instead of what actually should. With only me, no other family, I should be there for my sister and mom.

Every time I thought I was ready to decide, fear knotted my brain. *No, hold on to the dream, hold on to the here and now.*

I headed to the courthouse's bathroom stalls, where the flickering fluorescents droned above. I wiped the toilet seats and sinks with a bleach solution, which felt like a lost cause. The musty, acrid odors resurfaced every night. But repeating the tasks gave me time to think, examine every option, and fashion every loophole, like flying out every month to check on Mama and Cat and putting the debt on a credit card to worry about another day.

In my heart, I knew that "another day" had finally come for me as I reached into my pocket, fingers brushing against the unopened envelope that had been weighing me down for days. A response from Jericott Bank for my private loan request. The moment I had dreaded, holding the power to confirm or deny the path I'd been clinging to.

With trembling hands, I unfolded the letter, eyes scanning the words in stark black ink.

We regret to inform you ...

A leaden weight settled in the pit of my stomach, immobilizing me.

Lack of established credit ...

Breath remained trapped in my chest.

Insufficient debt-to-income ratio ...

My knees went weak.

No co-signer ...

I slid to the floor, sobbing.

With a heavy heart, I parked at the end of Wyatt's long, winding driveway after my shift. Each step along the familiar, dawn-lit path felt like a weight pulling me down. Determination drove each step forward despite the weight in my chest—his face and the truth waiting at the end of this path.Well, not the whole truth. But enough of it.

As I stood on Wyatt's doorstep, my hand poised to knock, a wave of nausea washed over me.

This was it. The moment that would change everything. I was about to close the door on a future that had seemed so confident, so full of promise.

I looked down at my chapped, trembling hands, thinking of the choices I'd made and how they led me here. Choices that had seemed so right at the time but now felt like a betrayal.

Taking a deep breath, I steeled myself for the hurt I was about to inflict. Then, I knocked on the door with a resolve I didn't know I had.

26

Now – August 2018

Second Expedition

The fury and terror of the flood are isolated from time itself. Thick, churning, and sinister, it's a reddish-brown current unrecognizable from the waters that sustain us. It descends upon us out of nowhere and all at once.

It lashes up to my waist when I'm only a few feet from reaching an alcove that would allow me to climb on a ledge of the canyon wall. The river's brute force knocks me down, the water burning my nasal passages and lodging into my ears as I tumble like a rock.

My desperate hands pierce the surface, grasping like pincers for anything to hold on to, my head bobbing for air. The velocity of the rapids pushes me downstream.

The current steers me closer to the wall, and I seize the chance to dig my fingers into the lifeline of its rough surface. The water bullies its force against all my strength. My inner forearm scrapes against the rock, peeling up a layer of skin. I yelp, losing my grip.

Water crashes over me as my body tumbles beneath the surface, grit filling my mouth as I claw toward the air. The world spins dark and murky until something solid slams against my spine—salvation in the form of a log tangled with bushes, catching me in nature's net while my heart thunders against my ribs. I whip my body around with all the core strength I can muster to climb atop the pile of dead brush. Mother Nature won't hold this net for long. If I'm lucky, I've got minutes to balance and scoot my body to the small, connecting embankment.

The water surges ferociously. With a white-knuckled grip, I maneuver across the log, the frothy torrent splashing bits of debris across my face and body.

When my hands touch the safety of the muddy bank, I collapse in relief. My clothing is a giant anvil gluing me to the earth, but I've never been so grateful for solid land under my fingertips. Muddy water burns its way back up my throat, each heave bringing another mouthful of river grit and bitterness.

I jolt to a seated position. Wyatt. Joss. The water hit her. Our group. Where are they? Muffled screams rise over the roar of the deluge. Then a shout.

God, please be alive. Please stay *alive.*

"Joss!" I call, still coughing. "Wyatt!"

I wipe my eyes, scanning upstream for heads or limbs. Joss is drenched, shuddering and clinging to a canyon ledge on the opposite side fifty yards away, the water teasing her ankles. Gear still gloms onto her back.

"Joss, hold on!"

"Laney!" Wyatt shouts from downstream.

Wyatt and Keaton wave wildly from my same bank side, about a hundred yards away, heading towards me. I close my eyes and exhale, warmth returning to my chest and limbs.

"She's up that way!" I yell over the water's roar, motioning upstream.

The minutes it takes them to reach me feel like hours. Wyatt envelops me in a wet hug with a force equally opposing and powerful as the flood raging beside us. His chest fuses against mine, and he pants, shivers.

"Thank God you're okay," he whispers.

Relief floods through me as my fingers finally release their grip. "Find me a rope to reel her in."

Wyatt hastily unzips his soaking wet backpack, retrieving one of our rappelling ropes.

"Where's Tommy Ray?" I ask.

The men look at each other, shaking their heads.

"He can't be far," Wyatt says. "I saw him run for the side."

"Help me get Joss," I say. "Keaton, go search for him."

"Tommy Ray's pack's got most of the gear," Keaton says. "Shovels, trowels, metal detectors." He bends forward to catch his breath. "When you said 'flood,' I chucked my pack onto the nearest shore, but it still might have gotten swept away."

"We'll find it." I head upstream toward Joss, dread hollowing my chest. "Wy, follow me."

Keaton heads back downstream along the elevated shoreline, scanning for Tommy Ray.

"Laney," Wyatt says, glancing around, the alarm evident in his tone. He swallows hard. "Where's your backpack? Is it gone?"

The terrible reality I'm without my gear hits like a sucker punch: warmth, shelter, necessities. I jump, clawing at my chest for de Silva's key on a necklace and the actual journal in its plastic baggie; the soaked exterior sticks to my skin and relief swells.

"Yeah, it's gone. But got the artifacts."

He palms at his gear gratefully. "Still got mine. Joss has the food. We'll pool everything."

"Think it can reach her?" I ask, motioning to the rope.

Joss screams for help, the water now biting her shins.

We must act fast.

"You stay on the shore along this side, anchoring the rope," I tell Wyatt. "While I scale the wall and pitch it to her. You'll have to hold it with the river velocity."

"I've got it," he assures me.

Damp hair pulls tight against my scalp as I jerk the elastic. "We got this."

Scaling the canyon wall and hopscotching creek boulders is agony—every movement straddles victory and catastrophe. One misstep could signal a lethal fall into the flood.

There's no choice, only moving forward. Fortunately, I'm agile enough to skirt wobbly steps and claw against slippery notches in the stone walls. Within ten minutes, we're knotting Wyatt's rope around an immovable boulder to chuck across the water to Joss. Wyatt keeps a hand on the line and the rock for extra safety.

Our first attempt to throw the rope falls short in the middle of the stream, where it flails like a ribbon through the rapids. Panic surfaces as we reel it in for a second try, praying it'll reach her. When she grabs it, hope flickers briefly before it slips through her hands. She loses her balance, falling on the submerged rock where she stands, water splashing in her face.

My muscles tense against rising panic while strength gathers behind a mask of courage. “Come on, Marwood! You got this!”

She looks at me, face dripping and scrunched, likely trying to hold back tears.

“We’ve got you!” Wyatt shouts over the water, giving a thumbs up and motioning for her to try again.

She obliges, limbs trembling.

“Ground yourself!” I shout, mimicking the stance for her to make. “Find your center of gravity, don’t reach too hard or fast—”

Joss visibly exhales before bending her knees while reaching one arm out.

“On the count of three!” Wyatt shows her three fingers before circling a lasso above him. “One! Two! Three!”

The cord sails above the rapids as the loop misses her right arm—one, two, three, four times.

The devastation and panic spread across her face. “I’m not gonna make it,” she wails.

“You are!” I point to my eyes. “Focus. Breathe. Again.”

Wyatt’s shoulders hunch with fatigue.

“Again, Wy!”

He breathes in deep, swinging the lasso above again—one, two, three ... success. The rope circles her arm seamlessly.

“Now put that over your head and around your waist,” Wyatt continues over the roar of the rapids. “And then pull. You should be able to tighten and secure.”

Once the rope is around her waist, she shifts her weight nervously from side to side. “Oh God! Are you gonna pull me through that?”

"I know it's scary," I say, determination etched in my voice. She needs confidence and hope. "You've got this." I pantomime for her to lower herself into the water. "We're gonna pull like hell."

Joss hesitates but obeys. We pull her inch by laborious inch, Joss straining her chin to the sky to keep it above water. Her body sends perpendicular ripples that cut against the grain of the muddy waters, as if the flood protests the outwitting.

When we finally pull her out of the water, she breaks into heaving sobs.

"We gotcha, you're safe," I say.

"The hard part's over, just a little farther," Wyatt says.

We struggle against the high wire balance of water and canyon wall, trying to navigate a trembling Joss and the soaking backpack dragging against her. When we reach the solid strip of the bank where we first split from Keaton, Joss collapses gratefully onto the ground.

"Breathe with me, Joss." I rub her back. "In ... and out ... in ... and out."

As she shudders and cries in my arms, a crushing guilt weighs on my chest. It was my plan, my call, and now they're all paying the price.

My fingers brush against something warm and wet. There's a gaping wound on Joss's quadricep, oozing blood through her ripped pants. Wyatt retrieves the first aid kit from his bag as I gaze towards the landscape, searching for any sign of Keaton finding Tommy Ray. The only sound echoing through the humid air is the tumultuous water.

"You help her, I'm gonna go help Keaton."

He nods, administering antiseptic.

I start to leave but pause. "Wy—I'm sorry."

There's no shred of admonishment in his eyes, only grace. "Don't go there with yourself."

My feet pound against wet rocks until Keaton's silhouette emerges through the spray. "No sign," he mutters.

Minutes later, an unnatural shape sprawls across the sloping bank, several yards ahead, dangerously close to the water.

"Tommy!" Keaton shouts, panic widening his eyes.

He charges ahead, and I breathlessly try to keep up, my pulse searing in my ears.

Please be Tommy Ray. Clyde's last breath flashes in my mind, sparking a hot ache. *Please let him be okay.*

Keaton crouches over the shape, and only when I move closer does my line of sight clear. He turns toward me, the tan drained from his skin, which makes me dread what I'm about to see.

He turns his head back to what lay before him. Then, I spot it. Tommy Ray, limbs outflung against the mud. A silent beat passes as my eyes focus on the horrific sight that leaves me lightheaded: eyes open, sputtering breaths.

A large branch has speared Tommy Ray's chest, staining his shirt with a dark crimson.

27

Now – August 2018

Second Expedition

The branch points like an accusatory finger toward the sky, its base locked into Tommy Ray's side, coloring the mud with an expanding deep red. His ever-rosy face is pale with shock, fleeting convulsions mark his body, and silent pain is tattooed on his unblinking eyes.

Keaton seems to shrink from the wound, mouth agape, his hands floating aimlessly around Tommy Ray. "I—my God ..." His voice is barely audible over the water.

"Can we move him?" I ask, urgency to fix him clawing at my throat. "Away from the water, at least?"

Keaton winces. "If we move him, we might as well be signing his death certificate. The branch—it's acting like a cork. Pull it out, or move him wrong ..."

"We need to signal help, get him to a hospital."

He chews his gum intensely, eyes darting from the rushing water to Tommy Ray. “Not sure he has that kind of time.”

The branch has skewered his backpack to his body, rendering it impossible to retrieve. “All our equipment’s stuck to him,” he whispers in my ear. “We need that.”

“To hell with that! We need to get him help. We can’t leave him here.”

Tommy Ray inhales a sharp, raspy breath. I bend down, nestling my hand into his cold, water-puckered palm. “I wanted to make Clyde proud,” he says, a current of shared understanding passing between us.

I squeeze his palm. “You have.”

“Find it for him, yeah?”

I nod.

He groans. “It doesn’t hurt that much. It’ll be alright. I’ll be good as new.”

I stand up as Keaton leans in. “His shock, it's the only thing keeping him conscious.”

Driven by desperation, I reach for Keaton’s backpack, fingers wrapped around the flare gun. “We’ve got to signal for help—”

Keaton's hand is a blur as he seizes the flare gun and tucks it into his waistband.

My heart stops. “What are you doing?!”

His betrayal stings sharper than the cuts on my dirty, wet skin.

“He'd turn on us given the chance.” Keaton's voice is hollow, resigned. “In his eyes, you can see it. Survival ... it changes priorities.”

His words are the cold splash of a new reality toward that forbidden line. The wilderness doesn’t change us; it exposes us, stripping us of our primal selves. And Keaton’s transformation is complete, all dead eyes and stony face, a predator at peace with his cruelty.

Fear claws up my throat, sharp and suffocating.

We lock into a battle of cold, silent gazes until Keaton mutters, "That's enough." Swiftly, he steps toward Tommy Ray, shoving him on his side by his boot before yanking his backpack from his limp spine with a squelch. "Sorry, man."

Tommy Ray moans as the branch pushes farther out his back.

Terror locks my limbs as my hands press against shocked lips. Keaton shoves Tommy Ray into the rapids. His pleas dissolve as the roiling water folds him under and carries him downstream.

Keaton whistles a few eerie notes of Taps.

He killed him. He killed him for his gear.

Then, he turns to me, his flinty eyes cold and calculating. The real danger of El Cobre stood before me, masked in human flesh.

He twirls his index finger around the gun's trigger guard with the reckless abandon of Russian roulette. "Not a word, yeah? You'll be better off to remember that."

My jaw fights to stay still as defiance rises against his looming threat. "Understood."

"We wouldn't want to scare them."

Sitting under a shady cottonwood, Joss and Wyatt look up when we approach. A surge of protectiveness rises; I can't let Keaton hurt them, too. I must get word to Wyatt while evading Keaton's suspicions.

"Didn't find him?" Joss asks nervously, rising.

"No, unfortunately." Keaton takes the lead, his somber voice ringing false. "Found his pack washed up on the bank, so I assume he drowned. Poor guy."

Tears well in Joss's eyes. "There's blood on his bag."

"He couldn't survive that much lost," Keaton adds.

My gaze drops to the ground as my defenses threaten to crumble. Wyatt's warm, grounding touch on my shoulder raises a question. He must know something is wrong.

"We're all gonna die out here, aren't we?" Joss asks.

"Not if we're careful and listen," Keaton says, his steely eyes flickering at me. "Also, Miss Delaney's a little tired and upset, so she agreed to let me lead us to the next leg of our trip. Right, Delaney?"

Grit from the floodwater scrapes my throat raw as I force down another swallow. "Right."

"And that means I'll need the two-way radio," he says, reaching his hand out to Wyatt, who appears confused but retrieves it for him.

He explains there's a clearing downstream before the creek winds into the canyon, where we might be able to find a detour.

Wyatt and Joss turn to me, seeking my permission.

My eyes fix on the dirt as the words come measured and cool. "That should work."

This is not the time to fight back. I need to gather myself and let the fury within my patience grow. I'll play along, bide my time, and find the right moment to tell the others what happened. Keaton's sharp gray eyes will watch for a slip-up, a sign of rebellion.

His arrogance and greed pulse like a vein waiting to be cut, each boast and sneer revealing another weakness ripe for exploitation.

In lock-step at my side, Keaton makes it difficult to convey anything to Wyatt, his gaze boring into me with every step.

Wyatt slowly brings up the tail of the group as Joss tries to keep up with my brisk pace with Keaton as if fearing a newfound connection that excludes her. If she only knew being in the dark is how I'm keeping her safe right now.

Finally, an idea begins to take shape in my mind, as a cliff dwarfs us in our path in the distance.

"I need to stop," I say, forcing myself to meet his eyes. "Bathroom break."

Keaton frowns, and I think he won't fall for it. "Fine. Make it quick. We need to figure out the next leg of this detour."

My eyes flicker to Wyatt.

"I need to go, too," he announces.

"Separate directions!" Keaton snaps before catching himself. "After last night, I don't want any misunderstandings."

I nod, knowing Wyatt will find a discreet way to converge in the foliage.

A few minutes later, Wyatt finds me behind a thick wall of mountain mahogany, away from Keaton's watch.

"He killed him," I whisper. "Threw him into the river. We need to do something."

Wyatt's eyes flash with horror. "Okay," he says, his voice steady. "Something he won't see coming. We can't underestimate him."

Hope flutters beneath my ribs as something bright sparks to life. "We've got that cliffside ahead before we get to the valley."

His eyes light up. "I think I have an idea."

Keaton's trademark whistle screeches through the air. "Wheels up, everyone, let's go!"

"Stay alert at the cliff. Follow my lead," Wyatt whispers before diverging back in the direction Keaton thinks he went.

When we reconvene at our rest stop, Keaton is eyeing us warily. The game's changed; we hope he doesn't even know it.

"We lost too much time today," he announces. "If we don't move now, well, then the whole day's a bust. We need a new way to Naranja Valley." He pauses. "Tommy Ray would want that."

"I think I have a way," Wyatt says, scanning his map. His high cheekbones rise, eyes gleaming. "It's going to be tough but worth it."

28

Then – June 2008

After First Expedition

The zinnias Dad had planted early last summer shriveled in shame as I pulled into the driveway the morning after my breakup with Wyatt. I'd let the flowers die. I walked through the front door, only to be greeted by more evidence of my neglect. Curtains were drawn shut, and dirty plates covered the coffee and side tables. Cat's action figures sprawled like dead soldiers across the battlefield of our dingy carpet. The sourness of sweat and stale food clung to the air.

"Where were you?" Mama demanded. "I've been on this couch since last night—Cat barely got me to and from the bathroom—"

It was a loaded question.

Following my cleaning shift at the courthouse it was time to tell Wyatt. His bedroom walls held the weight of tears as the truth spilled out—no Princeton money meant no escape, and definitely no fair chance at making distance work. My family chains pulled tighter than dreams. A slow realization had dawned on him that it meant we were breaking up. His amber eyes searched for a glimmer of hesitation from me, but there was none.

He'd pulled me into his lap, burying his face in my curls, hanging on as if our lives depended on it. The heavy silence begged me to remember how we were as one: the crisp brightness of the soap he used, the gentle cotton of his tees brushing my cheeks, and the way he embraced me with such conviction every time. Finally, I heard a muffled heaving and sniffling. I'd tried to pull back to meet his face, but he only pulled me in closer, burying his sorrow into my chest.

"Why isn't our love enough?" he'd whispered, his voice cracking.

My heart thudded painfully, his pleas hollowing out my last shreds of joy. The silent accusation was clear: I was the one walking away; I was the one breaking 'us.'

Distraught, I'd left his place, seeking solace at the bottom of a pint of coffee-flavored ice cream from the corner store. As I made my way from the back of the store to the register, the sterilized glow and brightly colored inventory felt harsh, judgmental even.

"D?"

The pint slipped from startled fingers, crashing to the floor. When I stood, there was Joss. She looked away, almost out of courtesy, like she'd caught me naked. In her hand was a bag of Almond Joys.

"I see you're uh—stocking up on that awful coconut crap."

She pursed her lips, motioning to the ice cream. "Coffee flavor. Must be a rough night."

My cheeks burned as the twenty-something clerk with a mohawk drummed his fingers impatiently for us to pay. "After you," I offered.

Joss was waiting outside after I'd paid, her eyebrows drawn together in concern. "You okay?"

Grief rose like a tide as my arms fought the urge to reach for her comfort, for someone to promise everything would be okay. "Yeah, I'll be fine," I'd muttered. "Broke up with Wyatt tonight."

Before I could walk away, her gentle hand grabbed my arm.

"My parents are in the city for the week," she'd said, nodding towards my bag. "If you need some company."

"Thank you."

We'd sat propped up by pillows on her bed, eating our ice cream and candy bars as the intimate crackling of Joy Division's vinyl "Love Will Tear Us Apart" softly played.

She didn't ask any questions. She didn't need to. The impossibility of a relationship with Wyatt was undoubtedly obvious to everyone but me.

"You know D," she'd whispered before we drifted off with the taste of sugar still on our tongues, "you don't have to be at some fancy school or with some guy to be amazing. You're already there."

The record fuzzed in my memory, blending with Joss's whispered words. But reality snapped back, sharper than the stale air of our living room.

"Sorry, Mama—long work night; I crashed at Joss's."

She crossed her arms bitterly, cocooned in her blanket on the couch. "You still could have called; that's only fair to your mama."

My breath shuddered out as my muscles coiled against the urge to strike back. *Give her grace she doesn't deserve. She doesn't know what's going on*. "I know. You're right."

My answer seemed to pacify her as she nestled further, cozying her arms beneath the well-worn fleece. "Come here, mija. Lay with me."

I wedged myself awkwardly alongside her as she enveloped me inside her blanket. It was this kind of rare, loaded affection that was my weakness, the kind where I'd do anything for her—and she knew it.

Her favorite Telenovela was on TV, a melodramatic dialogue about an evil twin unfolding between two lovers.

"I'm not going to Princeton," I said, void of emotion. "I'm going to stay here, figure out school later."

Mama's body relaxed from behind me. She lowered the volume with the remote.

"You're a good daughter," she whispered, kissing my head.

Cat came bounding out of our room in a feather boa and plastic crown. "There you are, Laney!"

My sister squeezed me tight, sandwiching me between her and Mama, suffocating and sweet at once. Pain crushes my throat and jaw as salty heat builds behind clenched eyelids, my body fighting the truth that right choices still carve holes in your chest.

29

Now – August 2018

Second Expedition

Wyatt's new proposed shortcut involves two dangerous parts that will require skill and nerve: first, we must find an egress point of the flash flood to ford where the water is lower. This will take us to a transition zone clearing beyond the bank, where it meets a different section of the canyon wall.

Second, we must climb that sheer canyon wall. With Tommy Ray's equipment and our rappelling gear, the plan is recklessly feasible. So many things could go wrong, yet I only needed it to go wrong for Keaton.

"When we reach the top, we'll only be a mile from the other side of that collapsed bridge," Wyatt says.

Keaton inhales stiffly, lifting his chin while his gray eyes scan the canyon and creek bank. He's assessing the plan, ensuring he won't come up with the short end of the bargain. "Alright, what are we waiting for?" he finally asks. He motions to Joss for her backpack, shoving it into

Wyatt's chest. "Why don't you be a gentleman and try out the water first?"

Wyatt gingerly treads the sloping bank and steps one foot in the water. It comes up to his ankle as he holds Joss's gear above his head.

His next move has the water up to his shin, and I hold my breath for his next strides to pull him deeper into its lethal flow, but it doesn't. The depth remains the same, with only tiny currents teasing his knees.

Keaton suppresses the smug satisfaction on his face, but his dimples give him away. "Okay, Joss, how about you next, please?"

She nods at him politely, blushing. If only she knew him for who he is. She crosses the water, arms in a T, as if on a gymnast's balance beam.

I'm last, cringing at the water, anchoring my boots to the creek bed. The wilderness feels different after another loss. The water is colder, the hills higher, the wounds more profound, the aches louder.

If we make it up the canyon alive, we will have one hell of a damp trek. And if we don't get dry enough by nightfall, the chill will create more problems.

Wyatt extends his hand, pulling me across the threshold with enough force that my chest meets his, igniting a heat between our slicked clothing. Our breaths are heavy and desperate.

"It's something with the climb, isn't it," I whisper, his chin skimming the top of my head.

"Hopefully. Just be ready."

A hostile finger-whistle from Keaton trills upstream, where he's already ten yards ahead.

"Let's go, lovebirds. We're burning daylight."

We pull back from one another, a simmering pot taken off the stovetop.

It's a strange sensation to yearn for Wyatt out here; it's too much reverie for the reality. This tenuous line between life and death forces a newfound clarity on all the things that are too little, too late. And before Keaton either puts a bullet in our heads or pushes us off a cliff, it may be worth telling Wyatt how I really feel.

How sorry I am for the last decade. For the choices I had to make, for not even trying to seek him out when things got a little better, out of fear. That seeing him again means I've fallen for him, but I expect nothing in return.

But there's no time to lay that all on the line. Instead, we traipse the transition zone silently for several minutes, flanked by a new common enemy.

"Okay, this looks manageable for top-rope climbing, shorter than other spots," Wyatt says as we gaze up from the base of a forty-foot canyon wall, striped by russet and beige colorations layered eons before us.

"I haven't rock climbed since we were sixteen," Joss says, pecking at the paint on her nails. "I can do a scree-covered wall, but these are too steep."

Keaton chews his lip, firing a hot glare in my direction. "Yeah, somethin' about this doesn't feel right." His hawk-like gaze scans the wall from bottom to top before he turns 360 degrees as if pleading for a shortcut.

"Like I said at the rest stop, it's the fastest way to reduce lost time," Wyatt says. "Three, four hours tops."

"You sure, Mr. Ivy League, no more brilliant ideas up there?"

"It has good hand and foot placement."

"Fine. You self-belay?"

Wyatt nods. "That's why I'll go first. Check out the safest route. I'll then secure the anchor at the top. Next'll be Joss and Laney."

Keaton glares at Wyatt, eyebrows arched with doubt.

"Well, ladies first, right?" Wyatt asks so casually I hold my breath.

Keaton's Adam's apple bobs nervously. "Now wait a sec—"

"Is that a problem?" Joss asks, hand on one hip.

Keaton whips his head at all of us, reserving a 'proceed with caution' expression for me, but I simply shrug, loving how it's all naturally unfolding to his disadvantage without me even trying.

"Unless we need the less experienced climbers to go first," Wyatt says. "If you want to go after me because you need extra help—"

"Whatever," Keaton says, his expression rigid. He points to Joss's bag. "But I'm keeping our food with me."

"You don't trust us?" Joss looks like she's been slapped, tears filling her eyes. "And D, you've been way too quiet—are you okay with this?"

"Whatever makes you feel comfortable, Keaton," I say. "It's been a rough day, and whatever we can do to help build that trust, let's do it."

Wyatt tenses. Next, he attaches his harness and ascends the rock wall with the ease of a lizard—lithe and nimble, each step soft and secure. Relief floods through me as his last limb clears the edge. The anchor snaps before my fingers find the harness straps, steadying them against Joss's shaking form.

"I can't do this," she says, on the brink of hyperventilation. "It's been so long."

Her fear takes me aback. City life has softened her, and all the callouses coarsened by life in Jericott have long been forgotten.

"You got this. You've done this before," I say, giving the harness an extra tug to bolster her confidence. "You've been through the worst of today already."

Joss flutters her lids like a blinking doll. "Guess you're right."

"I know I am. I'll guide you every step of the way. Be sure to engage your core, place your feet with intention, rest, and breathe."

"Namaste," Keaton says wryly. "C'mon, let's move!"Joss's ascent is slow, but Keaton groans once she's out of earshot.

"We're burning daylight," he hisses.

"And maybe murderers shouldn't be picky."

He leans his gaunt face into mine. "You try *anything,* and I will end you, too."

My breath quickens, but I maintain eye contact, waiting for him to break first.

A shout of relief echoes from the canyon wall above, and we turn away to see Joss collapse with gratitude into Wyatt.

They send the harness down, and I rush to hop in.

"Ladies first," I tell him, hoisting the harness strips into position. His jaw ripples with anger. "Wouldn't want to make things look weird, right?"

Sweat returns to my neck, remembering the first time I went rock climbing with Mama at age fourteen. I didn't want to go, but she insisted.

"If you want to do an expedition right, you need to learn," she'd said.

She'd probably laugh to see how right she was at this moment.

Years ago, my feet were impetuous, my arms spindly, and my thoughts scattered to the wind. I paid for it—a wrong move left me with a rock rash on my cheek and a broken arm.

This time, I'm seasoned and skilled, if not a little slower—I won't repeat the same mistakes.

My pulse hammers as I step into the harness, each tightening of the buckles punctuating my nerves. Slow and steady feet, inhale, exhale.

I thumb the harness, and then Keaton gives it a pull so strong I'm now inches from him. I swallow and look past his shoulder, trying to suppress the unease.

"Don't forget what I said," he whispers. "Not a word to the others."

My breath hitches. This is it. What happens on this cliff will be a point of no return—nature and circumstance forcing our hands.

Wind whips between my cheeks and the rock face, the mineral tang of dust and stone tickling my nose. My hands and feet curl gratefully into every secure notch they meet as I try to recreate the path forged by Wyatt and Joss. Thunder rips above with an angry grumble as I reach the halfway mark, disrupting my steady pace with a wobble. A cry of concern from Joss wails near the edge of the cliff. *I must block it out. One step at a time. Don't look down.*

A succession of plump raindrops pelt my head and arms, first steady, then building in speed. Danger lurks among slippery rocks and blurred vision; *speed it up*.

"It's okay, Delaney, keep moving!" Wyatt calls from below.

My fingers stretch toward the next hold as my leg pushes up, then terror spikes through me as my foot slips free—the world dropping away until the harness bites sharp between my legs, stopping the fall. Wyatt catches the slip before I plunge any further, but now I sway helplessly away from the rock, heart ready to crack out of my ribcage.

"Use your weight and momentum to pull yourself toward the rock!" he shouts.

Rain blurs the rock face as my hands slam against stone, the impact throwing me back into empty space.

"Keep trying! You can do it!"

Muscles strain against stone as fingers scrape repeatedly, each failure burning through exhausted limbs. The wall blurs into sheets of water, but stopping means losing everything. My body swings right, finding salvation in a curved ridge of rock. One grip leads to another until solid ground appears beneath trembling legs, water streaming into my eyes as Joss and Wyatt's hands find me.

"You shot through that last leg," says Joss. "Thank God you're okay."

"Anything to get the hell off that rock face."

As if the rain reserved its unruliness for my journey alone, it wanes to spittle when Keaton steps in the harness.

Be ready. Wyatt's words ring through my ears.

The darkness below frames Keaton's slow ascent as my body shifts closer to the edge. He doesn't have the skills of Wyatt, who'd scale rocks when we were kids like Spiderman, but Keaton's athleticism and wilderness skills support an easy ascent.

Wyatt mutters to himself. His chest rises in tight bursts as his body leans over the edge, chin dipping. Next, Wyatt rips the anchor from the earth and flings it over the edge. A skid of rocks, then a thud. And it all makes sense. The point of no return is to *be ready*.

My head pulses thick and buzzy with shock because it can't be real. We just lost someone hours ago, and now the man who I've known as a moral compass just cut a lifeline dangling above a canyon.

"Wyatt!" Joss shrieks. "Oh, my God. What ... what did you do?"

Wyatt says nothing as he coils the rope. Mouth gaping, heart pounding, I peer over the ledge to see Keaton crumpled in the dirt. Is he dead, alive?

I scurry to help Wyatt pack the rappelling gear and gather our backpacks. "We lost the food."

Wyatt grimaces, his full lips in a tight line. "We had to sacrifice something to catch him by surprise."

"Still, we got water. How far do you think he fell?"

"What the hell's the matter with you two?" Joss asks, clutching her chest. "This is unbelievable."

"No time to explain," I say. "I'll try the two-way radio. Get him some help and get him away from us."

I fetch it from my backpack, and once again, the radio only crackles. No signal.

"This… this is murder!" Joss's face is wrinkled with disbelief.

"Maybe broken limbs, but not murder," Wyatt says. "We need a lead on him. He's got a flare for a rescue. He'll be fine."

"You don't know what he's capable of," I say, looking Joss squarely in her face. "We have to get away from him."

Wyatt takes one last glance over the edge.

"He's stirring. We have to move."

30

Now – August 2018

Second Expedition

The lethal storm recedes to distant peaks in the north, a sinister blot of cerulean adjoining the light sunshine blue now canvassing our trail. Left in its wake are viscous patches of mud, wind-torn branches lurching from the safety of their trunks, frenzied insects high on humidity, and the scent of creosote.

The landscape isn't all that's worse for wear. An endless loop of the storm's sodden residue waterlogs us.

It rubs my feet raw with every spongey step, chafes my inner thighs, and glues my hair to my cheeks and neck like cobwebs. Every muscle is heavy and searing, ready to buckle at any moment. At this point, my mind laboriously puppeteers my limbs.

There's a stark silence among our trio. The universe has brought us back together after a decade marred by secret and raw chapters. There was no choice but to return to where we started. Older now, but unlikely wiser.

My mind flashes to Keaton squirming at the bottom of a canyon as the two-way radio continues to crackle with static. We are, without a doubt, all on our own.

Finally, Joss speaks, heading us off in our tracks. "There's no excuse for what you did. And you," she glares squarely at me. "I thought I knew you."

"And I thought I knew you, but you had no problem sending the Callahans to their execution—"

"They weren't a member of our crew!"

My anger flames out quickly because her ignorance balances her self-righteousness.

"He'll be fine," Wyatt says. "He's alive."

"It's not that I'm okay with it," I insist. "But it had to be done."

"No, it didn't."

A post-rain chill rises, and I shiver. "Tommy Ray didn't drown."

Her gaze bounces over my face, trying to understand. "But, I thought ... wait, you saw him?"

"Keaton and I found him. He was alive." I set down the gear pack, but the exhaustion doesn't make the load lighter. "He had a branch stuck in his chest. Keaton shoved him in the water while he was still alive and took his pack." My mouth goes dry thinking of Tommy Ray disappearing below the flood rapids.

Joss shakes her head, folding her body and knees until she's curled in a vertical ball on the cakey earth. "No, this can't ... this ... this is not how it's supposed to go. This can't ... he wouldn't."

"You don't know him, Marwood. That's what happens when we let strangers ..."

"He's—" She smears away tears from her dusty cheeks. "I trusted him."

"You saw all the blood on Tommy Ray's backpack."

"He's done so many hunts, crews rave about ... he's good—"

"Keaton's many things, but good isn't one of them," Wyatt says.

"He has a flare gun he can use for rescue," I say, rubbing my temples. "Plus, he's got Tommy's gun to fend off wildlife. He'll be fine. Best thing we can do is keep moving."

"But moving back toward Jericott, right?" Wyatt asks. "We can head west from here, instead."

"Wrong," I say too quickly. The expedition is slipping through my fingers. "I can't go back. If you wanna turn, fine."

"What if he intends to catch up and use Tommy Ray's gun?" he presses. "On us?"

"I have to keep going."

Wyatt grimaces, eyes flicking downward as he wipes his brow with the back of his palm. "Then we'll keep going with you."

"We're too close to turn back," I say, eyes trained on the peaks dwarfing everything in the horizon.

Joss gives a hollow chuckle. "Apple doesn't fall far."

Their fear and hopelessness gnaw at my guilt. I'm painfully aware of my obstinance, my tunnel vision, and I wear it like a scarlet letter.

Two hours pass. The sun is too far west to trek further. We still have significant ground to cover, but Mother Nature and Keaton conspire against us. At least the camp's vista is next to Naranja Valley and within view of the cliffs eight to ten miles east. As I bend the springy poles and dampened nylon into place for one of our two remaining tents, I steal glimpses of the limestone cliffs.

The dewy, post-monsoon sky blushes with vibrant yet diffused pastel hues plucked straight from an old MGM backdrop or Maxfield Parrish painting—Mama's favorite artist. I think she liked how Parrish conveyed the otherworldly splendor in the juxtaposition of desert and forest. A fantasy brought to life, the same way she revered El Cobre. My bones have a zingy, electric sensation—the treasure must be up there.

The heat is relentless by day, but once the shadows usurp the sun in the higher elevations, cold is the brutal ruler. Wyatt fashions a makeshift pump drill to create a fire when we can't locate the lighters in our gear.

The bow thrusts rapidly against the spindle, powered by Wyatt's rigid and determined muscles. Light smoke curls up from the tinder, a hesitant specter before mushrooming. Wyatt blows his lips ever so gently at the clod of dry grass on the improvised fire board—once, twice, before a glinting orange spark catches. I can already feel the heat.

"We'll need to take off our current clothes," I say. We exchange glances as the flames crackle to life. "Hang them up to dry before the sun goes any farther."

From a downed tree log, I peel off a damp sock and sweaty wrap around my ankle, still swollen purple and puckered from the moisture. I frown. A stupid ankle injury shouldn't slow me down. I rip open a new pack of gauze I find in Tommy Ray's gear, a pang of icy guilt tracing up my spine.

While our boots dry by the fire and a spindly tree doubles as our clothesline, I borrow clothing from Joss, who keeps her clothing packed in a waterproof sack. I'm also careful not to let her see the artifacts clinging to my body. I'll tell her about what the real map says soon enough.

Her clothes are a tight fit on my less taut frame, and I feel out of my element—she also loans me a baby pink zip-up jacket that makes me sweat and thermal leggings that pinch my waist.

My new look breaks the ice as Joss and Wyatt stifle smirks of amusement, having never seen me in such bright colors. My face blushes to match the jacket; I pray Mama's dark flannel and olive nylon jacket are dry by dawn.

Both Wyatt's and Tommy Ray's clothes are dense with floodwater. Wyatt refuses to wear the man's clothes, even dry ones. I can't blame him.

"I'll hang mine up right before bed. A little damp in the morning will be fine," he insists.

Next, Wyatt sets a perimeter trap around our camp, an early warning system for intruders, by repurposing some tin from our old trash and a series of ropes, rocks, and leaves. It's not foolproof, but enough to help us all feel safe enough to shut our eyes for a few hours.

Dusk deepens the sky, and shadows surround the camp as our empty stomachs growl over the silence. However, the food pack was the right sacrifice to lose Keaton.

The day, infinite and surreal in its length, has knocked us over. One person is dead, and the other is left for dead. And the unspoken question is suspended like smoke above our campfire: if Keaton is alive, will he try to come after us? Willful, greedy vengeance can be more powerful than any sustained injury.

Her hand drifts in soothing patterns across her stomach as firelight flickers across her weary features.

"Hey, you gonna be alright?" I ask.

Her eyes glisten. "I don't know." She hugs her side tighter. "Never could've imagined this. People getting hurt. Wish we could rewind all of it."

"We would've never done it," Wyatt says.

Sharp pebbles bite through denim as doubt settles in—his certainty feels like a luxury when survival leaves no room for looking back.

"I don't know what to think or believe anymore." Joss covers her mouth with clasped hands.

My thumbnail picks at rough skin while her words find the weak spots in my armor. "What do you mean by that?" I ask. "You've had a change of heart?"

"I learned from the best."

My anger is febrile. "You're gonna throw things that happened ten years ago in my face right now?"

"I didn't mean it that way. But wow, look in the mirror, hypocrite."

"Stop," Wyatt says. "Can we just—"

"Stay out of it, lover boy!" Joss snaps. "Funny how D seems to forgive you so easily—"

"Quit it, Joss." I grit my teeth, voice cold and stony. "Now."

She brings her knees to her chest.

"Listen, we need a truce. Please. We'll never find the treasure this way." Joss won't look at me; I touch her knee. "Please. I'm sorry. Let's put a pin in our drama. Resume it if you want when we get home."

"Fine," she says after a long silence, pecking at the dirt below her fingernails. "I'll be a good soldier."

She adjusts to the large rock she's sitting on when a hissing buzz interrupts the quiet. Her eyes shift to her left, their whites growing wide. Only her mouth moves. "It's. A. Rattlesnake," she mouths.

White-hot panic rushes through me. From my vantage point, I can't see the snake and its signature diamond-shaped head.

"Stay still," Wyatt whispers, slowly moving behind her and the snake.

Another one of his many talents is snake wrangling. He grew up surrounded by snakes, with Apache culture revering them and his family keeping king snakes around the garden.

The only question is if he can get to this snake before it strikes Joss. It buzzes its tail with a steady, hissing hum—waiting, warning.

"Shit, he's catching it with bare hands?" Joss whispers. "Impressive."

Wyatt fidgets his poised fingers, his eyes laser-focused on the serpent. In one light, instantaneous motion, he seizes the snake from behind its brown, bulbous head, its angry and defensive body flailing like a whip.

Joss and I let out a collective shriek and moved to the opposite side of the campfire from him, the three-foot snake appearing to dance over the flames.

"Where are you gonna take it?" I ask.

"Nowhere," he says, arm extended, the reptile thrashing. "We're going to eat it."

Joss recoils, wrinkling her nose. "Nope, no way."

My gnawing, cavernous belly tells me otherwise. "It's protein. Fat." Rattlesnake's no one's first meal choice, but it's what we have, and there's no way to know when food might cross our path again. "This isn't Cheesecake Factory."

While we bicker, Wyatt has already severed the snake's head a few inches behind the bulbous glands with his razor-sharp pocketknife. "Dig a hole to bury this," he instructs. "The reflexes—it can still strike on accident."

My fingers dig into wet earth as Wyatt slides the bones into their final resting place. Though it's dead, the burnished mosaic pattern of its scales sends a shiver up my spine.

Joss shudders. "I just—ew. I draw the line at snakes."

"You sure have gone soft," Wyatt teases, removing its entrails from a vertical belly incision. "Maybe you could at least find some good sticks for roasting? Being a chef should your stomach change your mind for you."

"Fine," she says, sulking. She scans the dark nervously. "You don't think there's more out there, though?"

"Of course there is," I say. "Look where we are. Grab a flashlight."

My hands work with Wyatt's to strip the snake's scales when a chirp cuts through the dark, sending my muscles rigid with fear before recognizing the sound from Joss's pocket. The sound nags at me, the unnatural way it so arbitrarily disrupts.

"Why do you even need that thing?" I mutter. "Phone alarms for city life?"

Wyatt hands me a long slice of raw meat. "Cut these into chunks."

Joss clicks on the flashlight and ignores me, trudging into the dark for twig skewers.

Before long, we're all holding rattlesnake skewers over the fire, even Joss, her face frowning in disgust. Mischief passes between us as Wyatt and I fight back laughter.

"Smells kinda like chicken," Joss concedes.

"Yeah, with something gamey or sweet to it," I add, my dry mouth salivating at the juices beading up on the meat.

When the skewered pieces are white and firm, Wyatt and I dig in, the warmth and delicate flavor radiating and satiating my hunger. I moan with relief.

"Thank you, snake—and Wyatt."

Wyatt bows his head before his next bite. "It's all thanks to the snake."

Joss takes a tentative bite. Then another bigger one. Within minutes, her skewer is empty.

With our hunger satisfied, we stare at the fire in silence.

"Is our perimeter going to hold up?" Joss finally asks. Flecks of fingernail polish catch the campfire's light as she chips away. "It's no one's fault, but I can't help but think it's a doomed mission."

"We'll be alright," I say, trying to convince myself. "We'll hear anyone coming."

My role reversal with her persists. She was the driving force until things got hard. With our truce, I pull back from my instinct to criticize her, even if it feels safe and familiar. Our souls are equipped with different muscles with varying pliability; what bends one breaks another.

"It'll be hard for Keaton to find us without some navigation better than the map," Wyatt says. "We've gotten through every challenge."

But what if the Callahans weren't traveling alone? That was a latent thought I hadn't allowed myself to mull over out of self-preservation. They may have had a third member in their crew, now that they were older, perhaps less agile. That person could come looking for them with weapons in tow.

"I got you," I say, swallowing hard. "At least the best I know how."

Joss cradles her sides with her arms and nods as if trying to self-soothe into deliberate ignorance. A hush falls over us, thick with our unspoken thoughts.

"I'm going to bed," Joss announces, stopping before heading into one of the two tents. "I need some time alone if that's okay."

Her eyes flicker with a split-second of mischief, a micro-expression in the corners of her lips only our history divulges. "Good night."

The empty tent catches my gaze, its loose flaps dancing like ghosts in the dark wind. "Guess it's you and me in there."

Wyatt's eyes meet mine, a current of understanding sparking between us. There's comfort in this, in the knowledge that as the wild swallows us whole, we have no choice but to turn toward one another.

31

Then – July 2008

After First Expedition

Two weeks after my breakup with Wyatt, I'd agreed that the latest all-out rager party being thrown by a nameless classmate was the perfect antidote for all my wounds.

"You deserve to let loose," Joss said.

"Not too loose," I joked. "I wanna remember the night."

"I will do everything in my power to help you have a good time," she said, squeezing my hand four times. "To make you forget the tough, shitty stuff."

Her transition to arranging my life flowed naturally like a river finding its old path. Perhaps she was making amends for the fissure she'd driven between us, or maybe she was appeasing her inner demons. Whatever the reason, tonight was a chance to continue rekindling our friendship, to snuff out the last few months.

The party, set on the sprawling grounds of a ranch, brought with it the heady smell of manure and the occasional disgruntled brays of horses.

"You don't think he'll be here, do you?" I asked Joss as we walked from her car down the long stretch of gravel driveway toward the house thrumming with a vaguely familiar synth beat.

"Mister Broken-Heart-Goodie-Two-Shoes?" she asked. "Please. I doubt he'd trade his bedtime stories for this."

Teeth dug into my inner cheek as old instincts rose to shield him, familiar as muscle memory. The night was just starting, and I needed to find another way to enjoy it.

We entered through a side door of the maze-like ranch house and were ushered immediately into a narrow hallway shadowed by colored pulsating lights, the walls vibrating with the music's bass. Joss grabbed my hand, threading us through crowds of stoners and tongue-kissers until we made it to the kitchen, which was bathed in the merciless glare of overhead lights. The air was thick with heated bodies and sweat. The contrast was disorienting.

The cold glass pressed into my palm as familiar faces blurred past, Joss's offering of liquid courage accepted without question. A large bag of ice rested in the sink; mixers blanketed the stovetop while liquor bottles took up every inch of counter space. From an adjacent sliding glass door, the cool night air summoned me. Every step I took toward the salvation of the outdoors was tacky with the residue of mystery liquors.

The backyard trees glowed with twinkle lights and paper lanterns and were encircled by rising cigarette smoke. For a second, it reminded me of the Altaha property—a memory I quickly drowned with a gulp of beer.

Some guy leaned over to whisper into Joss's ear.

She turned to me. "I'll be right back."

I glared at her; the idea of being untethered at this party was excruciating. She winked back. An empty foldout chair sat under a nearby cottonwood, and I beelined to it, hoping to avoid as many interactions as possible.

"Laney."

I jumped, startled by his voice. Wyatt.

"Hey." I struggled for composure, taking another long sip, stalling. "Sorry, didn't think you'd be here, thought you'd be packing or—when are you leaving?"

I already knew that answer—we'd circled our Jericott departure date on our calendars like the symbolic fresh start it would have been. But small talk was my safety net now, as anything deeper might cause my heart to bleed onto his.

"Two weeks from Thursday." He rubbed his hands together. "How's your mom recovering?"

"Okay. Slow but steady."

"Cat?"

"Fine. You know Cat."

"Good, that's good ..."

The muscles in his jaw rippled as if he were trying to clench back his anger and hurt. I wanted him to rattle off everything he didn't get to tell me; it was more than a fair punishment. He didn't, seeming to let go of the monologue he was owed.

There was still so much I wanted to say, too, that I could never say: guilts, what-ifs, and apologies that I'd resigned to keeping bottled up. I refused to allow a reopened discussion to lead him on—or myself.

He started to speak. "I was hoping you'd be here—"

"D, there you are." Joss had intercepted, filling me with a mixture of relief and disappointment.

"What are you doing?" she whispered, looping her arm in mine as we left Wyatt under the tree. "That's a slippery slope."

"You left me alone, and suddenly he was there."

She brushed off my defense, whisking me away to the kitchen. I needed to forget the last five minutes, and joining the current keg stand seemed the perfect answer. Before I knew it, I was inverted for a blood-rushing battle against gravity, a dizzying amount of cold beer flying down my throat.

When my world was right-side-up again, Joss whispered to the gorgeous cheerleader, Samantha, with her smooth brunette locks and smoother skin. They were giggling, and I felt unnerved and out of my element. I peered out the window to find that Wyatt was gone. Had he left the party completely, and that was the unceremonious last time I'd ever see him?

The party faded into a velvety soft focus as the beer settled into my bloodstream. Screeching ambient noise turned melodious to my ears as the warmth of kinship for strangers surfaced. The kind of mindset I shouldn't be in to see Wyatt again.

The shot glass slipped from Joss's grip into my waiting fingers, tequila sloshing against glass. "To new beginnings," I murmured more to myself than anyone else.

She smiled, shooting another, wincing. "Whoo!"

With a tight-lipped smile, I tipped the tequila into my mouth. Fire rolled down my throat, zapping away the anxiety churning my stomach. A burst of applause distracted the burn: it was the guy Joss had jetted off with when we first arrived, all rugged boyish charm and Josh Hartnett good looks. He seemed vaguely familiar.

"Never thought I'd have the privilege to see good girl Delaney Byrne pound a tequila shot," he jested. His smile, his recognition of me, unspooled a flutter of butterflies lubricated by alcohol.

"You'll see a lot more of me around here," I said.

These were my people now, after all. Jericott lifers, who scraped by every paycheck, worked at the mill and sustained the town with tourist-friendly charm. They run the sleepy shops that keep the town humming before settling into ritualistic binges like these before starting the weekly cycle all over again. It's not too different from how I'd lived, anyway. Desire could be reprogrammed like faulty wiring—dreams dimmed to a duller glow, heart settling for whatever scraps of connection came easy. Surely, that's all Wyatt had been.

"D, you remember Evan, right?" Joss asked. "Graduated, football team? Works at the mill now?"

Feigned realization washed over my face as my head bobbed in mock understanding. "Of course, yes."

An air horn wailed from the DJ's speakers, herding people toward the makeshift dance floor in the living room. Evan caught my eye, and with reckless impulse, I allowed him to lead me toward the pulsing lights and bodies in motion.

Each step was a tentative effort to distance myself from the gaping hole left by Wyatt. I could've removed my hand, turned on my heels, and stewed alone on the patio. But my body and heart moved with Evan without hesitation for several songs. We were a couple of Jericott lifers, and this was my path, my way to move on.

Joss and Samantha convened again on the dance floor, whispering and laughing in each other's ears before disappearing into the crowd.

Evan and I kept dancing, our hips locked in synch to the techno beat. It felt good; it was the first time that my summer decisions had felt lighter. Evan's firm hands on my waist felt uncomplicated and sincere, where I could just *be*, unmoored from consequence. Emboldened by the alcohol, I stared into his brown eyes, and as he grasped me tighter, I could tell he liked it.

My eyes met his, a wordless question lingering between us. Could a kiss rewrite history and make me forget? He was handsome, nice, funny. This could work. This could be my new normal.

His lips met mine until a techno rendition of Band of Horses—the song that used to be *ours*—filled the room. I jerked back as if his sloppy lips stung, the taste of his beer lingering in my mouth. It was like Wyatt himself had orchestrated this cruel joke.

My punch-drunk heart recoiled. He wasn't Wyatt. He would never be Wyatt.

I whirled around to see Joss beaming through the neon mosaic glow of the room.

My stomach churned sourly, revolting against everything I'd done. I darted to the nearest bathroom, heaving into the dirty toilet.

I wasn't only exhuming alcohol but overwhelming pent-up grief. Dad, Mama's issues, Princeton, Wyatt. So much lost, left behind by choice and without the privilege of it. There would be no Dad to catch me when I fell, no Ivy League achievements, no living life with Wyatt.

Pain ripped through my gut as the poison purged itself—burning eyes, heaving stomach, every pore trying to push out the darkness. Joss gathered my hair back. "Dang, honey, that was rough. You okay?"

Bitter acid splashed against porcelain before the flush swallowed it away. "Making sure I'm getting it all out."

She tore a piece of toilet paper from the holder, wiping my snotty, teary face. "Bright side? I think Evan's into you."

Bitter laughter caught in my throat as the hem of my shirt caught another trail of mucus. "Not after the way I fled from him."

My reply came easy and hopeful, and somehow, that was a relief. Because I knew. Evan wasn't enough, regardless of how hard I convinced myself otherwise.

Joss chuckled. "I think you underestimate guys."

My legs shook as I pushed away from the cold tile. "Can we go?"

Joss's cell phone buzzed. A brand-new model with a slide-out QWERTY keyboard. Joss angled the caller and message out of my line of sight. "Sure. Can we swing by the patio? Think I forgot something out there."

My feet dragged behind her urgent pull, each step sending daggers through my skull while bile burned on my tongue. The party's magic faded to grey as she yanked me through molasses air, trying to force my sluggish body back to real-time. "Geez, what's the rush?"

"Hey, you wanted to get out of here," she said.

She slid the patio door open, and the world shattered.

There, on the two-seater patio swing, Wyatt and Samantha were exchanging gentle, passionate kisses, his hands cupped on her face like he used to cup mine.

Tears mercifully blinded my vision. "That was fast," I said, my voice brittle.

Wyatt broke their kiss, turning to me with eyes wide. "Wait, Laney—"

My body carved a furious path through the crowd, shoulders colliding with strangers as rage propelled me toward escape. Wyatt and Joss's voices faded into darkness while my feet carried me blindly across moonlit grass. Finally, Wyatt grabbed me by the shoulders, halting me in my tracks. A moth-covered barn light glowed orange above us.

"She kissed me first, and I was angry at you," he said, his face twisted with desperation. "Now that I think about it, how can you be mad? You broke up with me." He paced between me and the barn. "You know I'd give anyone up for you, but you've moved on—"

"You have a lot of nerve speaking to her like that," Joss interrupted. "Leave her alone."

He ignored her and locked his eyes onto mine, breathless and desperate. "I ... I don't get it. I thought you wanted this." He jerked his head toward the house with a bitterness that made my heart drop. "That—that guy *you* were kissing back there, your message was loud and clear."

"It's not the same, Wyatt, and you know it," I shot back, my hurt flimsy and ragged. "I kissed Evan because I was trying to forget you, not because I wanted him."

"Don't you think I was doing the same?" he asked, his voice quiet. "Remember—she came onto me."

"Typical, blame the girl," Joss said. "Like you played no part leading her on."

He stepped back as if physically hurt by her words. "I ... I didn't mean it like that." He put his hands in his pocket. "We're not each other's type."

Joss's phone buzzed again.

This time, I saw the name on the screen—who was texting her. Samantha. She was probably looking for Wyatt. Anger flared through me, and I snatched the phone from her hands. "I'm gonna give her a piece of—"

"No!" Joss shrieked.

But it was too late. My bleary eyes racked into focus as a moth flitted around the screen's blue light. A familiar ache settled into my bones. I was reading betrayal, distilled and served cold in text bubbles.

SAMANTHA: He saw them, omg

JOSS: Your turn to swoop in

JOSS: Closed the deal yet?

SAMANTHA: Almost.

Dunno why I never went for him he's so hot and nice.

JOSS: Update?

?

?

JOSS: D coming

"What the hell is this?" I scrolled the screen again, trying to make sense of it. There had to be an explanation—there's no way she'd hurt me again. "Closed the deal? Did ... did you set Wyatt up? Wait, did you set me up? With Evan?"

She grabbed her phone back from my limp fingers. "I can explain—"

"Explain? What is there to explain, Joss?" Wyatt was fuming, pacing alongside the barn. "You're playing with us like we're chess pieces."

Joss looked like she'd been slapped. "I was only trying to help—to help you both move on—"

"We are none of your business!" Wyatt shouted, pulling the hair at his scalp in anguish, his fists clenched so tight I thought his knuckles might split. "Don't you realize what you've done? You can't just manipulate people's feelings."

"I'm sorry, I'm so, so, sorry." Tears swelled in her eyes. "I wanted to give you two a nudge to move on, be happy."

"You've always been so threatened by me," Wyatt continued.

"Oh, fuck you, dude, you have no idea! No real idea what you're talking about or what she must sacrifice." She turned to me. "D, I'm sorry, you know I'm always looking out for you—"

I waved her away with my hand. "Stop," I said.

"What?"

"Just stop. Stop. Both of you. I'm done." The ache in my head grew. My emotions were wrung dry, shattered and scattered. "Wyatt, setup or not, the fact we're both so ready to fill our emptiness with someone else—we probably weren't strong enough to weather the future."

Tears ran down his cheeks, the agony of his gaze swallowed by my numbness. "No, no—"

"Come on. I'll take you home. We'll talk in the morning," Joss said.

"I'm not done, Joss!" I said. "If you can't trust our friendship enough to let me live without your interference, then we have nothing. I'm tired of all this. I'm done. With both of you. For good. I'll find another ride home."

As I turned away, the heaviness was so overwhelming it was a wonder I could even breathe. I heard Wyatt choke on a sob, but I couldn't bear to turn back. The ranch house loomed ahead, pulsating like a dark, astray heartbeat. Their desperate cries faded into the distance, drowned in a night as unforgiving as my resolve. Each step I took was a small release, a letting go of not just two people but of past selves, of naïve hopes, of an unwritten love story.

32

Now – August 2018

Second Expedition

At my recommendation—for heat, of course—Wyatt removes his damp clothing, except underwear, to hang on our clothesline tree. When he crawls into the tent, I look away from his taut, muscled, brown skin, a buzz building in my chest.

"Sorry ... is this gonna be okay?" he asks. "It's the best way to stay warm."

"Yeah, of course."

We nestle into the extra-large sleeping bag, grateful for the waterproof bivvy sack that has kept it dry. The bag feels like a small blanket we wrestle between us. If I move an inch of fabric towards me, he flinches from the cold, and when he moves it, the chilly shrapnel of the air noses against my skin.

He stifles an awkward chuckle. "I think we gotta move closer. If that's okay."

My insides fight to suppress a quiver radiating from my core. I wish it were the cold. It's him. He's what I yearn for, but I'm terrified. Forced proximity while pining for him is beautiful and excruciating. Being used to pain, I'll accept the scraps of joy it'll bring.

I shimmy closer with my back to him. His hot breath undulates over my neck, and I'm unsure where my scent ends and his begins, an animalistic rawness of sour sweat, filth, and pheromones. I force my eyes closed, trying to remember the last time we were this close. It pains me that I can't remember every detail of being together before our breakup, only the way he made me feel.

"I replay that night of the party that summer in my head a lot." His voice is careful and measured enough to pierce my heart with guilt. "I went to that party to win you back, and I saw you with that guy. I can't help but think of if I hadn't kissed that girl, I wouldn't have ruined us for good—"

"You didn't ruin anything." My voice is less measured. "Life got in the way. Remember?"

"I remember."

The vibrations of his shivers ricochet through my back. Our faces hover close enough to share breath while his dark eyes hold mine, unblinking in the stillness.

"Something's on your mind, Firefly." His fingertips graze my elbow, and my nerves fail to say how I truly feel. I am afraid to love him too much.

I inhale, savoring the musk hovering between us. My eyes trail to his muscular chest and abs, masked in shadows, my imagination filling in what I can't see as he flinches and shudders against the worming cold.

"You're freezing," I say.

"It'll be fine, I'll be fine. It's not the Arctic."

"It might as well be. I have more heat than I need." Before my brain can catch up to my body, I'm unzipping Joss's puffy jacket. There's no shirt or bra underneath. Just the key. The fabric slips quickly behind me, hidden from his searching gaze. It's a yoke I can't have weighting the moment.

"Wait," he says, flinching away. "You don't have to ..."

"It's fine. You need to stay warm."

A guarded brightness flickers in his eyes as he eases back towards me. "For warmth."

I unzip the jacket further, slower, my hands trembling while removing the sleeves to blanket it across his back so it straddles us. His chest heaves deeper as the curves of my breasts appear. I try to obscure them with the sleeping bag cover while layering the puffy jacket on top of us.

"Sorry," I whisper.

"Don't be." His tone is light. "Nothing I haven't seen from you before."

My lips press tight against rising joy as arms wind around his neck, skin meeting the angle of his jaw. Our chests hover as close and far as they need to without touching. Old sensations ripple through muscle and bone as my body meets his, memories of bare skin and desire crashing back while danger masks longing as a necessity on this cruel mountain.

"Is this any better?" I ask.

His chin rubs against my cheek in a nod.

Countless minutes roll by too quickly in our sideways spoon until my hip, digging into the cold, hard earth, throbs in pain. I shift ever so slightly to reclaim comfort, pulling away from Wyatt. He moves closer in protest, entangling our legs as one.

"Talk to me, Laney." His voice is husky, laced with a softness that sends my pulse racing. "What's holding you back?"

Longing and terror tangle in my throat as the words stick like honey. "I want to be with you, but so much time has passed—"

"We can reclaim it," he says, tracing his touch along my jawline, warm and unhurried. "Nothing can stop us. Look at how far we've come."

Pain claws its familiar path through my ribs as I wrench my gaze away, remembering how close the last time came to breaking me completely. It feels safer to make what we had small, reductive. "Maybe our love—it was the childish kind."

Wyatt's hand gently cups my jaw, turning my face back towards his, filled with the tenderness I've missed, my resistance melting away. "Childish? That's the purest kind of love."

My heart swells, dangerously close to bursting, as I dare to imagine that he's right. I want to see myself the way he sees me and convince myself I deserve to feel this alive.

"Just say the words," he whispers into my hair. "And I'll give it all up for you."

His desire sends scorching longing through me, competing with my fear. I tuck my chin, burying my head into his chest. He hoists me to his eye level, fingers guiding my chin, dark gaze fixed on me, but I keep my lids lowered. It's too hard to face him. His mouth, so close to mine, exhales fervently, as he needs me, can't breathe without me.

"Say what I know you want to," he says. His lips move closer, ready to touch mine, lingering at a delicate standstill. "It's always been you."

"We can be us?" I whisper. "For real this time?"

My heart thrums in my ears. His eyes meet mine, shiny in the dim light. His impending answer is the biggest fork in our destiny.

"*You* were always my dream, Laney."

The corners of his mouth curl into a forlorn smile, and his struggle is evident: it's the shock of what would have been meeting the resignation of why it never was.

I wipe away a runaway tear before pulling him close, my head on his chest, clutching his bare back, rough with goosebumps.

"One step at a time." He pulls back, locking his eyes with mine. "But together, now. Yeah?"

I kiss him, his mouth sultry and deep.

There it comes again—that feeling and knowing. Our bodies never forgot each other.

Hello, old and true heart.

He cradles the nape of my neck with one arm, massaging my scalp with rough hands. Then, he glides the other hand along my torso, inside my underwear. I moan, stifling it with another kiss.

All at once, I'm seventeen at heart and twenty-eight in my mind. First love converges with the wisdom of second chances. We thrust, moan, and thrill in our favorite familiar places over our bodies until we come, pulsing, collapsing, and after-glowing.

"You think she heard?" Wyatt whispers into the contented silence.

"Maybe." I run my thumb under his chin. "I think she knew it was coming."

Wyatt chuckles, kissing my forehead.

The ruins of the day pale compared to being with him once more, my comfort within the danger, the two of us in the hurricane's eye. He was always my tranquil center.

Gentle touches ghost across my skin—his fingers drawing endless patterns, his face dappled in dance floor light during that first kiss, cotton sheets draped above us while storms raged outside. Those amber eyes and faint freckles had kept my world steady until they couldn't anymore. Until El Cobre's darkness swallowed everything whole. An owl's haunting call slices through the night, bursting my nostalgic bubble, the memories receding. And the afterglow fades, cold air nipping at my fingertips.

I swallow the painful knot in my throat. "What about your girlfriend?"

The thought of being "the other woman" jams me up with shame.

"It's over. She left, packed her bags, and didn't want to join me in Arizona. We fought about it, among other things." He pauses, voice heavy. "But it was never real love, not like what we have. I may have painted a different picture of that relationship to protect myself in case the door was closed forever with you."

Relief washes over me. "I get that," I whisper, knowing all too well the walls engineered around hearts to protect them from pain.

His arms fold around me like coming home, my body remembering every curve and hollow where we fit together. His fingers trace the familiar infinity swirls on my skin, soothing my heart.

Maybe we didn't get our decade, but we have the future.

My muscles relax as I realize how deep my exhaustion is, so vast that it feels like my consciousness hovers outside my body. I exhale long and hard as we ease again into the sleeping bag, arms wrapped around each other, spent after a bottomless twenty-four hours.

33

Now – August 2018

Day 3: Second Expedition

The glow of the pre-dawn backlights Joss's face through the gluey exhaustion in my lids.

"D, wake up, come quickly."

I shake Wyatt and sit up, fumbling to zip my jacket to my throat, but Joss appears too distracted to give me a knowing look. Wyatt trails behind us, the sleeping bag fashioned into a giant wrap. A light orange underbelly loiters on the darkness of the eastern horizon.

"Down by our clothes," Joss says, pointing to our clothesline tree. "I heard something out there, footsteps or something. I was too scared to go by myself—"

Wings flap above, a thunderous parting of the wind. I flinch. Joss yelps as a great horned owl flies to the tip of our tree, twitching its tufts in annoyance.

As my gaze breaks from the owl's dark shape, twisted branches claw at the dark sky like broken limbs. The beam from my pocket flashlight catches our clothes frozen stiff on lower branches, then slides across something else—something wrong. Light reveals wet fur and torn flesh, the creature's original form lost in a violent mess of red and matted hair. Revulsion rises as the corpse writhes with tiny bodies, maggots and ants weaving through the fur while death's sweetness fills my nostrils. "Please tell me the owl dropped that?" Joss asks.

I turn the flashlight to Wyatt for an answer. He's stoic, jaw muscles clenching.

"Owls don't touch rotting prey," he says. "They catch it live."

"What about a mountain lion?" I ask.

"No, not like this." He points to a higher branch. "Look, there's another."

Curtained over a second branch is a scrawny, fetid coyote, its gutted insides soaking its fur a mottled maroon, a lifeless tongue dangling off one of its white canines.

"Someone put them here," Wyatt says. "A warning."

"It's gotta be someone who was with the Callahans," Joss says, backing away.

"Or Keaton," I say. "If he didn't head to Jericott, he's out to get us."

"Keaton?" Joss says with a scowl. She rubs her opposite arms, trying to speed along the warmth of the sunrise. "No, it doesn't make sense; he wouldn't. This is gross."

"It doesn't matter who it was at this point. It's time to get the hell moving." I storm toward the clothesline tree to retrieve our garments, trying to cast my eyes away from the rotting, hung creatures. They're even more unsettling as the morning light increases, monsters without their masks. I breathe through my mouth, a putrid taste choking the back of my throat.

An unnamed anger rises off me like steam from a winter's lake. This journey shouldn't be easy, but this shouldn't be happening. All I want is to move forward. It's time to find the treasure and get the hell out.

I grab the clothes, dry yet chilled by the mountain air. I hear a twig snap and pause, my core warming with panic—a person. A light skitter follows, and I exhale with relief that its sounds match a smaller animal.

A busy silence takes over our campground as we hastily pack our gear. I excuse myself for the bathroom once we're minutes from pushing off.

Fifty yards away, around a bend of boulders and cloaked by leaves from long-limbed trees, I find a tiny nook of privacy. I crouch as if to pee, retrieving the map in the plastic zipped baggie tucked into my waistband.

If nothing goes awry today, we'll be in the right region to spot more of Rubio's signature markers carved into trees and rocks.

That thrill of the hunt flickers again as I thumb the delicate parchment of the original Rubio map. It's the push I need to drive past the fear and doubt. I zero in on the shaded ink of the cave entrance nestled in Diego Pass near the limestone cliffs. It's hard to imagine that the injured marquis could circumnavigate something treacherous, but the map reveals truth in the topography and markers. There must be an easy yet invisibly accessible path to the cave. If we make enough progress, all while keeping an eye out for the other hunters, we'll reach that ravine by tomorrow.

A faint rustle of fallen leaves causes tiny hairs to stand up along my skin, giving me the eerie sensation that someone or something is watching. I remain motionless, scanning the surrounding flora.

Two wild eyes stare back—citrine in color and rimmed in smoke.

A mountain lion.

Fear slashes through me, stealing my voice, binding my feet to the earth.

Mama told me never to turn my back on one. "El león, mirror its conviction and power, and it'll respect you," she'd said. "Turn your back, and it'll attack."

Sharp claws of fate dig into this moment as the mountain lion's eyes lock with mine, every nightmare becoming flesh. Its ears are neither bent in anger like in my dream, nor is it baring its teeth. The cat sits regally, curious, unblinking. Screaming at it seems unjustified.

If it really wanted to hurt me, I'd be dead already.

Instead, I rise slowly, taking one step forward, shoulders back. The cat flinches, moving back. Its ears twitch but remain neutral.

"Thank you. Now go." My voice is awkward, yet loud and assertive.

It retreats a few more steps before turning and flicking its tail. I exhale—too soon. The cat pivots back in my direction, pink tongue lapping at its whiskers. I hold my gaze and breathe, pulse thrumming louder in my head. It must hear my heartbeat.

Right before I feel like I'm about to pass out, the cat blinks and jerks its head to the right before darting away. Tears well as I blink with a relief that trickles down my cheeks.

"Laney?"

"Fuck!" I gasp and jump, crumpling the map under my jacket, yet relieved after my split-second reaction to see it's Wyatt. "Jesus, you scared me."

"Sorry," he says. "You were taking a while, and I got worried. Are you okay?"

"I ... I think so. I just saw a mountain lion."

Wyatt hunches in a defensive stance.

"It's gone—it was the strangest experience." My limbs hang still and heavy. "It just stared at me ... like we had a connection, terrifying as it was."

Wyatt's tense shoulders loosen. "Is that right?"

"It looked like a mountain lion I dreamed of the night before the expedition."

He gives a nod of reverence. "Sounds like a sign."

While the connection to the apex mountain lion was palpable at the moment, I'd never considered the cosmic purpose of what its appearance might be trying to tell me. Wyatt always believed in nature's unseeable, unknowable power, and I lean on him for answers.

"What do you think it means, then?"

"That I can't say. When the time is right, you'll know what it's trying to tell you."

My mind scrambles for meaning while adrenaline still courses from the lion's gaze. Wyatt's hands steady my trembling muscles until I find enough strength to lift my head from his chest, breaking our embrace. Joss's muffled calls echo from our camp.

"Let's head back," Wyatt says, pulling me in by my waist with one arm.

I look up at him, a reflexive flutter pulsing through me. That crooked grin spreads across his lips, hiding his gleaming white teeth. I want to tell him how much I loved him last night, but it feels too out of place right now. However, by his touch and tandem stride, I know he feels the same.

"Can we keep the lion thing under wraps with Joss?" I ask. "Her nerves don't need one more thing."

We catch up to her at the halfway point between camp.

Joss slyly raises her left eyebrow.

"What?" I ask, feigning innocence.

She smirks. "Thought you were in a big rush to go. Didn't know you were busy. Again."

Before we push off, I summarize today's trek: traipsing Naranja Valley and a few hillocks that lead to the western escarpment of Copper Peak. Then the day after, ascending the slope toward Cowboy's Saddle.

I'm about to tell Joss the truth about our destination—where we'll diverge from the group map to follow Rubio's authentic map to Diego Pass at the limestone cliff's base when a crinkling, clopping sound worms its way through the brush.

We all freeze. I desperately scan the downhill expanse, searching for the source.

I spot it—a microsecond vision. I'm almost hoping I can't trust myself: a dark blur, but a man no less. "Did you see him?"

They shake their heads.

"See who?" Joss asks.

Empty shadows stretch between twisted branches while secrets stay buried in darkness.

"Let's move. Someone's out there," I say, palming the outline of the knife in my pocket. "Following us."

34

Now – August 2018

Second Expedition

The brief serenity of the hillocks leading to El Cobre's western slope conflates the notion we're being followed—a would-be reprieve in our journey, gone. Fear and tension hang over the morning's cotton candy clouds. Every step through swishing tall grass, a plotted chess move, every word carefully whispered into the wind to keep our senses peeled.

Mama had no expedition partners except the three of us senior year because, selfishly, she needed me, and equally, I needed Wyatt and Joss. She'd always said survival and greed are a potent combo, that the way people act in the wild is different, and she preferred to work solo.

Would she have acted differently, been more ruthless with the Callahans, if we hadn't been there? Or did our presence save her? I wish I could have done this hunt alone and spared others the consequences of my decisions. Or perhaps going solo is why Mama only ever got so far. Time will tell.

It's noon, and the sun scorches our necks, yesterday's storm smothering the grass with a suffocating humidity. One more hill and a bend—as we near the escarpment, the landscape thickens. The grass is taller and reedier, untamed by humanity, and nature's needles prick our limbs. The cicadas are louder, and intermittent winds seem to howl in protest at our presence.

Our steps evolve into a soldier-like march as the height of the grass grows. Even as I wield a new, massive walking stick, my quads and feet burn as our pace slows to a sludge, dripping with jellied legs and parching thirst.

"D, we have to stop," Joss says breathlessly. I glance behind me to see her bent over ninety degrees. "Just for a bit."

"Just a little farther. We're on track," I say without stopping, even though I know she's right. If we can barely keep our pace, then maybe whoever is following us will lose our trail, too. We're getting to the part of the journey that feels like treasure's within reach.

"Please, we really should stop," Wyatt said. He inhales sharply. "Joss is right."

"There's a Rubio marker up ahead. C'mon!" The excitement and desperation are almost too addictive; at this moment, I'm my mother's daughter, and it's too hard to turn away from.

My walking stick pierces the dirt below the grassy reeds, and something feels different, unyielding. I pause as a furious hum grows. Slowly, I lift the bottom of the walking stick from the earth. A rippling black vortex is attached, and a swarming pestilent clump is unearthed.

Bees. Angry African bees.

A few rogue bees flit toward Joss's face. She swats one in a panic.

"No!" I shout. "It'll piss off the others—cover up and run!" Furious buzzing drones approach my ears, the bees circling and bumping into me, testing if I'm a worthy adversary.

My fingers fumble with buckles as gear falls away, jacket jerking up from my waist while fabric presses against my nose. The storm's bitter teeth await as my legs launch forward into white darkness, hope pulling the others in my wake. A hot needle sensation lashes my cheek. I keep running, enraged bees still hunting, their incessant hum loud and angry. Blurry and black in my vision, they bounce off my eyes and lids, trying to take hold of their target like heat-seeking missiles.

My brow stings with each impact as they streak past, flicking away the ones I can catch. Fabric shields my face until I'm running through darkness, guided by instinct as fire finds the small strip of exposed skin on my hand. Terror and fatigue claw at my muscles, but visions of Cat, Wyatt, and Joss flash like beacons in the dark, dragging my body forward when all it wants is to crumble. Then, the blindness catches up, my left shoulder colliding with something of greater mass—my body losing against the laws of motion. A loud pop erupts in my shoulder, followed by a fire surging through my body as I collapse to the ground. Intense pain radiates through my shoulder, sizzling the muscles and ligaments. My body curls tight into itself like a frightened pill bug, my head tucked away from danger.

A few moments later, I catch my breath enough to realize the buzzing and droning around me is gone. I sit up, more pain firing through my shoulder.

"D!" Joss removes my shirt from my face, crouching by my side. My brain can't form words for her. *Where's Wyatt?*

"I think you're in a little shock and—oh God," she says, eyes boring into my shoulder. "You ran straight into a tree trunk. Your shoulder's dislocated. It looks a few inches lower than your other side, damn."

"I'm okay," I say, clenching my teeth. "Find the med kit. Go help Wyatt."

We're quiet until I spot Wyatt over her shoulder, collapsing into the horizon as my memory hits like a thunderclap.

He's allergic to bees.

I tear toward him, screaming, frantic, my shoulder pain a distant sensation. Losing him again is not an option. When I reach him, swollen slits have replaced his eyes, a red invasion over his bronzed skin, and a thick wheezing accompanies his every breath. My trembling hands hover over his face, fearing anything else against his puffy skin could hurt him.

"Joss!" I scream. "Kit! Now!"

I glance up, anxiously looking for her. Heat ripples above the tall grass as a foamy layer of gnats and other diaphanous insects hover atop. But no Joss. The sound of air rattling in his throat thins until silence presses in. I pause and search for the rise of his chest, but the line between breath and stillness blurs until I can no longer tell if he's breathing at all.

Pain rips through my shoulder with each compression as half-remembered CPR lessons surface—some distant instructor talking about the Bee Gees while shards of agony burrow deeper into raw nerves. A curse slips through clenched teeth as my body fights to focus only on saving him.

Love and desperation press my mouth to his as I force air into his still lungs. Each compression sends fresh fire through my shoulder while time stretches and shrinks between heartbeats, muscle memory carrying my trembling arm through the motions of keeping death at bay. A jagged gasp breaks through his stillness, and I pull back, his lungs hungry again for air. Joss appears with the kit, hoisting one of his pant legs to his upper thigh. She removes the cap of an EpiPen and injects it forcefully into his outer thigh. I hear the pen click, and she holds it for several more seconds.

"How long will it take to work?" I whisper.

"No idea. Let's start pulling the stingers out. That'll only help."

Two stingers lance his forearms, haloed by huge welts as our fingernails scrape along his skin to plow the poison away.

I remove the final stinger from his leg when Joss grabs his wrist. "His pulse is evening out."

Relief surges as I check his face, cupping his jaw in my hands before two delicate fingers confirm the pulse in his neck, which resumes steady and strong.

"Thank God." I gently kiss his cheek.

"No way I'm leaving you that easy," he says weakly. The redness is receding from his face, and his eyes are now visible through the swelling. "Thank you, Laney."

"It was Joss who saved you."

She shrugs, handing him an antihistamine pill from our kit. "See, Wy, I'm good for something."

He chuckles weakly as I assist him with a sip of canteen water.

"Thank you, Joss. Sorry, I need a few hours, and then I'll be ready," he says. "I hate to be the reason we're slowing down."

"No, we can rest here as long as you need," I say.

He waves me off with a hand. With the chaos settled, he notices the unnatural angle of my arm and shoulder. "Whoa, you okay? Dislocation?"

"Yeah, she dislocated it pretty bad," Joss says. "Let's sling that shoulder. I don't know how to pop it back in place."

"Let me adjust it back." Wyatt tries to hoist himself to a seated position, but his weakness pulls him back down wearily.

"Wyatt, I'm fine," I say, even as the pain sears. "We'll deal with it later."

He and Joss exchange doubtful glances. "You're a good liar, D," she says. She turns to Wyatt. "Think you can talk me through it? I can do it. I can help. Shit, I'm the only non-injured one you've got."

Wyatt looks at me for permission, and I nod; anything to deliver me from the agony. "Sure, I can talk you through it." He instructs me to lie flat. "It'll hurt for a sec but set you straight."

Joss rubs her hands together. "I'm ready."

"Does her left hand or fingers have blueness or swelling?"

Joss checks them. "Negative GhostRider."

He smiles. "That's good. Okay, Laney, relax your muscles as much as possible."

Joss kneels to my left, facing me. She gives me a wink as she gingerly lifts and supports my arm at Wyatt's instruction.

"Now, abduct it to 90 degrees, and bend the elbow 90 degrees too."

Next, with her delicate yet self-assured hands, she grips my wrist and elbow, inching the forearm outward.

"Yep, keep that external rotation slow and steady," Wyatt says as I grit my teeth.

A plunking sound clicks as the ball meets the socket. My muscles flare with a surge of heat, and I exhale. The rushing pain in my shoulder and arm subsides to a merciful trickle.

"Oh, thank God," I say.

"Better?" Joss asks.

"Much. Thanks."

"Look at us, being the teamwork dreamwork," Joss says.

"Only took a decade," I tease.

Joss sticks out her tongue playfully. "Now, let's sling that sucker." She removes her jacket and long-sleeve tee, revealing a gray sports bra veined with sweat stains.

"Okay, steady your arm with your right hand," she says as she folds the shirt like origami.

In a swift series of slips, loops and ties, the shirt transforms into a sling. My shoulder is still in pain but stabilized, and I cradle the arm to my torso.

"Now, where'd you get stung?" Joss asks.

"I can take care of those."

"Not with one arm," she says, motioning to the target-like welt puffing on my right knuckle.

Joss uses her long, polished thumbnail to push and scrape across my knuckle, pulling the hook-like stinger and venom sack out of my top skin layers. I keep my focus on Wyatt and off the pain, also to make sure he's still recovering.

Joss flicks the stinger from her nail into the grass. "There. One down, just a few to go, and we'll get those cleaned out later."

She repeats the scrape, push, pull method on my eyebrow, cheek, and ankle. Her taking care of me is familiar and comfortable, and she rose to the occasion when I needed her most. It had been so long since anyone had taken care of me in that way, and I never found it easy to let them. If I let others take care of me, I was weak.

"I'd say you fared pretty well," she says.

I chuckle. "Not as well as you, apparently."

"That's because I copied what you were doing," she says, a tight-lipped smile dimpling one cheek. "Like always."

I squeeze her hand four times.

"Keep that on for at least an hour," Wyatt says. "You could do with some stabilization."

"Thanks." I rub my shoulder. "Sure you'll be okay to move in a few hours?"

"It's fine. Really," he says. "Feeling a lot better already. I'll be careful and keep the extra pens and pills right on me. Just in case it happens again."

"In case what?" I ask. "How would it happen again?"

"Sometimes there's a second wave allergic reaction that can be just as bad." He pushes down his pant leg. "Never had one, but you never know."

I stroke my fingers through his damp, sweaty hair. "Nothing's going to happen to you. I promise."

35

Now – August 2018

Second Expedition

Our humbling encounter with the swarm subdues our return to the trail. Every whisper is a risk, every spoken word a luxury.

Startled birds take flight from their nearby branches as a lone beep warbles from Joss's direction. I shoot her a sharp look.

"Sorry," she whispers, her face pallid. "Alarm. Forgot." Her words are flimsy in the heavy silence.

While the unease lingers, the lack of conversation gives me the head-space to strategize our evasion of who might be stalking us.

There was a possible third person with the Callahans. There was whoever set the snare trap back near Willow Creek. They could be the same. My mind even carries me to Lee Kowalski—I'd heard he'd resumed hunting in El Cobre in the last few years, and he'd never forgiven Mama or me by proxy. He'd even tailgate or antagonize me on occasion through town. I brush away the thought of the most likely suspect.

Keaton.

Logic wound through my racing thoughts—distrust proved right as pieces clicked into place. His body had to be broken from that fall. Even injured, he was dangerous, but now we had a chance. If it was Keaton, we just had to reach the point of divergence at Cowboy's Saddle, where the decoy map he had would lead him down a false trail.

The real map, weighted and clammy, is concealed against my body. There's a twinge of satisfaction for crafting such a ruse, knowing a sun-like blaze made from Rubio is ahead in our path—one Mama never saw on her trails.

By mid afternoon, the start of the Copper Peak escarpment unfolds ahead—a tall, layered sedimentary cake sitting perpendicular to the horizon where we'll hike up to Cowboy's Saddle. A massive, wilting lone pine stands before us, thick with waterfalls of sap and festering cankers, surely on its final annular rings. The tree is a hesitant welcome committee, a signal of changing terrain.

Mama never laid eyes on this tree, as she'd always taken a different route to the escarpment. Pride and pain tangle together as my eyes find the carved symbols high on the trunk—thirty feet of proof I'd already surpassed Mama's reach.

"Guys, look!" The excitement in my voice is palpable.

Joss squints, her voice trembling with disbelief, "Is that—?"

Wyatt grins. "Means we're headed in the right direction."

The blaze is a replica of the one drawn in Narciso Rubio's authentic secret map—a distinct circle adorned with fanning curlicues like a sun to denote we're on the right track.

When Rubio carved it hundreds of years ago, the blaze would have been at his height. But now, the blaze is more one with the tree than it ever was to its artist. Having aged with it—surviving against all odds over the centuries—wildfire, storms, drought, pests. A human-made marker that the wild could have easily swallowed up, a beacon to say, "Treasure's this way."

The blaze on the lone pine buoys our spirits for the afternoon.

Wyatt spots the next blaze. Two interlocking arrows are etched into an immovable boulder. "This almost always means a meeting point." He traces an index finger around its border. "Do you think it means we're closer than expected?"

I bite the inside of my cheek. "Not exactly."

Wyatt's eyes twinkle. "How do you figure?"

Discomfort crawls beneath my skin as I turn from his knowing look—the moment has come to share our true map with Joss. Rubio's symbols were enigmatic and deliberately confusing. His journal shows how contradictory they were to other blazes scattered across the world's treasure trails. If Rubio's swirling curlicues ended in a counterclockwise motion, it didn't mean to "go left" but "go right." The universal symbol for the wrong direction is the arrow nocked to the right, but Rubio's version translates to "keep going."

As the only one who's seen the real map's path and how to decode and retrofit the relative blaze symbols, I must enlighten them.

The more they know, the more they can help, Laney.

I've held it from Joss long enough. For all our differences, she's risen to every occasion where it matters: administering Wyatt's EpiPen, readjusting my shoulder, mustering courage to escape the flash flood, and challenging me to face my fears to embark on this adventure.

"Wait, what?" Joss doesn't miss a beat, picking up on the unspoken current between me and Wyatt. "What am I missing?"

"There's something you should know."

She looks at me with wide eyes as I retrieve the journal pages wrapped around my body and share the page with the sepia-inked sketch of the cave. "Look at these tunnels. It's there."

"Yeah, D. I can see that now." Her tone is clipped, and then she falls silent. "After everything," she says, face souring into a pinched expression. "Convincing you this is your legacy, your way out of your problems, then helping you organize, hell—saving you now *and* then—and you still hold back from me?"

"Please," I say as a puffy patch of clouds blots the sun. "Don't take it that way. Chalk it up to my trust issues. It was a good thing with all that's happened with the Callahans and Keaton. You knowing could've put you at risk—"

"Joss, you have to understand," Wyatt began, his tone calming, trying to mediate.

"Wait, *he* knows?" she asks, the hurt in her voice evident. Her jaw clenches, cheeks now burnished by our days in the sun. "I don't know how many more hoops I have to jump through for you, D." She shakes her head, storming off into the pines. "Hope if this is the wrong direction, you'll tell me."

Wyatt and I remain silent, exchanging loaded glances as my remorse expands.

More blazes dot our path—swirly suns, aimful arrows, and stark geometric shapes etched in rock faces and hulking trees.

Still begrudging, Joss finds the next blaze: a cairn of carefully constructed rocks with carvings in one smooth stone in the middle—a straight line followed by three slanted parallel lines.

"Alright, Keymaster," Joss says dryly. "What's the meaning of this one?"

I take her jab in stride—I deserve it. "Rubio doesn't make it easy, that's for sure." I pull out the map, comparing the centuries-old topography to our current view.

"I think he wants us to follow the escarpment from that side in that direction," I add, pointing northeast. "See how the slanted lines follow the same direction as the mountain line when standing at the cairn?"

"Feels off, though," Wyatt says, evaluating the tight-knotted pattern of rocks like a quality control inspector looking for a defect. "There's also the chance someone messed with this cairn, rebuilt it. This direction takes us farther away from Diego Pass than continuing more west."

"I'm inclined to agree with the land surveyor," Joss says, eyes narrowing into a harsh squint. "Over a pile of rocks, that is. We know where Diego Pass is. Let's get to it where we know we can."

My fingers hover over the fragile parchment as my eyes lift to search the distant skyline. "There's a reason his route goes this way. The cairn, the lines, the mountain, it all matches up."

Wyatt hesitates, combing his dark locks back with his fingers. "But taking the route you're suggesting leads us away."

"Please," I say. "At least give the cairn a closer look, see if it's changed all these years."

He takes the map from me, comparing it to the cairn, looking closely at the vegetation pattern. He nods. "It feels against the grain of what we should be doing, but by all accounts, you're right."

Joss sighs. "Guess we'll find out. Let's go."

As we trudge along, I see the glints of wisdom in Rubio's breadcrumb path to the treasure. We skirt another flood plain that we might have otherwise encountered, the rushing water hissing through the trees from afar. Treacherous gray gorges that slice the landscape bypass us. Slippery edges that can trip up the most skilled hikers we steer clear of, thanks to Rubio's directions.

The sun wanes earlier out here, hiding its glory behind the tall ridges and vistas we've crossed. Shadows now bathe us in a chilly blue veil as we prep to set up camp below the mountain's saddle, the rocky vastness dwarfing us. Wyatt joins me at the nearby rivulet to fill the canteens to boil while Joss pitches the tents for the evening.

The slant of our gait on a higher elevation slope ignites the pain in my ankle. I wince.

"You okay?" Wyatt asks, breathing heavily, his face worn with fatigue.

I nod. "How about you? You okay? Need us to slow down for a bit?"

"Nah." Wyatt places his warm, rough hand over mine as I screw on the canteen cap. "I'll be good."

"Still, got the medicine handy?"

He moves his hand from the canteen lid to the curve of my jawbone. "Always looking out, huh?"

Guilt shadows my deep affection. He wouldn't be in any of these perilous situations if it weren't for me. I tilt my head toward his hand, my lips brushing his palm. "Just tell me you'll be fine."

He smiles. "I'll be fine, but—" He scans the surrounding slopes.

"Think anyone followed us?" I ask, finishing his question. Our nuanced emotions have once again been brushed aside for survival. "I don't think so. Would've been hard to keep up with our pace, even when we stopped for you to recover. We're almost in the clear."

He nods. "We've been swift."

We sit in exhaled silence, the stream serenading our brief and blissful moment. One day, eons from now, its gentleness will have transformed into a gorge, redefining the landscape. Change is the only certainty, and I can't help but think Wyatt and I mirror that change. I hope it brings us together rather than apart again.

By dusk, we snuff out the campfire to keep a low profile, our stomachs roiling with hunger.

"I'd give anything for some of that rattlesnake," Joss mutters.

We huddle in blanketed layers instead, keeping our battery-powered lanterns on their lowest settings. The blue-tinted light illuminates our faces with an eerie hue. Wyatt's knee grazes mine as we sit across from Joss.

My words pivot away, dancing around the raw spot where map secrets still sting. "This time tomorrow, we could have our hands on the treasure."

She blows air into her palms and smirks. "As long as we can get to Cowboy's Saddle, right?"

"Yes, you know I'm sorry—"

Her blue-green eyes widen when she looks up, jaw gaping. A dark object swishes into my peripheral, followed by a thud. Wyatt had fallen to his side. Before I can turn around, the disembodied figure wallops the side of my head, and a throbbing pain branches through my nerves before everything goes dark.

36

Now – August 2018

Second Expedition

A burning assails my face before my eyes open to a roaring campfire, and a powerful headache matches its intensity. Through the flame's tentacles, against the indigo canvas and its infinite blips of stars, Keaton's sharp face emerges ghostlike.

"Evening, sunshine," he says to me, smacking his gum, the left side of his face tattooed with scrapes.

Somehow, it doesn't surprise me to hear his voice, given the skitters in the brush at dawn and the spooky rotten animals. But what does surprise me is the bristly rope binding my wrists behind my back. My skin burns at the tight bindings, but they seem to tighten even more when I try to move.

Keaton's laugh cuts through my panic.

"Your friends tried the same thing in vain." He removes items from his inner jacket pocket, and my heart drops. "Also took it upon myself to fetch these." He waggles the real map and key. I shudder, thinking of how he must have lifted my shirt and unclasped the chain around my neck. *How'd he found them? Was he close enough to hone in on our conversation?*

"Don't worry," he continues. "I was a perfect gentleman."

That's when I see Joss and Wyatt seated around the campfire. My heart clenches to see Wyatt looking tired and ragged, a large goose egg building above his brow. Joss's cheeks are tear-stained.

"So." He pauses as if for dramatic flair. "Last time I saw you, you left me for dead."

"You're dangerous," Wyatt says. "You left us no choice."

"You killed Tommy Ray!" I shout.

"And *you* tried to kill me!" The campfire pops and crackles. "So, I'd say that evens things out, yeah?"

I grit my teeth. "No—"

"Hey, you don't get to cherry-pick morality when it suits your means." He removes his gun from his waistband, buffing it with the hem of his shirt. "But maybe now, we can come to an understanding."

"You're deluded if you think I'm leading you anywhere near the treasure." Rage and humiliation churn in my gut as saliva arcs toward his boots, each emotion clawing for dominance while his betrayal stings fresh.

But he laughs, confident in his control.

A sharp pain pulses behind my eyes, echoing my regret for ever agreeing to let him join our expedition. Now, he knows the treasure's location and has the key to access it. I should have found a better way to leave him behind or kept trying to reach help through the radio.

But every choice in this harsh terrain comes with consequences. And if protecting Wyatt and Joss means paying a price, I will do whatever it takes.

Keaton's grin sends shivers down my spine, as it's wide enough to see the gum embossing his back teeth. "I don't just think you'll lead me to the treasure; I know you will." He brandishes his gun.

It's up to me to find a way out of this.

Wyatt wriggles in his restraints, kicking up dirt with his heels. "If you hurt her, I'll—"

"You'll what?" Keaton rests his hands on his hips, gun at the ready. "Kill me with your feet?" He removes his copy of the decoy map from his pocket before crouching beside me. "Now I know there's something here you're not telling me, something you're hiding. I know a liar when I see one."

"Yeah, check a mirror."

Joss sniffles. She's been quiet, and I only notice how her body trembles with silent tears as she hangs her head low. Joss's eyes dart to a sharp stone near Wyatt's foot. But just as Wyatt subtly shifts his position, Keaton's gaze follows Joss's, and with a jaunty kick, he sends the rock skittering.

"See what your poor leadership's done to your pretty little friend here? Shame, shame, Joss."

I stiffen.

"If you'd just listened to me, been a little more judicious, well, we wouldn't be here right now like this, would we?" He looks back at me, scrutinizing my face. "Are those bee stings?"

Silence builds my shield as his words hang between us. He turns, sizing up Joss and Wyatt in the fire's light. "Did you all have a little brush with bees?" He removes something from his jacket pocket: Wyatt's prescription labeled antihistamines and EpiPens, flashing them like a game show presenter. Panic cinches my breath. "Did some pocket-picking, and I'm guessing some friends had a little more trouble than others here—"

"Give those back!" I demand, the rope fibers clawing into my flesh.

He twirls one of the pens between his fingers with a sinister grin. "Oh, these?" He chucks them into the darkness with all his strength. "Whoops. Hand slip. Let's pray your guy here doesn't have a follow-up reaction."

Joss's cries are audible now, her head and shoulders trembling. A passing wind slants the campfire flames, which reply with a sizzling hiss.

"You bastard," I mutter.

"See, I know a thing or two about allergies. The EpiPens, all that. Me, the kid at school with the inhaler, can you imagine? Lucky for me, it's shrimp. The likes of which aren't anywhere out here." He kicks dirt in Wyatt's direction. "He's looking a little swell-y, eh?"

"If anything happens to him, I swear to God—"

"You're in no position to dole out threats. If you want to see this sister you've talked about again—"

Fury rips through my throat and explodes into the night air, primal and raw. "No need to get hysterical."

"What do you need me for?" I allow a dark, hopeless despair to numb the fury in my veins. In his ruthless game, I was a pawn like the Callahans and Tommy Ray. "You've got what you came back for."

"You make a good point." He sucks air between his teeth. "But I may have questions about this strange map." He unfolds its thin parchment from his pocket. "Stuff that still doesn't make sense. Plus, I want to see your faces when I take the treasure and leave you with nothing."

My body springs forward as rage takes control, only to jerk back sharply when the rope bites into flesh. "Sleep tight, everyone," he says, heading into my tent, keeping the flaps open. "We got a big day tomorrow, and I need everyone well rested." He points his index and middle finger towards his eyes before turning his index finger in my direction.

A series of strained, raspy breaths rouse me from the purgatory between wakefulness and sleep, my throbbing head and hunger muddying my reflexes. The embers of the waning campfire illuminate Wyatt wide-eyed, gasping in a fetal position, his hands still bound behind his back.

My tent is empty; Keaton is likely on a perimeter walk. Joss has drifted off to sleep.

This is my chance to help Wyatt. I wriggle desperately, pressing my pant leg against the ground to feel for my pocketknife. Nothing's there—Keaton must have emptied everything. Hopelessly, I scan the darkness in the direction he threw the medicine, knowing it's useless unless Wyatt's wheezing grows more ragged and desperate.

The fire. It can eat through the rope. Rope burns into my wrists as I inch backward toward dimming embers, every muscle trembling with restraint. The flames lick eager paths across tender flesh while tears blur my vision, teeth clenching against screams that could draw his attention through the darkness. The rope sizzles and smokes, fibers weakening as I fight against the instinct to recoil. I work in tandem with the fire, pulling my wrists in opposite directions. I grit my teeth, sweat dripping into my tear-blurred eyes.

Pull, pull, pull.

Finally, a release, freedom granted by what felt like the devil's own fingers. I pat and snuff out the sparks that threatened to light up my clothing.

Raw fire radiates from my scorched wrists as I force them to function, searching the shadows for the medicine that could save him.

I can't lose him. Not again and not like this.

37

Now – August 2018

Second Expedition

Relief floods through me as my fingers close around the EpiPen, and then my foot connects with hollow plastic—the rattle of salvation in pill form echoing through darkness as I race back to where Wyatt lies. There's no time for the technicalities of proper administration. I remove the safety cap of the pen and jab his outer thigh, his pants still on. Swing, push, click, hold. I massage the injection site once I remove the pen, rubbing with hopeful anticipation for his rasping to slow.

"Come on, Wy," I whisper while unknotting the ropes on his wrist, the roughness chafing against my burns. I need something to cut through it.

"D!" Joss whispers. She's now awake. "My sock. Right ankle."

A lumpy bulge inside her sock, on the medial of her ankle, reveals her pocketknife. "How'd he miss this? Why didn't you tell me sooner?"

"Just," she motions her head toward Wyatt, and I waste no more time cutting off his wrist bindings, "was waiting for the right time."

Wyatt's breath is now steady, his breath flowing effortlessly. I place a pill on his lips, which he swallows. Then, I turn to Joss, cutting her free.

"Where'd he go?" she asks, rubbing her wrists. "And how are we gonna handle this when he comes back? Pretend we're still tied up?"

"It's three against one," Wyatt says.

"No offense, more like two-and-a-half," Joss says. "You're in no shape—"

"I'll be fine. I have no choice."

"He's got weapons," I say. "We need to play this smart." I place a hushed index finger over my lips—only the low whirring of the waning campfire answers back. "The best thing we have going for us right now is the element of surprise. We set out looking for him, overtake him from behind."

"Or create a diversion," Wyatt suggests. "If we fan out, he can only go in one direction."

"I don't think any of those plans sound smart," Joss says flatly. "There's a million ways those could go both wrong and most likely, it'll get us killed."

"We have to work with what we got," I say. "Unless you have some other brilliant idea."

Joss scratches the back of her neck. "You're not gonna like it."

We wait in bated silence for her to continue with her master plan. "We do nothing. Keep the pocketknife and whatever other things handy on us, but—"

"Are you crazy?" I ask. "Let him win?"

"No, we're just postponing things, especially while it's dark. Nighttime is a huge disadvantage. Who knows, we may need his manpower at some point. Exploit what he could offer us."

I shake my head. "Absolutely not."

"Don't you want to be better positioned to get the gun and all?"

Frantic motion drowns out her words as my hands stuff gear into bags. "Pack quick. Look for weapons. Grab some food."

As Wyatt moves to help, Joss looks at me bewildered. "What?"

"I know you're scared," I say. "But I'm not wasting a chance now on a future chance that might never come."

"D." She crosses her arms. "I have this horrible feeling. Plus, I'm worried Wyatt is still recovering—"

"I'll be fine," he insists, despite his unreadable expression. He shoves the remaining pills in his pocket. "I won't slow you down. And if I do, I'll do what I have to."

His shallow breaths steady my racing thoughts as instinct whispers to trust him through whatever storms approach—each crisis will have to be weathered as it comes, and there is no other choice but to face the shadows one by one. "He didn't leave any weapons here," Wyatt says. "We only have our pocketknives."

"Shit. Okay." I turn to Joss. "We're moving. Please. Please trust me."

She scoffs, gathering her supplies begrudgingly. "Sure, okay."

We tread lightly through the darkness, only the essentials hoisted on our backs as we greedily stuff our mouths with the only granola bars we could find. Softball-sized volcanic rocks, porous and unbridled, create an obstacle course over the terrain.

I have only a general idea of the direction of Cowboy's Saddle; we may have to recalibrate our path when the sun rises. Our feet meet an ascent, quads laboriously working against gravity. Like the desperate prey I am, my eyes eventually adjust to make out the precipice of a steep hill to our left.

"Stay to the right," I whisper. "Drop-off is close."

When the ground levels out, I can make out a silhouetted cluster of pines and brush—an eerie bluish light flickering in its midst. We freeze, and I hold my breath, my heart racing.

"See that?" Wyatt whispers. "Keaton. Let's head a little south instead."

Multiple voices ring out. The curiosity of who is whispering in the lone darkness with our traitor is more magnetizing than the lure of a safer detour.

"Who is that?" I whisper. Wyatt tugs me back by my sleeve, but I wrestle free. "We have to know."

Meaning *I* must know. Who else am I up against, and what role do they play in Keaton's larger plan? Even in the darkness, I can sense the discord emanating from Joss and Wyatt.

"Don't be stupid, D," she hisses. "Let's go—or go back to camp."

No use—I'm a moth to a flame. The voices grow louder, but I still can't make anything out. They're hushed deep and low, tinged with a conspiratorial unease. I slowly descend to crawl on all fours; the abrasive ground is agonizing against my raw burns. The granola bar I ate morphs into a nauseous ball in my stomach. Joss and Wyatt follow suit, inch-worming across the dirt.

I faintly catch snippets of Keaton's voice as he explains the logistics of moving a treasure chest. He mentions "ropes and pulleys," while another indistinguishable voice chimes in about "a makeshift winch or sled," their voices carrying and diffusing in the dark. Who's the other voice?

We crawl another ten or fifteen yards over the sharp, prickly pine needles, which sear the campfire's rawness on my skin with a new wave of discomfort at every movement.

"I'm telling you, it'll all work out," Keaton says. The thick brush still masks who he's speaking to as I crane my neck for a better view. "I've got them right where I want them."

"We'll be ready at sunrise," one voice says, the recognition by sight and sound colliding into shock.

The sharp profiles of Harriet and Norm glow in the low-angled light of the lantern, carving unsettling shadows into their faces, bandages wrapped around their hands. Keaton's "proof"—their blood. A choked sound escapes before I can catch it, but those few betraying notes are enough to draw three faces toward our shadow. Harriet's smirk spreads slow as honey while metal glints in her rising hand.

"Good evening out there, Miss Byrne."

38

Now – August 2018

Second Expedition

Recognition jolts through us like lightning—even hidden by darkness, the glint of their weapons sends terror shooting down my spine as instinct takes over, legs launching into desperate flight. Joss takes off first. I can't see her, only hear her panting and crying. I head in the same direction, Wyatt's footfalls close behind me.

Two gunshots whiz past my ear as they gain on our tails. A lantern beam grazes over me. I dodge to the right, narrowly avoiding another shot that pierces the air where I just stood. The sudden split in our path forces Joss and me in different directions, her panicked cries fading into the distance.

My lungs burn raw from the cold as I can't move fast or far enough. I stub my toe on a rooted rock, and the momentum causes me to skid and slide forward. I land chest-first on the ground. The impact swallows up my air for a few frightening moments.

"Laney!" Wyatt's strong hands are scooping me up, pulling me to my feet.

Lacing his fingers in mine, he pulls my left arm along the dark edges of the wilderness, tree needles and brush scraping my face. We scramble on, our progress slow and arduous, until it feels like we've been walking for hours even though it's only been twenty minutes.

Relief flickers as I realize the footsteps behind us have long faded—just as my right foot catches air instead of solid ground. Wyatt squeezes my hand tighter as gravity pulls at both of us, my foot suspended over an abyss. I'm dangling over a cliff's edge, the depth to the bottom unknown. I clutch Wyatt's trembling arm, my anchor against the void.

"I got you." His voice is strained, and I'm unsure how long he can support me. "Grabbing on three."

One. Two. Three. I flex my core, swinging my body counterclockwise, free hand clumsily meeting his arm. The momentum sends him reeling backward, and I collapse on top of him.

But the safety is fleeting. We're exposed on this stretch.

"Follow me," he whispers as we scurry on our hands and feet to hide behind a large cluster of mountain mahogany. "Ready to keep moving?"

"Gimme a sec." My heart's racing, my lungs at capacity, and I am still reeling from the latest close call. I swallow hard; the sensation is raw and hot.

I take a moment to recalibrate my senses and register my surroundings. The unmistakable scent of smoldering juniper hangs in the air. I spot the faintest blush of white against the night of a newer moon, like a photo negative dredged across the sky.

Our panic didn't lead us too far astray. "We're maybe a hundred yards from the campsite," I whisper. "We've gotta find Joss before they find her."

"And when we find her?"

My eyes dart between gnarled limbs, searching the darkness through nature's twisted window.

"Find higher ground, for a 360—"

A sonorous grunt followed by a shrill scream reverberates through the cold air. Joss.

We charge out of the camouflage of dense foliage toward the direction of the cry without regard for what we'll find or fight against when we get there. All the pain and fear funnels into the focus of getting to her.

More cries ring out, followed by a "No!"

Then, a crackly blast: a discharged bullet. Terror locks my limbs for a heartbeat before survival kicks in, feet pounding earth until light glimmers through twisted branches ahead. Tommy Ray's bloody body flashes through my mind.

Please let her be okay.

A consistent pattern of thuds echoes louder as we sprint to the scene, stopping abruptly at the carnage unfurling near the knocked-over lamp. Bile creeps up from my stomach. I want to look away, but I can't.

Norm is sprawled face down, motionless. His pants are undone, revealing a bleeding wound on his upper thigh, likely from the gunshot we heard. My mind struggles to process the viscous, matted wound on the side of his head as Joss stands over him, her bra exposed, her pants ripped, and wielding a large volcanic rock. She's smashing it into the bloody crater of Norm's skull. Again. And again. And again.

The world warps around me as my shout echoes hollow and strange, disconnected as a dream. Between one heartbeat and the next, reality fractures—Wyatt's hands appear like ghosts, wrestling the blood-slick weapon from her frozen fingers while he drags her away from where Norm lies broken.

I run over, wrapping my arms around her. She trembles against me as Wyatt retrieves a gun from Norm's body.

The horrific scene bores through me, power-washing all feeling and sensation away until I'm a calcified husk. Joss sobs against my chest, forehead hot and damp against my lips.

As footsteps approach, Wyatt positions himself protectively in front of us, sliding one of the guns toward me, his at the ready.

"No, no, no! Norm!" Harriet is ready to rush to Norm's body, but Wyatt's loaded hands stop her.

Keaton stumbles upon the chaos, his eyes darting between us and Norm's lifeless body. His mask of control and bravado falters for a beat, a softened gaze lingering on Joss.

But Keaton, the opportunist, draws his weapon too, aiming at Wyatt with a calculated coldness.

Harriet's weapon emerges from her duster, icy blue eyes pooling as they fix on Joss and me. Yet, it's the shock and agony pinching her lips that feels heavier than the looming threat of her gun. A weary part of me welcomes their bullets—a relief from all the pain.

"You." Harriet's voice cracks the frozen silence. "You bitches. You couldn't."

Rage simmers within me, a growing storm.

"Your husband," Wyatt interjects with deliberate calm, "was a pillar of virtue, wasn't he?"

Before I can stop the words, they slip out, "Real solid guy there."

Harriet's hand wavers and the metallic click of the hammer pulled back cuts through the air. "Speak ill of him again. I dare you," she spits, though her voice wavers—a fissure in her steely veneer.

Keaton spews his defense, "You should've stayed at camp!"

I rise, bolstered by Wyatt's weapon and my anger. "No, you played a devil's game."

Keaton's lips spread into a scornful grin. "I cover my bases. It's just business, isn't it, Harriet?"

Her gaze never falters and is now hardening. "This hunt was my Moby Dick. You've been a thorn in my side—today and a decade ago."

"It's mine by birthright," I say. "You've done nothing but lie, kill, cheat—"

Harriet's laugh is bitter, "Look in the mirror, Red. You're no different."

She growls and charges toward me. Before I can react, Wyatt shoots. Harriet's right shoulder jerks back. She reels backward and hits the ground, howling. Keaton takes this opportunity to retreat into the darkened brush. Gun still pointed at us.

Wyatt sends warning shots toward the ground, first at Keaton, then Harriet.

"Just kill her!" Joss cries.

Harriet rebounds, scurrying off in the same direction as Keaton.

"They'll be back," I say before bending down next to Joss. "But it gives us time to gather our bearings." Joss has her knees curled into her chest, staring at Norm's motionless body.

Gentle fingers tuck stray hair behind her ear as my jacket settles across her trembling shoulders. “Hey.” I keep my voice soft. “Joss, I need you to look at me.”

Glazed and distant, her eyes flicker towards me without seeming to register anything.

“Remember how many times you protected me as kids?” A shadow of recognition flits through her eyes. “You were my rock. Decisive. Strong. I’m here to be the same thing for you now. And I’m telling you, we need to go.”

Her body remains immovable, eyes clouding with tears of pain. “This happened before. Senior summer.”

Before? What happened before? The revelation is almost too much to process, something worth more depth and exploration than this moment can allow. Painfully, we must set aside her confession.

"I can't imagine what you went through," I say gently. "Whatever's happened to you and what *he* did to you.” Our gaze falls back on Norm. “But we need to leave. Now. Tell me everything when we're safe.”

“He ... he ...” She can’t tear her eyes away from the bloody sight.

“I know.” I grip her face, forcing her eyes to connect with mine. “And I'm so sorry you had to experience that. But right now, we need to go for all of us. I promise we’ll get through this. Together.”

She seems to snap back for a moment. “D ... I didn't mean to ... I ...”

“It was self-defense. I saw it. Anyone would’ve done the same in your situation. But we need to move. Harriet and Keaton will be back. We need to be gone before then.”

“I can't ... I can't move ...”

Desperate, I look to Wyatt, who's already coming over to help me pull Joss to her feet before linking his arm with hers, with me flanking the other side.

"Easy there," I say. "We got you."

Heading west, we trudge toward Cowboy's Saddle, its black outline backdropped against the night.

39

Now – August 2018

Day 4: Second Expedition

There's no choice but to move forward. We're too far from home and too close to the El Cobre's X. And now that Keaton and Harriet have the route past Cowboy's Saddle, it's a race of wills to get through the high wilderness.

As the dawn slowly approaches, shifting the landscape into its proper form, I realize the de Silva cache should be the farthest thing from my mind. Yet it lingers there, an obligation I can't ignore. The saddle is in view, so close. I think of my sister waiting, hopeful, back home. I can't let her down. The only love that's never broken my heart.

Then, I look at the woman with the broken heart before me. Joss.

Sandwiched between us, she moves trance-like over the ascending terrain, her cold puffs of breath the only evidence she's still responding to stimuli.

"Let me grab something to eat for us," Wyatt says, motioning toward a verdant patch of bushes and trees. "We need to stop and rest, even for a bit."

We'd left behind so much back at camp escaping from Keaton. All we have are our canteens and whatever supplies we can comfortably carry on our backs, allowing us to conserve energy and make a quick getaway if needed.

Every ounce counts.

While Wyatt forages for pinyon nuts, purslane, and other wild edibles, I sit with Joss, hoping the non-judgmental silence will prompt her to speak first. I scan the horizon with its saturated hues and a sun-dimpled horizon ribboned by brown and blue wilderness. Any civilization nestled in its nooks is swallowed by the expanse and God's-eye view.

I rub her back gently.

"It came too easy," she murmurs, her voice like gravel.

"What did?"

She takes a deep, shuddering breath. "Killing him." Dirt-caked hands fly to cover her eyes, damming the emotional flood. "God, I wish ... I wish so much could be undone."

I swallow hard, my voice barely a thread. "Why easy?"

She zips her jacket up to her chin, a barrier against more than the cold. "It threw me back ... to senior year, the day before our expedition. My uncle ..." Her eyes dart away as if trying to pitch the memory and leave it on the chilled mossy earth. "My parents never stopped it. For years. Denied it. Back then, I was frozen in fear. When that Callahan monster started to ... I reacted. I had to."

Sorrow pummels me, making it hard to draw breath. A yearning to turn back time grips me—where I'd wrap her younger self in unconditional love. During those times, she told me in the wilderness or at Wyatt's party that it was *not about you.* Because it wasn't. The shame and regret blaze within me, almost as fierce as the thin mountain air strangling my lungs.

"I'm so sorry," I breathe out. "I should have been there for you."

Her embrace tightens fiercely, the fabric of her jacket rough against my burned hands. "It's okay, D. Life was heavy on both of us back then."

Old resentments wilt in the light of truth; I'm at a loss for how to reshape them. I can't deny how I felt, but can no longer deny her experience.

"Thank you for trusting me with this."

Her sad, open face tells more than words ever could.

"I see now why you did it. You defended yourself in every way that counts."

She looks down at her boots, worn and tattered from miles of walking and the weight she's carried. "Is it wrong that I don't regret it? Not yet?"

An ache of sympathy glows in my chest, replacing my sadness. "No, Joss. It's not wrong at all."

Still, her brows pull inward, her lips pressed into a grimace. "There's something else I should tell you—"

"I found another blaze and fresh tracks from Keaton and Harriet," Wyatt says as he rushes up to us. He checks the bullets in the gun from Norm. "We may be able to take them by surprise if we get a move on."

Words die in my throat as Joss waves them away, her gesture silencing whatever thoughts were about to spill out.

"Let's move." It's a stupid, desperate plan, but it's all we have.

Wyatt clears his throat. "Strategy at every step," he reminds us. "They can't see us coming. That's our best way to disarm them."

Thirty minutes into our ascent, with Wyatt tracking the lead, he stops, signaling us to halt with his arm. His index finger presses against his lips, a command to keep quiet. He kneels and rubs the dirt between his fingers before sniffing lightly.

The heart-pounding moves to my ears in anticipation. "Wy?" I whisper.

He rises, concern in his face. "We're closing in."

Joss nervously scans the surrounding terrain. "They could even be watching us."

The landscape relinquishes fewer trees, bushes, and grassy tufts; the air is dense with ozone. Without the map, Wyatt's tracking is our compass, combined with the small details I can remember.

"Your mom ever get this far?" Wyatt whispers as he hoists me up a large boulder; we're less than an hour from Diego Pass.

"No, I don't think she did."

Mama's markers—lightning bolts with swirled ABs—were used to guide her through El Cobre. I hadn't spotted a single one on this expedition, instead forging into the unexplored. Their absence tugs at me; I had clung to the hope that finding one might bring luck or her protection.

When we reach the boulder's summit, Wyatt locks his fingers in mine. "She's all around with you."

Her bright guidance wavers with each setback as our family's path spirals deeper into blood-soaked destiny. The path ahead is comprised of hulking, treacherous rock faces. Thorny but timid vegetation mingles with wisps of clouds. All I can do is hold on to Wyatt's hand for dear life.

Our breathing is laborious in the higher elevations, and our movements grow harder and slower. Wind gnashes against my eardrums. My lungs are thick and sticky with effort. A headache pulses with a tiny flame behind my eyes as we approach Diego Pass.

Hope flickers momentarily as we spot a Rubio marker signifying to *veer left*.

An eagle drifts overhead, landing atop a gnarled rock spire. It rouses its feathers, sending a shiver from breast to tail, cocking an eye toward us, and trilling a high-pitched, repetitive warning. Wyatt stops us again, confirming our enemies are heading in the same direction.

"She's in defense mode," he says. "We're not the first through here."

Fatigue drags like a chain down my throat as muscles beg for relief. In the shadow of the spire, we freeze. At the edge of a limestone outcrop, Harriet's back is to us, her eyes scouring the valley below, my map in her hands. Gear lies scattered around her, duster flapping in the wind, the sleeve darkened with dried blood from Wyatt's bullet.

Keaton's absence looms. My ribs tighten around my breathlessness. *Did she kill him?*

Joss's breathing shallows as my lips clamp shut to control my fear. Wyatt's gaze burns with resolve, his body coiled for action. We're out of time, out of options—Wyatt motions he'll attack first. I shake my head, but his eyes are wide and determined. We don't have the luxury to argue.

"I'm going." He mouths, gripping the gun, bouncing in place, ready to spring forward.

Joss reaches out to stop him, losing balance on her haunches, noisy pebbles splaying beneath her feet.

In one fluid motion, Harriet spins, pistol aimed and ready before Wyatt can flinch.

A satisfied, stained smirk spreads across her weathered face, as if relishing her marksmanship.

"Gun on the ground, now," she commands.

As we rise with arms in surrender, the ground feels unsteady against the fatigue in my knees and tendons.

"First bullet is for the murderer." She snarls, closing the distance in one swift step.

Before I can react, her hand grips Joss's arm, yanking her forward. In the same breath, the muzzle is jammed against Joss's forehead, and I can almost see the imprint of a red ring burrowing into her skin.

Desperation seizes me. "Wait! There's something else—something only we know."

Wyatt's glance flickers with cautious hope.

Joss's sobs sharpen as Harriet leans in, gun drilling into her temple. "Talk fast."

Before I can spin a lie, the sharp crack of gunshot slices through the strain. Harriet's body jerks, and she collapses, her neck snapping as she hits the ground with a sickening squelch. Dark blood fans out from her crown.

We hover, daring not to approach Harriet's still form. Our stunned silence swallows us. Her fiery and nebulous eyes stare at the sky.

The sharp scent of gunpowder wafts, tinged with metallic sharp blood, smelling salts to our survival instincts. Our heads swivel, searching for the shooter.

Joss, her sobs cut off by shock, whispers a single word. "Who?"

This is the third casualty in as many days. Harriet is dead, but safety is far from guaranteed for the rest of us.

40

Now – August 2018

Second Expedition

Wyatt signals us to cover and dives for the gun by Harriet's lifeless body.

"Freeze!" The familiar voice stops me mid-crawl from behind the rock.

Keaton steps out from behind a lichen-draped fir, his gun steady. "You all underestimated me," he rasps. "Thought I was gone, huh? Instead, I saved your necks."

Cat's bright memories crash against the dark terror of now, memories splintering until my body jerks away from both past and present.

Keaton's voice cuts through our shock. "Now, do I A) kill you, B) strip you and leave you, or—"

"Take whatever you want," Wyatt interjects, his voice heavy with surrender as he sits on the ground, inches from his gun.

"Just. Please," Joss says, her skin flushing and arms raised. "Let us all live."

Keaton's signature grin stretches wide as he winks, picking up Harriet's gun and showing us her empty cartridge before throwing the useless gun into the brush. "Oh, the irony. Or C) you tell me what you were about to tell Harriet."

He saunters over to Wyatt, his boot finding Wyatt's side and sending him sprawling.

Next, Keaton squats before me, his dirty fingers clamping my jaw with desperate strength. "What's this last piece of the puzzle you hinted at?" he snarls, his breath sour. Trapped in his vice-like hold, I'm sure his fingertips can feel my racing pulse.

Joss's face crumples, her gaze dropping to the ground, fingers curling into fists.

"Don't make this worse, Miss Delaney!" he pleads.

But my defiance surges, and I spit in his face.

Quiet rage flashes in his eyes as he wipes away the saliva. "Fine."

Joss screams as he wreathes her into a chokehold, his gun buried in her blonde locks, retreating with her as his shield. "I'll take my insurance policy with me."

Her tremored cries cut through me, sharper than any blade, but I grasp for calm. She needs that from me.

"I'm holding onto her until you explain what you told Harriet." Keaton continues to inch backward with Joss. "And if any of you stand in my way—"

His words are a blur of background noise as my mind races to pivot with some strategy, a way to obtain leverage and power.

"It was a lie!" I blurt, my voice betraying the conflict within. "I made it up." Wyatt winces in dismay; it's a risk, exposing our ruse, but I can't gamble with Joss's life. "Just let her go, Keaton."

Maybe it's a stupid move to give up our last piece of leverage when the timing to save her could be more advantageous later. But my heart gave me away. "Please, let her go."

Keaton's slate eyes, cold and calculating, flicker with doubt. He shifts, now shouldering his gear while maintaining his grip on Joss. "Clever play," he acknowledges with a twisted smirk. "But what now?"

He shuffles his grip on Joss. "One version is the truth," he says, grabbing his gear with one arm, the other locked around Joss. "But do I believe the *lie* was more convenient to you now or then? Bravo on the mind-fuckery. That's, well—Keaton-level stuff."

Joss's whisper, fragile and desperate, begs him to stop.

"There, there, sweetie." He patronizes her with a shush, his reassurance as hollow as the void it leaves in my gut. "This'll all be over soon."

Tears streak Joss's cheeks like indictments of my leadership as Keaton vanishes with her into the swirling mists of Diego Pass.

Guilt anchors me to the spot until Wyatt's steadying hand keeps me from crumbling. "We need to move," he urges, offering a jacket from our gear. "No time to lose."

"How could I have let this happen?" The self-reproach is a whirlwind I can't escape.

"You can't fix everything, Laney." Wyatt locks his hand with mine. "We can't control what's happened, but we can still take action."

We commit to rescuing her. Wyatt reveals his gun; my confession had distracted Keaton from retrieving it—a sliver of hope. My fingers, trembling but determined, found the dead woman's concealed knife—tools of survival.

We attempt the sheriff's radio with no luck. So, we forge ahead into Diego Pass, a labyrinth of limestone, sandstone, and wind-carved firs. Fog threads through it like a needle, clustering in patches.

Wyatt's tracking expertise guides us. The terrain is challenging, but memories of Mama's teachings alongside fragments of the map help fill in the blanks.

We slide down slopes and scramble over rocks. There's a primal energy here that rekindles a fire within me, even as we navigate the hazards lying in wait.

Our boots splash in crisp water as we cross a shallow stream. Clusters of late-blooming wildflowers pad our way, wispy patches of grass curling in the rain-blushed breeze. Under other circumstances, this untouched slice of wilderness would be close to heaven in another lifetime.

There's a small clearing fringed by firs, the porous and creviced rock face just behind it. The sentinel mountains loom around us as the pewter sky growls a foreboding warning.

Wyatt's steps slow before he finally stops to examine the mud flecked with moss and rotting leaves at the base of the pass. "Their foot placements are so much different from when we started."

"You think he's hurt her? Are hers still with his?" I ask.

"Yeah, she's with him still. But." His brows crease with concentration while his fingers delicately trace the prints. "When he took her, her prints dug in further, were sloppy. The result of being dragged and forced along."

"And now?"

"Now, they're softer. Side-by-side with his, or even pulling ahead, like here."

He points to daintier tracks ahead of deeper, larger ones trailing behind.

"What are you getting at?"

"That she's playing along. Maybe playing mind tricks on him."

A frisson of hope expounds. *She's a survivor. We're going to get her back safe.*

"Looks like their prints head right toward those trees," I say, palming the knife from my pant pocket.

We move past the crooked, wind-styled trees to find a three-hundred-foot crevice in the rock facing a stone's throw ahead.

I gape for a moment. "Cave's close. I don't remember the map going anywhere but straight." When I spot it, I walk up to the rock wall, palming its rough surface. "Wy! A Rubio marker."

The rectangular carving etched into the rock has hash marks slashed perpendicular in its center. To its left are small blazes of X'd circles wrapped in curlicue scribbles.

"Can you translate?" Wyatt asks.

A flutter rises from my chest to my head out of fear of it floating away. I've lived, breathed, and trained for this moment with Mama: to understand the meaning behind the symbols, to see the nightly bedtime story come to life in this very sliver of time.

"It says, 'treasure's this way, through the cave.'"

My hand clings and follows the wall, the stone increasingly damp. I come upon a twenty-foot boulder jutting out as if glued to the rock face, clogged with spindly brush and lichen. Peering around it, I forget and trade any danger for a blip of wonder.

Before me stretches the hollowed blackness of a cave's warm mouth, beckoning us to come inside. I gasp.

"This... is really it," Wyatt acknowledges, clearly struck by the same sense of wonder.

It's a tangible affirmation of a tale come true. De Silva did stow his treasure in the beating heart of the mountain. We ready ourselves to head into its unknown depths.

41

Now – August 2018

Second Expedition

Chills ripple up my spine as Wyatt and I enter the cave, its earthen walls like the moon's crust of pitted celestial rock. Musk and mildew haunt the stale air. Our flashlights catch bats roosting in the highest recesses and fungi, and snails idle on the ground. Water drops from slimy ceiling stalactites, which echo with eerie reverberation like a daring invitation to enter.

I flinch. Nestled in the corner next to an aggregation of rocks, a skeleton pokes out of the dirt.

The marquis.

Centuries of packed earth encapsulate him, the odd rib, femur, or phalange exposing itself to the cave's musty surface from the neck down to the ankles. The dirt-speckled skull, a creamy white, amplifies my reverent unease as my eye traces the scraggy lines of the sutures.

The marquis chose not to die right next to his treasure but in guarding it. I imagine his last view: the valley of Diego Pass beneath a blue sky.

Mama would be proud right now, her cheeks dimpling with pride, making the Sign of the Cross.

What is thy true bounty, she'd say. *Sometimes, it's worth it to die trying.*

For her, I place a cross of pebbles at the feet of the marquis, swallowing the teary knot in my throat.

Wyatt pays his respects with a solemn nod.

Salt stings my palms as they brush together, time slipping away with each wasted second. Two dark secondary corridors loom ahead. "Now, which way'd they go?"

He points to the narrower, more treacherous tunnel to the right.

The darkness of the passage swallows us within steps, the light of the entrance extinguished by arterial twists and turns, worming through the rock. My hand canvasses the veiny wall, treacly with condensation, to help lead where our flashlights can't.

In this cave with Wyatt, our shadows twisted by light and darkness, I reflect on our senior year lesson about the Beale Ciphers. They represent our thirst for answers, purpose, and leaving a mark. Although I'm driven to finish what Mama could not, I can't shake the feeling that my destiny is more than the treasure; it's finding my way back to Joss and Wyatt.

Air writhes at our backs through the tunnel, turning the acoustic whistles into groans. The tang of wet stone kisses our noses. The path narrows to single file, my flashlight guiding us along.

A thunderclap from outside reverberates through the walls, and I jump. A nagging feeling burrows in my chest about how unprepared we are: our pageantry of gear, packed with such care in Willow Creek Park, is useless. Helmets with headlights, extra flares, metal detectors, batteries, trowels, and food are now scattered across the mountain like descansos, commemorating our failures up against the wilderness and each other.

Yet there's hope whittled out of necessity that we'll come out of this with our pair of flashlights, a single rope with anchor, one gun, and two pocket knives.

Wyatt stops. "The storm. This cave might flood."

"And drown us."

He pulls me close, my forehead meeting his lips. "It'll be okay. Let's find Joss."

At least an hour into our careful steps, the cave's stifling breath dissipates into booming reverberations, replacing the humid hush of the entombing walls. The sporadic drip of water becomes a steady drumming in the darkness ahead.

"Looks like a chamber," Wyatt says, shining the flashlight around the walls and ceilings.

Stalactites and stalagmites several feet tall pierce the room's surfaces, menacing clusters of crooked teeth ready to chew us up.

"Have they been through here?" I ask, illuminating the shadows, poised with the knife.

"Yeah, but it's hard to tell where they went. It forks out into more tunnels. Watch your step for dropdowns."

Light catches the stagnant pool just before my boot crosses its edge, my path shifting to trace the fissured walls where Rubio's markings once lived before time and water wore them smooth. As we approach the X, the treasure cache continues to recede in my thoughts. Joss's safety and well-being are the new X, clinging to the fringes of everything.

My gut cinches to think of one more man being rough with her. He could lead her down a wrong turn where they're now lying dead or injured. I shiver, brushing away the intrusive thoughts.

We approach a column, its surface like a ghoulish candle with never-ending layers of melted wax fused from the floor to the ceiling.

Murmurs scatter through the chamber. They echo from nowhere and everywhere. We freeze.

"Hear that?" I ask.

Wyatt nods as we hover amidst the sound of water pearling to the ground. Muffled voices echo again, this time louder. I open my lips to call out for Joss when Wyatt cups his hand over my mouth.

I lip-read Wyatt's noiseless words: *A. Trap.*

We tread carefully around the melted wax column when I feel a sudden shift in the air—a cold draft—nipping from below. I motion silently to Wyatt.

We crouch gingerly on all fours, inching forward, hands touching rock and more earth until my right hand in front catches a few inches of air. I clutch solid dirt for dear life with my left.

A lower pit lies before us. I carefully nose our light down through the chamber, and only rocky terrain glimmering back. There is no sign of Joss.

Another ripple of thunder erupts as I stick an alloyed anchor into the ground. Distant rain patters from somewhere high above, like we're under a giant umbrella. Droplets inside the cave graduate to a thin yet steady flow.

Wyatt devises my makeshift harness out of our final rope, guiding it down in one smooth motion to the ground of the lower chamber about thirty feet below. When we both reach the bottom, three narrow, five-foot-tall corridors lie ahead.

"Eeny, meeny, miny, moe," I whisper as we shut our flashlights off to conserve battery power.

Footsteps pad toward the chamber. Wyatt trains his gun ahead as I scramble to turn on my beam. It catches Joss in the light, emerging from the far-right tunnel, the layers of darkness and humidity playing tricks on my senses—she's *leading Keaton by the hand*.

Under the grip of his weapon, Wyatt turns on his flashlight again, confirming it was no illusion.

Joss and Keaton. Keaton and Joss.

All sensation leaves my body as she points a knife at me with unsteady hands, her eyes steely and glinting through the shadows.

"What are you doing?" My head is swirling.

Wyatt's mouth gapes open. "Joss ... you're ... this is a joke. Right?"

"Just go," Joss says with a pained expression. She glances over her shoulder at Keaton, who is palming his gun and flashlight. "Please."

"You're scared—it's okay." I pocket my knife, raising my hands as a peace offering. "This journey, this place." It's that syndrome where one falls for one's captor. "It's getting to us all. Just put the knife down."

Instead, her fingers firm up around the weapon. Her eyes welling, Joss takes a tentative step towards me. "Leave. Please. Treasure's ours."

"You tell her, sweetheart." Keaton squeezes out from behind her with his gun, his flashlight beam lighting up his chin. It's like he's about to tell a ghost story.

Sweat seeps out of every pore, washing away all my hopes. The way he calls her sweetheart—not in the facetious Keaton way I expect, but in a serious, subversive way. All the scattered pieces snap into place like a lens finding focus, each ignored sign now blazing bright with meaning.

Their extra-long looks. The way they favored one another. Stories about a charismatic boyfriend captivated by the treasure's lore. Her rage when Wyatt cut his lines at the cliff. Parallel remarks about "the boyfriend" and Keaton himself having a tough time in the last few months. Keaton shoots Harriet to keep Joss safe. The unified, unresisting tracks leading to the cave make sense now.

I'd carefully laid out defenses against trusting her, but my vulnerability still muscled its way in. The pain grows hot through me.

"Keaton's your boyfriend."

"Ding, ding, ding!" he says.

My thoughts bounce and scatter, unable to grab onto anything concrete. "Why? Was this part of your plan all along? I was a means to an end?"

"D ... I'm—" The contorted expression on Joss's sad face suggests her ruse with Keaton took on a life of its own, but it doesn't make it feel any less than the worst betrayal I've ever known.

"Enough, Jossy. You don't owe her an explanation," he says.

Jossy.

"You've been planning this a while," I say. "Long before Mama died. How could you?"

She hangs her head. "You know what it's like to face impossible choices." The knife lowers as if too heavy in her delicate hand. "I never meant to hurt you like this."

"Yeah? In what way, then?"

"You don't understand." Her lips purse with something akin to remorse. "We're in deep with bad people, owing a lot of money."

My hand hovers over my pocket with the knife. "*He* broke into my house!"

"You almost saw me out that alley and along the street," Keaton adds.

Joss hesitates. "I'd told him about my hometown and the treasure months ago. With our payment due and his hunting experience, he got this idea—"

"Through the Darknet, I knew your mother had the final missing pieces to find the loot," he interrupts.

"Manipulating and inserting yourself into an expedition," I say, flushing with indignation. "You made her go to Copper Lanes while you ransacked my house."

Wyatt inches closer to me, trying to calm my rage. "Joss, you see, you're a pawn in all of this, the schemes he got you caught up in?" he asks. "He probably set you up, set all this into motion before he met you. You can still come back from this. Come with us."

She shakes her head, tears of denial gathering in the corners of her eyes.

"Jossy, they don't know our lives, our relationship. They wouldn't understand."

"But killing a man and sending him down the river is okay?" I fume. "And double-timing with the Callahans?"

Her eyebrows lift high as pain flickers across her features at the Callahans' name.

Keaton cocks his head back. "Spare me your holier-than-thou crap. You got outplayed. Period."

"The Callahans as allies could not have been part of your original plan," I say flatly.

"I like to improvise."

Ideas spiral through my mind like a gathering storm, searching for a path to freedom. We have no shot at escaping by the rope to the upper chamber. They're pointing their weapons at us, and three dark passages loom behind them, leading into the unknown. Getting through to Joss is the only way right now.

I take the slim opportunity, my shot in the dark.

"So, besides keeping the Callahans alive and in your pocket, what other secrets are you keeping from Joss? Besides using her?"

He grinds his jaw side-to-side. "Watch it."

"The first night," I goad, inching toward Joss as their guns follow me. "It was you attacking her in the tent, looking for the map, thinking it was me?"

Joss snaps her head toward Keaton. "Tell me she's wrong."

He shrugs, his voice flippant. "Okay. She's wrong."

My fingers lock around her wrist as her attention wavers, muscles twisting until metal clatters free from her grip. She squeals in pain. The struggle causes me to trip forward, and I drop the weapon, which lands in the shadowy folds of a small stalagmite cluster.

My diversion is enough to turn Keaton's head, which Wyatt exploits by pummeling him. Out of my peripheral, I see them pinning and punching one another.

Joss scrambles on all fours toward the knife until I seize her by her boot. I stab my knife to pin her pant leg into place. "Joss, this isn't you. He's lied to you—"

She kicks her other foot back and uses her upper body to propel herself forward. I use a swift pushup motion to lift myself to standing, retrieving my knife. I gain the lead over her, stepping straight in her path. "He's got you caught up in horrible things; imagine what else."

She pauses mid-crawl and rises. "Stop, just stop." A rectangular object falls from her jacket pocket; I pounce to retrieve it, examining it closer, disbelief morphing into an angry spark. "A sat phone? He has one too, doesn't he?"

Joss looks down, panting. We'd agreed they were too expensive to buy for the expedition, settling for the two-way radio.

All those vibrations I heard. Her "alarm." *That's how he found us.* "You sent messages to him," I say.

"They were his backup—"

"We could've sent for help this whole time. Saved Tommy Ray, called in the Callahans."

She winces.

A series of grunts reverberates through the chamber, followed by a punch and synchronized clicks. The men have each gained back their guns and resumed a standoff several feet apart. We freeze, back to square one.

My eyes land on Joss's face, each familiar line now warped by lies, but something stirs beneath her mask—her defense of Keaton ringing more hollow with every passing moment. "You may have started with him, but you don't have to finish this with him," I say. "You can still walk away with us."

"You don't believe that bullshit, do you, Jossy?" Keaton keeps his eyes and gun on Wyatt. "She's no friend, the way she's always treated you. I wouldn't mean to hurt you."

My fear turns into rancid anger. "I see what you did there. Told your girlfriend the perfect lie."

Keaton smirks while keeping his gaze on Wyatt. Almost amused that I can read between his lines. "How so?"

"*Wouldn't mean to* is not the same as *didn't do it.* You attacked your girlfriend, you psycho piece—"

"Enough!" he shouts, desperation growing by the minute. "We're getting the treasure, Jossy, then we'll work through it all like we always do."

"You said we'd find the treasure and disappear—no violence," Joss says, jaw tightening beneath her grimy cheeks. "You never said anything about murder or hurting them. Look at everything that's happened."

He snorts. "Things change. Plans evolve."

"People got hurt," I interject. I grip my knife tighter.

"You can't play in the shadows and not expect to get a little dirty."

A loud rush rumbles from above before a cascade of water bursts through the ceiling's opening, flowing over the anchored rope.

Cold metal presses into my side. Joss had found her knife again. "Please. Just go, I'm in too deep ..."

Keeping my gaze on her face, I pray this last chance to break her from his spell works.

"No, you're not."

Even in the hurt of betrayal, I want to save her and pull her away for everything she's been through, for everything we've survived together.

She keeps her eyes down. "I'm sorry, D."

A sharp tightness squeezes my chest as she backs away in step with Keaton. The pair aim their weapons at us until they disappear into the darkness of the middle passage, rainwater now lapping at our feet.

42

Now – August 2018

Second Expedition

Another set of choices stretches out ahead of and behind us.

The first—and smartest —choice is to turn back and climb the rope. We can cut our losses with a better shot at safety, albeit water-logged.

Cat surfaces, and I picture her at our treasureless reunion.

I'm just glad you're okay, she'd say, a glint of disappointment in her face.

The second, the reckless choice, is to move forward to face off against traitors Joss and Keaton for the treasure. We'll contend with not only them but possibly flooded tunnels and dark rooms, doubling the danger and uncertainty.

High risk, high reward is taking the most brutal way out of the problem. It's what Mama did to me and Cat. Now, my desperation toes that same fine line in her footsteps. I don't want to repeat her mistakes.

Days ago, this risk would've clammed me up with guilt and shame, but peace, forgiveness even, flows with grace for Mama now.

The choice is simple.

"You ready, Wy?"

He grabs my hand, gun at the ready in the other.

"Where you go, I go."

I lead us into the dark middle tunnel, where it quickly narrows to single file. Our flashlights do little to dispel the pitch black, only illuminating the slick, bumpy walls; by touch and sound, water squelches and sloshes our boots. This tunnel forks again, and we veer left. We wander through the rocky maze for nearly a half hour before coming to a dead end.

"Damnit." I wipe my brow as we start retracing our steps. "Gotta go back to that right one. They're way ahead of us now."

The ceiling height inside the right fork shrinks thirty paces in. We crouch-walk, my thighs burning. My light flickers, batteries stumbling toward a slow, winking death.

Next, the cave's ceiling opens about eight feet high, and we come upon a half-wall of two large boulders blockading the passage. It's too large and rooted within the passage for Joss and Keaton to have placed there, but I still wonder how they maneuvered beyond it—my elation blooms when I spot an elongated, three-foot-wide exit in the top left corner.

"Here, I'll give you a boost." Wyatt laces his hands for my boot, ready to propel me through the slim opening near the ceiling.

Before I can step into his hands, a rumbling begins from behind and above, and we freeze. A sickening sensation rolls from head to toe; we've been through this before. We exchange a desperate glance before a split second of silence followed by a whoosh.

Water gushes from behind us, thick, frothing, up to our chests, ready and greedy to swallow us whole as sheer force lifts us off our feet, hoisting us high enough to touch the ceiling.

My lungs swell with one last gulp of air as my arms cut through water, clawing toward the distant corner. "This way!" I shout.

Only silence answers back. I snap my head around as a wave slaps against my face, stinging my nostrils and eyes. Wyatt and his flashlight are nowhere to be seen. I death-grip mine, its beam still glimmering like a strobe light, but I'm unable to find him.

"Wy?"

The sluicing, droning water drowns out all other sounds.

Instead of turning toward the rock wall exit, I gulp in the air and dive under, opening my eyes in the murky water. A stinging jetsam of rock, bubbles, and dirt swirls in the fluctuating shadows, but no Wyatt. The panic invades my lungs, causing me to surface.

The boulder blockade remains intact and immovable, keeping us well-fed in the passage. I scream for him again into the watery void, the flood's depth increasing. Time is running out. The thought of losing him suffocates more than the surrounding tide.

Diving my head under again, I sense a swishing around me; I surface and see his face.

If we had time, I'd kiss him. That payoff will have to wait.

We know what needs to be done. Get to the exit in the rock wall. The water propels us toward the opening as we paddle in tandem.

Still relatively dry, the other side offers a bumpy landing, spilling us onto the hard dirt; the water trickles out behind us. My bruised limbs ache, though I push through the pain. We rise to our feet, soaking, panting, grateful for something solid beneath us.

"I don't wanna swim anytime soon." A half-smile surfaces on Wyatt's face as he wipes grime around his eyes.

I smile back, too tired and relieved to come up with a witty response.

"Let's go before this wall gives," I say.

"Must have been a microburst over the mountain."

The cave's winding pathway reveals a tunneled hole in the floor, slick, mucin-like algae lining its ground. It's not a dropdown but an angled descent.

"Our slide," Wyatt says. "Like Slide Rock in Sedona."

Sun-warmed stone presses against memory—his lips finding mine between whispered words, that last golden afternoon before summer crashed down on us. "I'll go first."

He kisses my forehead in an unspoken understanding. "See you on the other side."

I bend my arms, push from my triceps, and take off with surprising acceleration down the chute's darkened, butter-like surface.

My spine arches back toward the water while my eyes lock onto the black hole rushing closer. It's at once fast and slow, exhilarating and terrifying. Invasive, quick-fire thoughts flash before me of free-falling into another lower chamber from here, only to die at the foot of the treasure.

Then, a glow radiates through the slide tunnel—not artificial light but a pinky-purple luster. I hit an extra slippery patch of algae, and the tunnel whirls me upside down, around, and airborne. Without bearings, my pulse spikes, and I land squarely on my tailbone, cursing.

When I stand, and my spine crackles back into place, the tension and pain subside as remarkable wonder unfolds before me.

My neck cranes upward as the cavern opens before me, stone arching overhead like some ancient underground cathedral. Natural clearstory windows frame the wilderness while hiding the grotto in plain sight. It's a northeastern view. The rose-tinted evening sun diffuses the horizon, filtering the room with a dream-like quality.

Ornate stalactites and columns adorn the space like earthen chandeliers and Greek pillars. An icy blue pool bifurcates the room, fed by a gentle waterfall in one corner of the ceiling. I'm in awe at everything carved by the water's will.

There's a thump and yelp behind me as Wyatt lands equally awkwardly. I help him to his feet.

He goes slack-jaw, too. "Incredible."

"Almost worth it for this alone."

The scudding of distant footsteps interrupts the wonderment, and we fall back into defense mode. Joss and Keaton are in here, circling vultures eyeing the cache.

I point in the sound's direction—a rock bend next to the waterfall. Wyatt nods in agreement. He reaches for the gun in his waistband.

It's gone.

The floodwaters must have dislodged it. Wyatt looks back to the tunnel we came from as if it will just slide to our feet.

He grits his jaw and steps before me as I relinquish my pocketknife to him. We tiptoe toward the waterfall, then wade through the frigid pool.

No sign of the couple.

Now, mere feet from the mesmerizing cascade to our right, we approach a fissured rock bank. A gleam catches in my peripheral. I turn to the waterfall, my lungs tightening at the illusory movement—the treasure.

Lured by its promise, I slice through the curtain of water, the cold anointing me: *you finally made it.*

Nestled in its grave in the mud is the chest of Marquis Cayetano de Silva. It's about four feet by three feet—not as large as I'd pictured in two decades of imagination, though when considering its journey from Spain to the heart of this cave, its size is incomprehensible.

I throw Wyatt's backpack to the side of the chest and fall to my knees, quivering, heart drumming. The mud-caked wooden lid bordered by brass is ajar, and Mama's key is still in the lock. I pull it free, feeling its familiar weight as I loop the chain around my neck.

Our presence must have alerted Joss and Keaton just as they opened it. I whip around, anticipating they'll attack at any moment, but it's quiet as Wyatt stands at the ready in front of the waterfall.

As I lift the chest's lid, I feel destined to have this moment of solitude with the treasure.

Gold bars meticulously line the chest while coins from forgotten kingdoms nestle between palm-sized gemstones as luminous as the dreams that carried them. Dagger handles boast rainbow clusters of jewels, chains drape with the weight of pearls and diamonds, and a tiara, crowned with the fire of rubies, rests with regal grace, its luster undimmed by the passing of time.

It's a culmination of hopes and sacrifice so intense that it draws tears from the deepest parts of me, tracing my cheeks not in sorrow but in tribute to the woman who dreamed this moment bigger and harder: Mama.

Her love for the hunt was tightly knit through her identity, each expedition a thread that pulled her further from Cat and me, swallowing up precious fragments of her motherhood. The late-night planning, the

El Cobre trips that stretched into weeks, and the bottles of alcohol consumed spoke to a yearning for more—a dream she chased as vigorously as those times she chose to shine her love on us.

The dream felt like a betrayal, as she relinquished countless hours that could have been spent nurturing us as if treasure maps and legends would bridge the chasm between her and the love of her daughters. The drinking and the mood swings—these were the shadows of a woman caught in an internal struggle, grappling with a dream that nourished her bitterness with every new clue.

A realization flickers—Mama was both the fierce woman I admired and the flawed parent I wished would have been there more, and here in this cave, I'm at peace with love and disappointment living together in the gray.

"We did it, Mama."

I crouch, fingers trembling, drawn to a gold bar.

"Laney, look out!"

I duck as a sharp crack breaks through my awe. A bullet whizzes narrowly over my head, notching itself at eye level into the rock wall in front of me. I reflexively cover my arms and hands over my face and crawl behind the chest lid, which does little to shield me.

Through the side opening of the waterfall, I spot Keaton jumping from the rock bend onto Wyatt. A shower of pebbles falls as the two men wrestle for control. Wyatt slashes toward Keaton's face with his fingernails. Keaton yelps as four red slashes pool across his cheekbone.

"Bastard!" Keaton's eyes are wide with rage, his teeth bared like a cornered animal.

Keaton lunges into Wyatt's side, aiming for his abdomen. Wyatt reacts quickly, pushing Keaton's arm upward as two shots ring out. The hammer clicks back again in Keaton's grip—he fires twice more. But Wyatt forces Keaton's arm into the air, sending the bullets into ceiling columns—sandstone crumbles, scattering debris across the floor.

Wyatt lands a left hook and a slice to Keaton's arm. They tumble, locked in limbs and fists, battling one another.

The gold bar shocks my grip with its unexpected weight, cold metal biting into my palm. Each ounce promises the perfect tool for shattering his skull—I just need to ghost behind him while his attention drifts elsewhere, muscles already tensing for that one decisive swing. Ice jolts through my veins as unfamiliar fingers lock around my wrist, freezing my body mid-launch.

Joss. "Let me help," she pleads, fingers digging into my skin.

43

Now – August 2018

Second Expedition

"I can't do what he wants—take my knife."

Joss's face softens with a singular penitence as she hands me the weapon. I grasp it tightly, relief welling inside. After tucking it into my waistband, I use the gold bar to immobilize him before resorting to more drastic measures.

"Thanks. Stay here."

Joss nods and retreats, flanked by my backpack and de Silva's cache.

Adrenaline propels me toward them as Keaton's body pins Wyatt down. The gold bar swings in a desperate sweep, connecting with his skull while my legs launch upward, wrapping around Keaton's torso. My weight drags us backward as muscles strain to pull him away from Wyatt's prone form. It works, but not as well as I'd hoped. The bar skims part of his head before plunking into the water. I crash-land on my spine, air pinched in my lungs.

Keaton punches Wyatt's jaw in a sharp, brutal arc, sending him stumbling backward, arms flailing. His feet slip, plunging him into the water.

Before I can react, Keaton flings himself around, squaring me into the bullseye of his rage, his soiled fingers around my throat, his weight on my abdomen.

Thunder bellows with equal fury through the clearstory windows, shaking bits of stone loose from the walls and ceilings; our bullets and dreams are disrupting this dormant chapel.

"You fucking bitch." Bluish veins protrude from Keaton's sweaty face. "I promised Joss I wouldn't kill you. But you've ruined everything."

He squeezes my neck, and my vision narrows like a tunnel: light and sound garble. I try to shout for help, but only a wheezing breath ekes out; I reach feebly for his silvered-blue eyes before my hands plummet to my sides.

This is it, a nebulous, peaceful sub-consciousness tells me.

No. Fight, fight, fight, another voice urges.

In my hazy mind's eye, the immaterial mementos of my life rise to the surface: the purity of Cat, the love of Wyatt, the redemption of Joss, and Mama's determination.

Metal bites into my palm while his grip crushes my windpipe, each breath a battle against crushing pressure. The gun slides, cold and final, against my fingers as they find the trigger, hatred forcing the barrel toward his flesh. My hand shakes against his grip on the hammer while survival instinct wars with the last threads of mercy. A blur from the corner of my eye collides with Keaton. Joss throws herself at him, desperately trying to pry him off. Air rushes back into my lungs as his hands snatch the gun from me. Caught off-guard, Keaton's finger pulls the trigger reflexively. The deafening blast of a gunshot fills the air. Without thinking, I curl into a ball as if protecting myself from the bullet.

"No ... Jossy!" he cries.

Still gasping for air, I sit up, the scene before me crystallizing.

Keaton, his face stricken with horror, stares at the gun in his hand and then at Joss, a red stain blossoming on her clothes. *This can't be happening again. She risked her life to save mine.*

A sharp, icy stab of horror pierces my chest, and the cavern seems to spin.

We were supposed to survive this. I'd take never speaking to her again—anything over this.

"I didn't mean ..." Tears form in Keaton's eyes. "I didn't see you ..."

Drenched and gasping for breath, Wyatt emerges from the water, his expression taut with rage.

"You shot her! She was saving Laney from you!"

He ignores Wyatt, tears and snot streaming down his face, palm trembling over her wound. It takes everything in me not to pull him off Joss, to stop him from hogging up the moments with her.

A sob erupts from my throat. "Why?"

He's a villain, but not the one I want him to be—the kind I could put a bullet in the skull without blinking.

"I couldn't let you hurt her," Joss whispers, her cheeks ashen. "She's my best friend."

My muscles constrict as I pray and bargain with the universe to let her live. Keaton rises, wringing both hands through his hair, gun still clenched. "Babe, I'm sorry."

He kicks his boot through the pool, cursing as the storm grumbles outside, the cavernous rocks twitching and crackling. As the pink dusk makes way for the night, Joss's face disappears farther into the shadows.

"Keaton." I try to keep my voice as steady as possible as I rush to Joss's side, grabbing her hand. "Can we ... help her together, get her out of here? Please?"

"There's the sat phones, and you have a flare gun you can use outside," Wyatt says.

Keaton's lips twist into a sneer, nostrils flaring. He shakes his head.

A cracking sound reverberates from the rock walls. Wyatt scans his flashlight to the ceiling, where a fissure grows and branches in real time. Our presence alongside the storm has uncannily destabilized the cavern; for millions of years, it's stood strong, but now our intrusion could bring everything crashing to a heap of rubble.

"Delaney, we need to go, get help," Wyatt says. His voice is disturbingly gentle, sending dread through my veins.

He's telling me—without telling me—we must leave her behind.

She might not make it, and it's too hard to move herself and ourselves in her condition.

I'm not ready to let her go. I'll batten down the hatches.

Silent tears trickle down my cheeks, and I squeeze Joss's hand tighter, pressing my other hand on her warm, wet wound.

"No, I'm not leaving her."

Fabric whispers through darkness as trembling fingers strip away layers, desperate to stem the flow of red, until Joss's weak touch finds my arm and her pale lips press tight with unspoken words. Joss shudders. "No help. Just. Stay with me, D. For a little while."

I pinch my eyes shut. More tears run. "Joss, let Wyatt get help, you'll be okay."

"It's useless, D. For me. Just stay for a bit."

Resistance drains from my muscles as her silent plea wins out over battle instincts. "Whatever you want."

Meanwhile, Keaton is wading through the water with a blank look. Knee-deep in the pool, he steps into the waterfall's flow, its cascade enrobing him as if in absolution. Wyatt keeps the flashlight pointed at Keaton, who retreated behind the fall, his watery silhouette plucking part of the cache from the chest. In a clanging shower, he stuffs the loot into our backpack—our only way of carrying treasure out of here—before heading back to Joss.

My feet anchor a careful distance away while their pain unfolds before me, muscles tensed to maintain this fragile space between intervention and allowing grief to run its course. He returns to her side, our backpack loaded alongside the rest of his gear, kissing her forehead and her lips, their agony and longing palpable.

"I'm sorry," he whispers, slinging on the backpack. "I wanted things to be better." Emotion chokes off the rest of his words. "I'd carry you out of here if ..."

"No use."

Their love is a strange, toxic swirl of manipulation and redemption.

Keaton shakes his head. "I'll leave my gear. We'll take the treasure on my back, sat phone, I'll patch you up, carry you—"

"Won't do any good. My adventure ends here." Joss winces. "It's okay, Key. Go. It's what you wanted, right?"

He closes his eyes, kissing her palm. "I'm sorry. I love you. I'll make it count for both of us."

My heart sags as I realize the emptiness in our pursuit of fortune and glory. Tommy Ray impaled by a branch, the Callahans dead, and now Joss's body shuddering in its twilight. The treasure is a fool's gold.

For I shall die with nothing, the marquis had said.

We watch Keaton give his girlfriend one last kiss and allow him to disappear with our backpack full of treasure into the slide tunnel, leaving us with nothing but what's in our pockets. Rain spits sideways through the high wall openings as another peal of thunder fractures the surrounding rock.

Wyatt approaches us and sits a few feet away. He nods solemnly at me, knowing, respecting, that I won't let her die alone. My heart pounds loudly in the silence of the cavern. I won't leave her. Not now. Not ever.

I turn back to her, summoning a smile. "Glitter Twins for life."

44

Now – August 2018

Day 5: Second Expedition

Keaton's departure is solace, not only to me but also to the cave, it seems, which breathes its own sigh of relief—the fissures ceasing, the stones quiet, the storm moving westward, dwindling to a murmur. It's as if the mountain had an acute rejection of Keaton, removing him like a foreign object before its pulse weakly resumed. The cavern suffered irreparable damage, but we're afforded precious borrowed time.

A wet chill binds to the darkness, and we collectively shiver in damp clothes. I don't have time to worry about what the cold will do to me. My goal is to make Joss comfortable.

We have flashlights for light, but we have little to make a fire. Wyatt thinks he could devise something with the flint rock in his pocket, lip balm, and hair strands as tinder, even in the damp conditions, but it could spark equally devastating consequences. The heat could cause the rock to expand, causing more cracks and sending entire chunks raining upon us.

He won't say it, but if it's crossed my mind, I'm sure it's crossed his: Joss won't last long enough to bother with a fire.

Still, we try to make her comfortable; I gently lift her head and place it on my lap. Wyatt removes one of his two jackets and drapes it over her body.

"Thank you, Wyatt." Her voice is a permanent whisper, every soft syllable requiring meticulous attention. "For giving me the last thing I deserve right now. I was cruel—"

My fingertip brushes softly against her mouth to hold back the coming words. "No need for apologies," he reassures her. "Kindness and forgiveness from here on out."

She nods, blinking back tears. "I've been so bad." Remorse punctuates her tired expression. "It's finally caught up to me."

"Stop." I stroke the blonde hair from her forehead, combing her scalp. "It's okay." She exhales.

She motions weakly to the northern corner of the room, in the opposite direction of the waterfall. "Over there. My belt bag. He didn't take it."

Wyatt takes charge, so I don't have to leave her side. He returns with the hip pouch, retrieving a small, worn leather notebook from inside.

"Your flower press journal," I say, leafing through dozens of pages, which goes back over a decade.

Next to each delicate bloom is the handwritten name, its scientific name, the year, and where she found it.

Rosa, red rose, Seamus Byrne's funeral, 2007.

Aquilegia formosa, red columbine, expedition, 2008.

Lupinus perennis, purple lupine, Wyatt's graduation party, 2008.

Antirrhinum majus, snapdragon, night I met Keaton, 2016.

Bellis perennis, daisy, from Keaton after positive pregnancy test, 2018.

"Do me a favor?" she asked. "Add this." She'd pulled a small, bruised cluster of tiny white blooms from her pant pocket. "Achillea millefolium, yarrow, second expedition ..." Her voice strains through every word.

A tear slips down my cheek. "I will."

"Symbolizes healing. Love."

Each flower, pressed and preserved, is like our friendship; beautiful, always fragile, and now nearing an end.

The silence is heavy, stippled by the distant waterfall trickle and Joss's labored breaths. She smiles, wincing.

"Need me to adjust anything for you?" I ask.

She grimaces. "No. It's fine."

A stinging sensation threatens to choke my words. We must stay on track with the things we need to say before it's too late. I think Joss knows it, too.

"The treasure ... it was never about ... using or hurting you," she says, her voice trembling. "It was about proving that I wasn't that same person. That I could ... *do something right* for once." Her eyes glisten with the bitter recognition of how deeply she'd been led astray by his lies. "Keaton said the treasure could be that proof. That it would make you see me differently."

Damp toes curl inside my boots. Angry tears streak down my cheek. I want to grab her, shake her, tell her what I wished I could have told myself: *it's not your fault, it's not your fault, it's not your fault.*

I lace my fingers between hers. "I've wasted too many years wondering if I made the right decisions." I glance at Wyatt; his eyes smile, but his face is solemn. "But it was the only thing that made sense. And I've gotta find grace for that. Just like you do."

She grasps my hand with all her strength. "Why's it take death to wise us up?"

Her question cuts sharply into my heart, shattering it into a million shards.

"You're not dying," I whisper, my voice trembling with fear and sadness. "Please, no." The weight of her hand in mine feels heavier now, as if she's still holding on just for me.

We watch each other weep, our pain and parallel paths soldered by tears. After drifting in and out of a light sleep for a few hours, every twitch or long lapses of her stillness rouses me to an alert state. Somehow, Joss clings to consciousness, her grasp of my hand still strong.

I trace my finger along her damp forehead. "You know I forgive you, Marwood." I don't know if she can even hear me. "I hope you forgive you."

"You ... do the same."

I nod vigorously, a tide of peace pooling over. "Okay."

"Thank you."

"For what?"

"For one last adventure ... and the chance to feel ..." Joss inhales sharply, the flashlight's diffused beam highlighting the growing pallor on her face. "To feel loved ... unconditionally."

My grip tightens around her, muscles quivering with rage. The familiar burn of sorrow spreads through my chest as I imagine Keaton deserting her and her having the nobility to let him.

"I can't let you go. Let us go find rescue."

Her eyes twinkle with resolution. "You need to let go. So, I can, too."

Salt and grime mix against my skin as the back of my hand swipes beneath my nose. "No, not yet."

"Always were stubborn." Joss smiles stiffly as the cave groans again, pieces of the ceiling sharply cracking and skittering to the ground. "Promise me ... you'll get out. Before it's too late." Her gaze moves in Wyatt's direction. "You've got a life worth ... loving. Don't let it pass you by. Not again."

Her words are more laborious, stretching farther apart. The quantity of blood loss is unnerving, reaching from her stomach to the edge of the pool, where it drips into the water, diluted into nothingness.

I kiss my fingertips and place them on her cheek. Tilting her watch face, I see it's just after three in the morning.

"Did I make it ... at least one more day?" she asks.

"Of course you did."

The weight of Joss's head, her fine blonde hair, sinks heavily in my lap, pressing against the nervy pins in my legs, which haven't budged in hours.

A splintering crunch rattles through the cavern as a deluge of fine dust surrounds us. Our flashlights catch a large fracture spanning the ceiling and a damaged column drooping under its weight.

Wyatt rushes over, his face taut with urgency. "Ceiling's about to give way," he warns.

I look at my friend resting in my lap. She smiles brightly, tears hostage and glimmering in her eyes.

"Go, D."

I refuse.

"Yes," she says firmly. "You will."

Wyatt cradles Joss's head with a tender touch and then firmly grips my arm, urging me to move away from the danger.

"Joss, no ..."

"Sorry. Say what you need, Laney," Wyatt says. "Joss, may your spirit soar."

She winks at him. "You're alright, Altaha. I love you, D."

The chamber groans, and more splintering erupts from every corner.

Joss squeezes my hand four times as Wyatt pulls me in the other direction, hoisting her waist bag around his arm. She lets go before I do.

"I love you more," I say one last time.

Wyatt and I sprint towards the slide tunnel, splashing through the water. My legs, numb and heavy, struggle to keep pace. As we dive into the tunnel's entrance, the compromised column crashes down behind us with a thunderous roar. More ceiling rock bombs the water, churning the pool. A cloud of dust rises, hiding Joss from sight. A raw cry escapes my throat, echoing in the cavern.

I forget to look back for the treasure chest.

45

Now – August 2018

Second Expedition

There's no time to breathe or grieve. The cave threatens to swallow us at every turn for disturbing its peaceful hibernation. Our destructive wake is deafening as the ear-splitting avalanches hurry our slippery ascent up the rock chute.

I'm gasping, chest palpitating in the claustrophobic, shadowy space, which feels so narrow now that it could collapse at any second.

"Almost there, Laney!"

The mucus-like tunnel walls, as if we're trudging through the nostrils of a mountain giant, are so dark that I can barely make out any shapes in the bobbing beam of the flashlight.

Wyatt's hand finds mine in the shadows, pulling me out of the slide tunnel's slippery threshold.

Ahead, we see the wall of boulders with the ceiling opening still intact, the ground soaked in mud.

"Looks like the water stopped." I place my hands on my knees to catch a gulp of air into my burning lungs.

"You're right. Let's hope there's no swimming pool on the other side."

Keaton's fresh prints are embossed in the mud. Anger smolders in my belly. "And here he was."

Wyatt boosts me to a foothold that can propel me to the ceiling opening. My heart drops when my flashlight catches the murky brown stretch of water unfolding ahead.

"Damn. Flooded, but shallow."

Sloshing ankle-deep in cave water to the next chamber, I can't recall when I felt dry on this trek. The September heat is a fuzzy memory in this puckering, bone-chilling wet. It chafes everywhere, adding to the aching reminder that Joss is forever gone.

Dwelling on any of these thoughts for too long could be deadly. It means adrenaline and flight are tapering, and hypothermia is ready to assume her icy throne. Every time the cold damp tries to distract me, I flick it away.

Mind over matter, mind over matter.

Terror crashes over me as memory floods the chamber—where hope had lived, betrayal now lurks in the shadows. "Goddamnit, he cut the rope."

A shorn rope teases us far out of reach from the lip of the ceiling hole, an intentional middle finger from Keaton.

"They didn't come down here with a rope, though," Wyatt says, acoustic water drips bouncing off his words. "And it's too far to jump. There must be another way."

They must have found a different path through one of the two passages flanking the middle tunnel we came from.

An ominous crunch followed by a thump erupts, and I flinch, my pulse spiking. The rock avalanche in the treasure room set off a chain effect threatening to ripple throughout the cave, ready to spit us back into the wilderness or bury us in its catacombs. Either way, we can't stay in here much longer.

I point to the left. "I'll try this one. You take the far right."

"We shouldn't split up."

"We don't have time," I say. "Holler if your tunnel's the way out."

"Laney, wait."

My flashlight flickers weak patterns across his face, catching the sadness pooling in his eyes. "Save it for when we get out of here. Because we're sure as hell going to."

He squares his shoulders and nods before retreating to the passage on the right. I creep through the left tunnel, a small trickling stream masking any possible footprints. The stream runs toward me, the first hopeful sign; it must be running from an opening, an origin spot. Rock scrapes against both sides of my arms as the passageway narrows and ascends, my legs bending, working harder to clamber through. A faint breeze, warmer than the surrounding air, tickles my face.

"Wyatt!" I yell, the echo of my voice loud and garbled. "It's gotta be this way."

I call for him again. No response. I keep calling as I return to the lower chamber for him.

A crash howls through the walls, then a breathy groan. My heart quickens, and my nerves rattle. I race through the dark right tunnel, calling his name. I only hear faint moans in response.

He has to be okay. Now that I have him back, I can't lose him—not after Joss.

I approach his tunnel, my unease escalating as a cloud of dust powders the flashlight beam.

"Wy!"

"Laney!"

Wyatt's on the ground, lying on his stomach in a crumpled heap, rockfall piles surrounding him and sealing off the tunnel. I edge closer to find a small gash on the back of his head, a mound of sand and pebbles burying his back, a foot-long rock on his hamstring—and his left arm wedged at the bottom of the rockfall.

"It ... happened so fast," he says.

I squeeze my eyes shut, skin beading with sweat. *Breathe.* "You're gonna be okay. I'm gonna get you out of here."

First, I remove the small boulder from his leg. He exhales with relief.

He waggles his free arm butted up against the wall toward his waist.

"There we go, that's good," I say. "See, you'll be out in no time."

The cave walls creak in protest.

"Laney," he whispers. His handsome, dirt-covered face is inches from mine as I furiously dig with my hands. Pained yet full of love, his expression is like Joss's in her last moments. My panic is a riptide, as every scoop of sand I remove is fruitless as more seems to replace it.

There's no time. I keep scooping sand, but it's like silt slipping through the neck of the hourglass.

"Firefly. If my arm doesn't break free soon, you must go."

Tears blind my vision as I dig faster. I'm not losing anyone else; I refuse. "Nope. Not allowed."

"Think of Cat," he whispers. "I can't let you stay. I love—"

"Shut up. Not like this. You're getting out."

Splintering echoes around us. This time, louder, closer. I blink the tears away and resume digging with a sharp piece of rock rubble to help free his shoulder. He could wrestle free with enough room to angle his body and limb.

"Try pulling now."

He pulls a few inches, and I jolt before his arm won't budge. My hope drops.

"Laney ..."

"No! Wy, I need you to fight. I need you to want it with me."

He pulls again, grimacing, howling in pain. The rockfall relinquishes a few more inches of his arm. "Yes, Wy, yes. Keep pulling as I dig."

Dirt flies as I scrape and shovel, the minutes dragging slowly until everything aligns. In one smooth motion, we pull his arm free. He winces, examining his bloodied hand and contorted fingers. Holding him fiercely, I never want to let go.

I'm panting, wrapping his good arm around my shoulder, hobbling toward the tunnel exit. "You ready?"

We pass through the chamber as rocks from above sprinkle onto its puddled floor. Wordlessly, we pick up our pace into the left passage: if we don't reach the upper chamber soon, there will be nothing but a gaping hole to suck us back into the depths of the cave.

The tunnel narrows to an army crawl passage. A lighter shade of darkness radiates through a small opening ahead, a tiny distinction magnified by our newly nocturnal eyes. Through the small opening, we're thrust back into the familiar crooked mouth chamber full of sharp, canine-like dripstones. We don't linger—only long enough to glance back at the severed rope knotted in the alloyed anchor.

There's at least an hour ahead of winding through these catacombs. For now, the loudest, most threatening rockfalls subside to a distant grumble. I don't take for granted that we're out of danger by any stretch.

Cool mountain drafts hit our faces, a beacon to the surface. The empty cavern mocks us now—what had been a whispered promise of rescue and riches just hours ago twists into hollow echoes of broken hope.

Finally, the darkness ahead is no longer pitch black but a dull slate, and I know we're nearing the proverbial light at the end of the tunnel. There's only moving forward until we see a hopeful sliver of dawn. It greets us as the crash of stones and water wallop in the tail-ward distance, erasing where we've been.

46

Now – August 2018

Second Expedition

As we emerge from the cave, I'm born into a new world—a world without Joss. The air, trees, and mountains are muted, no longer carrying the same vivid hue.

Estrangement for ten years is one thing, knowing she was in the world. I could hang on to the memories and resentments as I saw fit because they were still malleable, not conclusive.

Death—there's no more molding the clay. Our relationship has been baked into its final shape alongside a curio of delicate memories of Mama and Dad. Sometimes, it's too hard to touch them for fear they'll break, and I won't remember how to put them back together.

I remember the delicate blue kintsugi bowl Mama gave me the night of the winter formal, forged by golden tributaries that show flaws don't stop one from being whole.

That love and acceptance transcends time to mend our deepest fractures. Mama and Joss knew they weren't perfect, but that didn't stop them from loving and trying.

It's the blue hour of morning, right before dawn, a gentle transition from the cave's humid darkness. Wet and exhausted, Wyatt and I stop at a grassy clearing shaded by a group of wind-sculpted trees. He works on a new pump drill to make a fire to not only warm us but also pin a hopeful, smoky SOS to the sunrise for a rescue team.

"Let me help," I say, seeing how his hurt hand slows his trademark skills.

"I think I got it."

My hand grazes his, and he winces sharply, the ring and middle fingers marbled with purple bruising, bent out of their joints. Crusted blood and dirt extend from his elbow to his wrist.

Carefully, I touch his shoulder. "Wy, please."

He stops working on the pump drill. The damp flannel peels away from my shoulders as tender fingers work to clean his wounds; Mama's old fabric, now pressed gently against torn flesh. I inspect his fingers with a gentle thumb and kiss them, grateful for their warmth, pulling him free from the rock, and that we made it this far.

"Not used to someone caring for you?" I ask.

"Seems neither of us are." He caresses my hair with his other hand, his own black mane mussed and flecked with a thick coat of silt.

I give his crown a tousle and push the hair away from his forehead, my blood running warm with the way he looks at me. "We're quite the pair."

"The kind that can move mountains."

I kiss his injured hand again, a sense of lightness sweeping through my body. Using twigs, I measure a few to his finger length to create a splint before ripping a strip of Mama's flannel to wrap and tie around his fingers. "Should at least stabilize your joints."

The blue hour now scatters to the wind, and I trace my hand from his forehead to chin, haloed by the coral sunrise. Once the fire is roaring, smoke peppering the air, my body and nerves relax for the first time in hours. It's far from our last stretch on the journey, but I can breathe knowing Wyatt is safe. We split the last of the foraged stash in our pockets. A headache throbs behind my eyes, and my throat is needle-dry.

Twenty yards away from our fire is the stream we crossed before we came upon the cave. Now full and clear from the storm, it swirls down the mountain. I cup my hands into its crisp current, its cold nectar healing my throat. I drink until I almost burst before sprawling beside the fire with a grateful, distended stomach.

But the respite is brief, as temperamental as the breeze shifting directions. A chilly gust nips at my face, and I tense again, reminded of how far we're from Jericott.

I nibble at a hangnail as I stare into our fire.

"Laney, you okay?" Wyatt knows my tics.

"Everything's just hitting me, I think."

"Shelby won't leave us hanging. We'll find a way to signal him, or he'll see the fire."

A restless shiver prickles my neck. "God, I hope so."

Alongside the little we carry, hope is in low supply, too. We don't have what we need to survive our way out of here alone.

Wyatt grabs my hand as I'm about to stand. "You need to recharge. Rest. Just for a bit and give the smoke a chance to attract attention."

I concede, resting back on the grass. "You're right. It's hard to turn off the panic."

Our instincts don't subside just because the biggest dangers are behind us or dead to us. My defenses remain ready to attack and fight back.

He leans in, rubbing his thumb over my cheek, then kisses my lips. Reality melts away for those thirty seconds.

"Feel better?" he whispers.

I smile, nudging closer. "A little. Promise to always keep me grounded?"

"Always. That's a promise."

Digging into my jean's coin pocket, I fish out the piece of heart-shaped wood he made for me ten years ago. "Remember this?" I rub it between my palms as he plucks it with his splinted fingers, marveling. "It's never left me."

"You never left me either," he whispers into my hair before stilling his amber eyes on my face as if reaching back into our lightning-bottle moments senior year, centered in our vignette.

He kisses me again. More profound, longer—a kiss that doesn't waste a second chance. Every tiny ripple in the universe, so brilliantly choreographed, brings our souls together to this point. A melty heat radiates from my body, thawing any lingering chill.

Deep exhaustion, a full belly, cool air, and warm fire while in Wyatt's arms are the perfect sedative for drifting off. Within the folds of light sleep, hours or minutes pass when my brain registers the sun bathing my face.

A swish cuts through the breeze's natural rhythm, the sound distinct and wrong against wind-rustled leaves. The padding of assured footsteps, a wheezy exhale. A clicking, chewing sound. The scent of artificial cinnamon.

A bleary human form, backlit by the sun, looms over me.

There's a pause, and then a chillingly familiar voice whispers, "Rise and shine. Our game isn't over yet."

47

Now – August 2018

Second Expedition

Keaton and his gun stand between us and the fire; the heat is powerful, and every fiber in me is set alight with fear and determination. I push myself to a seated position, eyes locked on his.

"You're too old for games," I challenge.

"I'll make an exception for you," he says raggedly, the elevation vying for his breath.

Clotted with wet dirt from head to toe, stubble shadowing his sharp jaw, he carries a roguish, animalistic quality like the Callahans. But still, I can see a flicker of humanity in his face, fresh pain from losing Joss—a dark monster struggling to make his way toward the light.

"Why'd you come back?" I ask, my voice sharp. A few yards away, his backpack bulges with treasure; a gold bar's outline stretches against the canvas. "You were free."

"*You* shouldn't be free." He flares his nostrils, tilting his head high. "Saw the smoke from your campsite."

I rise, temper flaring, as his fingers fidget near his gun. "Who are you to judge? And who stayed with Joss in her final moments? Did she get a say in how you did all this?"

His brows harden into a rigid line, motioning me toward the cliff's edge with his gun. "She rarely knew what was best for her."

The vein in Keaton's temple bulges as if ready to break the skin in equal parts fury and sorrow, the mountain's brutality snapping something in his psyche. He doesn't care what consequences civilization might have in store.

I can't let him stew in his downward spiral. "Keaton, she loved you." I swallow hard. "She would never have wanted this. This isn't justice. It's madness."

Survival instincts sharpen my senses as stalling tactics spin through my mind—each word needs to keep him talking while my eyes search for that one vulnerable moment when his guard might slip.

"Keaton, if you do this, you'll never get off this mountain alive," Wyatt says gently. "As much as we hate it, we need each other."

Keaton sniffs emphatically, shaking his head, reaching for his gun, and checking the cartridge. I shudder. The wind nudges hair across my eyes. I look through the strands of red, silvery green oblivion ahead and below, ready to take us.

Suddenly, Keaton's gaze darts away, his eyes widening momentarily as they flick to something in the shadows behind me. His body tenses as if he's seen a ghost, which makes the hairs on my neck stand up.

"Please," Wyatt begs. "You'll be no better than the Callahans. Do you want to be remembered as that?"

His attention refocuses on us, lips flattening into a stern line, fingers curling and flexing on the grip of his gun.

“Let’s end this,” I say. “No more bloodshed. For Joss.”

A tear stains the side of his nose. Slowly, his gun falls to the ground as he mutters incoherently. Wyatt darts to his side, ready to snatch it, but the sudden movement seems to snap Keaton out of his fugue of remorse.

Keaton lunges at me, and I instinctively sidestep his charge. In my spare split-second, I thrust out my leg to catch him off balance.

Time stretches, languid and thin, as Keaton stumbles toward the precipice, his eyes wide, reflecting raw terror. Panic grips me. I lunge, desperate to catch him, fingers inches from his, but the void claims him.

Keaton disappears over the edge, silent and without fanfare.

Metallic bitterness varnishes my throat, shock paralyzing me. I struggle to breathe between the waves of horror and relief. I will myself to look over the ledge, stepping gingerly—a dark green and brown expanse blankets the world hundreds of feet below, dotted with low-hanging clouds.

Wyatt breathlessly pulls me away from the ledge as if nature and fate will change their minds. My chest sags with exhaustion, and I melt into his embrace, which smells like earth, fire, smoke, and something akin to home.

Over his shoulder, emerging from the shadows, my eyes catch *hers*—those same citrine, smoky eyes as days before *and in my dream.* The mountain lion. She blinks slowly, flicking her tail, before retreating over a hill of tall grass and disappearing into a line of trees.

"Keaton's sat phone," I say.

With trembling hands, I unzip the backpack; the slide fastener's chattering plastic teeth reminiscent of my old schoolbag, stuffed with textbooks and crumpled papers of unfulfilled promise. This time, paper dreams give way to reveries of gold.

A hefty gold bar and jewel-encrusted dagger rest at the top of the bag. Beneath it is a throng of gold coins. Heart racing, I dig my fingers down, the cool metal brushing against my skin like beans or rice grains from a bulk bin. I chuckle to myself, a giddy bubble of elation rising—this is what Scrooge McDuck must've felt like diving into his vaulted sea of coins.

My fingers plunge into glittering wealth, diamonds and rubies catching light as they surface. Another dive beneath the treasure brings an unexpected shape—smooth and oval rising into view as an emerald the size of a bird's egg, its deep green faces fracturing the morning sun into brilliant forest fire. It's the gem Joss and I had forever zeroed in on within the El Cobre stories, the one that held that shiny promise that we could achieve something more. A knotted lump constricts my throat as I clutch the emerald tight.

Wyatt squeezes my shoulder. "If your mom could see this now." He rests his head against mine. "Everything she ever dreamed of."

My index finger strokes his cheekbone, a tired smile spreading across my face.

We kiss, the emerald pressed between his cheek and my palm, cocooned in our bittersweet victory.

"You did it, Firefly."

The crown jewel near the bottom of the backpack is the satellite phone, nestled between gold coins and precious stones.

My heart jumps into my throat when it rings for the Sheriff's office. Shelby picks up.

"You can say I told you so," I say.

An hour later, fuzzy droning hums from the west.

Warmth races up my chest. *Rescue. I get to see Cat. I'm going home to my sister.*

Wyatt races out to a small grassy hill nearby to scour the sky. I rise slowly, taking one last look toward the cave. "Love you more, Glitter Twin," I whisper.

I gently place the emerald in my bag and hoist it on my back. The load feels lighter than when we began—carried by both victory and loss.

Helicopter blades chop through the air.

"Laney!" Wyatt calls from a distance, barely audible over the din of the aircraft.

The copter's now cresting over the peak, close enough that I can make out the pilot wearing aviators—and Sheriff Shelby.

Wyatt motions to the backpack. "Want me to carry it for you?"

I grin, shaking my head. "Not this time."

The helicopter bellows overhead in its approach, disrupting the valley's wild terrain with its own brand of chaos: blinding us with dry wind, flattening the grass to a shimmering green carpet, angling trees that have barely seen civilization. With the chopper's skids on the ground, relief and finality swell.

Shelby jumps out of the aircraft first, bent almost ninety degrees, rushing over to us. I embrace him with a ferocity that even surprises me.

"Thank you," I whisper in his ear so he'll hear it over the helicopter.

"And Joss?" I see him mouth the name and bite my inner cheek, shaking my head. His face twists with sorrow as he places a hand on my shoulder.

We settle into our cramped seats with headsets on, and I'm wedged next to Wyatt, gripping his hand like it's the only thing keeping our mountainside spark alive. Shelby sits across from us in the cabin with a droll smile.

"Thankful you're both okay." His voice crackles over the headset.

I tilt my head onto Wyatt's shoulder and smile. "I can't thank you enough, Sheriff."

He shrugs off my gratitude, cheeks pinking as he smooths the hair of his mustache. "Found a print match from your home, too. I know who broke in."

My nerves twinge as Keaton's terrified expression before the fall flashes in my mind. "I know." I can't meet his eyes, so I look out the window. "Doesn't matter now. I just want to go home."

I crane my neck to take in the view and spot a fleeting frame of the mountain lion darting between the trees. Then, the pilot veers the aircraft up and out of the valley, the g-force whirling my stomach.

I'm ready to see my sister.

48

April 2019

Jericott

With the expedition in our rearview, there was what happened—and an alternative story we shared with the world. Only Wyatt and I know the truth.

We convinced everyone we left the mountain with the full treasure, insisting there was no grand chest as the legend claimed. Better to kill curiosity than risk more lives in that treacherous cave for the remaining jewels—some secrets, perhaps, are best left buried.

Traces of Harriet and Norm turned up piecemeal over the next few months, scattered by the elements and predators. Since authorities wanted them for their illustrious rap sheet of lethal global expeditions for years, their remains and recovered belongings went to federal agencies. And with higher-level government involvement in their deaths, Shelby assured that anyone behind Relics Ltd. would cut their losses rather than searching for a piece of the treasure.

Wyatt and I sold the authorities on a convenient truth of the "Callahan Pirates" before they delved deeper. We told them Keaton killed Harriet and Norm defending our expedition group, Norm at our first encounter, and that we tried to play nice with Harriet, who forced us to keep the hunt moving with her, but that she ultimately turned her weapons on us later in the trail, so Keaton shot her.

A few hikers found Tommy Ray in the mud cracks of an arroyo a week after our return. The Jenkins clan quietly collected his remains from the county coroner's office before slipping back to their Verde Valley compound.

They never inquired after the treasure or the circumstances of his death. Their latest controversies—including a drug bust—may have warded off any attempts to claim Tommy Ray's share. And with the expedition contract he signed, they had no legal ground to collect.

I thought of giving Joss's family her share of the treasure. Then I thought better of it, reviewing her expedition contract. She'd opted out of a next of kin beneficiary—and added mine and Cat's names instead.

Her confession on the mountain about her uncle yielded too little time to give the topic the dialogue it deserved. And with only pieces of the picture, I had to shade in her truth and wishes.

Perhaps she'd put that voluntary next of kin clause in the expedition contract for herself, that her parents didn't deserve financial redemption for how they handled what happened to her senior year. I donated her portion of treasure money to a sexual abuse prevention non-profit in her honor.

Our public narrative concluded that Joss perished in a rock collapse in the cave before we could save her and that Keaton fell while trying to lead our descent.

I never intended for Keaton to get off so scot-free. The Sheriff did add my home burglary to his list of offenses with the Phoenix Police: DUIs, drug possession, and a handful of parking tickets.

After which, Shelby was skeptical of his mountainside heroics, but I insisted Keaton saved us all, that his bravery eclipsed his troubles with the law. His story could live on untarnished in her memory, scrubbed clean of desperate choices and dark moments—a gift of selective remembering that preserved only the light.

Sheriff Shelby assumed the role as the face of the El Cobre hunt. Wyatt and I instantly shied away from the media attention, so he stepped up to the spotlight, telling us we'd suffered enough in that cave that we didn't need to go through the court of public opinion.

Wyatt and I keep most of the showy glory at bay. Local shops and tourist spots tried to capitalize on Jericott's updated claim to fame. No longer was our town famous for the folklore, but home to real-life treasure and expeditioners. Our tiny local museum requested the chest key, which I gave them. Devin, my former diner boss, asked us for autographs and signed memorabilia to display, and I gladly said no, basking in his groveling.

While we live quiet and inconspicuous lives, there are a few noticeable traces of treasure in our daily lives. Cat proudly wears a dainty diamond and ruby necklace, a custom-made treasure just for her. And I, with my small emerald earrings, cut judiciously from The Big Green Egg.

We invested most of our riches into secure ventures and secret stashes while also embarking on an ambitious renovation project. Our dream home—a charming Craftsman house on three acres of land near Wyatt's parents' property—hit the market shortly after our return from the expedition.

Cat is overjoyed to have a room of her own for the first time, with plenty of shelf space for her beloved Buffys and Captain Kirks, though I often find her curled up on the floor next to my bedside in the wee hours of the morning.

We pour our hearts and souls into reviving the Craftsman's low-slung gabled roof, worn wood floors, and expansive front porch. Its gaze is fixed westward, towards a lush grove of sycamores and maples that promise to be ablaze with fiery reds and oranges come autumn.

Nestled among the trees, our home shields us from viewing El Cobre's imposing mountain peaks that still evoke tender memories. Each day, those recollections, alongside Wyatt and Cat, lose a little of their sting.

I couldn't entirely give up Mama's house—it symbolized how far we'd come—but there was no rush to get rid of it. I paid off the mortgage.

For all El Cobre Mountain took away from me, it gave back.

Today, I sit on the front porch swing of our new home in a billowy sundress, which drapes protectively over my very pregnant belly. My feet swell, an early spring heat sticking in all the wrong places, and I swear my future daughter's elbow wedges between a rib.

And I couldn't be happier.

Her name will be Leni, which means *lion*. I think Mama and Joss would've liked it.

She's due in a few weeks, and we think it all began that second night on the mountain.

It's been a collective breath-hold for nearly nine months, walking on eggshells for this miracle the universe gifted us. I try to swat away the guilt of my blessings as if being an El Cobre survivor makes me deserve them less, that I don't have to continue to wear hardship as a badge of honor.

I think back to the poor, scared, overwhelmed, overworked eighteen-year-old embittered by her mother's choices. And then, I see myself in the mirror today, cultivated by forgiveness and resolve. My daughter will have the mother she deserves.

Every day, Wyatt's fingers trace infinity swirls over my pregnant belly, a silent promise that nothing can part us again.

After all, we're star-written.

The screen door squeaks open, and Wyatt appears with a handful of daffodils from the garden. He settles beside me, and I can't help but smile at the sight. "What's the occasion?" I ask, already knowing his answer.

He leans in for a quick kiss on my cheek. "Does there have to be one?"

"True," I say, nudging him playfully. "You celebrate anything these days."

"As we should." His soft gaze falls to my belly. "For her."

The baby sends a series of rapid flutters through me, and I pat my belly reassuringly. "I'm learning to."

Wyatt singles out a daffodil from the bouquet, shimmying it out of the bunch. "I thought we should put this in Joss's flower press book. She didn't have one in there."

Unfallen tears send a needling sensation between my nose and throat. "Yeah?" I whisper, the hush guarding them from spilling.

"Narcissus is their fancy name," he says as I thumb the lemon-yellow petals. "They mean rebirth, new beginnings."

"All things hopeful."

He nods, burying his face in the crown of my hair with a kiss.

Cat bounds out of the screen door with a clatter and a large, ice-clinking glass of lemonade in her hands, which she proudly hands to me.

I wipe the captive tear from my eye. "And what's the occasion for this?"

She scrunches up her face in mock annoyance. "I made it, that's what!"

The rush of sugar tingles my tastebuds. "Needs more lemon," I joke.

Cat's mouth puckers. "You're so picky, you know that?"

I wink at her. "You got to balance sour and sweet. Needs a little more zing."

Wyatt runs his fingers through my hair, brushing the damp strands from my neck. "So, a little more of you then," he teases.

I laugh, and the baby kicks again, a series of bubbly, popcorning motions. "She likes it, though."

Cat places her hand next to mine on my belly. Her eyes light up, feeling her soon-to-be niece under her palm.

"Means she likes sweet stuff, and she's sweet like me," Cat says.

The three of us sway gently to the rhythm of the breeze rustling through the sycamores, and I can't imagine a sweeter dream.

THE END

Acknowledgments

Because this is my first book, this might get a little long—so skim for your name if you have to!

First, and most importantly, I'd like to thank those who enabled me to dream big, and then go bigger: my husband and children—Richard, Annabelle, and Will. The loves of my life, my everything. Your encouragement and loving reminders at every obstacle sustain me and remind me what the creative journey is all about. Thank you for your patience while I finished that "one last thought/paragraph" and for showing me how those late hours after work do eventually add up to a novel. Belle and Will, I hope you dream just as big for yourselves.

Mom and Dad, thank you for always keeping my spark for storytelling bright and alive—whether it was illustrating my first book (which I wrote for my elementary school library) or indulging me by driving me to poetry jams to share my bad rhymes on stage—you're the best. Any semblance of a knack for writing comes from both of you and your immeasurable talents. And I hope Pop-Pop would've been proud, too. I love and appreciate you both, always and forever. And Brian Peddicord—when the rubber meets the road, you're there. Love ya, dude.

Patty and Rich, thank you. Your generous enthusiasm, love, and support in so many facets of this journey mean the world to me. I'm so lucky to call you family.

Now, you, Alexandria Brown—I owe so much to you. From the moment I nervously pitched this book, you put me at ease, and we just clicked. It didn't hurt that you were an equally enthusiastic Bravo fan.

Your leadership, friendship, and the beautiful way you edited this book to the finish line equal my undying gratitude. Thank you for taking a chance on me.

Tina Beier, I have so much appreciation for your brilliant and incisive edits—you truly helped me check myself before I wrecked myself. Thank you so very much.

From complete strangers of the Four Corners to what I know will be lifelong friends, my critique group—Patty Barrué, Sara Flannery Murphy, and Inna—endless thanks. Your wisdom, insights, and talent from this story's earliest stages helped shape the backbone of every scene, and your encouragement through the ups and downs means everything. I treasure each of you. Patty and Inna—you're next.

Special thanks to the lovely Alyssa Matesic for helping me craft this story into something presentable and singular, and for all your encouragement at each early stage.

Thank you to my local writer besties—Christelle Lujan, Elizabeth Lyons, and especially Neely Tubati Alexander—for paving the way while introducing me to so many amazing people. Your publishing experiences and insights have made me feel so heard and not alone on this wild ride. I'm so lucky to know you all.

Many thanks to the Jolliest Bunch for all the laughs, encouragement, and support of my crazy dream during our 9-to-5: David Keeps, Mark Schulte, and especially Becky Majewski. Bex, the better half of the Wonder Twins, I'll always remember your happy tears when I shared my news. You're the best. And Amanda Rochon—I love how writing brought us together. Thank you for introducing me to the productivity of writing sprints. I just need your cool prizes every time I finish one!

Some of my all-time besties, Noelle Kranz and Alex Macias—I can't go without mentioning you. You've seen so many versions of me and have cheered me on in everything for 20+ years. And Les and Diana—you always remind me that friendship can pick right up where it left off, no matter how busy life gets, and being there when it counts. Laney and Joss could learn a few things about friendship from all four of you. Thank you.

Early readers: Brian Speer, Jenna Helgeson—love you guys. (Our kids like you the mostest.) And Marchella Leone—thank you for putting down your cool dragon books to read this in its baby stages.

Many thanks to Nat Mack for the gorgeous cover. You brought my vision to life in such a perfect and glittery way.

Thank you, Katrina Escudero, for championing this book with such precision, heart, and enthusiasm.

And lastly, to the writing community at large—including fellow Rising Action authors, WFWA and TSNOTYAW (if you know, you know)—you all make this writing life so much richer and more fulfilling.

About the Author

After more than a decade in the corporate world of advertising, Jill Beissel turned her attention to fiction. Her stories explore the complexities of female relationships and women wrestling with what it costs to want deeply and live honestly—set against atmospheric backdrops and infused with emotional suspense. She lives in Phoenix with her husband, two kids, plus a very old dog who insists on curling up at her feet while she writes. *Glitter and Gold* is her debut novel.

When Sofia loses her coveted job, her American dream is on the line. With her U.S. work visa hanging by a thread, a job interview at a top Miami marketing firm is her last shot at staying in the country. But as she navigates the high-stakes competition, she finds herself irresistibly drawn to her chief rival for the position—charming and ambitious Esteban.

Esteban embodies the glamorous Miami lifestyle Sofia has always admired, and he's unbothered by their rivalry. But for Sofia, everything is at stake. She can't bring herself to tell him how much this job means to her, nor that her future depends on securing it. With her visa expiring, mounting family pressures, and bills piling up, Sofia faces an impossible choice: win the job, or risk returning to a life she fought so hard to leave behind.

Can Sofia claim the career—and the love—she longs for, or will her dreams slip through her fingers just as they're within reach?

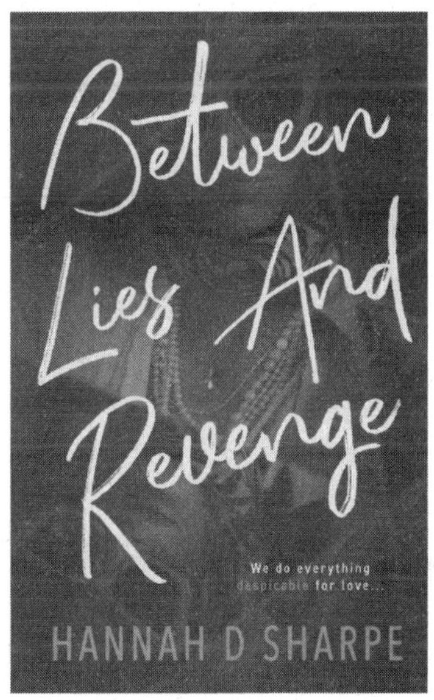

Years after the death of her brother and the theft of her heirloom jewelry, ex-con Elle is on the run ... until she spots a stranger wearing a signature piece. Determined to take back what is hers, Elle stalks and befriends the woman, using her gemology skills as a ruse. Elle offers to appraise and clean the jewelry, replicating and replacing the pieces instead.

Olivia is drowning. She maxes out credit cards behind her financially-strict husband's back in order to pay for fertility treatments, keep her blackmailing father at bay, and maintain appearances with her wealthy friends and their cultist MLM social circles. When Olivia meets Elle, she finally feels understood ... and inspired. With Elle's expertise and Olivia's connections, the two start a side-hustle by way of home jewelry appraisal parties. When this isn't lucrative enough, they develop the perfect con: switching rich housewives' gems with fakes. But their hidden truths get in the way of their success, and each other. Before their secrets bury them, they must confess their lies to one another and trust their final con will exact the revenge that'll secure their freedom, and their lives.